THERE WAS A SEASON T.V. OLSEN

Set against the brutal Black Hawk War, *There Was A Season* is the story of a brave young officer, a determined woman, and the trials and perils their love must overcome on the sprawling and magnificent American frontier.

Lt. Jefferson Davis: He'll risk anything for his ideals and the woman he loves. But even as he struggles to fulfill his dreams of glory, he runs head-on into an invisible enemy bent on destroying him.

Chief Black Hawk: Feared by all who would harm his tribe, he swears his people will be safe from the white man's treachery, no matter how high the price of defiance.

Sarah Knox Taylor: Spirited and courageous, she battles the dangerous frontier and her own father's fierce objections to be with the man who's captured her heart.

ABOUT THE AUTHOR

T.V. Olsen was born in Rhinelander, Wisconsin. "My childhood was unremarkable except for an inordinate preoccupation with Zane Grey and Edgar Rice Burroughs." He had originally planned to be a comic-strip artist, but the stories he came up with proved far more interesting to him than any desire to illustrate them. Having read such accomplished Western authors as Les Savage Jr., Luke Short, and Elmore Leonard, he began writing his first Western novel while a junior in high school. He couldn't find a publisher for it until he rewrote it after graduating from college with a bachelor's degree from the University of Wisconsin at Stevens Point in 1955 and sent it to an agent. It was accepted by Ace Books and was published in 1956 as *Haven Of The Hunted.*

Olsen went on to become one of the most widely respected and widely read authors of Western fiction in the second half of the twentieth century. Even early works such as *High Lawless* and *Gunswift* are brilliantly plotted with involving characters and situations and a simple, powerfully evocative style. Olsen went on to write such important Western novels as *The Stalking Moon* and *Arrow In The Sun,* which were made into classic Western films as well, the former starring Gregory Peck and the latter under the title *Soldier Blue* starring Candice Bergen. His novels have been translated into numerous European languages, including French, Spanish, Italian, Swedish, Serbo-Croatian, and Czech.

The second edition of *Twentieth Century Western Writers* concluded that "with the right press Olsen could command the position currently enjoyed by the late Louis L'Amour as America's most popular and foremost author of traditional Western novels." His novel *The Golden Chance* won the Golden Spur Award from the Western Writers of America in 1993.

Suddenly and unexpectedly, death claimed him in his sleep on the afternoon of July 13, 1993. His work, however, will surely abide. Any Olsen novel is guaranteed to combine drama and memorable characters with an authentic background of historical fact and an accurate portrayal of Western terrain.

THERE WAS A SEASON

T. V. OLSEN

LEISURE BOOKS   NEW YORK CITY

*To "Custer" and Mary Olsen,
my father and mother whose help in those years when
things were less than good made this book possible.*

A LEISURE BOOK®

September 1994

Published by special arrangement with Golden West Literary Agency.

Published by

Dorchester Publishing Co., Inc.
276 Fifth Avenue
New York, NY 10001

Printed in the United States of America.

*For everything there is a season, and a time
for every matter under heaven....He has
made everything beautiful in its time; also
he has put eternity into man's mind, yet so
that he cannot find out what God has done
from the beginning to the end.*

ECCLESIASTES 3: 1, 11

AUTHOR'S NOTE

Among many source works that contributed to the writing
of this novel, special credit must be given to *Jefferson Davis:
American Patriot,* first book of Hudson Strode's definitive
three-volume biography. As a fictional treatment of true
events, *There Was a Season* should never be cited as a source
of facts. Most of those scenes not founded on known
historical events were suggested by factual or speculative
anecdote. The rest, along with such internal detail as
dialogue, were supplied by the author's imagination. A few
minor characters have been invented or, if drawn from life,
disguised for what seem good and sufficient reasons.
Accounts of the romance of Jefferson Davis and Sarah Knox
Taylor that are (relatively) uncluttered by speculation may
be found in several good biographies of Davis and of Zachary
Taylor.

PROLOGUE

He was brought from the courtyard room and up to the parapet between two men. On his right was Brevet Major General Nelson A. Miles; on his left, Sergeant T. L. Grogan. They held his arms securely but not roughly.

The sunlight hit his eyes like a fiery fist.

"Wait," he said.

Miles and Grogan halted. So did the six guards behind them. The prisoner braced himself for a jolt of the neuralgic anguish that always felt like live acid flung in his eyes. But it wasn't too bad. About ten seconds of quivering needles behind his throbbing eyelids and he could open them again.

Not bad at all. The light was golden, the shadows cool and long. He stared hungrily at the landscape and marked the day in his mind: August 27, 1865. The first moments outside his cell in three months . . .

Three months. It seemed an eternity. The federal authorities had lost no time in whisking him north after his capture in Georgia.

"Can you stand by yourself, sir?" asked Grogan.

"I think so. May I try, General?"

Miles nodded curtly. The two men stepped away, and he took a few hesitant paces to the edge of the parapet. Drank in the broad green ramparts that rolled away from it. Sunlight glinted on the Engineer's wharf; silvery scallops danced on the riffled surfaces of the moat and the James River beyond. He was glad of his thick overcoat of black pilot cloth: the early evening was turning chilly. That, and a kind of caramel haze showed autumn's soft attack on the Virginia countryside. *The roses at Brierfield will be fading.*

Somehow his mind veered away from that thought.

He turned his gaze on the outside of his prison. His precise memory promptly clicked off the dimensions: thirty-foot walls of gray granite, some of its solid proportions up to ninety-five feet thick. Running a mile and a quarter around, with an eight-foot-deep moat that was more than a hundred feet across. Fortress Monroe—"the Gibralter of the Chesapeake"—was the most impregnable of all the federal forts. He studied with mild irony the fifteen-inch Rodman guns standing *en barbette* from the bastions. He himself, as U. S. Secretary of War (another time, another life), had been responsible for their introduction.

General Miles moved up beside him, lighting a cigar. Holding it so the smoke wafted across the prisoner's face. Perhaps a deliberate gesture. Perhaps not. Miles was twenty-six, dynamic and fiercely ambitious; he wore his black Kossuth hat at a jaunty angle.

"Like the view, Jeff?"

Jefferson Davis glanced at him. Badly wanting a smoke, he was careful not to let his eyes rest on the cigar. "I'd like it better from across the river, General."

He easily masked his irritation at the young man's brashness. He'd early considered calling Miles "Mr. Miles" (in pointed token of his being only a general of volunteers before Secretary of War Edwin M. Stanton had appointed him Jefferson Davis's jailer) but that would be playing Miles's own antic game. He did not know why Nelson Miles hated him, but it neither disturbed him nor surprised him. He had never provoked neutral reactions from other people.

"No doubt," Miles answered with his thin imperious grin. "Not the same as chains, but it may give you an idea how your slaves felt."

"No people of mine ever wore chains," Davis said coldly.

"Not even on their souls?" Miles blew an idle haze of smoke at him. "Well, you've learned a bit about chains here, eh? You should be more appreciative, Jeff. You could also learn a useful thing about the value of humility in defeat."

"You can defeat a nation, General. Not a man. A man can be killed. Defeated, never."

"Very lofty. But drivel." Miles touched his mustache. "That aphorism can be as easily stated the other way around."

He nudged the older man playfully on the arm with a gauntleted thumb. Davis loathed such familiarities, but he had submitted to enough real indignities to make this one seem minor. The least of it—since in this Miles was only carrying out orders—was being locked for three months in a bricked-up gunroom with a single barred window facing nothing but the gray moat water and the parapet's solid masonry wall, two guards pacing the damp sweating cell all day and night, more guards pacing outside the door, on the glacis, on the parapet, on the ramparts below it. Seventy-odd soldiers to guard one sick, frail, fifty-seven-year-old man.

"I prefer it the first way," he said.

Miles shrugged, losing interest in the baiting. He turned to T. L. Grogan. "A half hour, Sergeant. Then you'll escort America's only President ex-officio back to his cell."

"Aye, sir."

Miles descended from the parapet and disappeared inside the courtyard.

"Awright!" Sergeant Grogan barked at the half-dozen guards. They were all German mercenaries, trim, boot-tough, muffled up like thick blue bears in their caped kersey greatcoats. "See what you can do about looking official, you slabby krautfaces.

March! Up and down the parapet. Up-down, up-down! *Eins, zwei, drei—*"

They whipped smartly to attention, gloved hands smacking the butts of their Springfields, swiveled in a unit, began the slow pacing.

"Goose-stepping squarehead babies," Grogan muttered. "Wind 'em up and leave 'em run." He turned back to Davis, regarding him with tough, merry eyes. "I'd wager, sir, you'd enjoy a bit of a stroll down on them Erin-style ramparts."

Davis smiled. "Think the general would approve?"

"Gave no direction otherwise, did he?" Grogan looked woodenly sober. "And my memory's that rotten, I forgot to ask."

Grogan was a mountainous slab of weathered Irish oak. He was, Davis guessed from the seams in his gnomish face and the wiry gray curling in his red hair, close to his own age. But easily capable of subduing a frail statesman-prisoner. He wore a Colt revolver at his hip, but Davis had never seen him take it out. He was a good man: direct, shrewd, devoted to his duty. And the only friend Davis had among the guards.

The prisoner began to descend from the parapet. The effort was too much; he tottered. But Grogan's brawny arm was there, supporting him over to the easy-graded slope.

"Best you don't try walking alone awhile yet, sir."

"Thank you, Sergeant."

He continued to let Grogan's arm take his weight as they walked slowly back and forth below the parapet.

Davis had no mirror, but he had seen his reflection lately on water or other shiny surfaces. The months had taken a shocking toll of him, reducing his light frame to bone and sinew. He looked far older than his years; his hair had gone completely gray. The skin was stretched transparently across his cheekbones, deepening the aristocratic hollows beneath them.

Bitter months. Memories of defeat. Indignities. He had no possessions but the clothes on his back and his Bible. He ate with his fingers because his jailer professed fear that he'd commit suicide with a utensil. ("With a spoon?" he had asked. Miles had only grinned.) He never left the cell: a portable commode was wheeled in while the guards looked on. A lamp was kept burning day and night at the head of his cot; two-hour shifts of guards eternally paced his cell, their stiff service-issue shoes squeaking every second. He slept (when he slept) badly; his head ached always, there was fire in his joints. The neuralgic pains that periodically ravaged his eyes were worse than they'd ever been.

A few motes of hope. His wife, along with friends like Horace Greeley and former President Franklin Pierce, working to build up public sentiment in his favor. Their appeals to President Andrew Johnson to get him an early trial. Which was all he asked: a chance to plead his own case and that of the Confederacy. At least the danger that they might hang him without a trial was past.

It had been a tall ladder to tumble from. U. S. Army officer, prosperous planter, hero of Buena Vista. Senator from Mississippi, Pierce's Secretary of War, and—until less than four months ago—His Excellency, Jefferson Davis, President of the Confederate States of America, confidant of monarchs, prime ministers, and Pope Pius IX himself.

Now he stood accused of sedition and high treason. Of masterminding Lincoln's assassination. Of even (God save the mark) trying to escape in women's clothes at the time of his capture outside of Irwinville, Georgia. Now he was scapegoat of the South's bitterness. Butt of all calumny and insult in the Northern press. "The most dangerous man in America" and Everyman's candidate for a hanging bee at a sour apple tree.

He permitted himself an astringent smile. "Tell me something, Sergeant," he murmured. "In a war, what makes a man a criminal?"

"Losing, sir." Grogan was perfectly solemn.

"I'm afraid so. Think I'd like to sit down for a bit, if you don't mind . . ."

They had walked a little distance from the wall. A weathered stone bench stood under a big oak. As they neared it, a dust-brown bird left its pickings at the bench base and flew away. Davis followed its flight as long as he could.

Grogan eased him down to the bench, then fumbled a ham-like paw in the pocket of his caped greatcoat. "Brought along an exter pipe, sir. Thought you'd not be averse to a smoke."

"Thank you," Davis said gratefully. His own prized briar-wood and tobacco had been taken away.

Grogan handed him a handsome meerschaum, then took out his own stubby, blacked cob. He wiped a match into flame, shook away a sulphurous flare of sparks, and lighted both pipes.

Davis puffed with reverent care, leaning his head back against the oak's furrowed bark. The cold wind blowing in from Chesapeake Bay and the Atlantic smelled of brine and freedom. It drove a cotton-ball cobbling of clouds overhead, slicing the sky into blue wedges. The sun softened Monroe's grim walls. For the first time in longer than he could at once remember, he felt at peace. With himself. Even with the world.

The worst aspect of imprisonment was the way the long, idle, motionless hours stretched out. The Bible's comfort had cloyed. For a man who'd always burned with energy that needed physical or mental outlets, it was maddening. No man attained the age of fifty-seven without a burden of ghosts. But few had to be cursed with such a lack of diversion that each ghost had to be pulled out and wrestled down all over again through idle hour after idle hour. The crisping feel of fall intensified the feeling. It always did. It was the worst of times at the best of times. Locking into his thoughts with a savagely nostalgic bite.

At such times, he'd think mostly of the North where he had soldiered as a young man. Falls in the North were the coldest and brightest and most intense.

Saddest? That too. Damn.

He restlessly, absently rubbed the memory of the welt on his right ankle where it rested across his left knee. Then realized what he was doing. And shuddered. Those damned leg shackles. He had worn them for only a week, but he would never forget. Never. It had taken four burly guards to hold him while the prison blacksmith had secured the irons on his ankles. He had wept, had even begged them to shoot him.

He had been unmanned a few times in his life, but not many. The shame of it still sickened him.

"Aye," Grogan said gently, removing the pipe from his mouth. "It's a feeling clings on like a cocklebur, ain't it, sir? Even when the shackle's gone, it's still there."

"I suppose they all say that."

"Sometimes they do. Others, they don't need to come out with a word. It's in the faces, sort of like death, and not just the chains either. You, now, way you watched that bird. I been serving in these walls thirty-six years come this fall, and I seen but one other who'd watch a bird just so. Old Black Hawk, it was."

Davis gave him a sharp glance.

"The famous Sac chieftain, sir."

"I know who you mean. That's right . . . Black Hawk was imprisoned here, wasn't he?"

"Through the spring of '33. They wintered him at Jefferson Barracks, then brought him here."

"I know," Davis said quietly. "I was the man who brought him to the Barracks. Down from Wisconsin."

"You, sir?"

"I commanded the troop detail that brought him, I should say."

"Now there's a caution," Grogan said thoughtfully. "Myself, I was the young soldier with the task of guarding Black Hawk on his walks on these ramparts . . . as I'm doing with you today, sir." He bent over and tapped the bench with his stubby pipe. "He liked to sit where you're sitting now. Only him, they kept the irons on his legs all them months. Little mincing steps he had to take, like a prissy girl. God, what a comedown for that old devil! And the look of him! If ever there was a hawk in a cage. Did you know the old gentleman well, sir?"

"He was quite a man, Black Hawk. That I knew. And the most brilliant military tactician I ever knew, bar none. If his stratagems had been perfected by a general of a white and civilized nation, he'd stand in the books with Alexander, Caesar . . ."

"Is that so!" Grogan was properly impressed by these words from the commander-in-chief of such as Bob Lee and Old Stonewall.

True words. But evasive ones. Davis was aware of a biting lump in his throat. He rubbed his hand on the abrasive stone of the bench. There was a conspiracy in this day . . . the nostalgic fall, the confrontation with (so to speak) Black Hawk's specter, the sweet bitters of backward-turning thoughts. He couldn't remember when things that the mind held at bay had swarmed at him so strongly.

The young men, all the young men, comrades in the golden times when nothing could go wrong no matter how many things went wrong. When each day had a taste of forever. Albert Sidney Johnston. His dearest friend, his favorite general. Killed at Shiloh. And Robert Anderson. That gallant friend, that gallant enemy. Major Bob Anderson, whose personal heartbreak had come not at war's end, but at its beginning when it had been his lot to surrender the federal garrison at Fort Sumter. Gone, all of them. All the young men. Old or dead. Or split apart by destiny's scarlet scythe and four warring years.

Well, there was still the other kind of memories. Thank God. The ones that time never stained.

Youth. In youth, a man foundered in his own conflicts, never knowing what he wanted. By early middle age he was hardened into certainties; ideals became beliefs. Finally the flaccid erosions of cynicism began. And with them, the battle to hold his soul intact.

In that respect, maybe, his road had been smoother than most. He thought of his words to Miles: *A man can be killed.*

Defeated, never. It took a strength held to through long years of living to let a man say that and mean it.

Strength which had taken some harsh tempering. A lot of it.

Davis's fingers ached from gripping the edge of the bench. The memory was always there. A thin running pulse so near the surface that he could lightly, fondly touch it at will. But thrusting itself full and burning now into the front of his mind.

The seasons came. They went. Year after year. And not a jot of memory ever dimmed.

"Ten more minutes, sir," Grogan said. He had discerned the prisoner's mood and, respecting it, had been silent for some minutes.

The glossy oak leaves whispered. They dappled the lawn, the stone bench, the man sitting and the man standing.

But to the man who sat, the tongues of the present said nothing. His thoughts had frozen and retreated. Across a thousand miles and thirty-three years of time. . . .

PART ONE

A Season for Anger

1

For most of the day and through the swift March twilight into darkness, the two riders had been hemmed about by an oppressive cling of virgin forest. It was quite late, not yet midnight, when the trees began thinning away. Overhead, a black webbing of naked branches made a frosty filigree on the metal-blue sky.

The road they had followed south was still little more than a widened game path. Slashings littered the trailside; raw stumps and the stubble of cut saplings and brush sculptured a thin topping of new snow. Though the powdery mantle sparkled with a milky starshine, the men picked their way carefully through the night.

This winter of 1831–32 had been the bitterest in the memory of the Northwest. The snow had retreated, fallen, melted. In late March it had fallen once more, covering the drab earth like a sugary icing. With it came a dry ironlike cold that still gripped the eastern fringe of what would become the Territory of Iowa. The days were only cold. The nights taloned like death into the marrow of the unlucky traveler.

The horsemen had gone for two days and most of a night with no rest. In their numb exhaustion, they were almost oblivious to cold. They rocked slackly in their saddles, patiently alert to the horses' progress.

Almost unexpectedly they left the last trees and came onto the crest of a lofty well-grassed knoll. The view was panoramic. To west, to south lay an undulating wilderness of forest and prairie. Down to the deep left of them was a sprinkling of lights.

The younger of the two men broke an hour's silence: "Dubuque. A fair sight about now, James."

"It's that, Mister Jeff."

Cradled among the gray battlement bluffs and wooded slopes that flanked the upper valley of the Mississippi, the village seemed to tumble off the steep hillsides toward the river. Its scattered buildings lay in tight pockets that climbed off the riverbank. Pockets so thickly wooded that the town, except for those spatters of light, had more of a wilderness aspect in the night than the bald white-cowled hills that girdled it.

In spite of its still-raw look, Dubuque's frontier genesis was nearly a half-century behind it. In 1788, Julien Dubuque, a French-Canadian, had gotten permission from the Indians to mine lead on the site. Eight years later, obtaining a grant of one hundred and eighty-nine square miles, he had founded a settlement; but it had vanished following his death in 1810. Now, like the fabled phoenix, Dubuque had risen again. And so had a red flag of danger.

The raw, hectic sounds of a boom town's late-night revelry drifted faintly to the ears of the two men. They listened a moment, then started down the slope, trampling dead crusted grass flattened by wind and a winter weight of snow.

Suddenly James raised a long arm. He said, "There, sir," but the other was already swinging in the indicated direction, toward a bivouac line of tents and fires coming into view from behind some forested hummocks.

The fires were hot beacons in the frost-bright night. The encampment was set in such a high-angled way as to strategically command the town. A handful of greatcoated sentries paced their watches in and out of the firelight which glinted fitfully on their bayoneted muskets.

The horses drummed the frozen ground. The guards were alert; the two were picked up and challenged before they reached the aura of firelight. Having identified themselves, they were directed through the bivouac rows to the tent that housed the detachment's two officers.

As they rode up, Lieutenants Gibbs and Wilson were crouched by their small fire outside the tent's flap, intent on the battered miniature chessboard which was set on a camp stool between them. While one contemplated his move, the other would hold his ungloved hands to the fire's warmth. Both pretended not to notice the newcomers.

"George," Jefferson Davis said, "Denny."

"Hullo," said Wilson, not glancing up from his game. "Did you hear something just then, Dennis?"

"Couldn't say," Gibbs said laconically, gazing at the fire. "You know how this cold weather deefens us Southern boys."

Davis dropped off his horse, stiff with weariness, and handed his reins to James Pemberton. Walking to the fire, he peeled off his fleece-lined gauntlets, saying dryly, "Well, gentlemen. Don't get all excited on my account."

Wilson sprang to his feet and pumped Davis's hand. "For God's sake! Look who's here, Denny. It's young Jeff Davis!"

"By God, it is," Gibbs drawled and rose, extending his big-knuckled hand with a broad grin. "Hoddo there, ole Southern boy. You have a nice trip down?"

Davis briefly shook their hands, then held his own half-frozen ones to the fire. "Don't doubt it for a moment," he told them. "Dawdled shamelessly in only the most sumptuous brothels and taprooms between here and Prairie du Chien. Canary in every glass and a harlot in every—"

"I say, Dennis," Wilson broke in. "Do you feel that Brer Davis is giving us a bit of a chafing?"

"Dunno about that," drawled Gibbs, "but if any of them-there fine and nifty doodads ole Jeff is alluding to was inside fifty miles trailside by the way he came, ole Jeff would have found 'em out sure, you bet."

"Gentlemen, would you both do me a great favor? Would you both please go to hell? Please."

After two days of almost continuous riding, the fire's ruddy warmth was a bone-deep luxury which sloughed away some of his exhaustion. Standing by it, Davis made a strong light figure, robust and not quite slender. Most people called him tall, but he wasn't exceptionally so. His jackboots added an inch to his five feet eleven inches; he had a straight military bearing that gave the effect of height.

The firelight glinted on the darkly golden hair which curled along his temples under his tall leather cap. His forehead was square and high; the inquisitive, strong-arched brows hooded his eyes. Their color played from blue to gray around the matrix of his moods, which were positive and intense. His mouth was finely formed, his nose aquiline. The cheekbones, high and prominent, gave a slight hollowing to his jaws.

"Jolly good to see you and all that," Wilson said, "but wherefore alone, old boy? A week ago we dispatched one of the Winnebagos with a message requesting more troops. Didn't he reach Crawford or didn't we sound imperative enough?"

"He reached it." Davis spoke without turning his head. "Colonel Morgan died a few days before your runner arrived."

"I say—Willoughby Morgan's dead? Of course we knew the poor old fellow was weakening steadily. Then . . . Lieutenant Colonel Taylor is post commander now?"

Davis nodded. "I guess it's a permanent assignment. His brevet colonelcy came through at last. And I understand his family is coming up from Louisville to join him."

"Is that a fact? All the Taylors?"

Denny Gibbs's quiet drawl had sharpened with such interest that Davis glanced at him.

18

Gibbs, a towering youth of twenty-two, had a smooth boyish face that was wind-chapped and apple-cheeked from the cold, making him seem a lot younger. His blue eyes were as mild as his voice; his flaxen-pale hair and long mustaches were soft as cornsilk.

"Wouldn't know," Davis said. "They hadn't arrived when I left Crawford." He turned, warming his back. "I needn't tell you fellows that Zachary Taylor is a man with definite ideas. He's resolved to settle the Dubuque trouble once and for all. Without bloodshed, if possible."

"I shouldn't bank on that," Wilson said. "Last night a clutch of the Dubuque chaps stole up here and shot at the tents. We routed them directly, nobody injured, but the men are in high dudgeon. Want to go in and clean out the town at bayonet point. Can't say I blame them. Within our rights too, eh?"

George Wilson was the easygoing Gibbs's opposite. Small and dark, wiry as a catamount, with eyes like black gimlets. At times his energies built to such explosive peaks that he'd take dips in half-iced streams in the dead of winter to take his edge off. Usually he carried his high spirits with a wickedly cheerful impudence. He wore his Eton schooling like a badge, but both he and Gibbs came from leading families in Kentucky.

"Right or not," Davis said, "you'll sit tight for the time— pending further instructions. Old Zeke's orders."

Wilson groaned. "And what are *your* orders, Brer Davis?"

Davis grinned. Since October of last year, when General Macomb had ordered Fort Crawford to dispatch troops to Dubuque in order to prevent the white settlers from encroaching any deeper into the Indian lands, the detached force had been under strict orders to avoid any show of arms except in self-defense or to prevent an attack on the Indian villages.

"Don't laugh too hard, George, but the colonel hopes I can persuade the whites to move off the non-treaty lands peaceably."

Wilson laughed about as hard as he could, bitterly. "God,

man, d'you think we haven't talked to 'em? We've argued, we've reasoned, we've wheedled, we've all but gone down on our knees to these damned jakes."

"Maybe you lacked a telling argument."

"I suppose *you* have one?"

"Maybe. The government's about to conclude a new treaty with the Sacs that will cede the Dubuque area unconditionally to the United States. For a guaranteed annuity."

"Treaty, eh?" said Gibbs. "Jeff-boy, how much you reckon a treaty means to these red peckerwoods? Black Hawk and his Injuns are priming this minute to grab off lands that were ceded to us long ago."

"Well, Denny," Davis said wearily, "they just might figure that the Grandfather in Washington City and his honorable electorate have given 'em more than provocation enough. Not the first time the whites have invaded the Indian lead country. Five years ago they moved into the Fever River area just across the Mississippi and seized all the Winnebago diggings at Galena. Almost set off a full-scale rising before the Army threatened both sides into capitulation. But the upshot was that two years later, the Treaty of Prairie du Chien ceded all the Illinois lead country to the whites. I was there. The Indians considered it outright thievery. The Sacs and Foxes have laid claim to this Dubuque area since time immemorial . . . and are getting a shade tired of watching their lands seized under one flimflam excuse, then another."

Gibbs shrugged. "I just don't see getting steamed up about these bloody beggars' 'rights.' Hell, they were squabbling among themselves over rights before there was a white man in this country. Then took sides with the French or British as suited their damned fancies."

"Or interests," Davis said. "But it's all academic to us. We follow orders, gents. The War Department feels it's essential to show the tribes our good faith. The Winnebagos and Ottawas and Potawatomis—not to mention all the Sacs and Foxes who

20

haven't taken up for Black Hawk—are watching and waiting. Even the friendly chiefs have grave doubts about our intent. You can't blame them, all the whites squatting here in open violation of past agreements. So before negotiations proceed further, the squatters have to go. I'm empowered to make a detailed record of each claim. Claimant can repossess his property directly the treaty's concluded."

"And who," Wilson hooted quietly, "is going to walk down there and tell them *that?*"

"I am."

The other two exchanged glances. Davis had no reputation for diplomacy.

"I say, Jeff," Wilson blinked. "Have you noticed what's going on down there?"

"Whatever it is, it's on the lively side."

"Oh, quite. They've been carrying on in Slone's groggery four nights running. Drinking, brawling, talking themselves to a fever. Much as a man's life is worth to be seen down there in uniform. They've already shot at some of our men. And sent word that any officer who shows his face will get sent back in chunks."

Davis walked to his horse, opened the flap of a saddlebag and took out a brass-mounted pistol. The weapon was already charged, a cap crimped on the priming nipple. He thrust it into his belt.

"Be obliged if you fellows can assign us accommodations for the night. See that the horses are cared for, James. I'll be back before midnight."

"You can't face that drunken trash alone, Mister Jeff."

Davis looked at him. A tall, superbly built man with a pale brown skin, James Pemberton was a griffe, only fractionally Negro. His Creek Indian blood dominated his ax-blade features, high cheekbones, and straight inky hair. Two years Davis's elder, he had been his body servant for nine years. His manners were gentlemanly, his voice soft as summer dusk.

"Wish there were the choice you infer, James. There isn't."

"Sir?"

"Thunder, lightning, and hail won't budge your backwoodsman stuck fast on an idea. Shake the government and the Army at him and he spits in your eye, bedamned to the consequences. But he respects cold gall. Let a man show enough of it, he'll hear him out."

"Look, Jeff-boy," Gibbs put in, "we all know the Lord so loves you that he lined your guts with boiler plate. But this is a pure foolishness. Those miners won't believe you even if you get 'em to listen. All they'll hone for is to notch a nice fresh-faced second lieutenant's ears."

"Yours, maybe. They don't know me. New face, voice of different tidings, all that. Besides, I've spent the past six months logging on the Iowa River. Frostbite, sore muscles, pickled pork, and lice. But damned little excitement. Now if one of you will kindly direct me to Mr. Slone's . . ."

Wilson sighed. "Of course—of course."

He and Davis passed through the tents and the sentries to the long rim of the hill.

Dubuque clung like a toy village to the flanks of forested hills that fell away to the small business area. Hills that virgin prairie grass had covered before the Indians' surface scrabblings for the plentiful "float lead" had caused woody mottes to spring up. The newer diggings showed everywhere as ugly ocher scars.

Wilson pointed. "That far light at the south end of town . . . that's Slone's. By the way, Jeff." He cleared his throat. "Before you left Prairie du Chien, did you by chance, uh, say hello to Miss Street?"

"Miss Street is well and sends you warm regards. To put it, I'd imagine, fairly mildly."

"Blast your levity. I say, what if those jackasses won't even listen?"

"In that case, I'd suggest you draft another note requesting

22

those extra troops. Look, George, quit worrying. I'm going down to talk to them, not take on the whole camp."

"Always provided," Wilson said dourly, "that a checkrein is kept on the celebrated Davis temper . . ."

Going down the slope toward the lights of Dubuque, Davis felt his exhaustion slip away. A sudden reserve of energy warmed him against the stiff wind knifing off the Mississippi. It was, he thought, the pure foolishness Gibbs had called it; yet he walked as if there were springs in his heels.

He passed the outlying cabins and frail shanties that, scattered through the ravines and shouldering hills, housed Dubuque's rough, transient population. In places, lacking lumber, the miners had burrowed like badgers into the hillsides, hollowing out and sod-fronting their caves. These were almost indistinguishable from the many horizontal drift shafts or "sucker holes" that tunneled into the bluffs.

Lead. Galena. Gray gold, some called it. By whatever name, it was the key to all settlement across eight million acres east and west of the Northern Mississippi Valley.

At this hour, Dubuque's main avenue was a deserted trail chopped to a mire by wheels, hoofs, boots, and frozen into miniature ridges and craters. Davis slogged to the lower street with its jumble of warehouses, brothels, and taverns. He could have located Slone's place, a rambling log tavern, just from the boozy blare of noise.

He reached the porch, stepped up and around a man who sat there with his face in his hands drunkenly groaning, pushed open the hide-hinged door and went in.

The taproom stank. It reeked of cigar and pipe smoke, blackjack rum and bad whiskey, unwashed clothing and bodies. The only furnishings were two crude puncheon tables, some half-log benches and a bar formed by whipsawed logs laid across a pair of whiskey barrels. The saffron fog of smoke dimmed the candlelit room; his eyes stung and watered.

The din stopped. So did the banjo someone was plunking in

a kind of dismal cadence to it. Davis shouldered his way to the bar, not turning his head when somebody spat at his boots.

A man spoke to him: "How-de-do, sojer boy."

He was a big rawboned youth leaning against the bar with his arms folded, grinning fiercely. His lean jaws sparkled with fiery whiskers; a coonskin cap topped his tangle of dirty red hair. He wore grease-blackened buckskins and a bearskin coat whose stink wasn't quite lost in the saloon's myriad stenches. A huge buffalo pistol was shoved in his belt, which also held a sheathed Arkansas toothpick: the frontier dagger. Two-edged, pointed like a needle, designed for fighting and killing, and nothing else.

Davis peeled off his gloves and slapped them on the bar. "The name is Lieutenant Davis, mister."

"The name is Rafer Beal, sojer boy. Don't answer to no mister."

The sudden twang of a Jew's harp in a back room, the ensuing shriek of a woman's laughter, were explosive slashes in the stillness. Davis, his face an easy mask, nodded at the man behind the bar. Squat as a drum, the fellow had cold-humored eyes that did nothing to liven his doughy face.

"Mr. Slone?" Davis made his tone cool, unconcerned, faintly insolent. "Wonder if I might use your place as a kind of town platform? What I have to say should interest all your, ahem, patrons."

After a grudging moment, Slone nodded. "For pure brass, young 'un, you cut it finer'n anyone I met. You go ahead and see what it gets you." He raised his voice. "Lads, this fellow hain't come with soldiers at his back. I 'low that earns him a say."

Davis leaned back against the bar, hooking his elbows on it and facing the room. He looked at the weathered, bearded, stolid faces, the anger lurking thinly beneath. Some of them would be the scum of the river: cardsharps and whiskey traders, coaster and swillpots. But most of them, he guessed, were typical

24

of the simple, hard-living frontier breed. Hunters, trappers, miners, rivermen, they knew a rough democracy; they'd listen. For a little while anyhow.

"Men, the government's about to conclude a treaty with the leading chiefs of the Sac nation. You all know what it involves . . . what's at stake for all of you. All we ask is that you demonstrate fair intent by removing yourselves lock, stock, and barrel to the Illinois side. Then—"

"Hell." Rafer Beal tested his dagger's edge with the ball of his thumb, grinning. "We-all heard about that. Ain't likely the gov'ment sent one of their tin sojers just to give us that say-so. You just one little ole bluejay, boy. They reckon you can spank a whole den of bearcats by yourself?"

"I'm here to try to *keep* the peace. If you'll hear me—"

"Don't reckon we will."

Beal pushed away from the bar. His rawboned ungainliness was deceptive: he moved like a cat. A flick of his wrist drove the dagger into the bar's plank top; it froze a golden sliver of light.

"Boy, there ain't a soul don't know what you sojers is doing here. Pertecting them goddam redskins against the little man claiming his rights."

Davis looked at him casually, then went on: "As most of you know, the administration of mineral lands in the public domain is now under the jurisdiction of the War Department. That means the Army, and I'm here as its spokesman. Empowered to register each and every one of your claims. Bring me a detailed description of your property and I'll record it. Each claim will receive proper recognition on the day the treaty's signed and sealed."

Gruntings and rumblings stirred the men. They looked at him owlishly. He pressed the argument: "Gentlemen, as of now, you're all squatters who could be legally dispossessed any time. You've a clear chance to make your claims secure for yourselves and your heirs. Be obliged if you'd see the word's passed along to everybody with a squatter's claim."

He paused to let the magnanimity seep in. "You've resented the presence of troops here. All right. They'll be withdrawn once the treaty goes into effect—"

Beal chuckled mildly. "Well, boys, you know I 'lowed all along this here whole treaty business is a goddam trick to steal our land. Ain't us them sojers is here to pertect, it's them red bastards. Goddam paper don't mean shucks. Gov'ment does what it pleases. Goddam gov'ment is got the Army, and the little man fools with them, he gets a bayonet up his ass. But we stand together, the Army will shy off quick. Shooting up civilians would make heap big stink clear to Washington City. Them big politicos don't want that."

Davis eyed him again. "I'm wondering, Beal, just how much land you claim hereabouts?"

"Talk's cheap, bluejay. You want to tell us there hain't no more sojers coming to Dubuque if we don't come to taw here'n'now? Go on, now. Tell us."

"I needn't tell you a damned thing, fellow."

"There you are!" Beal flung out a gaunt arm, sweeping the room with his stare. "You ain't gonna get no straight answer off'n him. Do like he says and after a while it comes about that treaty business never meant shucks. Seems the gov'ment and the Injuns couldn't reach no fare-thee-well and the treaty's off. You come back, there's an Injun squatting on your claim and a mess o' bluecoats with bayonets pining to cut you to mincemeat. So-jer boy"—he straightened with a soft movement—"I do make you a goddam liar, for certain-sure."

Davis's voice stayed smooth and pleasant. "I think, my friend, that you want a sound caning to teach you respect."

Beal gave a rumbling chuckle. And moved like a rattler. Coming at Davis from the side, clamping a powerful arm against his throat, forcing him backward across the bar.

Davis strained at the arm. It held like a bar of iron, thrusting back his chin at an angle that threatened to crack his spine. He thumped his fist against Beal's ribs. Like hitting a side of frozen beef. He had the cold realization that Beal was putting out about half his strength; the man could almost as easily break his back.

There was a tug at his belt, the pressure left his throat. Beal stepped back, holding up the pistol he'd yanked from Davis's belt. Chuckling, still holding Davis at the end of his arm, he tossed the weapon on the bar.

Davis used the respite: his hard sudden twist broke the hold, and he spun away.

Beal leaped, but not toward Davis. He ripped the impaled knife from the bar. Just as swiftly he sprang to a clear space in the middle of the packed-earth floor.

He stood between Davis and the door.

"Now," he grinned, "you guard that pretty gizzard o' yourn, sojer boy."

He came at Davis in a dainty weaving motion, dropped to a knife fighter's crouch. Davis gave ground step by step. His hand settled in the deep pocket of his greatcoat. No, he thought, that's no good. It will spoil everything. But you'll be dead if you don't . . .

"If you will kindly move aside there," a voice said politely. "Thank you, gentlemen—"

Men took one look. They fell over their neighbors in a stampede to create space. An alley opened magically between the cleared spot and the door.

"Goddlemighty," someone yelled. "A crazy Injun with a shotgun. Don't nobody make him mad, for Christsake!"

James Pemberton stood in the doorway, holding Davis's double-barreled fowling piece. No way to tell whether it was loaded with birdshot (wicked enough at this range) or something worse. And nobody was curious enough to provoke the answer.

Beal turned a mild and interested glance on the tall body

27

servant. "Why, boy, I am plumb flabbergasted. You-all know you are pointing that there young cannon at a *white man,* boy?"

"This shotgun is not overly particular, mister. At just this moment, neither am I."

Beal roared gleefully and swung back to Davis. And gazed into the muzzle of a small Allan's patent pistol. It needed only a tug on the trigger to lift the hammer and detonate the cap.

"Sojer boy, you ain't even cocked that bitsy thing."

"Not necessary with this little article. And it is a fleabite beyond a few yards, but at a short range—say from me to you— one can put a ball nicely through a man's unlovely gizzard."

Beal chuckled in the smoky silence; he slid the dagger back in its sheath. "Why, sojer boy, you are a caution, sure enough."

Davis nodded. "Thank you, James. You saved Beal's life. Don't obey orders too well, do you?"

"Not always, sir."

Beal seemed delighted with the turn of things. He sagged against the bar, his sides quaking. "Migawd, you bullies, we been took proper by these high-talking bastards. We got us a pair of South'n wildcats here, boys!"

Davis retrieved his other pistol, belted it, and looked again at the crowd. "Well, gentlemen. You've thought over my proposition. Suppose we drink to its success." Danger, as usual, had a genial effect on him. His manner was crisp, friendly, positive. "Mr. Beal—I insist. The treat's mine, Mr. Slone."

Beal smacked a hamlike palm between his shoulder blades, the friendly gesture slamming Davis against the bar. "You're awright, Army. But my name's Rafe, goddam you! I don't answer to no goddam mister."

Davis glanced at Pemberton. "You can go on back now, James."

"I hardly think so, sir."

Pemberton walked to a bench in one corner and seated himself, the shotgun across his knees. The atmosphere melted: it flowed with warm conviviality as the miners swarmed around

28

Davis and Beal. They were vociferous and thirsty. The excitement had whetted every spirit alike.

With one ordeal behind him, Davis braced himself for what he considered a worse one. An evening-long round of free drinks, awful racket, and back-slapping in as foul a dive as he had ever seen.

2

In the spring of 1832, most of the great Northwest—containing the present states of Illinois, Indiana, Ohio, Michigan, Wisconsin, and part of Minnesota—still belonged more to the wolf, the cougar, and the Indian than to an increasing trickle of white traders, miners, and settlers. To it, the young United States had laid a doubtful claim since the Revolution, established it as the first U.S. colony with the Ordinance of 1787, and firmed its supremacy with the Treaty of Ghent following the War of 1812. A handful of military outposts protected the American whites and the interests of an expanding nation. Otherwise the spired oceans of timber and swelling seas of prairie had changed little in the two hundred years that the *voyageurs* of New France had tramped and trapped them.

From upper Illinois northward, rivers were still the favored mode of transportation, and settlement followed the rivers. Roads were few and far between. Usually mere hoof-mired trails, usually half-completed. Grubbing out tree roots was so costly that it became simple expediency to saw them off close to the ground. Roads followed stream bottoms where possible, corduroyed across marshes, forded shallow streams and bridged the deep ones on precarious stringers with puncheons laid across. Here and there a native might swell his skimpy poke by establishing a raft-and-pole ferry.

Jefferson Davis and James Pemberton, returning from Dubuque, were in no hurry anyway. Real spring had blown in on a light wind from the south. A thaw wind. The rotted ice went out of the Mississippi with a roar. The churning floes filled the days and nights with a brittle drumming as they rode north from Dubuque by way of Panther Creek to the mouth of the Turkey River. Coming to Dubuque, they had crossed the mile-wide Mississippi on solid ice; by now even the bobbing flotilla of ice blocks had almost subsided, and Walker's treadwheel ferry was back in service. It carried them across to Cassville, and they stood again on the soil of Michigan Territory. This—the half west of Lake Michigan—was still four years from being declared the Territory of Wisconsin.

It was just a hop from Cassville up to Prairie du Chien. And while Davis didn't exactly dawdle in reporting back, he held to a trip of easy stages. The muck-deep roads and flooded streams were adequate official excuses and the weather was the best of all personal excuses. Every day had brought sunny breezes. The brown prairie grass was starred with blue windflowers; pussy-willows burst their sepia sheaths and poured gray catkins to the sunlight. Nights were chilly, but a cozy camp and a fire crackling with pine pitch made up for it.

For a while they followed the Mississippi northward, then cut over to the military road that angled up to the Wisconsin River Valley. They encountered no one on the road; the few log cabins along the way were often tumbledown and deserted, the efforts at land-clearing reclaimed by weeds and second-growth timber. Reminders in this soft spring beauty of the North's grimmer face.

To cross the broad Wisconsin and reach Prairie du Chien, they had to hit it at the point where Leclerc, the surly French Canadian, had his ferry. It was a rough crossing. The wine-colored thaw water tore angrily at the tilting weighted raft, spraying creamy riffles across the men and their skittish stiff-legging horses. The choppy dance of sunlight on the Wisconsin only hinted at its easy power as it coursed deep and silent on its crooked prowl to extinction in the Mississippi a mile down.

Leclerc, familiar with the river's temper, phlegmatically enjoyed his passengers' discomfort and, once across, over-charged them for "the ver' rough passage this time year." As Davis counted out the coins, he heard, from a little distance downstream, the measured strokes of an ax.

"Sounds like a wood detail from the fort."

"*Non,* is new neighbor building. Robier the trapper. Thank you, m'sieu . . ."

In saddle again, they swung west along the Wisconsin's north bank toward the meeting of the rivers and Fort Crawford. Midday warmth swirled humidly in the bottoms. Davis was tired; there was a spreading ache across his back and shoulders. It would be good to get back. The continued sound of the un-seen axman's labor made a pleasant refrain to his thoughts of a hot bath and change of clothes.

He could report on a successful mission. For two days he'd sat at a table in Slone's taproom, duly registering those who brought him their claims on mining or farm property. Patiently extracting the necessary information from each claimant, he hadn't bothered to argue with the many he knew were faking or overclaiming. Let the government smell out its own rats. His job was done. Accomplished without striking a blow or shed-ding a drop of blood.

Within another couple of days, Dubuque had become a ghost town. The miners had commandeered every craft available—keelboats, flatboats, bateaux, rafts, pirogues, birch canoes—to convey them and their belongings down and across the Missis-sippi to Galena on the Illinois side, where most of them would wait it out till they could return legally. Lieutenants Gibbs and Wilson would remain encamped with their detachment till orders came relieving them, which in all probability would be soon, with the Black Hawk trouble coming to a head.

Would the temporary removal of the miners from the Sac lands help head off a war? Davis doubted it. A mote in the wind. A few Sac and non-Sac chiefs would be more inclined to negotiate than fight, that was all . . .

He and Pemberton rode out of the steamy bottoms and up a long hill clad with old gnarled oaks. Sunlight freckled the amber shade; dead leaves still clinging to the branches rustled in the tiny monsoons of late March. Passing over the hill, they dropped down to a dead-grass stretch of prairie.

Davis heard a sudden tattoo of hoofs. A horse running. The animal burst out of the oak woods to their right. It was saddled and riderless, a golden chestnut whose coat rippled like live gold. An Arabian, from its fine small head and arched neck. It saw the two men and hauled up snorting, then crashed back into the woods at an angle, disappearing again.

"James, do you know the horse? He looks familiar."

"Yes, sir. One of Colonel Taylor's thoroughbreds. And that was a lady's saddle."

"Catch him up . . . I'll try to find the lady."

He twitched his sorrel's head around and put him into the forest at the angle from which the chestnut had charged. A saddled runaway meant that the rider had probably been thrown. Davis rode briskly through the sun-fogged glades and damp shadows, emerging into a wide slash of clearing.

The girl was sitting on the ground, her back against a large oak. He swung out of his saddle and walked to her.

"Are you hurt, miss? What happened?"

She was a small girl, not much above fourteen, he guessed. Her big hazel eyes stared at him with a kind of half-tearful shock. Her face was oval and small, the high forehead and full rounded chin impressing him as both stubborn and unbecoming. Her pink mouth was small, thin-lipped, almost stingy. For all that, she was pretty enough, or would be with a few more years on her. Her riding habit, a puff-sleeved and full-skirted cashmere twill, was too bulkily stylish for her slim urchin figure. At least he assumed it was stylish, being four years behind on the edicts of Paris and London. A dark fur toque with a yellow plume rested on her glossy brown hair which, parted in the middle, was divided into four spiraled curls that hung to her bosom.

She gazed at him blankly. She raised a hand and rubbed at her cheek. It was streaked with brown leafmold.

He bent down. "Miss, listen . . . are you injured?"

He grasped her lightly by the elbows and shook her.

She gave a little anguished scream, her whole body stiffening. "Oh, don't—don't, you fool! What are you about? My arm— let go!"

He jerked his hands back, realizing why she was holding her left hand cuddled against her waist. The dead white of her face was the bloodless pallor of pain. But now pain was almost canceled by the anger flooding her eyes.

"You *fool!*"

"I'm sorry . . . I didn't realize."

She blinked, her eyes like wet brown pebbles. "Help me up, please." She extended her right hand.

"Are you sure you can stand? Perhaps . . ."

She wiggled her fingers imperiously. He took her hand and gingerly eased her to her feet. Her brows flew together in a spasm of pain.

"Mister Jeff!" Pemberton called.

"Over here, James."

Pemberton came riding through the trees, leading the girl's chestnut. He swung down. "Is the young lady hurt, sir?"

"No, not at all," the girl said. She was blinking rapidly, biting her lip. "This *gentleman* almost removed my arm, that's all . . ."

Davis flushed. "I'm very sorry."

"I should think so."

He was tired and out of sorts, which always made him more thin-skinned than usual. But he held his temper. "Can we be of any service? If you live nearby . . ."

"Haven't you done quite enough?"

"Listen, little girl." He said it very quietly, spacing every word. "I didn't know you'd hurt your arm. But I didn't do that. You must have been running the horse too hard . . . probably over rough ground—"

That hit a nerve. She drew her small body very stiff. "*If* I was, it's hardly any of your affair."

His control slipped another notch. "No, in spite of which I undertook to help you."

"I didn't ask your help, did I?"

The devil! He wasn't taking such backtalk from a child, hurt or not. "I should have warmed your bottom instead, you snippy little vixen!"

Her eyes blazed. She turned toward Pemberton with frigid dignity. "I will take my horse, if you *please*—"

A tottering little step. Then she moaned and slipped to the ground.

Davis hurried to her, knelt and turned her gently on her back. He rolled back the sleeve of her dove-gray habit. No bleeding. But the flesh of her arm was puffy and discolored. He felt carefully along the bone.

"I can ride to the fort and bring Dr. Beaumont, sir."

"I don't think that'll be necessary. No break or fracture . . . perhaps a sprain. We'll take her to where that fellow's chopping. Couldn't be a hundred yards away, and he might have a drop of spirits . . . something to bring her around."

He gathered the girl up in his arms and started back toward the riverbank. Pemberton followed, leading the horses. They came to the trail and swung westward. The oaks were so densely crowded along the bank that the dusty sunshafts plunging in frail isolation through the branches rarely touched the spongy ground.

They were close to the chopping sound when Pemberton said quietly: "Someone is following us, sir."

Davis halted, listening. Brush crackled from somewhere to their right. The sound stopped. "Keep a watch," he said, and walked on.

Another hundred feet and they entered a clearing set back from the bank in a motte of sugar maples. A man was notching out the corner saddles of a building timber. He stopped work and nodded courteously.

"*Bon jour.* I am Vitelle Robier." His chest-deep voice had a dry dark music. "What is wrong with the ma'm'selle?"

He was about fifty. Short, lean, muscle-trim, with hulking shoulders and unusually long arms; his skin was like saddle leather. His wide, rather brutal mouth and thick blade of a nose would have dominated his face except for his eyes. Kindly eyes, the deep calm blue of a twilight glade. He wore a linsey shirt and breeches of tanned deerhide.

Davis said flatly: "Who's that in the brush?"

"My son. I hear the noise, a horse running, I send him to see what it is."

"I don't like a man skulking at my back."

"*Pardonnez-moi,*" Robier said curtly. "That's his way." He raised his voice sharply: "Jean!"

The son trotted almost noiselessly into the clearing. He came no farther than its edge, then dropped on his haunches and laid his musket across his knees. A half-breed, Davis thought; he could have passed for a full-blood. He wore buckskin and his hair was scalp-locked. Proud, sullen, burning-eyed, he had the slim rawboned look of a young puma. He was about eighteen.

"I asked a question of you, m'sieu." The friendly tinge had left Robier's voice.

"I beg *your* pardon," Davis said. "She was thrown by her horse . . . arm injured. I don't know how badly. Would you have a drop of spirits about? Whiskey or brandy?"

Robier shook his head. His brows twitched upward like

quizzical black commas. "If m'sieu wishes, I will look at the arm."

He laid down the ax and glanced toward the lodge at one side of the clearing. A typical Indian dwelling: dome-shaped and walled with mats of skin and bark fitted over a frame of bent saplings.

"Ceclie! Come out. Bring a blanket, eh?"

The deerskin covering the entrance was pushed aside; a girl came out, a rough trade blanket folded over her arm. Not over sixteen, she had a nubile full-curving body that her scarlet leggings and short dress of soft-beaten doeskin did little to de-emphasize. Her skin was pale bronze; her hair, clubbed in the Sac fashion, glistened with colored beads—and what was no doubt bear grease. Despite her broad cheekbones and wide full mouth, she was pretty by more than Indian standards. Usually Indian eyes eclipsed the white. But hers were bright green, large, flashing like jade.

"*Comment vous portez-vous,* m'sieu?"

She dropped a proper little curtsey. The words and decorum clashed with her attire. Not to mention with those minxlike eyes.

Davis nodded. "*Je vais très bien,* ma'm'selle."

She unfolded and spread out the blanket, and he laid the girl down. Robier knelt and flexed his fingers lightly along her arm, past the bruise up to the elbow. His fingers were long, callus-tipped, but not insensitive.

"Eh. I think sinew is pull' around the joint. See—here is the swelling. It will get worse. I think there be much pain for the lady." He looked askance at Davis. "My Ceclie can make the cure to take down the swelling. M'sieu has perhaps heard of the *Midewiwin?*"

Davis sat down on his heels. "A little. The so-called medicine society of the Sacs and Foxes."

Robier smiled. "This so-call' medicine makes the cure no white *docteur* has learn'."

"With chants and rattling gourds?"

"With herbs and boiled leaves I have myself seen cure. There are four ranks in the *Midewiwin.* My wife's family was of the first rank. Ceclie knows their skills."

"Well . . ." What harm could it do? "That would be a kindness, sir."

Ceclie went back to the lodge and returned with a bundle of soft furs and a handful of wet leaves. She pillowed the white girl's head on the furs and pasted the leaves across her forehead. Davis watched the bloodless face with a quickening concern. She hadn't stirred a muscle. Perhaps he should have sent Pemberton after Beaumont . . .

She did stir suddenly. Her eyes quivered open and moved blankly over the three kneeling beside her. Starting to raise her left hand, she gave a little moan. She stared at the swollen purpling arm.

"Oh. Where . . . where am I?"

Robier gravely explained, introducing himself and his family. Her reply couldn't have been more gracious. Suddenly she seemed older than Davis had guessed. By several years. But her eyes still had a frozen angry look for him. He had the uncomfortable feeling that her pride wouldn't let her mend the bad start they had gotten off to . . . and he was too proud himself to like attempting it. But he'd better try.

"I am Sarah Knox Taylor," she said. "Colonel Taylor is my father."

The words froze on Davis's lips. The Old Man's daughter. Dandy kettle of fish. What did he say to that?

She made a small movement as though to rise. "Oh—" She bit her lip in pain and vexation, and lay back.

"It is best, ma'm'selle, that you rest where you are awhile or maybe you fall off the horse again." Robier looked at his daughter. *"Petite chou,* you will make the cure, eh?"

As a Southerner, Davis was familiar with outlandish pet

names for children. Names like "Lamb Pie" and "Honey Pot." But "Little Cabbage!" Leave it to a Frenchman.

Ceclie went to the lodge again and came back with a fat buckskin bag. From it she took two small pouches, removed shredded leaves from one, a reddish dried root from the other, and dropped both in a pot of water which she set by the fire flickering in a ring of sooty rocks.

Sarah Knox Taylor looked faintly alarmed. "What is all that?"

"My Ceclie makes the cure. Your arm, soon it be all well."

"Really—it's not necessary!" She began to raise herself. "I'm sure I can manage if you'll—"

Robier scowled. "Ma'm'selle had better lay still. The cure is good. You rest now. You will see."

"My man and I will wait," Davis said. "As soon as you feel able—"

"You need not wait, sir."

" we'll escort you back to Prairie," he said thickly, then stood up, turned on his heel and walked away. He had to observe the ordinary courtesies. But damned if he had to sit still for insults from this petulant little chit.

"You may as well water the horses, James."

"Yes, sir."

Pemberton led the three animals down the long bank to the river. Remembering his manners, Davis introduced himself to the Robiers. At the same time, with a Southerner's instinct for sizing a man as trash or quality by his habits, not his possessions, he glanced over the camp. Well-ordered, all the gear necessary to create a rough comfort in the wilds. Robier was building his cabin slowly, but building to last. He'd dug a trench to hold the base logs and these, already laid, were cottonwood cuts that wouldn't rot in the ground.

Robier lighted up his pipe and began to chat comfortably, ignoring the strained quiet between his guests. He had lived for many years among Keokuk's Ioway Sacs; recently, after his

Indian wife had died, he had decided to introduce his children to the white man's civilization. Prairie du Chien, three quarters of its population made up of mixed bloods, had seemed a good place to settle.

Ceclie removed the pot from the fire and took out the steeping leaves and roots. Ignoring a possible scald burn, she macerated them between her palms, then knelt beside Sarah Knox Taylor and had her hold up her arm. She began smearing on the brownish stuff. She frowned her dissatisfaction with its consistency, spat twice into her palm and rubbed the spittle into the leaf-root mash. Then smeared away. Sarah Knox Taylor's expression was controlled. But her face, which had regained a rosy tint, again lost some color. For a final touch, Ceclie filled a cup with the murky brew that the mash had steeped in and handed it to her. Miss Taylor drank it off to the last drop, neither quickly nor slowly, to show that it didn't faze her in the least.

Robier, his French-Canadian funnybone tickled, screwed up his face in mock anguish. "Ho! Is pretty bad stuff, *non?*"

"Quite." Miss Taylor smiled with an effort. "Have I your permission to leave now?"

"But yes. Ho ho!"

"Thank you very much. Thank you, Miss Robier."

Davis assisted her into the sidesaddle while Pemberton held the bridle. She coldly thanked them, nodded to the Robiers, and rode away, keeping the hurt forearm hugged lightly to her side.

Davis sighed. "Come along, James. She may fall off again."

3

Prairie du Chien lay on a broad flood plain of the Mississippi. Long ago, early Jesuits and *voyageurs* had found a village of Fox Indians on this spot; the chief's name, Alim, meant "dog," so the French had dubbed him "Chien," a name applied in turn to the village. Prairie du Chien was the romantic appellation that had stuck with the arrival in 1754 of the first French-Canadian settlers, through the taking over of New France by the British nine years later, and into the American era. In the thirteen years they'd occupied the Northwest, the British had built fur storehouses at Prairie du Chien and brought a boom to the fur trade that the Indians had carried on for centuries at this confluence of the Wisconsin with the Mississippi.

Davis and Pemberton kept Sarah Knox Taylor in sight all the way to the village. She had the sense to ride slowly and Davis had the sense not to overtake her, knowing it might provoke her into another foolish run.

The town was on a long climbing flat a little distance above the Wisconsin's mouth. On the west rolled the Mississippi, a sheet of sun-wrinkled blue mottled by tan silt sworls from the rising meltwater. A semicircle of grassy bluffs ended the flood plain on the town's east flank. Part of the settlement was on a long island slotted away from the main shore by a turbulent slough. Now, at high water, the island was largely inundated. Only the high ground where the buildings of Astor's American Fur Company stood was untouched. Across the slough, the eastern part of the village consisted of Fort Crawford and a scatter of log houses, less than a dozen of them white men's homes. The rest were hovels belonging to Indians and French-Canadian half- and quarter-breeds who made up the trapping brigades of *engagés* sent out by the American Fur Company. A sprinkling of Winnebago lodges rimmed the village.

Davis and Pemberton weren't too far behind the girl as the three of them rode in along the landing. It was a hive of activity at this time of year. The waterfront on both sides of the slough was crowded with keelboats, flatboats, bateaux, and canoes. Hunters from the West were coming in with buffalo hides, trappers from the North with bales of furs. The traders from St. Louis were up with boatloads of goods for sale and barter: blankets, guns, traps, trinkets, and whiskey. Bronzed, breechclouted Indians mingled with *voyageurs* in bright plaid shirts and colorful capotes, all of them hammering out talk in an atrocious patois.

A graveled road led from the landing up the slight eminence where Fort Crawford stood. Axes and hammers were clattering; construction still went on in "the new fort" as it had for the past three years. The first American log fort here had been destroyed by the British in the War of 1812, the second ruined by the rioting Mississippi. Hence the decisions to locate on higher ground and build of quarried rock. The present construction, begun by Colonel Taylor during his first tenure as commander, was still far short of completion. Outside the walls, some soldiers were splitting logs with L-shaped frows and wooden mallets while a young officer looked on.

He glanced over his shoulder as the riders came up, saying pleasantly, "Hullo, Knoxie. Have a nice ride?" He saw Davis behind her; he yelled, "Jeff! Land o' Goshen . . ."

42

Davis swung to the ground. "Hello, Bob."

They shook hands, grinning at each other.

Lieutenant Robert Anderson was a handsome pink-cheeked young man of twenty-seven with large brown eyes and thin lips that fluted ironically up at one corner. Sardonic and easy-natured, he had been among Davis's few close friends since his West Point days. They had seen little of each other in the last six months, having spent the fall and winter in separate sawyers' camps directing the cutting of timbers for the fort construction.

Still grinning, Anderson glanced at the girl. "Presumably you've met my old comrade, Jefferson Finis Davis . . .'."

"Yes." Her voice was very flat.

Anderson raised a brow. "I see you have. How nice. I say, did you hurt your arm?"

"Ask your friend." She clapped her heels against the chestnut's barrel and rode on past the fort walls.

Davis handed his reins to Pemberton and told him to go from the stables to their quarters and prepare a bath. The body servant rode away toward the complex of barns and stables beyond the fort quadrangle. Davis peeled off his gauntlets, looking quizzically at Anderson.

"When did the colonel's family arrive?"

"Two days ago, St. Louis packet. Sharp-tongued lass, what?"

"You seem to be well-acquainted. Colonel's daughter, eh?"

"He has three. Sarah Knox is the middle one. Our family and the Taylors have owned neighboring lands in Kentucky for two generations. My brother Charlie and I grew up with the Taylor girls. So I know how trying Knox can be, though you're the first who ever twisted her arm."

"Is that so?"

"Charlie was her sweetheart for years. Childhood sort of thing, but then they haven't seen each other in some time. More recently, our friend Gibbs has led Miss Taylor's beaux pack."

"Denny?"

"Sure. Their fathers are old friends. He's squired her about Louisville during his leaves the last two summers."

"Look, she fell off her horse, I didn't even see it, and not to change the subject, but is the colonel about?"

"Ah yes. The old paragon of sartorial splendor will be eager to hear your report. How was Dubuque?"

"Later. Is he about?"

"Saw him heading for his house awhile ago . . ."

Not even pausing to report in to the adjutant, Davis skirted the fort buildings and headed for the commander's home. Usually immaculate to a degree just this side of foppishness, he had learned not to let his own peccadillos cross the colonel's. He was grimy and bearded; his old uniform, which was almost falling apart, smelled of sweat, horse and saddle leather. He wanted nothing more just now than a hot bath and change of clothes. But Zachary Taylor, who did not give a tiny damn about punctilious dress, would want to know the outcome of his mission without one damned pinch of delay. That was Old Zeke.

The log-and-frame house where Fort Crawford's commander lived was Judge Lockwood's old place. It was set off by itself in a poplar grove beyond the barracks quadrangle. Two-storied and gabled, it boasted shuttered windows and a big glassed-in piazza with a railed balcony above. The first frame building in Prairie du Chien, it was a thing of rare splendor in the raw Northwest. The fort commander represented the government in this lonely *entrepôt* and outpost. He was expected to offer hospitality to all military, political, and social dignitaries that passed through, and more often than not he had to entertain beyond his means.

Davis went up the flagstone path. He knocked at the door, then doffed his shako and cradled it on his forearm. The windows were open to the spring breeze; a pianoforte was producing a fractured melody. While a small girl's bored stubborn voice droned *"One-two, one-two,"* a woman was saying,

44

". . . have Dr. Beaumont look at that arm. Knoxie, did you hear me?"

Davis knocked again.

"Knoxie, will you please answer—never mind, I will. All right, dear; that's enough practice."

The instrument ceased on a limping chord. The piazza door opened. The colonel's wife was dark and delicate, somewhere in her mid-forties; she showed her years lightly.

"Good afternoon, Lieutenant."

"Good afternoon, ma'am." He bowed. "I am Lieutenant Davis."

"Of course, the young officer sent to Dubuque. I am Margaret Taylor. Come in, Mr. Davis."

She showed him into the parlor. It had been transformed since Davis's last visit to this house, when Willoughby Morgan was commander. The Taylors must have brought their best things on the steamboat route from Louisville. The old shabby furnishings had been replaced by quality ones: a rose-patterned rug, brocaded settee, ladder-backed chairs, a tall clock, the gleaming pianoforte, and a mammoth sideboard of black walnut.

Zachary Taylor was slouched forward on the settee, a little boy of about five beside him. The two had their heads bent over a crackling pile of maps spread out on a low table.

"Now here, Dickie, this is The Portage, this little neck of land square in the middle of the territory where these two rivers, the Fox and the Wisconsin, swing almost together. And d'you know what?"

"No, Papa."

"Well, the Wisconsin runs south, clear down here to Prairie du Chien, and the Fox, which bumps almost against it, runs north. That's remarkable, d'you know? And Fort Winnebago is right here, smack on The Portage—"

"Zacharias," his wife said.

Taylor glanced up. Davis, bemused by the colonel as a family man, snapped into a belated brace.

"Lieutenant Davis reporting, sir!"

Taylor smiled and rose, casually returning the salute. "Welcome back, Mr. Davis. Was just explaining divers logistics to my boy here. Yonder's my daughter, Miss Elizabeth, and this is Master Dick."

The very pretty girl of seven standing properly by the pianoforte bench was a young replica of her mother. She dropped a curtsey. "How d'ye do, Lieutenant Davis?"

The little boy stepped up and offered his hand, a bit pugnaciously. "Was you ever at Fort Winnebago?"

"For two years. Matter of fact, I helped build Fort Winnebago."

"Honest Injun?"

"Honest."

Dickie grinned, obviously taken with one who was a builder of forts. "I got a frog this morning, Lieutenant. A big frog! Want to see him?"

"Knoxie!" Mrs. Taylor called. "Dickie, I'm sure the lieutenant might enjoy that another time, but—where is that girl! Knoxie, we have a guest!"

"Coming, Ma." Sarah Knox Taylor came tripping down the hall from the kitchen, a white bandage around her arm. She halted in the doorway. "Oh."

"Miss Taylor and I have—" Davis began, but Miss Taylor, her jaw set, was already marching across the room to the staircase.

"Knoxie!" said her mother.

She went up the stairs without a backward look.

"Now what's ailing her?" the colonel demanded.

"Afraid it's my fault," Davis said. "You see, I—"

"Of course." Mrs. Taylor smiled and nodded. "You're the young boor we've heard about."

"I hope not, ma'am."

She sighed. "Never mind, Lieutenant. Getting the facts straight has never been one of her virtues. She did neglect a point or two, such as your name and that you were an Army soul."

She glanced at the two children, the boy champing to be gone, the girl hanging on every word. "Both of you—scat. And Betty, stay away from the river with that dress, d'you hear?" Dickie went out the door in a rush; Miss Betty dawdled after.

"Excuse me," Margaret Taylor said crisply, and went up the staircase.

"Sit down, Mr. Davis, sit down."

Taylor was embarrassed; he crossed to the sideboard and produced a box of cigars. Standing, he was of medium height, but his width of shoulder, thick chest, and short legs gave him a squat and bulky appearance. His ill-fitting uniform, only vaguely regulation as to color and cut, did nothing to mitigate the impression. The unending flow of jokes about his tightwad ways and sloppy dress had contributed as much to his reputation as had his prowess in the field. His head was heavy and leonine with a great Roman beak of a nose; his wide mouth had a perpetual grim pout and his eyes were small and bush-browed. His thick shock of dark graying hair and full side whiskers curved around his broad face like a shaggy helmet.

"I'm afraid, sir," Davis said uncomfortably, "that I got off on the wrong foot with Miss Taylor."

"The devil you did!" Taylor gave a rueful deprecating snort; he shoved the box of cigars under Davis's nose. "Don't take spirits or tobacco myself, but a friend on assignment in Florida supplies me with these Havanas which I'm assured are choice. Take one. Hell, take a handful. Must ask you not to smoke 'em here; the weed makes my wife actively ill."

From the floor above, Davis heard Mrs. Taylor's low voice and Knox's short sullen reply.

Taylor sagged onto the settee next to Davis, shaking his head. "When she was little, I understood her; was younger then myself. Now—thank the Lord for Dickie, and plague take all female children. Damme, if that girl doesn't have a case of vapors—of the head. Well, about the Dubuque business . . ."

Davis was glad to talk about the Dubuque business. Taylor heard him out without comment, then gave a spare complimentary nod. "A job well done, Mr. Davis. You'll write out a full report, of course."

The map over which he and Dickie had been poring had curled; the colonel spread it out and flattened his palms on the edges.

"Look here, mister—"

A quick scan of the map oriented Davis: he was familiar with a hundred duplicates. The three forts guarding the upper Mississippi Valley were inked in heavily. Northernmost was Fort Snelling at the mouth of the Minnesota River, farther down was Fort Crawford at the Wisconsin's mouth, then Fort Armstrong at Rock Island, Illinois. Halfway between the Mississippi and Lake Michigan lay The Portage and Fort Winnebago—linking the Fox and Wisconsin waterways, which in turn linked Fort Crawford with Fort Howard over at Green Bay. That string of forts, no scrap of treaty paper, gave the United States mastery of the Northwest against Indian and Canadian British alike. Scattered through Michigan Territory were the usual little civilian stockades and blockhouses dignified with names like Fort Apple Grove and Camp Walnut Stand—good enough for militia stand-offs; in case of real trouble, soldiers were dispatched from the big forts.

Taylor's blunt fingers moved on the map. Stopped at a point on the Mississippi roughly a hundred miles below Rock Island. "Black Hawk's wintered here . . . at the mouth of the Des Moines River. We know he's been negotiating with the Winnebago and Potawatomi, but hasn't yet secured any concrete promises of aid. We don't think he will—nor find much more among his own people either. Big Sac Chief Keokuk is advising against any belligerent action, and the braves are split. The success of your Dubuque mission will help damp any martial spirit"—Taylor twitched another complimentary nod—"and put a firm period to any ideas of a grand alliance. That still leaves us with Black Hawk. Imagine you never met him."

"Yes, sir. Briefly."

Taylor's brows went up. "Oh?"

"Last June, at the Rock Island truce council. As you know, Colonel Morgan sent four companies down to Rock Island to deal with the trouble. I commanded Company B."

"I'm aware of that, mister."

"Yes, sir."

Naturally he'd familiarized himself with the records of officers who would serve under him. And with the whole background of trouble to which the new commander must fall heir.

Last spring, while the warriors of the Rock Island Sacs were on their winter hunt, white settlers had invaded some villages, burned the lodges, beaten the women and plowed up the ancestral burial grounds. Into other villages they'd brought whiskey, cheating befuddled Indians out of horses and furs. This was the situation Black Hawk and his men found when they returned to start the spring planting. Black Hawk had retaliated with lightning raids against the settlers' property and livestock. Whereupon Governor John Reynolds of Illinois had sent out a call for militia. These had given blundering pursuit to the Sacs, who'd evaded them with incredible ease. By midsummer, it had seemed more sensible to arrange a truce. As usual, the Indians were left with the short end: they must retire to the lands west of the Mississippi and agree not to recross without consulting Illinois's Great Chief and Washington City's Grandfather.

The Sacs' grumbling acceptance had turned to swift rage when, their food running short, they were refused permission to return and gather roasting ears from their old cornfields. Black Hawk had made angry appeal to the British, who'd appear

49

ently given him vague promises of support. He was further goaded by The Prophet, a half-Sac half-Winnebago mystic whose fierce hatred for the whites had led him to stir up Black Hawk's bitter jealousy of Keokuk—a leader convinced that resistance to the Americans must result in defeat. And the extinction of his people. By fall, Black Hawk was vowing to cross the Mississippi in the coming spring and make corn grow on his lands in the old way.

"I take it, sir," Davis said, "that you've no doubt of Black Hawk's intent to carry out his threat?"

"Intent be damned. Ability's the word. He doesn't command much status outside of his band; he's neither an hereditary nor elected chief. Just an aging headman with a kind of mesmeric influence over his own Rock Island Sacs. His personal attributes are another thing, as I've tried to explain to those War Department ninnies. They see him as a sixty-five-year-old fanatic with a few hundred primitively armed savages at his back. Half the picture. Fighting his way on his own ground, Black Hawk could make fools of Bonaparte or Wellington."

True, Davis thought. But Taylor was salving an old wound too. In 1814, as a young major, he had been ordered to fortify Rock Island against the British and their Indian allies. Raging against the incursion on his ancestral home, Black Hawk had borrowed cannon from the British: his braves had caught Taylor's troops in an indefensible position and routed them. Though he'd established Fort Armstrong, that remained the one engagement in which Zachary Taylor had ever failed to make a foe strike his colors.

The domestic fracas on the floor above was getting spirited. A peremptory word from Mrs. Taylor ended it. A moment later, she descended the stairs, a bit flushed.

"Would you care for whiskey or brandy, Mr. Davis?"

"Neither, ma'am; thank you."

"Coffee, then?"

Davis had forgotten what a good cup of coffee was like; he

said so. She exited to the kitchen. Overhead, Knox Taylor began to pace her room, making each step a vicious little explosion.

Taylor glanced dourly upward. "That girl wants a good hiding," he muttered. "As I was saying, Black Hawk will surely come, and noting how he's delayed till spring, I'd hazard he's girding himself for a campaign that'll last till snow flies."

"What's been done, sir?"

"Why, not enough by half. General Atkinson's coming up from Jefferson Barracks with six companies to assume command at Fort Armstrong. Why in hell wasn't it done months ago? Those savages have been high-blooded since last fall. We should have fortified, garrisoned, warned, threatened—done everything possible to impress on Black Hawk that however costly he makes it for us, it'll be far costlier to him. As it is— you know how ill-prepared we are by the condition of our own garrison: two hundred and twenty-five troops and eleven officers. Threats failing"—Taylor paused—"we shouldn't have hesitated. Should have treated Black Hawk and his 'British band' like a gangrenous limb and chopped 'em off before they pollute the whole body. Isolated as you'd quarantine any disease and exterminated."

Davis said nothing. He didn't go along with the "tame-'em-or-kill-'em" philosophy held by nearly all whites. When stationed at The Portage, he'd gone out of his way to learn the Winnebagos' language and customs; he had hunted, wrestled, run foot races with the young men—and had worn with pride the sobriquet they gave him of "Little Chief."

He felt Taylor's dourly appraising stare. "I take it, mister, that you don't approve of such stark sentiments."

"It's hardly my place to approve or disapprove, sir."

"Exactly."

"It merely seems to me that a powerful government can afford to leaven firmness with charity—"

"Charity! Black Hawk is a red Nat Turner, no better."

"Turner led an insurrection of slaves, sir, and the Indians, after all, are free nations with territorial rights, a point we've already recognized in numerous treaties."

"Distinctions be damned! Turner was a butcher, Black Hawk's a butcher. You don't coddle butchers. You've never seen an Indian rising, have you? I don't mean a whiskey skirmish or tow, I mean an all-out blood-letting, a border war. Let that savage take an inch today, tomorrow it's a mile. Today he has five hundred followers. Tomorrow, five thousand!"

The colonel's vehemence had climbed several octaves. It even caused Knox Taylor's rapping steps to pause. After a moment, they picked up again.

"I believe, sir," Davis said stubbornly, "that with all you say, the Indians' rights . . ."

"Rights! Damn and blast, man, are you aware that in various treaties since 1804, the Sac and Fox chiefs have ceded all their lands east of the Mississippi to us in return for an annual payment of a thousand dollars? That they retain privileges of living and hunting on those lands so long as they remain part of the public domain?"

"I am, and also that Black Hawk resisted each treaty in its turn. That he warned the chiefs that for every foot of ground they yielded, they'd lose ten more. Rather accurate prophet, that old savage . . ."

Margaret Taylor's entrance defused the situation. She was carrying a tray with a graceful silver pot and cups. She halted and gazed up at the reverberating ceiling.

"Knoxie, stop that at once!"

The clatter ceased. Mrs. Taylor walked to the table, brushed the maps aside, set the tray down and poured the coffee. Taylor scowlingly picked up the string of maple sugar lumps, broke off a piece, dropped it in his cup and sipped the steaming brew. Mrs. Taylor seated herself in a chair; Davis felt relieved. Her presence should damp the argument nicely. When would he learn not to let himself be baited into issues with superiors?

He felt the colonel's knifing glance. "Had something in mind to tell you pending your return. I'll be needing a trustworthy aide; I'd settled on you."

Davis nearly swallowed his coffee wrong-way. An aideship . . . and an extra ten dollars a month! Well, he thought resignedly, you may learn someday.

"Ordinarily," Taylor continued, "I don't engage in touchy dialectics with subordinates. But when I'm going to work closely with a man, I want to know more than shows on the record. Trifle unfair, I admit, provoking you. You have the gall of an Army mule, my friend, but I like your integrity. We'll get along, provided you keep your political opinions, particularly as regard our red brethren, to yourself. Agreed?"

"Yes, sir. Thank you."

The relief he felt mingled with the sardonic thought that if Taylor had provoked a disagreement deliberately, there'd been nothing assumed about his heat once it was under way.

"Zeke," Mrs. Taylor put in quietly, "if orders could come at any time, hadn't we best plan something for the men? A convivial occasion? You've been working them so, and"—she answered his frown with a smile—"as I've often heard you quote Napoleon: 'In war, the morale is to the physical as three to one.' "

"Well, madam, what do you suggest?"

"Why not a dance for the garrison and the village? Not a military affair, a real Western hop."

"Need I remind you that the Fort Crawford ballroom is an unfinished building lacking both doors and windows?"

"What of that warehouse that the Astor company donated for a school? I'm sure that if you ask Mr. Rolette—"

Which touched a genuine sore point with Taylor. "I'll ask nothing of that damned fellow. Nothing!"

"Very well. I shall."

"Outflanked," muttered the colonel. "Mr. Davis, take note. I am set upon, beleaguered, and tyrannized in my own home. I am literally bullied into acquiescence by an avalanche of domestic viragoes—wife and daughters. Never marry, boy, go hang first. If you have to be a fool, at least avoid being a live one."

Mrs. Taylor lowered her eyes and sipped her coffee with a little smile. Upstairs, a measured knock of heels began as Knox Taylor defiantly resumed pacing. The colonel and his wife looked at each other. Mrs. Taylor sighed.

4

"Heat up the water a little, James."

"Yes, sir."

Pemberton scooped a bucketful of steaming water from a faintly bubbling pot set on the fireplace dogs. Davis cramped up his knees as the body servant emptied the bucket into the wooden washtub. He groaned with pleasure as the hot cloak of water turned even hotter; his skin was already a boiled-lobster hue.

"Fine, James, fine. Lay out my new uniform, will you?"

Since his return to Fort Crawford two days ago, he had quickly found that his new status as the commandant's aide did not at all interfere with his ordinary routine—as far as the duty roster was concerned. He had spent all of this morning on the wood detail. Wood-gathering was a year-around chore; big open fireplaces were the only means of heating each barracks room. Luckily Davis had a friend in the regimental sergeant major who, in exchange for the last remaining bottle of Napoleonic brandy that had been a gift from his brother Joe, was willing to take some paper duty off his hands. He was still stuck with all the colonel's legwork.

If an undermanned garrison meant a doubling of his duties, it also enabled him to have these splendid quarters to himself.

The single stone-walled room was comfortably large. It contained a big clothespress and, to either side of the door, a bed, table, straight chair, washstand, and slop pail. The puncheon bookshelf above Davis's bed held a well-thumbed Bible, *The Tragical Plays of Shakespeare,* and a volume of Burns's poetry.

Someone knocked on the door.

"Who is it, male or female or—"

"An angry father."

Davis laughed. "Come in, Denny."

Lieutenant Gibbs entered, sporting a cane and a pronounced limp.

"How in the devil did you collect that leg? Close the door, damn it! When did you get back?"

"Just this morning." Gibbs pulled a chair around and eased himself into it, holding his stiff right leg out straight before him. "Our overweight adjutant, Lieutenant Barry Sholder, hastened to assign details to Wilson and me as soon as we reported in. George gets all the fun—out tracking a black bear who had a set-to with some garbage buckets back of the mess hall last night. Me, I pulled construction work."

"Don't tell me."

Gibbs nodded sheepishly. "Tripped over a piece of scantling and bunged my kneecap. Just came from the hospital. Beaumont says stay off it as much as possible for a few weeks. Even lent me his gout cane."

Davis suppressed a smile. The big Kentuckian was the most accident-prone individual he'd ever known. "That's a rotten way to get out of a war," he gibed. "Didn't think you and George would be relieved of the Dubuque duty this early . . ."

"Neither did we, boy. Colonel Taylor's runner arrived yesterday with orders to get our tails back to Crawford. Northbound steamboat came by a little later, so we made prime time. George and I reckoned it means the Black Hawk thing is brewing fast."

Davis grunted, soaping his back. "The men think so, for

sure. Been more than the usual rash of desertions. The Winnebagos came in yesterday with six of our runaways they'd tracked down. Old Zeke had them flogged and branded on the parade, in front of the whole garrison."

Gibbs moodily twirled his cane. "Gadzooks. What a hell of a way to get left out of a war! If a man has to have an accident, why not a grievously romantic one like blowing off a couple toes with one's own pistol?"

"You probably haven't heard the worst. Did you know there'll be a big gumbo ball tomorrow night?"

"No," Gibbs groaned.

Davis told him the gala plans. Mrs. Taylor had persuaded "King Joe" Rolette to provide his building; she had marshaled the ladies of the garrison and the village to decorate the place and prepare refreshments. It would be an all-night stomp; word had gone out for miles around.

Gibbs glumly fished a cigar from his pocket. "The Gibbs luck holds true. I can't even promenade with this damned knee."

"All right, James."

Davis stood up; Pemberton sluiced him down with a bucket of cold water. Toweling himself briskly, he went to the cot where James had laid out fresh linen and the new tailored uniform that Joe had sent up by steamer from Vicksburg. He dressed, studied himself as well as he could in the foot-square cracked mirror above his washstand and decided he cut a devil of a figure. Gleaming made-to-order boots hidden to the heels by long blue service trousers. Short dark-blue coatee with a flared chin-high collar trimmed by white tapings; ten gilt-brass buttons ranged in close single-breasted "herringbone" form, long blind buttonholes running up from them. He especially admired the new insignia for second lieutenants: the Army had just done away with the old sleeve chevrons, and he was the first officer at Crawford to sport a pair of the new silver epaulets.

"Beautiful," Gibbs said. "Just beautiful. Want to promenade me over to the sutler's? I got to shop for a new dress pattern."

Davis laughed. "All right. I need some tobacco."

The two of them stepped out into the sunny morning. Davis paused to adjust the white waist belt that supported his saber and run a modestly proud eye over the graveled parade and stone-block buildings with their paved porches and neat colonnades. He had been personally in charge of much of the construction. Officers' quarters and company storehouses occupied the two long one-story stone buildings at north and south ends of the parade; these also formed two walls of the fort quadrangle. The long east and west walls were built of pine logs, stockade-style; they enclosed four long stone buildings, two on each side of the parade with the east and west gates centered between them. These housed the company barracks, non-com staff quarters, blacksmith and carpentry shops, bakery, guardhouse, post library, and sutler's store.

The young ladies had entered the east gate and were coming up the paved crosswalk that intersected the parade at right angles. One was Sarah Knox Taylor. The other was Mary Street, daughter of General Joseph Street, the Indian agent.

Gibbs said, "Shall we join the ladies?" And hurried down the walk without waiting for an answer.

They met the girls at the walk intersection. Both men touched their shakos and bowed. Knox was wearing a dark blue calico dress with a matching calash. A white silk sling cradled her left arm. She replied with cold politeness to Davis's greeting, warmly to Gibbs's.

"Denny, how wonderful to see you. What's happened to your leg?"

Gibbs stammered a reply. He couldn't take his eyes off her. Even prepared by Anderson's tidbit of gossip, Davis was surprised at the change in Gibbs's usual lazy, drawling manner. Still he knew that Denny's easygoing ways were deceptive. He could be damned intense about some things.

"Knox," he got out, "have you an escort for tomorrow's dance?"

Mary Street's blue eyes sparkled. "Why Denny, she's had scads of requests. You can't just up and ask a girl the day before."

"Well," Gibbs floundered, "I just got back."

Mary laughed. "Wouldn't that be a sight, though. Dancing, and crippled up like a pair of pensioners, both of you!"

"Oh," Knox said solemnly, "Dr. Beaumont said I can discard the sling tomorrow. But, Denny, your limp, you were joking, of course. Weren't you?"

Gibbs's face froze, then sagged. The girls burst out laughing. Davis grinned. Denny's expression was something to see.

"Do you mean . . . you will, Knox, won't you?"

"Of course I'll go with you, silly."

Davis nodded at the empty baskets the girls were carrying. "I assume you ladies are headed for the sutler's. If so—"

"Indeed you may."

Mary handed him her basket, linked her hand in his arm, and the four of them went down the walk toward the quadrangle's southeast corner and the sutler's store. The powder magazine with its three-foot-thick walls of notched blocks was located in this quarter; beside it stood a newly erected shot tower. A squad of soldiers was melting lead ore and pouring molten lead from the tower's top into a vat of water, "freezing" it into perfectly spherical pellets that would be sorted according to size for musket balls. War signs, Davis reflected. Bullet-making. Hours of palm-blistering practice on the target range. Precision drilling and field maneuvers. And of course the pick-up in desertions. But Zachary Taylor's shrewd instincts kept the general tension of the garrison in a fine pressure of balances. He saw that even the men's spare hours were filled with light fatigue detail that occupied without exhausting them. It kept their nerves cool, their performance at keen highs.

Odd how everyone felt it, though there were nothing but

unofficial whispers. After all, gossip ran, wasn't there a good chance that bloodshed could be averted? Wasn't General Atkinson parleying with Keokuk and his leading headman, Wapello, in hopes that the big chiefs could dissuade Black Hawk from any belligerent action? Davis, as Taylor's aide, was privy to all the colonel's information. There had been no confirmation of hostilities, no definite orders.

Yet something was coming. You knew, that was all.

The two couples swung west along the parade under the awning of the southwest building. Mary, Davis thought amusedly, was a chatterbox. But a witty and delightful one. She was a tiny sunny-haired girl, pert-featured and quick as a bird.

"Jeff," she murmured, "d'you reckon Denny's her favorite? Quite a few others did ask her to the hop."

"I wouldn't doubt it for a moment."

Mary gave him a comical brow-lifted glance. She must know about his encounter with Miss Taylor. Which meant that soon the whole garrison would know.

He diverted the subject: "If Gibbs is here, can Wilson be far behind?"

She laughed. "George did manage to drop in by our back door—armed to the teeth like a Barbary pirate—before hying on to the woods and heap big game. What an Indian that man would make!"

Mary's flippancy masked the bittersweet flavor of her two-year romance with George. Old Joseph Street had sworn that no Army man would ever marry his little girl. Particularly not a smart-mouthing high-stepping pseudo-British jaybird like George Wilson. Must be hell, Davis thought, to have the usual travail of an Army courtship complicated by an angry parent.

They entered the aromatic gloom of the sutler's store. It was a commissary, grocery, drygoods store, and trading post all in one. The counters and shelves were stocked with all kinds of perishables, meat, cheeses, flour, and molasses; yard goods like calico, shirting, strouding, merino, and plissé; hard goods

60

that ranged from candy, raisins, sugar, salt, spices, smoked meats, tobacco, and whiskey through pots and kettles, crockery and glassware, axes, knives, leathers, firearms and powder and shot. MacDougall, the cadaverous red-bearded sutler, was dickering with an Indian. The two girls went at once to the shelves of yard cloth. Knox had Gibbs pull down various bolts of material for her inspection. Grinning, Davis inspected a rack of brass-mounted muskets. Denny was acting like a pet bear. A serious case, no doubt of it.

"Denny, your knee, I'm sorry," Knox said suddenly.

"It's all right."

"No, you sit right down here. I insist."

Gibbs seated himself gratefully on a keg.

"A blanket," MacDougall snapped, "and a 'nest' o' copper kettles. Not a farthing more. Take it or leave it."

"Mac plenty damn thief," said the Indian. He threw a couple of swanskins and some otter pelts on the counter, grabbed up his trade goods and went out. Softly smiling, MacDougall waited on the girls.

"Mother and I are setting up practically from scratch," Knox said. "We'll need a lot of goods in quantity. Flour and molasses and so forth."

"Best make your choices from my storeroom in back, miss. Meantime I'll wait on the lieutenant."

As he came over to Davis, Vitelle Robier and his daughter entered the store. The trapper gave Davis a friendly nod. Ceclie gave him a shy-bold glance. She looked quite fetching in a red blouse and blue skirt, both fashioned of coarse trade stroud and trimmed with beads and quills. A bright, barbaric costume that emphasized her sun-colored skin and sooty hair. It was plaited in smooth braids interwoven with strips of scarlet worsted and seemed to glisten from a recent washing rather than from grease.

"*Bon jour,*" Davis said. "Where is your son?"

Robier grimaced. "He does not like towns."

61

"What'll ye have, Lieutenant?" asked MacDougall.

"Some tobacco. I want to look over your liquor stock too. Why not wait on Mr. Robier while I'm selecting?"

Davis walked to the back of the store and cast an eye over MacDougall's stock of "special items"; farm implements and tools for the villagers and settlers; blankets, earbobs, looking glasses, beads, and ribbons for the Indians; costly wines and whiskeys for the fort's officers. He studied the whiskey labels. The open door of the storeroom was just to his right.

"Isn't Jeff Davis handsome?" he heard Mary murmur. "And that new uniform! Gracious, he looks almost too good to be true."

"I agree. Certainly a vain puppy, isn't he?"

"Oh, I don't think so."

Knox laughed quietly. "That's it exactly. A vain overbred bird-dog pup."

Davis grabbed up a bottle at random and returned to the front of the store. He set the bottle on the counter, giving his hot collar a tug. Damn all service collars; they were regular gorgets.

Ceclie Robier was looking at him. She smiled. Her green minxlike eyes seemed to dare him. And she was damned pretty. He smiled back. And spoke without really thinking:

"Miss Robier, I wonder . . . might I have the pleasure of escorting you to the dance tomorrow evening?"

Robier was counting out payment for the few items he had bought. He turned slowly from the counter. "I am a kloochman," he said quietly. "My daughter is a *mitiff* . . . a half-breed. And this is as it is. But a man does not make the sport of her. This you understand?"

"Perfectly. And you, m'sieu, should let a man finish. You will accompany us?"

Robier's face relaxed. *"Excusez-moi."* He looked at his daughter. "Well, *petite chou?*"

"Mais oui! Yes—yes, Papa! I have the dress, the fine dress I

make but do not wear—" She laughed, trying to show by excited little gestures how pretty the dress was.

"I think one thing more." Robier grinned at MacDougall. "Give us a bar of your good soap, sutler."

5

With Ceclie Robier on his arm, Davis walked through the April twilight toward the big lighted building. Vitelle Robier strolled behind, his pipe pungent on the wind; his son ghosted along at the rear. Ahead of them, men's, women's, children's voices mingled in a fever of celebration. People had come in from miles around, many on foot or horseback. A blaze of light from the hall's doorway and windows picked out ox carts, *calèches,* and other equipages hitched under the oaks in front.

"Mademoiselle is lovely tonight," Davis said.

"Merci!" Her eyes were fixed forward; her dark mouth half-smiled.

She wore a dress of bright scarlet calico that clung to her waist and the rounded cones of her breasts, the neckline scooped to bare a velvet vale of shadow. Décolletage less daring than some he had seen on Vicksburg belles at highly social cotillions. Her touches of adornment seemed bolder: an Indian belt of colored beads and three-stranded necklace of white-and-purple mussel-shell wampum. Her hair, gathered back in a thick club and tied with a red trade ribbon, shone like a crow's wing. Best of all, she had used the good castile her father had bought.

They entered the former storehouse. It was both broad and

lofty, more like a drafty barn. The addition of a puncheon floor and rows of half-log benches made it a schoolhouse and, on occasion, a playhouse for amateur theatricals. Soldier's lamps—bayonets with candles wedged inside their rings and thrust into the walls—provided an ingenious lighting. The benches were pulled back to the walls; tables at the rear were laden with tureens of thick savory gumbo and platters of cornbread.

The place wasn't too crowded as yet. Davis scanned the room for Colonel Taylor and his family; he saw them with Denny Gibbs at a table in the corner. On impulse, he took the Robiers over to pay his respects. Though social lines were loosely structured here, he was curious to see how the Taylors would react.

Taylor rose with a courteous greeting. He acknowledged the introductions pleasantly; so did Mrs. Taylor. Davis had never seen the colonel so relaxed and affable. Tonight he seemed to have put everything else aside and was enjoying himself.

Knox Taylor sat between her mother and the two scrubbed and curried younger children. The sling was gone from her arm; she was wearing a pink cashmere frock with a molded bodice and belling skirt; her hair was dressed in curls and gathered into shining clusters by a cunning mesh of ribbons. The bulky riding costume he had first seen her in, Davis realized, had done her no justice. She was less slightly built than he'd thought, and no fourteen-year-old. Seventeen, he guessed, or eighteen.

As they chatted, a stumpy figure of a man came up. "Well, Davis," he barked, "what are you up to now? Who's the young lady? See her father is along as chaperon. Shrewd fellow."

"Miss Robier," Davis said dryly, "Mr. Robier, may I present Dr. William Beaumont, Fort Crawford's surgeon and resident granny."

"You can shut up now," Beaumont snapped. Not a large

man, he had a large stubborn lantern-jawed head; his hair tumbled in black burs over his tall brow. Rumpled and untidy, he was a forty-seven-year-old bundle of volatile energy, noted for an inexhaustible lack of patience and a pungent vocabulary.

"Sir!" His eyes pronged Robier's like brown darts. "Will you kindly tell me what in blazes was in that herb mixture you put on Miss Taylor's arm? It did some good—or I'm a fool."

Robier smiled. "You will have to ask Ceclie. She is *la docteur.*"

"Ma'm'selle?"

Ceclie shook her head shyly but firmly. "I cannot say. It is secret."

"Won't you all join us?" the colonel asked.

Dr. Beaumont declined; he had business elsewhere. Davis and the Robiers accepted the invitation. When they had loaded their plates and seated themselves, Davis and Ceclie were directly across from Knox and Gibbs.

"How's the leg, Denny?" Davis asked.

"It's not a leg," Gibbs said morosely. "It's a pure blight on my evening, boy."

Knox Taylor smiled briefly and wiggled her fingers at someone. Davis, glancing across his shoulder, saw that General Street and his daughter had entered. The Indian agent was in his fifties, a white-haired man of ponderous dignity; he spoke gruffly to Mary when she smiled and waved back at Knox. Davis looked around for George Wilson. He was standing with Anderson and some brother officers and pretending not to see the Streets.

The big room was starting to fill up. The few empty tables had been taken by the first arrivals; latecomers filled their plates and sat on benches. Others promenaded in idle circuits, eating, laughing, talking. The farmers were easy to pick out in their linsey and butternut, some of the younger men sporting shirts of bright red flannel. The tradesmen wore black broadcloth; their ladies were more flamboyant in gowns of fluttering calico and bombazet. No silks or crinolines here. The young girls strutted for the stag line, flirting handkerchiefs perfumed with oil of cinnamon.

With the sluice gates of talk down on every side, you had to speak up to be heard. The Taylor corner was dominated by the colonel's expansive and vigorous talk: exactly the unsoldierly sort any gentleman planter might make. On how the Southern levees were holding, his recent purchase of three hundred acres of Louisiana farmland, last year's tobacco crop on his Kentucky plantation.

Robier showed interest. "The fur trade soon be gone. The gentlemen wear hats of wool and silk, no longer so much beaver. So now I have the new place. Nothing big, a few *arpents* to clear and farm."

"Good," Taylor said. "Never saw better than this prairie soil. It'll be covered with fields one day. Wheat. Corn, oats, rye . . ."

Knox ate her soup with a gusto that made her frail slimness seem contradictory while she carried on a stream of chatter with her mother and (in fluent French) with Ceclie. It kept Davis in a wire-fine awareness of her. Before long he found himself moodily conjecturing that everything she said was indirectly aimed at him. It was irritating.

Members of the regimental band struck up a Virginia reel with fiddles and a banjo. Couples began taking the floor. Davis smiled at Ceclie. "May I have the pleasure of this dance?"

"I—I'm not sure how I be, m'sieu. Papa show me how a little, but . . ."

"You want to try, don't you?"

"Oh yes."

Robier nodded his approval. Davis glanced about for young Jean, to note his reaction. He was nowhere to be seen; probably he hadn't even come in with them.

He took Ceclie onto the floor. People were stepping out on all sides; others clapped their hands in time. To the ladies' bright frocks was added a sudden whirl of red, green, and yellow sashes and capotes. A number of *voyageurs* had come barging in the door as if at one signal; they promptly swung out the prettiest girls. The soldiers, sensing the Army's honor at stake, came onto the floor in a rush of blue and white. The men, greatly outnumbering the available girls, cut in right and left. No lady was captured more than a few seconds by any one partner.

As an officer, Davis enjoyed a temporary immunity. Ceclie was awkward for the first minute or so, then was suddenly picking up steps and rhythm. He was amazed at the sensitivity with which she followed him, her body as quick and pliant as a young animal's.

"Ma'm'selle is enjoying herself?"

"Oh, yes. Yes!"

He felt a hand on his shoulder. A grinning Bob Anderson took Ceclie away. Davis walked back to the sidelines. Mrs. Taylor had taken Betty and Dick to a refreshment table where women were serving the children switchel, a chilled drink made of molasses, water, and a dash of vinegar. The colonel had crossed the floor to chat with his friend, Captain Thomas F. Smith. Robier was with them. Only Gibbs and Knox remained at the table. Denny looked glum. His injured knee was really a godsend for his partner; he was a buffalo bull on the dance floor. But no doubt she knew it.

Lieutenants Abercrombie and Belton were already swooping in on Anderson to relieve him of his partner. Belton got there first and danced Ceclie away. Davis wondered if he shouldn't have given her warning. In the near-womanless world of a frontier garrison, a pretty new face was a magnet for the young subalterns. Competition was fierce; duels were fought sometimes. And for half-breed girls, no lines were drawn after dark.

He gazed at the soft pink petulance of Knox Taylor's mouth. Should he make another try at smoothing the waters? She was aware of his look and wouldn't meet it. She nervously smoothed the ruffles of her white fichu.

"Denny," she said, "would you bring me a glass of switchel, please?"

Davis said: "I'll be glad to."

Gibbs swung awkwardly to his feet. "I can do it." He sounded irritable; he limped away as fat Lieutenant Barry Sholder came up, shy and perspiring.

"Oh, ahem, Miss Knoxie, may I have the pleasure of this dance?"

"Of course."

"You'll be sorry," Davis said idly.

Sholder gave him a resentful stare. Miss Taylor rose and swept around the table, taking Sholder's arm. "It will be *my* pleasure, Lieutenant," she said clearly.

Davis folded his arms and settled back to watch, faintly smiling. Among his fellow officers, poor old Barry enjoyed the sobriquet of "Goosebarry." He had a knack for making an ass of himself under the most ordinary circumstances, and the more he tried, the worse he made matters. A clumsy man with any sense would vaguely emulate the motions of a dance and let it go at that.

Not Sholder. He had to dance or be damned. He tackled the steps with a rigid fury, ignoring the music, hugging his partner in a rib-cracking embrace, bulling his way into other couples.

Gibbs came back to the table. "Where—?"

"There." Davis pointed with his chin.

"My God, not Sholder. Look at that! The fool stepped on her foot." Gibbs was genuinely distressed. "Jeff-boy, can't you sashay out and do her a kindness?"

"If you say so," Davis drawled.

He walked across the floor, threading between the couples. As he approached Knox and Sholder, the latter bumped into a young farmer and his girl. The lad spoke strongly.

Sholder, startled into releasing his partner, said: "I beg your pardon!"

"I really should beg yours," Davis said politely. "Thank you kindly, Goose—"

He whisked Knox away just that casually, leaving Sholder flat-footed. Relief flickered across her face. And vanished almost at once.

"This time," he said pleasantly, "Lochinvar has come out of the South. How's your foot?"

"Thank you," she said coldly. "May we sit down now?"

"I would like to speak with you, Miss Taylor. I suggest that we step outside a moment."

"Sir!"

He danced her inexorably toward the doorway. She strained tentatively against his arm. "Let me go, please!"

He tightened his arm. "You can always create a scene, Miss Knoxie," he murmured. "But perhaps you'd like that. Any little old tribute to your charms, eh?"

Her eyes blazed.

They were close to the door as the reel flourished to an end. He simply shifted his hand from her waist to her arm, her good right one, and propelled her outside. Under the trees, men were talking in groups, here and there sampling a sly jug. Young as the evening was, couples were walking out already in the early dark. Davis noticed young Robier sitting on his heels almost out of the light.

Knox firmly halted under a tree some yards from the building. She jerked free of him, then placed her back against the tree. She touched her kerchief to a sheen of moisture at her temples, eying him with a cool distaste.

"Very well, Lieutenant. Have your way."

"Thank you. I'm merely curious. Why do you dislike me?"

"You are too cocksure and arrogant by far."

"You must have decided as much when we met, then. Second sight, Miss Taylor?"

"You're a boor, sir, and you wear the facts of your nature like medals."

"Then you'll hardly blame a boor for following his nature—"

He swept her into his arms and kissed her, brief and hard. She twisted away; her hand swung. His ears rang with the flat stinging slap.

He pulled her back and kissed her more thoroughly. When he let her go, she slapped him again, this time so hard that he fell back a step.

Picking up her skirts, she turned and stormed with great dignity back to the building. He rubbed his jaw, his ears still ringing. Frail? Not by half!

He almost laughed. Almost. But the strange riffle of excitement in him was no laughing matter.

Gibbs came boiling out of the building at a wild limp, stalking over to him. He halted, his face taut as a drumskin. "Jeff, if you've insulted Miss Taylor . . ."

"I wouldn't call it that."

"What happened, then?"

"Denny, it's none of your affair."

He started past Gibbs, who slapped a hand on his shoulder. He wheeled, slamming his palm against Gibbs's arm and knocking it away. Gibbs, in midstep, surged off balance. He thrust instinctively with his hurt leg to catch his weight. A grunt of pain left him and the leg folded. He stabbed his cane at the ground; it skidded and he fell on the raw clay.

"Denny . . . I'm sorry."

Davis bent down to help him. Gibbs had struggled onto his good knee, the front of his uniform smeared with sticky clay. His face was dead white. He struck Davis's hand away, got up with the help of his cane and limped away in the darkness toward the barracks.

Davis shook his head. Damn! The jagged mood ran out of him. He was about to turn back into the hall when he saw the Indian.

He came out of the darkness at a soft padding trot, a shadow among the shadows. He wore only a breechclout and leather leggings that partly bared his lean buttocks. Copper bands gleamed on his arms; his brown torso was silvered with sweat. Seeing Davis, he came over to him. Davis recognized Man-Who-Walks, the Northwest Army's best runner.

"How, Little Chief. I come from White Beaver. At fort, they say chief of soldiers is here."

Davis felt a stir of excitement. White Beaver was a name the Winnebagos had given General Henry Atkinson—commander of the entire Western Department of the Army. He told Man-Who-Walks that Taylor was inside, and the Indian trotted into the building. Davis followed. Man-Who-Walks approached Taylor, opened a parfleche at his hip and produced a slightly crumpled envelope. The colonel broke the seal and removed several folded sheets.

Davis glanced at the floor. Ceclie was still creating a stir among the single officers; they'd practically cordoned her off against civilian interference, taking turns swinging her onto the floor and guarding her jealously between dances.

He also looked around for Knox Taylor. She was chatting with Mary Street as if nothing had happened. His latest clash with her came to a confused head in his thoughts, webbing them like a drug.

"Ladies . . . gentlemen. Your attention, please."

The colonel rapped his words across the music. The fiddles stopped; the dancers shuffled to a halt.

"I have a message from General Atkinson at Fort Armstrong. Black Hawk has crossed the Mississippi into Illinois."

The hubbub freshened.

"When—where?" somebody called.

Taylor raised a hand for silence. "Three days ago—at the Yellow Banks below the mouth of the Rock River. Four to five hundred braves along with their squaws and children, all their animals and domestic stock." He crackled the papers in his hand. "The entire 1st Infantry is ordered to Fort Armstrong, where regulars and militia will be organized into an allied force. Governor Reynolds of Illinois has issued a call for militia volunteers; they're to organize at Beardstown, whence they'll be sent to Fort Armstrong. I imagine they'll recruit from all the border states.

"All able-bodied men wishing to join the militia may accompany my troops. I am sending out runners to Mineral Point, Dodgeville, Blue Mounds, Helena—" He named a half-dozen, more settlements. "They will spread the word among the inhabitants and ask for militia volunteers. We'll embark from the Prairie du Chien landing day after tomorrow—crack of dawn, please note. As garrison personnel will enjoy an active day tomorrow—commandeering all available river craft, loading on provisions, seeing to their gear—taps will sound at nine rather than at midnight as we'd expected. Enjoy yourselves till then."

The music picked up; couples swung out. Davis looked for Ceclie again. She was sitting this one out, surrounded by admirers. There would be no getting to her for a while.

The dancing turned frenetic; Davis gave himself to its furious gaiety. He danced out two more sets, whirling the buxom country girls from partner to partner. Afterward he went out under the trees where the young fellows were passing the jugs and the tall stories. Davis excoriated his belly with fiery pulls of forty-rod till his brain felt as inflamed as his gullet.

As usual, the drinking was accompanied by outlandish tricks. He wasn't quite sure how it happened, but he found himself the center of a gang of roistering bumpkins, balancing a full glass of whiskey on the flat summit of his shako while he drank from another glass. The idea was to drain every drop from the one in a minute flat without tilting his head enough to tip over the other or spill any of its contents.

Anderson and Wilson chose that moment to stroll up and provide comments.

"I say," Wilson said soberly, "even if old Jeff weren't an aristocrat, you'd have to agree he's the portrait of one."

"I certainly do," Anderson said. "Distinguished as hell. You mean he's an aristocrat?"

"Of course he is. My God, man, can't you tell?"

"Time!" crowed the young settler holding the watch, just as Davis finished and held the emptied glass upside down. "Gentlemen—" He carefully lifted the glass of whiskey from his shako and handed it to Anderson. "Would either of you care for a drink? Please try to choke on it."

He returned to the hall, none too steadily. Parents were gathering up their drowsy younger children and noisily reluctant older ones; once they were evacuated, things would get livelier. Davis's blood glowed with whiskey and excitement. All the people, every object, seemed to give off bizarre auras.

A marching song was struck up. He looked for Ceclie. She was laughingly shaking her head to offers to be her partner in the marching and swinging games about to begin. Her admirers were loudly wondering why as Davis came up.

"Because, messieurs—" She came lightly to her feet, her sea-fire eyes sparkling. "I came with M'sieu Davis, who asked me first . . ."

Couples were beginning to promenade in a hall-wide circle, one voice after another chiming in:

> *"We're all a-marching to Quebec—*
> *The drums are loudly beating!*
> *The Americans have gained the day*
> *And the British are retreating!*
> *The wars are o'er and we'll turn back*
> *To the place from whence we started!*
> *So open the ring and choose a couple in*
> *To relieve the broken-hearted!"*

Ceclie turned up her face, laughing at him; her eyes kindled wildly, then softly. "Open the Ring" was sung out: the dancers

joined hands, a solid circle was formed. One couple split off
into the center, nucleus for the rest as they twirled to the
familiar tune of *Skip to My Lou.* The marching burlesque allowed for all kinds of improvisings and shennanigans. Each
one kept tune in his own way, the rhythm as much a thing of
the body, the arms, the head, as it was of the feet. The part-
ners skipped, bowed, knelt, promenaded, double-shuffled, even
kissed.

> *"Green grow the rushes O!*
> *Kiss her quick and let her go!*
> *But don't you muss her ruffle O!"*

There was a wiry, feverish non-stop quality to the fun. The
men from the garrison, facing an early curfew and a campaign
in the field, went at it with hard abandon. Young fellows from
the farms, most of whom would enlist as volunteers in their
damned good time—next week would be soon enough—were in
no hurry. Bred to the wilds, they knew how to savor life close
to the bone, letting the night grow with a will of its own and
have its way with them till the shank of the evening wore to a
gray nub.

The marching play soon turned into private dancing. Mountain dances brought north by the new American breed of
settlers from Virginia, Kentucky, Tennessee. Hoedowns, four-
handed reels and square sets that would continue into the small
hours, whipped out to tunes like *Monnie Musk* and *Zip Coon,*
till tingling nerves and twitching feet wouldn't permit even the
most staid to linger on the sidelines. The fiddlers rounded into
Weevily Wheat, grand old reel of the Scottish Jacobites, and
made it swing:

> *"Oh I don't want none of your weevily wheat*
> *And I don't want none of your barley—*

> *But I want some flour in half an hour*
> *To bake a cake for Charley!"*

Knox Taylor and Bob Anderson had paired off. Davis caught her glance in the whirl; her eyes slashed at him. He thought that she formed *boor* with her lips. Then she laughed, as if at something Anderson had said.

> *"The higher up the cherry tree,*
> *The sweeter grows the cherry—*
> *The more you hug and kiss the girls,*
> *The more they want to marry!"*

Music and redeye made a roaring medley in his blood. He spun Ceclie away, he held her close, he matched the best of the high-steppers. Some were "cutting the pigeon wing," springing into the air, clicking their heels together, yelling "Whoopees!" as naturally and exuberantly as the "Amens!" at a camp meeting.

> *"Yes Charley he's a fine young man,*
> *Yes Charley he's a dandy—*
> *He loves to hug and kiss the girls*
> *And feed 'em stripe-ed candy!"*

Davis leaped into the air with an ear-splitting whoop. He bucked and wove and clapped his hands above his head, never losing a step. He wasn't sure afterward of all he did. Only that he cut many weird capers and the crowd ate it up. Badinage and laughter and shouts of encouragement washed at him from every side.

On the sidelines, faces clipped into focus. Robier's dark unreadable one. And the colonel's. Davis had a moment of trepidation till he saw on the next turn that both Zachary Taylor and Captain Tom Smith wore broad grins.

> *"Grab her by the lily-white hand*
> *And lead her like a pigeon!*
> *Make her dance the* Weevily Wheat
> *And lose all her religion!"*

As he swung Ceclie close by the doorway, Davis had a glimpse of young Jean Robier. He had pushed to the edge of the circling dancers, his proud young face murderous.

The hell with you, my friend, Davis thought. And swayed by his churning mood, he did a foolish thing: whirled Ceclie so close to her brother that they brushed him in passing.

Young Robier took a step forward. His knife flashed from its sheath.

A woman screamed.

Davis thrust Ceclie from him and wheeled, dropping his hand in his pocket where the little Allan's was snugged. Ordinarily he didn't carry the small pistol charged, but it was good for a bluff.

Vitelle Robier came swiftly across the floor, but Zachary Taylor reached them first. He stepped between Davis and the young half-breed. Said four words and cracked each one like a whip.

"Put up that knife!"

The dancers milled to a stop; the music ended. Robier came up and spoke sharply in French. Young Jean sheathed his knife. His eyes flamed darkly. He said: "You American pig. Should you ever touch my sister again, I will kill you." His French was flawless.

Robier slapped him across the face. But his thick hand was too heavy for slapping: the blow swiveled the youth's head. Blood spurted from his split lip. He never took his eyes off Davis. Robier stared at his son with a gray defeat in his face.

"Come," he said.

He walked to the door. Young Robier slowly followed him, and the two went out.

The colonel eyed Davis with cold disapproval. He etched his words with acid: "I would suggest, Lieutenant, that you conduct this young woman to her family. Then I would suggest that you retire to your quarters."

Davis offered Ceclie his arm and sent a casual glance around the races. He did not see Sarah Knox Taylor's. They walked from the building, the murmurs washing together behind them. Robier and his son were standing a short distance away.

The trapper's face was like stone. Without a word he turned and tramped toward the dock, pushing his son ahead. Davis and Ceclie followed at a distance. A rind of moon picked out their way. A whippoorwill cried softly; a screech owl luted the spring mood. The revelry in the hall continued, spilling across the night.

"Mademoiselle danced in beauty . . . but I have spoiled her evening."

"*Non*. I will always remember tonight."

They clasped hands, walking a bit more slowly. Stars sheened the murky slough ahead of them. Robier and his son had reached their pirogue; in the darkness steel clicked on flint as the trapper readied a torch. Yielding to impulse, Davis halted, gently turning Ceclie to face him.

"'She walks in beauty like the night of cloudless climes and starry skies; and all that's best of dark and bright meet in her aspect and her eyes.'"

"M'sieu?" Half-smiling.

"Poetry."

Their lips found a fierce fusion. She strained up on tiptoe, her supple body arching like a young willow. She broke away and backed off, pressing a hand to her mouth.

"Ceclie!" Robier called.

"Oh, m'sieu," she whispered. Then turned and ran angling down the slope to the dugout. Robier applied a glowing chunk of tinder to an oil-soaked flambeau and handed it to her. He and his son pushed off. The pirogue moved down the slough, haloed by a smoky bronze glow.

Davis walked slowly up the incline toward the fort, whistling softly. Then he frowned; his steps slowed. His mind ran back across the evening. He felt a little puzzled and, for some reason, obscurely cheated.

He stood listening to the darkness. Wind combed the dead prairie grass; it rattled dry milkweed stalks. The night had not changed. Yet it felt different. As if something had drained out of it. Something . . .

PART TWO

A Season for War

6

Brevet Brigadier General Henry Atkinson assembled his Northwest Army at Fort Armstrong. It was a ragtag heterogeneous force made up of regular infantry drawn from American forts north and west of Missouri and volunteer infantry mustered by state and territorial militia throughout the Northwest. A sizable force. But Atkinson needed time to whip it into fighting shape. Frontier duty had kept his regular troops crisp and seasoned. His big headache was the sixteen hundred civilian volunteers who formed Illinois Militia under the command of Samuel Whiteside. Rough and roistering backwoodsmen who scorned such military posturings as close-order drill and field maneuvers. Sneering that they could outride and outshoot the bluecoats any day of the goddam month. All a man had to know in a ruction was what was to the right of him, what was to the left and what was up ahead. The general threw all his commissioned officers and non-coms into the task of bracing the rowdy crews of rednecks to a semblance of military style.

On May 4, Atkinson called a meeting of all regimental and battalion commanders. "Gentlemen," he told them painfully, "a certain rumor can be discarded. Our scouts have reported in. No sign of hostiles between here and The Prophet's village. As would be the case by now, had they really turned back."

An agonizing confession from the man who commanded the entire Right Wing of the Western Department of the Army, which included most of the frontier north and west of Missouri.

Black Hawk, in his efforts to raise a large fighting force, had dispatched messengers to chiefs of the Northwest tribes, asking for warriors. His hope had been dashed when the Winnebago chiefs had met in council to declare their friendship for the United States and the neutrality of their people. The Potawatomi chief Shabbona had added insult to injury. When part of his tribe had threatened to take the warpath under Big Foot, a sub-chief, Shabbona had had his braves spread the alarm among whites across northern Illinois, from the settlements at Peoria, Peru, La Salle, and South Ottawa to Chicago itself.

Panic had been the first fruit of that warning. The Northwest rumbled with terrified rumors: the Sacs and Foxes, united with the Sioux and Winnebago and Chippewa, picking up Potawatomi and Ottawa as they went, were sweeping clear to Detroit—killing, raping, looting, burning. Hundreds of settlers had fled to the protection of Forts Winnebago and Howard, to Fort Dearborn at Chicago, and to Solomon Juneau's post on the Milwaukee River.

As yet, actually—and as the military knew—not a shot had been fired.

After crossing from the Trans-Mississippi lands into Illinois, Black Hawk had marched his band boldly past Fort Armstrong and up the Rock River going northeast. Atkinson, still placing hope in his negotiations with Keokuk, had made no effort to block his advance. A mistake. Keokuk's overtures had proven useless. Now it was early May; Black Hawk had penetrated deep into Illinois, still following the Rock.

Then a second blunder. A rumor had reached Atkinson that prudence had won out; Black Hawk was retreating by the way he'd come. At the time, the bulk of Whiteside's Illinois Infantry Militia was still organizing at Beardstown. Atkinson could have sent a message directing them north to a point on the Rock River where they might cut off Black Hawk's march. Instead, believing the rumor, he had ordered a concentration of all regulars and militia at Fort Armstrong.

The general admitted the error.

"We can now be sure that Black Hawk is in the neighborhood of Dixon's Ferry. Our scouts report that he supped with 'Father John' Dixon and his family several days ago. Told Dixon he was going sixty miles up the Rock. Which could mean nothing, but the scouts found enough to indicate that he's still on the move upriver. Accordingly, I'm sending an expeditionary force in pursuit of the Sacs. Colonel Taylor, you'll assume command of four companies of your 1st Infantry and six more companies to be drawn from my 6th. Mr. Whiteside, you and your Illinois volunteers will accompany the colonel's regulars and will be under his direct command."

Atkinson paused heavily. "For the present, Colonel, your only instructions are to set up a field headquarters at Dixon's Ferry. It will serve as nerve center of future operations. Under no circumstances are you to attempt contact with the enemy." His glance circled their faces. "I hardly need remind you that we've a potential tinderbox on our hands. One careless spark will ignite the whole border."

"Sir!" said a young officer. "It seems to me that Black Hawk's crossing into Illinois in violation of the Rock Island agreement should be treated as an act of war."

Atkinson gave him a jaundiced look. "That's just fine, mister. But there are still scores of settlers in easy striking distance of him, and damned if I'll move against him without being in a position to contain him . . ."

Next morning, the troops began their sixty-five-mile journey up the Rock. And Jefferson Davis had his first taste of field action in a real war: a dirty, grueling, inglorious trek. A flotilla of overladen flatboats had to be maneuvered up a wide crooked river across long stretches of boiling rapids laced with boulders and sunken logs. Men poled for hours against the current, muscles twitching with agony, palms raw with blisters that broke and bled and blistered again. They cordelled past the worst places, a shore party dragging on the ropes. Tangles of forest and underbrush hampered the land contingent; the old military road that followed the left bank was largely overgrown, and teams of men sweated out each day cutting and clearing for teams and baggage wagons. It was still too early in the season for the clouds of mosquitoes that would later breed in the plentiful bogs and sloughs along the Rock River, but the trees dripped hordes of woodticks that infested men's clothing and burrowed into their flesh.

By the time twilight cloaked the river and a halt was called, spring armies of frogs would be bassooning the night with mating sounds. But nobody cared. They were too spent to do anything but strip and shake their filthy clothes clean of woodticks, smear hoglard on their cracked and blistered palms, wolf their rations and topple into their blankets. When reveille shocked them awake, they shuffled into rank for assembly, inspection, muster roll, and mess. Then the nightmarish cycle began all over . . .

When the flatboats beached at Dixon's Landing on May 12, John Dixon came down from his post to greet Taylor and his officers. A tall, gaunt, craggy man in his fifties, he had the appearance as well as the reputation of a patriarch. The Winnebagos whom he served as adviser and banker had named him Nachusa (Long Hair White). He and his wife and five children were still the only white people living on the river. Five years ago, his brother-in-law, O. W. Kellogg, had broken a trail from Peoria to Galena to facilitate overland travel to the lead mines. Where the trail crossed the Rock River, Dixon had established a simple flat-bottomed ferry. Later he'd built a rambling log building that served as home, hotel, tavern, post office, and trading post. He had a reputation for generosity and fair dealing; he was a favorite with the regulars because of the vast amounts of credit he let them charge up.

He shook hands all around and said: "Colonel, might you and your staff join me for a tot of grog?"

"Later, sir, if you've no objection. With your permission, I would like to set up a camp at this place."

It was a beautiful spot. May had spread in a soft green explosion across the prairie meadows rolling back from the riverbank. Blossoming wild crabapple trees made a pink fog daubed with the flowering white of craggy plum. A restful sight to river-weary eyes.

"You're more'n welcome. I'll tell my old woman to fix a good feed for you and your officers. You sup with us tonight."

"Kind of you, sir. I must tell you I'm declaring your taproom off-limits to all men in the ranks."

Dixon smiled. "Was about to ask if you mightn't. Don't mind setting up for a patrol now and again, but blamed if I need a whole army drinking me out of home and hearth. That's if there was a stick left standing after the first night."

The fatigued, muttering gangs of regulars and militia trooped onto and off the flatboats, unloading ordnance, baggage, and barrels of flour, beans, and pickled pork. Taylor stood watching them, legs braced apart and hands clasped at his back. His campaign outfit was something to see. Most of the uniforms were sketchy, casualty to frontier duty, pieced out with odd garments of homespun and buckskin. But Taylor outdid everyone. In a green frock coat, disreputable pantaloons, and oilcloth cap, his jaws furred by a week's pepper-salt beard, he'd have passed for a shabby peddler. His cheek was pouched around a wad of tobacco which he worked with the slow, relishing regularity of a man who had to get far from home and a watchful wife to indulge a favorite vice.

He turned to Lieutenant Robert Anderson, whom he had assigned the nicely ambiguous post of Assistant Inspector General of Troops in the Field. "Mr. Anderson, when the unloading's done, have soap issued. I want this herd of boars cleaned up. Tomorrow I'm declaring a day of rest . . . we'll dole out a little hooch too."

A wise order. Whiteside's "Sucker Army" was in an ugly mood. Only utter fatigue had kept them from tearing loose. It was necessary to restore morale, and though he had check-reined wholesale drinking, Taylor now gave an order that the militia be supplied on a strict daily ration from the Army's own whiskey. Enough to prime the pump, not flood it. Winfield Scott had just abolished the Army's long-time whiskey dole on the grounds that it led to chronic drunkenness and increased the desertion rate, but Taylor had always ignored every Scott-ordained regulation that he safely could.

Orders were given for disposition of baggage and equipment, unhitching and turning out the mules, digging latrines, pitching tents, and distributing rations. Men hurried back and forth, barking commands or carrying them out. As Taylor had shrewdly surmised, the prospect of a swim bolstered all spirits. Soon hundreds of men were congregated behind a birch-cloaked point, stripping down and plunging in, diving, sputtering, splashing one another.

"Gentlemen," Taylor said, "let us repair to that potation mentioned by Mr. Dixon. 'Hem, I'll stand the drinks."

His staff managed to keep straight faces.

Dixon's house was ninety feet long, built in three sections; a cluster of Winnebago lodges stood off behind it. The left-hand section combined a tavern and trading post; two small windows paned with greased paper admitted the only light. The officers ranged themselves on two benches flanking a long table. Dixon concluded a trade with a *voyageur* and his Indian wife, filled some pewter mugs from an oak barrel, set them on a tray and carried it to the table.

"Health, sir." Taylor raised his mug, but (constant in this regard) barely touched it to his lips. "Kindly open an account for Z. Taylor in your books, Mr. Dixon. Charge these drinks."

"My pleasure, Colonel."

"No, we're imposing on you as is. We'll pay for what we eat and drink. I would like to ask some questions."

"Judged you would."

"I'm told you entertained Black Hawk when he camped over."

"Him, Neapope, and The Prophet broke bread with us. Wouldn't swear to it, but I thought the old Hawk was having his second thoughts about a war. Other two seemed to egg him on."

"I know The Prophet—White Cloud," Taylor mused. "He was with Tecumseh in 1812. Neapope, I know, is Black Hawk's right-hand man. Evil genius or whatever."

"He's a medicine man, damn young for the part, don't take whiskey nor tobacco. Close friend o' White Cloud's, which is how The Prophet got Black Hawk's ear. Reckon he give ear to that pair against his own good judgment. Thinks The Prophet speaks with the ghost tongue, the voice of Tecumseh."

"Any idea how large the Sac force is?"

"They done a considerable brag on how many Potawatomis and Ottawas joined 'em, but it sounded like heap wind. Still I made it about eight hundred braves." Dixon weighed the colonel's frown. "I hazard that's more'n the Army reckoned."

"By about three hundred." Taylor tapped a blunt thumbnail on his mug. "With your permission, I will erect a fortification on the meadow. I think conditions warrant it . . . and I need a general headquarters." He flicked a smile. "Of course we'll call it Fort Dixon."

Dixon stroked his chin. "Black Hawk told me his heart is bad, but he don't want no fight. All he wants is to make corn on his land in the old way and be left alone. Come to a face-down, I'd take vow he'd settle for that."

"The government won't. Black Hawk's violated a solemn agreement. Let him bring it off and we open the door to a score of risings, finally a territorial bloodbath. I haven't asked where your sentiments lie; perhaps I should."

"I'm a loyal American, Colonel, even if I try to see all sides. My Winnebagos keep me up on all that's afoot in the country. Want to know where Black Hawk is this minute?"

"If you know that, sir, you're well up on the Army."

"No offense, but that's no great trick. Word is Black Hawk has left his main band on the Kishwaukee River and has gone with forty of his braves to the mouth of Sycamore Creek. Seems all the big chiefs and sachems of the Potawatomi are holding big powwow there to decide whether their medicine is that strong they can override Shabbona's word and join the Sacs."

"That's bad news. If they should go over to Black Hawk—"

The door opened; a sergeant of regulars entered. He came to the table and saluted. "Begging the colonel's pardon. There's riders coming up Kellogg's Road from the south. Whites, sir, a good-sized party."

Taylor pushed to his feet. "Some late-arriving volunteers, no doubt."

They went outside. A party of several hundred mounted men was coming across the southern prairie. Suddenly they spurred forward, whooping, waving their hats, firing off muskets. They were a motley-looking contingent in buckskins and homespun. They halted; two men left the group and rode over to Taylor and his officers. One, a rugged beak-nosed man in an old-fashioned uniform and cocked hat, said:

"Have I the honor, sir, of addressing Colonel Zacharias Taylor?"

Taylor nodded curtly.

"I am Colonel Isaiah Stillman of Fulton County. This is Major David Bailey of Tazewell County." He indicated his bland-faced companion. "We have a combined force of three hundred and forty-one men raised from our respective bailiwicks. We heard you were concentrating here and are placing ourselves at your disposal."

"On whose orders?"

"Well, on our discretion." Stillman reined in his prancing

iron-gray. "Governor Reynolds asked us to patrol Kellogg's Road between Peoria and Dixon's. I assure you, sir, that we've done so assiduously. But no sign of hostiles these many weeks, and settlements along the southern routes are hardly in danger. We felt we should offer our services where they may prove useful."

"I can use 'em now. My men are dead spent, in no shape for marching. Step down, gentlemen." They dismounted; Taylor pulled a map from his pocket and unfolded it. "Here's the mouth of Sycamore Creek. The Potawatomi leaders are holding council there. According to Mr. Dixon, Black Hawk has joined 'em, leaving his main band on the Kishwaukee. I want you to go roughly twenty-five miles up the Rock and make camp here, on Old Man's Creek. You'll be in proximity to the Potawatomis, but not near enough to alarm them. Your presence will be a pointed warning, nothing else."

Disappointment flickered across Bailey's moon face. "We been counting on a chance to engage the reddies."

Taylor fixed him with a flinty eye. "No hostilities have broken yet, mister. And nobody'll say the first shot was fired on my order. You'll post sentinels and hold yourselves in readiness. Under no circumstances are you to proceed farther except on my order. No scouts, no sorties, no provocations. Should the Indians attempt a friendly contact, you are to respond in kind. You are not to fire unless fired upon. Understood?"

"Of course, sir," Stillman said.

Taylor ran an eye over his officers. "Mr. Wilson, you alone seem so chipper that you can hardly bear it."

Wilson grinned. "True, sir."

"You will ride with Mr. Stillman and Mr. Bailey. Gentlemen, you'll be in charge of your own men, unless a doubtful situation arises. Should that occur, you'll defer to Lieutenant Wilson's judgment as you would to my own . . ."

Davis's duties as aide kept him hopping. On the evening of

the second day at Dixon's Ferry, he had just managed to down a sketchy supper when Taylor's striker hurried up saying that the colonel wanted him on the double.

He crossed the meadow at a trot, working the rubbery cramps out of his muscles. A copper-gold sunset flooded the prairie, but the twilight threnody of crickets and whippoorwills was violated by a bedlam of noise from the militia side of the sprawling encampment. Nearly all the volunteers, nine-tenths of them originally from Kentucky and Tennessee, were born to the saddle; all were crack shots. Horse races, foot races, shooting matches, and wrestling falls were going on all over the camp. Soon after setting up bivouac yesterday, the irregulars had found mysterious whiskey sources of their own. Grogged to the gills, they had raised Cain all last night and most of today.

On the side where the regulars had pitched their tents, men moved quietly back and forth at their duties; lazy tendrils of smoke wove up from well-tended fires. The regulars had spent the day working on a log fortification by the ferry crossing, but it would take a few more days to complete. The colonel's tent was set under a big oak. He was seated in a camp chair in front, papers spread out on a small folding table, iron inkpot at his elbow, grimly laboring over one of his long, tedious, and highly involved reports to the War Department. He looked up at Davis and threw down his pen.

"Where the devil have you been? I've got . . . what is it now, Ruggles?" This to the sergeant who had hurried up, throwing a hasty salute.

"It's them milish, sir. Gang of 'em are taking shots at them Indian lodges."

"Damn and blast! Did you tell 'em to quit?"

"Yes, sir."

"Take along a squad and tell 'em again, this time from behind a line of muskets."

Ruggles went off on the run.

"That's what I wanted to see you about, mister. The way

92

things are going, we're like to have a war here and now. At Dubuque, you made a gang of these wild men listen to you by getting the ear of their spokesman . . ."

"Yes, sir. Rafer Beal. He's here . . . ran into him today. The Dubuque miners who went over to Galena joined up with the Jo Daviess County Volunteers. It seems they've elected Beal their captain."

Taylor's brows rose. "Is that so? Good. You can try your influence with him again. He could be a great help to us, calming this rabble down."

"I don't know, sir. At Dubuque I had only Beal's own crowd to deal with. Less than a hundred men . . ."

"I'm aware of that, but it's the same general breed and your friend Beal may be a natural leader. All we need is someone who can keep these rednecks in line."

That was the whole problem. A leader. Samuel Whiteside was well-known as an Indian fighter; he had served under Taylor in 1814. At the outset, the colonel had been pleased by Whiteside's appointment as militia commander; but as a leader of men, he had proven a bitter disappointment.

"I'm afraid you overestimate my influence with Beal, sir. He's utterly independent and couldn't care less about our problem. It would depend on how his fancy is tickled."

"Then tickle it properly, mister, or I'll have to crack some heads together. Atkinson wants the milish handled with velvet gloves—and I'm bound to say he's right. We'll need all the trained woodsmen and rangers we can get before we're done. Tomorrow I'll split Whiteside's army, send some to join Stillman and Bailey at Old Man's Creek, but for now . . ."

Davis crossed to the volunteer camp, which sprawled across the prairie like a squalorous fungus. The dusk was alive with points of flame. What tents the irregulars had were pitched haphazardly among log half-shelters; gear was strewn everywhere. Most of the militia fires were smoking and badly tended, their builders too drunk to care. Davis's nostrils twitched to the greasy taint of frying sidemeat, scorched johnnycake, and coffee boiled to a black syrup. Walking through the camp, he caught scraps of pungent talk and laughter; men took drunken notice of him; some cursed him.

The Jo Daviess crowd was ganged in a loose circle near their crude scraggle of shelters, watching a ruckus of some sort. Davis was almost ignored as he threaded through them. Two men were tussling in the firelight, both still on their feet. One was Rafer Beal; the other, a gangling black-haired fellow built like a plank. But a plank turned out from knotty oak. His sleeves were rolled up; his lean forearms were corded with muscle.

The watchers urged the two on, cheering lustily.

"Get a crotch hoist on him!"

"Chaw his ear off, Rafe!"

Momentarily the gangling youth had Beal at a surprising disadvantage. Davis had felt Beal's strength; he'd have sworn the rawboned riverman could break in half any man in his size and weight class.

"Slide away, Rafe! Slide away, dammit!"

The trick of "sliding away" caused a scramble for advantage that sent both men to the ground.

"Dog fall! Dog fall!"

Which declared the contest a draw. The two men got to their feet and gripped hands. A broad grin crinkled Beal's face.

"Well, I catched some sockdolager for fair. You take the bright honors, Abe."

"No, you took me down clean enough, Rafe. I give you the contest."

"Clean, like hell! Why, I—" Beal's glance found Davis; he grinned vastly. "Why, how-de-do there, Army! Reckon you ain't met my adver—adversity—"

"Adversary," said the other wrestler.

"By crumb, that's right. Jeff Davis here. Army, this big hock o' country ham is Abe Lincoln. He be cap'n of the Clary's Grove boys from Sangamon County. Can tell stretchers like nobody

94

you met. Also can whup any man in Illinois but Rafer Beal."

Lincoln's face was oddly plain and striking: all bony ridges and gaunt hollows. He was even taller than Beal, around six feet-four or -five, but his spare and ungainly frame ran all to knobby joints and lengthy limbs. In fact he was so gawky that, weighing him against Beal's heft and grace, Davis wondered that he'd escaped breakage. Then his hand was pummeled in the lanky captain's grip; he ceased wondering.

"Servant, General," Lincoln drawled.

"Believe I saw you drilling your men this morning, Captain."

He'd seen Lincoln marching a column toward a clump of trees. Apparently unable to remember the command to halt or turn them, he'd yelled: "This company is dismissed for thirty seconds, when it will fall in again on the other side of the trees!" Causing a mad scramble.

"Didn't that take the rag offen the bush, though?" Lincoln said good-naturedly. "Reckon a duck'd take to molasses better'n an old piney woods boy like me does to soldiering."

"You be looking for something, Army?" Beal asked.

"A word with you."

Beal took him by the arm and walked him to the edge of the camp, where the gaunt firelight barely reached. Beal bent and scooped a double-eared jug out of the tall grass.

"Ahhh. Ole 'Nongahela. You see that handkerchief a-hanging from Lincoln's belt?"

"I noticed."

"Means he be the champeen wrassler in the country. No matter howbeit booked, he bested me three out o' three. Had both underholts once and he throwed me clean. Dragged him down on dog falls both other times." Beal tilted the jug on his forearm and hooked thumb and took a thirsty pull. "First time we wrassled, couple year ago, we was both flatboating Galena lead down to Nawleans. Mostly he whups me, then gives me the match."

Beal chortled and passed Davis the jug. He braced himself,

closed his eyes and drank. When he thought he could trust his voice, he said: "A little weak, isn't it?"

Beal's shoulders shook. "Sojer boy, I never see your beat. Man has need of boiler plate in his belly 'fore he takes on ole 'Nongahela rye. Believe you would plumb strangle 'fore you let on." He took back the jug; his Adam's apple bobbed for five seconds. He slapped in the cork and set the jug down, his eyes bright as a masked coon's. "'Low you been sent to knock our heads together."

"In a manner of speaking. Things are a little out of hand, wouldn't you agree?"

"Looka-here now, Army. You can't tree yourself a whole forest o' wild bearcats 'thout mixing in some sockdolager and painter sweat. Talk agin these boys' fun and you have yourself underholts on a wildcat. Take my advice and leave her be."

"Can't; I'm here under orders."

"Part of which'd be to prime ole Rafe to he'p you, eh?"

"Will you?"

"Looka-here, hoss, I ain't got all that much voice outside my own crowd. We's each of us a bearcat climbs his own tree. All I can tell you, you bluejays go trying to bust up the ball, you be chawed up and spit out. They's four times as many o' us."

"If this sort of thing goes on much longer, you'll be at our throats anyhow. A pity, seeing we have a common foe who'd be delighted to see this army fall to pieces. One who'll give you all the fighting you want before long."

"Well, then, you're a-bracing the wrong man, Army. Abe Lincoln would be a rightful choice."

"Why him?"

"He's one of us right enough, only different. Got a jag o' learning for one thing, only that ain't it. Makes you laugh fit to split with them stretchers o' his, but that ain't it either. All I know, he can whup 'em into line even when he ain't got a mind to. Hell, he didn't want to captain his own company. I be told that Clary's Grove crew drug him right outen their own line where he's trying to hide and give him a voice vote, three fourths o' seventy men. He's a balky man, Lincoln is. Got to rope him up and tie him down."

"Suppose I tried, would you help?"

"Not by a damn sight," Beal said happily. "Wouldn't miss 'er for the world, though. You rile him, maybe you will catch some sockdolager."

"I knew I could count on you."

They returned to the fire. Lincoln was sitting cross-legged on the ground, telling a story. All his height must be in his legs, because seated, he looked of average stature. He spoke deliberately and gravely, but a vast chuckle was welling under the group's silence. When he'd finished and the men had roared their appreciation, he looked at Davis and Beal.

"What can I do you gents for?"

"For me, nothing," Davis said. "For your state and your country, perhaps a good deal."

The young captain blinked at him, then looked soberly around the circle. The men exchanged small sly grins. "That so? Well, suppose you grease up your talk gear, General, and we will give good ear."

Davis did—painfully aware of how pompous his talk of principles must sound to such men. Their loyalties were boundaried by their regions; high-flown talk from an outsider merely amused them. There was silence when he finished, a kind of ribald waiting.

"Very interesting," Lincoln murmured. "Puts me in mind some of a toy I had when I was a tad. Little shiny lead soldier it was, on horseback. Well, sir, I lost it. And my pap said, 'Don't you be a-fretting, boy, he will turn up sometime.'" He eyed Davis, nodding thoughtfully. "Did, too."

The men roared.

Davis felt the blood crawl into his face. "There is only one answer to that, and if I were not in uniform and on duty, you would have it."

The volunteers laughed harder. Lincoln, who hadn't cracked a grin, lounged angularly to his feet. "Cool your bile waters there, General. I say I wouldn't help you?"

Beal took each of them by an arm. "'Fore we commence to lay down the what-for to all them bearcats, we best prime the pump with some gollywampus."

"*Now* you'll come along?" Davis said.

"Why Grandmaw suck eggs, boy, course I will. Reckon I'd miss seeing the pair o' you massacreed?"

They walked to where Beal had cached the jug. Davis, his anger not quite cooled, looked at Lincoln in the dim throw of firelight. "Did you find it essential to qualify your acceptance with an insult?"

"I detect a spot of old Kentucky in your tone, General?"

"I doubt it. I was born there, later educated there. But my family moved to Mississippi before I was two."

"Too bad you didn't get born in a log house. Might have added a spot to your education."

"It had glass windows, but it was log, all right. So was the first school I attended in Mississippi."

Lincoln sighed. "So was mine, but ones I went to never shined off the rough edges. Takes a passel of learning for a man to unlearn his roots. General, I laid it to you a-purpose. I will flay you up and down and crosswise before we're done, and if you was raised about this breed, you should know why."

"I believe I do."

"Well, then, you get as warm's you please. It'll lend the picture some fine touches. Just don't get so hot you shoot me."

Beal took a long pull and nudged Lincoln's arm with the jug. The Illinoisan shook his head. "I don't drink whiskey."

"Forgot." Beal winked at Davis and passed him the jug. "Ain't that a hell of a note? Him a-running for office too."

"Office?"

Lincoln grinned, a little sheepishly. "Illinois legislature."

Davis took a nip of the jug for camaraderie's sake. This

second jolt didn't seem as bad. "I understand that war service has its political uses."

"Well," Lincoln said, "what I tell folks, I got tired of clerking in Denton Offutt's store in New Salem. But I got to admit one month smack here on a man's behind 'ud be worth three of stumping it. Another reason—well, her name's Ann. Might be she'll see me in a kindlier light if she don't see clean through me."

Beal took another healthy swig and whacked in the cork. "Abe, you know where all this ruckus is been a-flaring from? Bo Scullers's outfit."

Lincoln nodded. "That's a Pike County company, General . . . Scullers is captain. Ever logged any? Drive of logs jams up, a riverhog bucks her open by busting out the key log. We'll just sashay to that shebang first . . ."

The three crossed to the Pike County camp. Some sort of commotion was going on, punctuated by bursts of jeering and gibing. As they walked into the firelight, Davis saw a large whiskey barrel set in a cleared space. It must be full, for the biggest and strongest were taking turns clamping their arms around the barrel and straining to lift it enough to take a sip from the bunghole. They were so entranced by the sport, they didn't notice the newcomers. A young giant swaggered up to the barrel; he stooped and seized hold. His muscles stood out like cables; veins swelled in his forehead. The barrel stirred. Raised an inch. Two inches. The youth groaned; the barrel thudded down to an accompaniment of hoots and jeers.

"I'll take a whirl, nobody objects," Lincoln said.

Men turned and saw a uniform. An acrimonious rumble ran through them. Davis caught a raw reek of whiskey. He almost laid a hand on his belt pistol. A bantam of a man in shiny black buckskins stepped forward.

"Y'ain't welcome here in that company, Lincoln."

"All sot up to take on the American Army, are you, Bo?"

Scullers stabbed a dirty finger at Davis. "I know what this

sojer boy wants. He come to give us the law from that big-bird colonel and you be along to grease the griddle." He laughed feistily. "He don't look like no Moses to me. And your name ain't Aaron."

"Abraham it is," Lincoln said good-naturedly. "Come to lead the flock out of error."

Scullers spat. "How you aim to do that?"

"Anyways you want it, Bo." The warmth had run out of Lincoln's tone. "You may not want to dance the jig, but you will lend the tune a sober ear."

"I don't get you, Lincoln." Scullers's eyes squinted to bright slits. "You appointed yourself this bluejay's keeper?"

"Him?" Lincoln jabbed a scornful thumb at Davis. "Don't be a damn fool. I got no more truck with a fancy-fine cotton-mouth like that'n any man here. But this army is got to hold together. You go busting her up and it's your kin—yes, your wives and babies—that could lose their scalps. This army stands between them and a whole nation of blood-crazy Injuns. You know that's so."

Before he had finished, they were hooting and clapping their hands in rhythm to drown him out. The black-haired captain took it with a grin, mallet-like fists cocked on his hips, till the noise tapered off.

"Boys," he drawled, "there ain't but one way you can shut me up tonight. That's if any of you cares to undertake spiking my gun."

Scullers snorted. "You're too slippery. Ain't a one of us you can't throw galley-west." His finger stabbed again, this time at the whiskey barrel. "That's the only way you'll make this bearcat give ear. Lift her clear and drink hearty."

The others yelled approval.

Lincoln walked to the cask. Bent-kneed, he embraced it and gave a tentative heave, testing its bulk and weight. Then straightened and rolled his gaunt shoulders, opening and closing his fingers. Bending again, his clasped the barrel with great care, as though it contained rare china. His fingers splayed with a tremendous pressure. The barrel rose by slow inches. When it was a foot above the ground, he paused. Lincoln's face was masklike, but the sinews of his arms were corded ridges under the brown skin. Again the cask moved upward. When it was two feet above the ground, he tilted the bunghole to his lips. Slowly, slowly, the barrel settled back to the ground.

Cheers went up. But a man yelled: "Hell, he didn't even swaller!"

"You went and done it, Abe!" crowed Beal. "You took a drink of whiskey. Ho ho!"

For answer, Lincoln spat a mouthful of liquor on the ground.

" 'Y God," Beal said with his overpowering grin, "that Abe'll make a goddam politico sure. Got more twists to him than a sidehill gouger."

The men surrounded Lincoln with backslaps and cheers. "A Scullers never goes back on his word," Scullers growled. "All right, bluejay. S'pose'n you say what'll make ole Big Bird Taylor happy."

"Not very much," Davis said. "The colonel prefers that you take orders from your own elected officers. But a general order was issued yesterday forbidding the unauthorized firing of guns. We'd like to see it observed. We'd also appreciate the captains seeing that whiskey consumption is kept to a tolerable level—and the jugs kept corked after tattoo."

Getting a border recruit to listen was a far cry from making a dent in his willful nature. But Lincoln took care of that. Once Davis ceased speaking, he was into the breach with a drawling, whimsical speech on the same theme, the tone of it light as thistledown, pointed as a needle, personal as all get-out, taking on hooters and gibers until, as he warmed to his task, even his most ferocious kibitzers had collapsed in laughter. The caucus ended with a half-dozen pair of brawny hands seizing on the barrel and filling cups for a belly-toaster. And then it was time to move on to the next bivouac . . .

They didn't visit every camp. Beal insisted that he had an unerring nose for the most troublesome and disorderly ones, and his judgment wasn't found wanting. Lincoln had his say with each, standing hipshot in the firelight, one hand rammed in the pocket of his jeans, the other combing his unruly mane. He handled each audience according to its temper—skeptical or suspicious or downright hostile. He joshed, he twitted, he cajoled. His eyes twinkled gravely at his own lusty jokes, of which Davis was frequently the hapless butt. In spite of himself, he felt his temper warmed several times; the tall, still-faced Illinoisan was enjoying himself as much as his listeners.

As the evening wore on, his resentment wore off. He was watching more than the antics of a backwoods buffoon. Lincoln swept the strings of his hearers' feelings, biases, tempers, with a masterly touch, at the same time ringing each man with a homely understanding. Which was quite a trick with a militia whose ranks held a ragtag conglomeration of miners, rivermen, farmers, storekeepers, border lawyers, adventurers, loafers, and plain ruffians. Men who had joined up for every reason under the sun. Patriotism, termagent wives, boredom, easy government pay, Indian hatred, a lust for excitement, or the farcical military record that would underpin a shaky platform in upcoming state elections . . .

Well after midnight, the three men finished their circuit back at Lincoln's camp. Lincoln and Davis had feigned their drinks, but Beal had toasted copiously at every fire. They had to support him between them, stumbling through the near-dark, Beal bawling a highly tuneless rendition of *Old Soomer Licked the Ladle*. When they eased him down beside the fire, he started laughing fit to kill, slapping his knees to a tune somewhere in his head.

"Whee-oo," Lincoln said. "What a night. Done enough stumping for ten campaigns. Lord deliver me from any more wars."

"Careful," Davis said. "That's a pretty definite statement from a politician."

"Well, treat it like a vow, General," Lincoln grinned, "for it's sacred. I am wore out like the greased pig at a county fair and have teased up an appetite like a baby buzzard. Can't offer but sowbelly and corndodgers, but would be proud to have you pitch in."

Davis gathered enough wood for a fire. Lincoln produced a sack of cornmeal from his heap of gear. He mixed cold water, a quart of meal and a finger of salt, patted the mush into thick pones and laid them in a skillet. "Soon's we got a nice bed of coals, we will whop up those dodgers with a mess of pork. No better eating less'n they go hard on you, then you could knock down an elk with a chunk."

Having noticed several books amid the mound of Lincoln's gear, Davis was glancing through a couple of law texts. "Rawle's *On the Constitution.* And Kent's *Commentaries.* We studied those at West Point. What's this—a grammar?" He turned to the title pages. *"English Grammar in Familiar Lectures accompanied by a Compendium of Punctuation, Exercises in False Syntax, and a Key to the Exercises, designed for the Use of Schools and Private Learners. By Samuel Kirkham."*

He must have sounded doubtful, for Lincoln chuckled. "Look through it, General. Ask me any question."

"All right . . . what is a phrase?"

Lincoln pulled his long nose. "A phrase . . . is an assemblage of words not constituting an entire proposition but performing a distinct office in the structure of a sentence or of another phrase."

"I didn't know that."

Lincoln grinned, looking pleased as a boy. "My ma primed me with that one. Not my real mother. She died when I was a tad. Pap married again. Her I'm owing for the books and study . . . and a feeling for some good things."

Beal sighed and toppled over on his side. Chuckling, Lincoln threw a blanket over the snoring riverman. "Old Rafe has damped down one fearful dry in the cause of amicable relations." He sat down again, crossing his amazing legs tailor-fashion. "Well, we cooled things down to a tolerable simmer for tonight, anyhow, General. Can't say how long it'll last."

The pones were delicious. And the talk was good: Davis was surprised at the range of his companion's knowledge and interests. During a pause, he curiously studied Lincoln's long, peculiarly sad face as he gazed into the fire, arms wrapped around his knees. The man was considerably more than a whimsical bumpkin with a knack for knocking other bumpkin heads together.

"General, you ever consider going into politics?" he asked with a sudden grin.

"God forbid!" Davis said fervently.

A smoky false daylight had crawled out of the east when Davis said a good night and headed back for the regulars' camp. The prairie was quiet in the ghostly predawn. The noisy revelry had ended hours ago, the last of the drunks having sought their blankets. The grass was freckled with wet opal; pulses of peach and old rose were climbing the eastern sky. The morning was beautiful, man's effacements erased for a little time.

Suddenly he stopped. He thought he heard a creak and rattle of equipment. The sound came from the woods on the up-river road. Davis moved on, angling in that direction. A pallid grayness still clung to the prairie, but he could see the limping file of men emerging from the forest.

Stillman's and Bailey's volunteer force. They trudged along in tired bunches, no sign about them of the boisterous, bragging crew that had left Dixon's Ferry two days ago. Some had lost their horses; some even lacked rifles or muskets. Davis recognized George Wilson and ran over to him. Wilson was slumped in his saddle, chin down. Bareheaded, a blood-browned rag tied around his scalp.

"George—"

Wilson wearily raised his head. "Hullo, Jeff."

"What happened, for God's sake?"

104

"Huh? Oh . . . they ran. The bloody bastards ran."

"Who ran?"

Wilson shook himself, looked around like a man coming out of a bad dream, then reined out of the column. He pointed at the volunteers. "They did. These gutless goddam poltroons!"

Nobody looked at him. They slogged on.

"God, Jeff." Wilson rubbed a shaking hand over his face. "He wanted to give up. Black Hawk. Sent us three of his braves under a flag of truce. Had five others stand off to see what would happen. Soon as the Sac spokesman said they wanted a peace parley, one of these bastards took his rifle and—cool as you please—shot one of the truce bearers. Killed him, you know, as he would a dog. Other two managed to escape. Then these, these *bastards* went after the five Sacs who were watching. And they killed two of *them!* The shooting brought Black Hawk himself . . . it wasn't quite sunset, he was easy to single out. White buckskin, white horse. Swear he hadn't a handful of warriors at his back. I dunno . . . maybe he was crazy enough after what happened to make a suicide charge on us. Or thought he was. He didn't reckon with the stanch militia who had him outnumbered by, I should say, a good eight to one. They turned tail, Jeff, just turned tail and ran like sheep . . ."

"But where was Stillman? Where was—"

"How in hell do I know? I tried to rally 'em, but you can't rally sheep. There's a lot sheep'll do, mill and bleat, run, throw away their guns, provisions, a hundred more valuable things, so they can run faster. The one goddam thing they will not do is *fight!*"

Wilson shook his head haggardly. His voice sank. "That was our chance, you see. Our one and only. A chance to nip a war in the bud. Save hundreds of lives. Whatever his reasons, Black Hawk meant to surrender. *Surrender!* And these damned fools killed it . . ."

7

"Knoxie has a beau-*o*, Knoxie has a beau-*o*—"

Betty did a little skip dance in back of her sister, who was bent over the hearth stirring a seething kettle of tallow with an iron spoon. Knox looked up, wiping a straggle of hair out of her eyes.

"Go away, snip, or I'll box your ears."

Mrs. Taylor sighed. "Betty, go out and play. Find your brother. Anything."

The seven-year-old edged circumspectly around Knox to reach the door. She paused. "Knox has all *kinds* of beaux! Everyone says—"

Knox whirled from the kettle. "I vow, if I get my hands on you!"

Betty popped out the door, her small-girl voice trailing sing-song taunts. Margaret Taylor, her face pinkened by the warmth of candlemaking, straightened up, wiping her hands on her tallow-spotted apron.

"What in the world has gotten into you lately?"

"Ma, that child is enough to try the patience of a Spartan—"

"True," Margaret said dryly. "That hardly excuses you. Flying off the handle at every least little . . . do be careful, you're dripping tallow on the floor."

"Oh bother!" Knox clattered the spoon down on the stone hearth and sulkily threw herself into a hand-carved armchair.

"Another tantrum?"

"And why not? No matter what I say or do is wrong. No matter what that nasty child says is excused—"

"That will do. It wasn't Betty's actions that started all the talk. She merely picked up and is repeating . . ."

"Of course. Knoxie's all to blame. Knoxie's at fault as always."

"Well, you did 'walk out' with Lieutenant Davis, and you should have thought how it would look, half the town there and all those clacking women knowing that you'd come with Denny, then Mr. Davis doing that scandalous dance . . ."

"Into which all their sweet minds read the nastiest implications possible. I suppose I'm to blame for that too."

"Well, you shouldn't have gone outside with the lieutenant."

"Mother, if I have to explain once more! I told you he practically dragged me out the door, which I couldn't prevent without creating a scene."

"Oh? I can't quite recall the last time you were so concerned with appearances that you neglected to have your own way." Margaret cocked her head a bit to one side. "Knoxie, did . . . ?"

"What?"

"When you stepped outside with Lieutenant Davis that night, did anything—happen?"

"What on earth *could?* We weren't gone two minutes."

"I didn't notice when you'd left. Only that you returned looking quite fussed and bothered."

Knox smiled. "Why, Mother."

Margaret blushed. "Well, the way you've behaved of late is enough to make a body wonder . . ."

"Wonder what, Mother mine?"

"Whether you aren't generating an excess of animal spirits."

Knox hugged her knees, almost rolling out of the chair with laughter.

"Do you really find a mother's concern such a source of hilarity?"

Knox stopped laughing. Margaret was hurt, she saw. And stood up at once, going over to her and slipping an arm around her. "I'm sorry. Really I am."

After a moment Margaret patted her hand and smiled. They stood in companionable silence, listening to the riffle of retreat drums from the fort parade. The sound quickened to a heavy roll, then crashed into stillness. The evening cannon boomed. They smiled at each other as the familiar notes of retreat were bugled out. Retreat, for the Army soul, was the flourish that punctuated the day. Mess, tattoo, taps would follow; but it was the sunset gun that rounded out another day of fatigue detail, garrison punishment, all the aspects of a military day.

For the Army's women, as for its men, retreat brought an unraveling of the day's knots. It was an old story to them both. Knox looked around the big kitchen, much nicer than kitchens she'd known at other posts. The hand-carved chairs and heavy table of whipsawed boards whose making had filled many a winter hour for idle-handed soldiers were the only furnishings left over from Colonel Morgan's occupancy. He had been a bachelor, his culinary needs few. The big room now held all the paraphernalia of an industrious homemaker. Margaret's favorite pot, a forty-pounder, hung on the lug pole of the big stone fireplace, the rotary clock jack for turning meats, hooks hung with copper kettles and small brassware. By the hearth, a potato boiler, dye tub, and Dutch oven. Strings festooned with dried apples, peppers, and pumpkin rings stretched overhead from wall to wall. And the comfortable litter of candle-making. Two long poles resting on chairs, the eighteen-inch candle molds that had been used by Margaret's mother and grandmother laid across them. Filled with double-wick candlewicking, the molds waited for repeated dips into the tallow kettle; sections of bark spread beneath protected the lye-scoured floor from drippings.

"Hadn't you better go change?" Margaret said. "Denny will be along directly."

"Lordy, I forgot. And I forgot to tell you that I invited him to dinner."

"Knox, look at the kitchen! Everything in a mess, and you know I'd only planned on sandwiches and tea."

"What's the difference?" Knox laughed. "Serve Denny sawdust between lathboards and a cup of dishwater and he'd never notice."

"Oh, go along with you."

Knox hurried up to her room. It was small, furnished with a bedstead, bureau, and clothespress, the walls decorated with a few childish samplers of Betty's fabrication. Starting to unbutton her dress, she paused, remembering, then went to the window and drew the curtains. She was always forgetting that her window angled toward the officers' barracks this side of the parade. While as an "army brat" born and reared, it was impossible for her to forget that some officers were no more gentlemen than the commonest tackie in the ranks. She slipped out of her dress and a sticky burden of petticoats and small clothes. She sighed with relief—what a freight for a muggy day in mid-June. She poured water from a pitcher into a basin, soaked a cloth and sponged her slim body from head to toe.

She smiled, thinking of Denny Gibbs. *Serve Denny sawdust between lathboards* . . . That was unkind perhaps, but not unfair. The young officer who had seemed the image of dash and excitement to the girl she'd been two years ago when they'd met at his father's home in Springfield, Kentucky, had become such a commonplace to her that she could forget she had invited him to dinner. Two years ago . . . the summer she had awakened to a realization of her womanhood. Bob Anderson's brother Charlie (to whom she had been secretly engaged since they were both six) had suddenly seemed a mere boy. The attentions of a tall, good-looking officer, a graduate of West Point, had flattered her. Denny, though naturally shy (and little exposed to girls because his father had reared him among stern masculine surroundings), had been well-trained in the courtly ways that would delight a romantic girl.

Their fathers' long friendship was a catalyst; they watched the budding match with clucks of approval and saw to it that their children were together often that summer and the next. Letters were exchanged. But that second summer, at Louisville, things had seemed different. Little traits of Denny's, awkwardly boyish *faux pas* that had been endearing and amusing the year before, began to annoy her. She was aware of a fray in her feelings. Yet she'd continued to like him very much. She'd become more aware of his real qualities, the seriousness behind his shy courtesies and drawling sense of fun.

She was growing up, she supposed. Nothing was ever perfect. Denny loved her, she knew that. And she had met nobody that she liked better. But was it enough?

That question, among others, had plagued her lately. A summer spent far from the social whirl to which she'd become accustomed, soirees, lawn parties, concerts, and friends, was partly to blame. But her discontent went deeper. Lately her appetite had faded; with it, ten pounds of weight that she could ill spare. She slept lightly and fitfully; the least sound jerked her awake. Sometimes she was nervous and cross, prone to lose her temper for no cause. At night, tossing sleeplessly, she would wet her pillow with tears. Animal spirits. Maybe her mother's ridiculous phrase was right . . . but the pain and depression of her periods only intensified what she already felt. She just didn't know.

She had dressed in clean linen and a frock of sprigged pale muslin, all coolness and summery frills, and was pouting at herself in the mirror when she heard a knock at the door downstairs. Her mother answered it; she heard Denny's voice. Taking all the time in the world, she dashed a brush many times through her bell of curls, pinched her cheeks for color, and went languidly down the staircase, touching each of the railings and counting them off in fives. Finally she entered the kitchen. Margaret had swept aside enough paraphernalia to let Denny take a chair. He came stiffly to his feet, grimacing as his still-game knee caught his weight.

"You look stunning, Knox. Really!"

She smiled and thanked him, wishing he could turn a compliment without looking abashed as a schoolboy. Margaret, busying herself with sandwiches and tea, said: "Tell us about your day, Denny."

"Little to tell. The wood detail again." Gibbs sighed. "A man joins the Army to fight Indians. Instead he spends three years building roads, cutting lumber, quarrying stone, making hay, gathering wood, drawing water, herding cattle, building barracks and stables and hospitals. Not to mention all the spring and summer botanical and horticultural activities. Gardens and orchards!" He looked disconsolate; he tapped his bad knee with his cane. "Then directly a war comes along, I have to trip on a blasted . . . excuse me, ladies."

"What about the war?" Margaret asked. "Any news at all?"

Gibbs nodded. "Good news for a change . . . I was at headquarters today when Captain McRee received the dispatches. Three days ago a party of Sacs, thirteen or so, jumped six farmers who were planting corn over by the Pecatonica. The Sacs left five bodies, no trace of the sixth."

"*Good* news?"

"Well, that, no. But eighteen militiamen led by Colonel Dodge of Dodgeville gave pursuit and overtook the red devils. Wiped 'em out to a man. First victory for our side since the war's begun!"

Knox wrinkled her nose. It was all barbarous. How stupid war was, particularly this war. Since a handful of Sac braves had routed Stillman and Bailey at Old Man's Creek (a fiasco jeered throughout the territory as "Stillman's Run") it had taken one drearily farcical turn after another. And Black Hawk, having failed to gain an alliance with the Potawatomi chiefs, had merely wished to surrender! As it turned out, he'd not only taken eleven militia scalps but enough booty—equipment and provisions, many bulging saddlebags, a baggage train of six wagons and oxen, an abundance of powder and shot, and numerous rifles dropped by the terrified whites in their flight—to continue his war. A few days later the butchered bodies of fifteen white men, women, and children were found on Indian Creek twelve miles north of Ottawa. Later it came out that this hadn't been Black Hawk's doing, but the work of a half-breed renegade named Girty, a fact barely noticed amid the panic and confusion that followed. Black Hawk and his band had already escaped up the Rock to its source at Lake Koshkonong in Michigan Territory, where a swampy wilderness had swallowed them like smoke. From there, Black Hawk had launched a campaign of harassment and terror against the border settlements. Once again it was old Shabbona who had spread the warning; hundreds of settlers had fled to forts and blockhouses. At least two hundred had not made it . . .

The children were called; they sat down to eat. Margaret plied Denny with questions. The never-ending round of a woman's day, especially in the warm months—cooking, washing, gardening, feeding chickens, skimming milk, making butter and cheese, putting up jellies and preserves—left her little time for outside gossip.

"They're still flocking in," Gibbs said. "Droves of settlers demanding protection. Everyone hates the Army till they need it."

"But what of news from the field?"

"Well, General Atkinson has made his headquarters at Peru, Illinois, and has raised another army of four thousand volunteers. General Henry's rangers and Colonel Frye's—oh, and more regulars have been ordered up. Winfield Scott himself is coming from Fortress Monroe in Virginia with nine companies."

112

"Oh?" Margaret raised her brows. "If the Army's first commander is taking the field, I'd guess the War Department is somewhat less than ecstatic over General Atkinson's conduct of the campaign."

"Well, I can hardly speculate as to that." He smiled. "Last, but not least, Colonel Taylor's troops are still encamped at Dixon's Ferry."

"Waiting," Margaret murmured. "No doubt poor Zeke is fit to be tied . . ."

Supper over, Knox and Gibbs took their usual evening stroll away from the fort quadrangle. The evening was quiet and windless. They passed the stables and open-sided haysheds and skirted the big truck gardens beyond. The prairie soil was so rich that the annual plantings of corn, potatoes, beans, tomatoes, carrots, beets, and onions kept the garrison supplied year-round. They idled across the meadow between the fields and the bluffs, Gibbs whacking the heads off dandelions with his cane. He was almost able to get along without it now.

"Denny, please stop swinging that thing about. You make me nervous."

"Say, did I show you this? It's a sword cane. You twist on the head like this . . . and presto!"

She made a face. "What a wicked-looking thing. Put it away, please."

He did so, looking a little hurt.

"What do you need that for, anyway?"

"I don't know . . . one can never tell when he'll be called on to defend his own honor. Or another's."

"Oh, is that it? . . . Look, Denny!"

She caught his arm and pointed. A big buck stood roe-coated and handsome at the edge of a cornfield. His head was arched; twilight sheened his magnificent antlers. Suddenly he turned and bolted away, his whitetail flag bobbing, and vanished in the woods.

"Beautiful."

"Yes," Gibbs cleared his throat. "There's something I've meant to ask you . . . I hardly know how to say it."

"If you're going to propose, Lieutenant, you might at least wait for a little moonlight."

"Don't laugh at me, please."

"I'm sorry."

"It's not a proposal," he said lamely. "But a rather important matter . . . at least I think so. Please don't be offended."

"How could it possibly offend me?" She laughed. "Out with it, sir!"

"That night of the gumbo ball"—he spoke quickly—"did Jeff Davis insult you?"

Knox was silent a moment, swishing her feet in the grass as they walked. Finally she said carefully: "Is that really any of your affair, Denny?"

"If you say not."

"You've been listening to the gossips, I suppose."

"Well, you looked angry when you came back in . . . and I did hear talk later on."

"What did you hear?"

"That he kissed you."

"Twice," she said evenly. "And I slapped him. Twice. I hardly think anyone's honor was affronted. If it was, I satisfied it. Does that satisfy you?"

"I shouldn't take it so lightly. But if you say so . . ."

"I do. Please let the matter drop."

He was stiffly silent as they walked. A smile brushed her lips. She knew from the talk that Denny had tried conclusions with Davis that same night. And had come off badly. One bit of gossip had it that Davis had knocked him down; if so, no mark had resulted. She'd made a point of studying his face next day when he'd come to apologize for his action in suddenly leaving the dance and returning to his quarters. His explanation that his leg had been paining him something fierce hadn't satisfied her at all . . .

114

"Brighten up." She laughed, pressing his arm. "It can't be all that serious. I know that you and Jeff Davis have been friends a long time."

"Seven years. How did you know?"

"You always spoke of him, silly. 'My friend Jeff.' Wasn't that Davis?"

He smiled reluctantly. "That was Davis. He was already a second-year man when I entered my plebe year at the Point, but he never hazed a fellow as most upperclassmen did." He paused sheepishly. "Guess I did act pretty much the idiot that night . . . I suppose you've heard."

"I suppose I have."

"Jeff's a fine chap. Not usually brash—really a gentleman. Oh, a bit prickly. Goes with being one of the 'cotton aristocracy,' I suppose. He was born in the Kentucky backwoods— and his father, I understand, was a failure at most things he put his hand to. Jeff's brother Joseph, on the other hand, is one of the half-dozen wealthiest planters in Mississippi."

"Davis surely isn't an aristocratic name. Is he defensive because of his roots?"

"No, I wouldn't say so. It's more or less in his nature to cut a swath that's high, wide, and handsome."

"I've noticed."

Gibbs chuckled. "Carved himself a legendary niche at West Point. In his junior year, he was one of the ringleaders of the worst riot in the Academy's history. Got arraigned before a tribunal and officially dismissed . . . then talked the tribunal out of it! Accumulated demerits as a squirrel stores up acorns. Earned himself a bad name that became the envy of his peers, the boast of his friends—"

"Yes, I can imagine."

"Don't mistake me, there was plenty of bottom to Jeff's flamboyance. As one instructor learned to his regret. He told Jeff that in a real emergency, he'd be unstrung by his own mediocrity. A few days later, in the explosive magazine, the same fellow was conducting a class in the making of fireballs—that's a fused grenade, you light it and throw it—and the fuse of one became fired. Jeff turned to the instructor as though he were asking the time of day: 'What shall we do, sir? This fireball is ignited.' 'Run for your lives,' the instructor yelled. Jeff waited long enough for the pandemonium to become a rout, then picked up the fireball and threw it far out the window.'"

"Good Lord! Wasn't that taking a terrible chance with all those lives—even an instant's delay?"

"Oh, Jeff said he was sure there'd been time to try the fellow's mettle fairly."

"And *that* made it all right?"

"You don't see my point," Gibbs said tolerantly. "If he hadn't kept his head, the building might have been demolished, a lot of cadets killed."

Knox sighed. "All right, let's not belabor the point. I take it you admire the man."

"I guess envy is the word. He has the guts to try almost anything. And the flair necessary to bring it off. The affair at Dubuque, for example. Funny, for he's really reserved; has few close friends. Anderson, Wilson, Dr. Beaumont, myself—in our garrison. But everyone likes him."

"I don't. And do you think we might change the subject?"

She fanned herself with her hand as they strolled. The day's heat was lifting, but she felt unwontedly warm. She did not want, just now, to be reminded of Davis. The way he had kissed her. It had been too natural, ever since, to measure that memory against the way Denny kissed. In a chaste, almost brotherly fashion.

The wide circle they were walking had taken them nearly back to the river. They passed through a belt of oak and beeches which ended at the riverbank. Red-winged blackbirds rustled in the cattails; the air keened with wild mint. The dusky water caught the evening star like a diamond. From the island town across the slough, a nameless *voyageur*, drunk or lonely, was singing.

> *"A la claire fontaine*
> *M'en allant promener—*
> *J'ai trouvé l'eau si belle . . ."*

Her breasts felt faintly constricted by the tight bodice of her frock. Her nerves were sensitized to Gibbs's tall bigness beside her, the touch of his arm where her hand rested.

"I know exactly how that fellow feels."

"Do you, Denny? Show me . . ."

He took her in his arms. In the usual way. As if afraid that she might break. She almost jumped as something gouged the small of her back.

"Will you put down that silly cane, *please—*"

The cane thudded on the ground and rolled against her heel. The silky tickle of his mustache made her feel like sneezing. She felt like crying in exasperation too. That brotherly, dispassionate kiss again! She pressed herself to him; she flicked her tongue against his lips and was a little shocked at herself. But it had the desired effect. He crushed her against him.

When the long kiss ended, she broke free in a half-panic and turned from him, pressing her hands to her face, her heart pounding crazily. He moved closer behind her, his big hands circling her waist. "Knox, Knox—" His lips nuzzled her hair and neck and ear. She turned in his arms, twisting her face to the rain of his kisses, returning them with equal passion.

"Oh Denny, don't, oh darling, we mustn't—"

The endearment, a reflex of the wild tumult in her, only inflamed him more. His hands moved.

"Denny!" She clasped her hands over his and jerked them away, stepping back.

"I'm sorry, Knox." His big hands twisted with a small-boy abjectness. "I don't know what got into me—"

"Oh, for—! Do you have to *apologize?*"

The anger she felt, mostly at herself, mingled with the violent pulse of her blood. He stepped close again and took her hands in his.

"Dear, won't you, can't you tell me how you feel about me . . . really?"

She pulled her hands away. "Not now, please. Don't ask me that now." Her arms were goosefleshed; she rubbed them with her fingers. "I want to go in now. Denny?"

"You're cold. Here . . ."

He unbuttoned and whipped off his coatee, pressing it around her shoulders. His arm was big and warm and gentle around her as they walked back through the trees. Threading the confusions that iced her mind was an awareness of that strong protective arm. She turned her face suddenly, tightly against his shoulder as they walked.

The Taylor house was set just beyond the grove. In a few minutes they stood by the veranda. The night air slid like cool black silk across their faces. He pressed his face against her hair, murmuring.

"What?" She felt languidly secure in the haven of his arms, eyes shut, voice muffled against his shoulder.

"Would, um, would it be all right if I considered us engaged?"

What a way to put such a question! Denny's way. Kind, terribly sweet Denny. Who could bring such fire to her and soothe the burning with such balm. What did it mean? Yes. Say yes.

"Yes. But—"

"Oh, Knox!"

"But we shan't tell anyone, not for a while. We, we have to be very sure, Denny."

He pressed his mouth to her hand. "You will be," he said fervently. "*I'm* sure."

His good-night kiss was forceful. So forceful that her truant passions were aroused again and she clung to him.

Slipping through the dusk-filled parlor, she went quickly up the darkened staircase. Paused a moment, hearing her mother's low pleasant voice from the children's room, reading a bedtime story. She entered her room; Margaret had left a lighted candle on her bureau.

She began to undo the neck of her dress. Her fingers were shaking; she looked at the mirror. Her mouth was a dark trembling stain. Strange . . . he had asked her a score of times to marry him. Always she had put him off. Yet not so long ago—no more than a few months really—if he had kissed her as he had tonight, then asked, she would have said yes. And with no qualifying but.

She gazed at herself, palms flat to her cheeks. She had not wholly committed herself to Denny. But why not? Why couldn't she be sure? How could she feel so with a man and not be sure?

8

"Them reddie bastards," muttered Corporal Mulrooney. "Faugh! What a job. Poor devils. Only a bloody Englisher could do the beat o' that. Wager Frenchy ain't see the like since Waterloo. Eh, bucko?"

"*Sacre nom de Dieu,*" Sergeant Champeau swore offhandedly. "Still your tongue, you bloodthirsty Hibernian! Even the Emperor called the British a civilized foe."

"Saints!" grunted Mulrooney. "I needed one good laugh this day. Ye've given me grist of it, me lad."

Lieutenants Jefferson Davis and Robert Anderson were riding at the head of the column, greatcoated shoulders hunched against the cold rain slashing down into the narrow trail.

"Wish those two would let up," Anderson muttered.

"Let 'em get it out, Bob."

"I am." Anderson sighed. "Jesus. There are times a man wants to throw off—at least verbally—the cloak of officer and gentleman."

He was right. Even a pair of old soldiers like Mulrooney and Champeau had been so shaken by what they'd seen today that, unable to sentimentalize without embarrassment, they made its horror halfway tolerable by reducing it to an exchange of brutal banter. Very simple, Davis thought. Unless you were an officer. Or unless you saw beyond the double-edged implications of butchery and atrocity to the homicidal rage of a people betrayed too often, goaded past all endurance.

To counter the press of dull routine as Taylor's aide, he had prevailed on the colonel to send him on patrol. He wished he had foregone the request.

They'd come on the smoking ruins of the farmstead at midmorning. Riding into the yard, they had been met by the householder's head. Just his head. Cut off and skinned and impaled on the picket fence. Beyond it, the five bodies. A man, a woman, three half-grown boys. Five crimson corpses from which the skin had been flayed in tiny scallops. They might have been left alive. None, thank God, was alive now. The rest was typical. House and outsheds burned, cattle and hogs slaughtered, horses run off. Unwillingly, the mind formed images. Silent coppery bodies slipping through the brush in the misty dawn. A family caught with the night bar off the door, probably at breakfast. Details? Too many details already. Forget it.

With the whole patrol pitching in, the burying had gone quickly. By the time they were through, a chill drizzle was slopping out of a dismal stew of sky. They should have sought shelter, but no one had the stomach to linger. They headed back for Dixon's Ferry in the steady rain.

Back to trouble, no doubt. With those stanch hearts and brave souls, the State Militia of Illinois.

For a time, regulars and volunteers alike had been like a gang of youngsters released from school. They had loafed away the lazy golden days, hunting, fishing, swimming, eating, drinking, gambling, roughing each other in tumbledown games, making a zestful romp of the whole business. Farcical business. Farce was the only word for this miserable war. A few hundred grubby half-starved savages had presented the United States Army with its toughest challenge in twenty years. Against Black Hawk's swift mobile strike-and-run style of warfare, conventional strategy was useless. A large modern army commanded by the nation's leading strategists was unprepared, paralyzed, floundering helplessly. The old Sac had accomplished the impossible. Burdened with upward of eight hundred warriors, all their women and children, to be fed, concealed, moved unseen through the wilderness with their livestock and belongings, he'd successfully eluded hundreds of seasoned white woodsmen. Laid false trails. Sent out raiding parties to focus attention miles from his main advance. Now, from a secure base in the sprawling bogs and forest at the headwaters of the Rock River, he had buckled down to a flurry of quick savage strikes that had reduced scores of farms to smoking ruins and made mutilated corpses of scores of whites.

From Fort Dixon, Zachary Taylor had sent out constant patrols to Fort Deposit, Kellogg's Grove, Apple River Fort, North Ottawa, Galena. Chasing down rumors. Following hazy scents. Fighting ghosts. Again and again, nothing but burned farms and deserted campsites. A brief skirmish now and then. A few trifling triumphs. Dodge's coup at the Pecatonica. And last week's heroic resistance by the defending settlers, mostly women, at the Apple River blockhouse against a hundred and fifty howling Sacs led by Black Hawk himself.

If that weren't enough, the militia was grumbling mutinously. Their ranks had thinned, large numbers being mustered out after their three-week enlistments expired. Desertions were commonplace. For a time, the colonel had damped the fires of revolt by breaking them apart for patrols. Until several hog-wild and drunken gangs had burned and plundered villages of peaceful Indians, including Shabbona's town at Pawpaw Grove —Shabbona, friend of the whites. The few of their number who might have exerted control, men like Rafer Beal and Abe Lincoln, had finished up concurrent enlistments and gone home, indifferent to or disgusted with the whole business. The Honorable John Reynolds himself, Governor of the State of Illinois and commander of its militia, had simply quit—his example setting off another rash of desertions. Then the weather had turned foul. Each dawn came gray and raw; chill rains drizzled out of gunmetal skies. Unprepared, many of the troops had no tents or waterproofing, no warm clothes. Dry wood was scarce; the misting damp that the rednecks called "mizzle" seeped into everything. Meat rotted, flour mildewed. Provisions were low, rations halved; the weather seemed to have driven all the game in the country to cover. John Dixon had slaughtered all his oxen, milch cows, and other livestock to feed the troops . . .

"What d'you say to an early camp, Bob?" Davis shivered as an icy dribble trickled inside his collar. "We'll soon be wet throughout. Can't make Dixon's before nightfall anyway. Maybe it'll let up before morning."

"Let's wait till we've crossed Boomer Creek. Trees are thicker over there; we can find shelter of sorts."

They were following a crooked game trail through a forest of tall hemlock. Suddenly the trees opened to the broad cut of the creek. But where they'd made an easy crossing yesterday, the water rushed in swollen fury, hammering to spray against round smooth boulders. Sergeant Jules Champeau, a slight, grizzled ramrod of a man, reined up between the two officers. A veteran of the Napoleonic Wars, he had been a colonel in the Grand Army; it let him take liberties with the normal constraints of rank.

"It is very rough and deep, sirs. One should go across first to try the footing."

"I will."

Davis put his mount down the bank into the water. The current roiled up past the animal's knees; he balked. Davis urged him with his heels. The horse went forward with mincing reluctance, wary of a drop-off. A hoof skidded on a slick rock, throwing the animal to its knees.

The current flung horse and rider sideways into the water. Davis's elbow hit a rock; the shock of pain and cold water momentarily numbed him. The current tumbled him into deeper water. He was swept downstream a good thirty feet before he grabbed hold of a shore-hugging boulder. Anderson and Champeau came scrambling along the brush-grown bank; they dragged him clear.

"We'll get you dry, my lieutenant," said Champeau. "Come, under the trees . . . Mulrooney, find dry wood."

"Easier fetching a chunk o' fire from Hell," growled the wry-faced corporal. "Simms, Watson, lend a hand."

A little way off the trail, trees rimmed a tiny clearing and arched over it, almost roofing out the sky. Men attended to horses and gear, others scoured for wood. A single deadfall they kicked to pieces yielded a harvest of tinder-dry slabs. Davis strode up and down in his squishing boots, beating his arms across his chest. Fitful gusts of wind cut him to the bone; his teeth chattered. When, wet clothes discarded, he huddled in a blanket next to a roaring fire and drank coffee laced with whiskey, he felt only a little better. Fever triphammered in his temples, his belly seemed to boil.

By midnight he was burning up with fever. Sluggishly rational, he pooh-poohed Anderson's concern. Objected as the men built a crude shelter, thatched it with hemlock boughs and laid more boughs on the soaked earth underneath.

"Stop complaining," Anderson said. "How many get their personal comfort seen to by the Assistant Inspector General of Troops in the Field his own self?"

The rain had nearly ceased. Mizzle hissed on the coals. The men huddled in damp blankets, their parsoaked clothes steaming on sticks propped by the fire. Champeau knelt by Davis's open-sided shelter and proffered a silver flask.

"Cognac, sir. The sovereign remedy."

Davis took the flask. "Does this stuff have all the healing efficacy we attribute to it or is that another excuse?"

"Well, my lieutenant, you have the damned good excuse."

Davis gave a febrile chuckle and let the fiery dark liquor glide down his gullet. . . .

He slept in spurts. And dreamed. Weird inchoate dreams. Savages yelled in the deeps of his fever; fire and blood painted them red; they danced demonlike across charnel heaps of headless flayed bodies. Then he was five years old, grasping his sister Mary's hand as they fled through the twilight woods toward their father's cabin, a "bogey" (or some heavy animal) crashing through the brush in pursuit. Again, half-lucid moments and knowing they'd piled blankets on him to sweat out the fever. Wide-eyed, tight-jawed, he breasted wave on wave of pain. His body doubling up till his knees jackknifed against his chest. Next arching backward at a spine-wrenching angle. He vomited up the last particle of food in his belly. Then dry-retched for hours.

It was close to dawn when his tortured body finally relaxed. He drifted into an aching, troubled sleep. He dreamed the "bogey" dream again. Same black forest. Same crashing menace at his heels. But when he looked at the girl to whose hand he clung, it was Knox Taylor. And when he turned to face the "bogey," it wore the face of Old Zeke Taylor.

He woke suddenly. He was bathed in sweat. The sun was high; a breeze feathered his dry skin. His muscles were raw, he felt weak as a cat. But his head was clear, and smelling pan bread and coffee cooking, he was hungry.

He put away a good meal, then insisted that he was well enough to ride. Anderson had seniority, but he didn't argue. They took up the march at an easy pace. They should reach Dixon's with daylight to spare.

The men's damp spirits had lifted. Excitement salted their talk; all were eager to get back. Just before they'd left Dixon's, word had come that General Atkinson would take over personal command of all troops in the field: he was marching up from Peru with his new militia army. Between the lines, every man read that the tedious weeks of bivouac at Dixon's Ferry were ended. The Northwest Army was preparing to move in force against Black Hawk.

Davis, who ordinarily honed for action, paid the talk little attention. The fever and cramps were gone, he was stronger. But little waves of dizziness came and went. His throat was scratchy and raw, his chest ached as if steel bands enclosed it.

When they reached Dixon's Ferry, sunset was building a fiery fresco across a silver sky. The doubled size of the encampment and hum of fresh activity were apparent at once.

"Atkinson's here," Anderson said exultantly. "If . . . look. Isn't that Sid Johnston?"

It was. Lieutenant Albert Sidney Johnston, General Atkinson's adjutant and Davis's closest friend of West Point days. A tall young man in a grimy buckskin shirt, he had a strong high-browed face with an irregular nose. Few cadets who'd moved in the Academy "set" of which Johnston had been the leader would have recognized him in the leathery frontiersman he'd become.

They dismounted. Exchanged greetings.

"We arrived this morning," Johnston told them. "Well over four thousand militia in three brigades, under joint command of Posey, Alexander, and Henry. Damn, it's good to see you fellows again! Jefferson, you look a mite peaked."

"Is Winfield Scott here?" Anderson asked slyly.

Johnston grinned, not altogether humorously. "Don't be subtle, young lieutenant. No, Scott hasn't arrived yet. The Old Man's still in command."

"Titularly anyhow, eh, Sid?"

"All right." Johnston lowered his voice. "Everyone'll guess as much anyway. President Jackson's so disgruntled with the Old Man's handling of the campaign, he's sent Scott specifically to take charge of the strategy. Imagine what a sore spot it is with the Old Man, then multiply by two. Now I'd suggest you two get over to the stockade without delay. The general's conferring with all the staff and line officers, and I'm trying to chase down some absentees."

"Could it be," Davis said dryly, "that we may be permitted to fight Indians after all?"

"Dunno about that," drawled Johnston, "but doubt we'll leave you to languish here in luxury . . ."

Davis and Anderson turned their horses over to Champeau and crossed to the meadow to Taylor's stockade. General Atkinson's tent was tucked in the evening shadow of the palisade. The officers were grouped around a field table. Zachary Taylor stood a little apart, feet braced, hands clasped at his back, chin tucked down and broad underlip pouted. He gave the two subalterns a curt nod, reserving a curious stabbing glance for Davis. He must look as drawn and liverish as he felt, Davis thought.

The general cleared his throat and tapped a finger on the map spread before him. They quieted down. A North Carolinian of fifty, Henry Atkinson was a spare and rugged man with a gauntly imperial face and shelving jaw. He looked stubborn; his nature was careful, and he mended fences better than he tore them down.

"Gentlemen. Those of you whetting for action will have your wish—" A tendril of wind snapped up the map's stiff edge; Lieutenant Barry Sholder swooped a thumb on it. "Well done, mister. I hope that Black Hawk can be pinned as readily." A pallid chuckle from the officers. "I doubt it, however. Our keenest scouts have failed to turn up his main band." The general's finger crackled across the map where the jagged worm of the Rock River crawled northeast into Michigan Territory. "The marshes and wilderness around Lake Koshkonong are a varitable maze. A stronghold and a striking base. What can we do? Only answer is, establish our base of operations in Black Hawk's own stronghold. Infiltrate the region with camps and patrols. Pour on a pressure that'll force him wholly on the defensive. He's accomplished the incredible. Kept fifteen hundred people, half of them women and children, on the move, lying low, managing to live off the land, raiding the while. But picture the cost to the old butcher. Not only is his band hard-pressed and exhausted, but half-starved—"

Zachary Taylor cleared his throat. "Wouldn't count on it, General."

"I beg your pardon, Colonel?"

"Horses."

"*Horses*, sir?"

"Yes, sir. Since Stillman's Run, the Sacs have prosecuted horse-stealing with great vigor. Any luckless owner who attempts recovery is invariably ambushed and killed. Black Hawk's developed a hell of an efficient light cavalry. Whole key to the quickness and mobility of his raiding . . ."

Atkinson frowned. "I'm aware of—"

"But he has a more urgent need for horses. As evidenced by the remains of horse feasts we've turned up at many an old Sac campsite. Only horses can be moved quickly over long distances. Where they've butchered cattle and hogs in the raids, they've driven the horses to their camps. Best horseflesh becomes war ponies, rest is eaten. Black Hawk keeps a traveling butcher shop on the hoof and keeps it constantly replenished."

Atkinson looked as discomfitted as any leader who had failed to note and weigh in a master stroke of enemy logistics. "You might have mentioned this in a dispatch, Colonel—"

"Assumed you knew as much, sir. Common knowledge. Assumed your scouts would have . . ."

"Yes." Atkinson coughed. "Your point is abundantly clear. Gentlemen, we'll proceed up the Rock to its headwaters at Lake Koshkonong. Should have our headquarters established in less than a week. I want a five o'clock reveille tomorrow. We'll start loading flatboats and baggage wagons directly after mess. Order of march will be as follows: 1st Infantry in front, 6th

Infantry to rear. An advance guard to be drawn from the 1st Infantry will precede the column. Flank guard from the 6th will be thrown out at two hundred or more yards. Rear guard will consist of the Illinois Militia, Henry's troops on the right wing, Posey's and Alexander's center, and Colonel Dodge's Michigan Volunteers on the left . . ."

At the first steely hint of dawn, the troops were bugled out of their blankets. Within the hour, mustered and messed, they were engaged in a flurry of preparations. Men ran to and fro along the riverbank, boarding drawn-up flatboats, dropping burdens of gear, hurrying back for more. A train of mule-hitched wagons creaked under loads of beans and pork and flour.

Taylor and Davis tramped back and forth, the colonel taking note of everything, his aide jotting down his comments. Davis's throat felt like a raw kiln, his head ached miserably. He had developed a hoarse wracking cough. He carried himself board-straight, trying to show nothing, but nature finally conquered. A spasm of coughing exploded in his chest, doubling him up.

He straightened to meet the colonel's pointed stare.

"Little under the weather, mister?"

"Weather, sir, yes." He fought a nasal twang from his voice.

Taylor made no further comment. Thank God. What a grim irony if he were invalided out of his first campaign when some action was finally in the offing . . .

Line officers were readying the regulars for the march. By now the volunteer companies were straggling to the bank, their captains and non-coms cursing them into the usual formless knots. A militia muster was something to behold, men ranking themselves in every possible deviation from a straight line. Some sat, some squatted; the rest leaned on their long rifles and looked bored. Many were hungover, surly as sore-footed bears.

"Look at 'em," Taylor muttered. "The velvet glove! High past time for a mailed fist . . ."

For nearly two months, against all his instincts as a soldier, he had swallowed the raw gamut of militia insubordination. Atkinson's arrival with abundant supplies had relieved the food problem; then what was the trouble? Mostly that the war had gone on too long. It was no longer fun. Not even the prospect of killing Indians whetted enthusiasm.

Lieutenant Wilson came up, saluting. "Beg pardon, sir, a word from that bloody milish captain, Scullers—"

"Yes, he'd be the source from which all discord flows. What's the trouble now?"

"Well, sir, the little beggar wants me to tell General Atkinson that his company enlisted to fight only in the state of Illinois. If we follow Black Hawk into Michigan Territory, it's quits. More, he demands flatboats to take his men down to the Mississippi. I, 'hem, thought I'd tell you first."

"Flatboats, eh? I'll give 'em flatboats."

Wilson stared. "I say. You can't do that, sir. Yield to these chaps and it'll infect the whole milish. We'll have a bloody revolt on our hands."

"Exactly."

Taylor turned on his heel and started down the riverbank at his choppy, rolling stride. Davis and Wilson exchanged glances, then followed. Passing clots of bearded, seedy militiamen, they were hooted and jeered. Taylor halted and looked at the two subalterns.

"Gentlemen, you'll wait right here."

"But sir . . . !" Wilson spluttered.

Taylor was already walking on. He stopped twenty or so feet from the Pike County Volunteers. Bo Scullers stepped out slowly, grinning.

"That bluejay o' yourn pass the word, Colonel?"

"Yes. To me."

"Figured he mought." Scullers looked toughly confident. Also

130

pleased. He wanted to tangle horns with the meaner bull: Taylor. "We get them flatboats?"

"You get 'em. But your sense of direction is faulty. Your way's upstream, not down."

"Tell you somep'n, mister. Us border boys is swallered all your brasshead spit'n'guff we gonna. You either pure loon-crazy or you think we are. Which is 't?"

"You are boarding those flatboats. Your possibles will be brought to you. Your horses too. Don't concern yourselves about your liquor supply; I'm confiscating it."

A chorus of anger broke from the volunteers.

"Answers it. You're the crazy 'un." Scullers's sun-boiled face was wolfish. "Well, sir, 'most every man of us can bust a squirrel's eyes with a long piece, you want to think about that."

Taylor turned abruptly and tramped up the bank. A bray of derision went up from the volunteers. On the high ground, Captain Tom Smith was mustering his company of 1st Infantry Riflemen. Taylor approached him; they conferred briefly. Then Taylor headed back for the bottoms, Smith at his side.

A sergeant barked commands. The columns of Riflemen, weapons shouldered, marched down the bank and right-angled across the front of the suddenly silent groups of volunteers. Formed a double line facing them.

"All right, Zeke," Smith said.

The two men were alone in the fifty feet of space between the Riflemen and the militia.

"Captain Scullers," Taylor said, spacing his words. "In the past two months, you've been repeatedly informed that while united under my command, you people are part of the United States Army. Expected to observe its regulations and obey its orders without quibble. You have uniformly ignored me. Jeered and insulted me. You have sabotaged discipline. Disgraced yourself and your country with your drunken and disorderly antics. Now I am telling you, sir, that I will countenance no more of your damned insolence."

The mutterings had trickled into silence. An osprey wheeled over the water, its cry shrill and piercing. The colonel never stirred a muscle. But his words fell like hammer blows.

"Facing you are one hundred Infantry Riflemen. I can certify to you that their weapons are the equal of your own and that they have been drilled to the nines in their use. I can certify that the first line of fifty men can fire, drop down, recharge, load, and prime those weapons by the time the second line has fired. I can further certify that at Captain Smith's order, they will do precisely that. Finally, I can certify that if you do not commence to file onto those flatboats in one minute flat—by my watch—I will tell Captain Smith to give that order."

Taylor palmed his watch and snapped open the case.

Davis began counting off the seconds in his mind. His mouth was dry as a cotton ball. He knew his colonel; this was no bluff. But did the militia know it? The sallow dawn put a liverish stamp on the scene. On maroon mud and gray water, on the Riflemen's green hussar uniforms, on dark trees and stark hulks of boats, on men's faces. Time was suspended like a grease drop in water. Taylor and Smith stood in place like stocky monuments.

Bo Scullers's face crinkled with a small hard grin. "All right, Colonel, you got it. Boys, step aboard."

"Just a minute!" Taylor rapped. "Before you touch a toe to the boats, straighten up those ranks, mister."

Scullers's grin faded; he swallowed. "Yessir." He pivoted to face his company. "Brace up your lines, you goose-livered cottonmouths. Snap into it!" The men made vague shufflings. Scullers straightened up to his diminutive height. "I'll take you on two at a time," he bawled, "and thrash the whole goddam company! *Now straighten up them lines!*"

The trickles of movement were slow. But they obeyed.

The loading continued. Taylor seemed determined to oversee every detail of the embarkation personally. He tramped ceaselessly back and forth, and Davis followed, feeling sicker by the minute. Another fit of coughing seized him. He stumbled and nearly fell. His eyes blurred, he could hardly keep from vomiting. When he recovered, Taylor was watching him intently. He said nothing, and Davis regarded the silence as ominous.

When the loading was finished, Taylor said: "We'll clean off my 'desk,' Mr. Davis. Which will conclude our sojourn at Fort Dixon."

They walked to the stockade, where Atkinson and his staff were assembling their baggage. Taylor conferred a few minutes with the general, then entered his sod-roofed quarters. The puncheon writing table was stacked with sheafs of papers. The colonel rammed a sheaf into a courier's pouch and handed it to Davis.

"These are the dispatches for Fort Crawford."

"Yes, sir, shall I give it to one of . . . ?"

"You'll take it to Captain McRee yourself, Mr. Davis."

"Sir." The word croaked from his whetstoned throat. "A regular courier could as well—"

"No need to waste a courier, is there?"

"I take it, sir, that you spoke to Anderson."

"I did. Last night. You looked ill and neglected to mention why. So I asked Mr. Anderson. Had to convince him he was doing you no favor by reticence. He finally confessed that he didn't think you'd live through whatever it was that laid you low while on patrol."

"A few chills and cramps, sir—"

"So I've kept a particular eye on you. Are you aware, Mr. Davis, that you act like a man drugged or drunk?"

"Sir, I'm a little shaky from yesterday is all."

"You're plain damned fatigued," Taylor snapped, "inside as well as out. The lesser part of valor, mister. The government has not provided you with a costly and elaborate training to be thrown away killing yourself on a spate of goddamned heroics! How long since you've had a furlough?"

"Three years. Sir."

"A damned sight nearer four."

"But, *sir!*"

"That's enough!"

Davis clamped his jaw.

"I consider that I'm permitting you an outsize dignity by not sending you downstream with the keelboat conveying the sick to Fort Armstrong. But I see no reason, since you're on your feet, to make you spend a week riding a boat deck down that miasmic damned river. You can make Crawford in a couple days by Kellogg's Road. Once you've delivered the dispatches, I want you to take a month's leave, not a day less, to—where the hell is your home?"

"Woodville, Mississippi. Sir."

"Just so. Wipe that look off, dammit. You're not surrendering a fistful of glory. Just a dirty, miserable, grueling chase after savages. Dismissed."

9

As the day wore on, the weather soured again. Matching Davis's mood as he rode northward. He made early camp at the stage stopover in Kellogg's Grove. His glum spirits were slightly buoyed by convivial company and a warm fire. Later it was good to again sleep in a bed that was warm and dry while wind and wetness tore at the eaves. The next day dawned sunny though cool. Riding on, he felt better, but not much.

His bitterness at being removed from the campaign ebbed into resignation. He might as well enjoy his enforced leave. Try to. There *was* a bright side. The last time he'd seen his family was on a brief furlough following his graduation from the Point. It had been four years . . .

He nooned at Apple River Fort and stayed over that night at Galena. The Sacs had struck at both places and at settlers' cabins between. He saw burned homesites; he spoke to tense, scared people braced for more swift and savage assaults that could come at any time.

By early afternoon the following day, he reached Prairie du Chien. He was passed into Fort Crawford's parade by four brisk guards; the garrison was on the alert. Reporting to the adjutant, he learned that Captain McRee had gone on patrol this morning, chasing a rumor of a Sac war party camped ten miles up the

Wisconsin. Also the furlough for which Davis had applied to the War Department had finally been granted; his papers had arrived. Very timely of the red-tape boys, he thought bitterly.

Leaving the dispatch pouch in the adjutant's hands, he went to his quarters where James Pemberton greeted him and prepared a bath. Davis stripped off his soiled uniform and soaked while Pemberton went to the dock to book two passages on whatever downriver packet was available. He returned with the information that the stern-wheeler *Arabella* had been delayed in unloading her cargo and taking on fuel. The captain had said she'd cast off at eight this evening.

"Is that agreeable, sir?"

"Fine, James. Lay out my clean uniform, then pack our luggage and take it to the boat."

"Yes, sir. It'll be good to see Mister Joseph again. And your mother."

"It will." Davis climbed out of the tub and briskly toweled himself. Suddenly he was half-doubled by a coughing fit.

"Sir, that doesn't sound good at all. Hadn't you better see Dr. Beaumont?"

Fifteen minutes later, clean-shaven, a feel of fresh linen and a clean uniform on his back, Davis trudged up to the hospital. He had to pass the commander's house, and he slowed as he neared it. Margaret Taylor, wearing a faded dress and poke bonnet, basket on her arm and shears in hand, was gathering cuttings from a mass of rambler roses that rioted over an ancient trellis.

He paused by the gate, touching his shako. "Good afternoon, ma'am."

"Lieutenant." Her nod was brief, her tone distinctly cool.

"I am just up from Dixon's Ferry."

"So I see."

She continued to ply the shears. No curiosity. No queries about the colonel. He could guess why. Well, no harm in trying.

"I wonder . . . might I speak with Miss Knox, if she's about?"

"That might be ill-advised."

He removed his shako and gazed down at it, fingering its white infantry ponpon. "If it's not too much to ask, I would appreciate your speaking plainly, ma'am."

"Very well. Your conduct at our farewell dance of two months ago became the talk of the village—"

"The hoedown?" He raised a sardonic brow. "The slack mouths must be hard up if they continue to bandy about an incident that stale."

"The talk has died down, of course." Her face pinkened. "But your behavior with that girl was disgraceful. Suggestive and—unnecessary. One thing for a tackie in the ranks to carry on at such ribald cut-ups. And quite another for an officer. Especially when the matter involves my daughter in loose talk."

"Talk . . . I don't understand."

"Gossip. Scandal. How many kinds of loose talk are there?"

His face warmed. "If there's any talk such as that, it's a lie."

"I'm aware of that. But true or not, the effect's the same, the damage is done. What a grand melange they've cooked up! You and that Robier girl. And my Knox's name coupled with hers in presumed feud for your favor. It's disgusting!"

He stared at her. All that out of a little innocuous horseplay? He knew what wildfire distortions gossip could shape, but this was ridiculous. For a moment he couldn't think of anything to say.

"I, well, I apologize for any distress my actions may have caused you or yours. But all the more reason that I speak with Miss Taylor."

"Why? Haven't you done enough harm?"

His hand gripped the gatepost. "Mrs. Taylor . . ." He stopped, not knowing what he wanted to say.

Most of his private thoughts of the last two months hadn't been of the war. There was more. How much, he wasn't sure;

it had stayed unfocused under the surface of his mind. A memory that was half-excited, half-resentful, completely irritating. All he knew was that behind it lay more than met the eye.

There had to be when two people hit sparks off each other as he and Sarah Knox Taylor did.

He wanted to see her again. Had been counting on it all the way here. And in his sudden surge of disappointment, he could admit to himself just how much.

"I am not making too much sense . . . even to myself, I fear. But I do wish to see her. To convey my apologies personally. May I?"

She studied him a moment. "That, Mr. Davis, will be entirely up to her." It was a small concession; she went up the path and entered the house. "Knoxie!" he heard her call.

In a minute she came out, wearing a faint smile. "Apparently Knoxie isn't inclined toward your company. Betty says that she saw you coming and left by our back door. Are you satisfied?"

"Quite," he said coldly, and bowed. Not elaborately, for that would have been a gesture, the insolence of defeat, and he despised such gestures. "Thank you, ma'am."

He moved up the path, his thoughts tauter than he liked to admit. She must have been confident that he was coming to see her. And completely repelled by the fact. Or was she? Damn. He tried to grin. But it wasn't funny. A kind of desperation grabbed him. He *had* to see her . . .

The hospital and surgeon's quarters were in a long fieldstone building on the sloping ground back of the fort. It contained a large ward, a smaller one, a dispensary, a kitchen, and a big north wing that housed the surgeon's quarters. Davis opened the north-wing door and entered a large untidy room. Dr. Beaumont was puttering amid a clutter of apparatus of which only he and God knew the purpose. He stopped puttering and glared in a friendly way.

"So you're back. What the devil do you want?"

"Some professional service. Am I interrupting anything?"

"You're damned right." Beaumont peered at him. "My God, you look terrible. A complete examination, I think. Strip."

As he removed his coatee and trousers, Davis described his condition of the last few days.

"I can diagnose already, but let's check you over anyhow. Sit down." Beaumont stepped behind the stool and began to palpate—pummel was a better word—his back and shoulders. "Suppose you slept out in the rain every opportunity."

Davis grinned. As his own health wasn't the best, Beaumont had avoided going off to war, an arrangement that he found eminently satisfactory. A depleted garrison meant few patients and plenty of time to pursue his experiments.

"That's war, they tell me, Doctor."

"Hell it is. When we stormed York, Canada, in 1813 and I spent thirty-six hours cutting off arms and legs and trepanning heads, *that* was war."

"I know. We're all familiar with what a harrowing life you've led . . . ouch!"

Beaumont had stiff-fingered him in the abdomen. "That hurt?"

"You're damned right it hurts! Are you trying to stick a hole in *my* stomach too? Not that I ever believed that story."

"What d'you know about it? Sit still, dammit. Was ten years ago this month . . . I was surgeon at Fort Mackinac when this trapper, Alexis St. Martin, got in the way of a shotgun blast. Whole charge entered his body below the left breast, opened up chest and abdominal cavities, fractured ribs, lacerated the diaphragm and punctured the stomach. Jesus, it was a mess. Dug out part of the shot and some pieces of clothing and predicted he wouldn't live two days. I was wrong."

"That's hard to believe."

"Try to shut up. Next day he seemed better, so I dug out more shot and cloth. Completely recovered except the goddam hole in his gut wouldn't heal. Formed a freak fistula between the stomach and the abdominal wall. Even grew a valve or flap.

Ten months later, unable to work, he was declared a common pauper by the civil authorities."

Davis raised his brows mock-wearily. "I know, Doctor. I was only joking. You have one claim to fame, and everyone knows the story—ouch!"

"Stand up. I took in St. Martin and began observations. Kindly appreciate that this was the first time in history that the actual process of digestion was observed firsthand. I lowered food into his gut on silk strings. Raw salted pork and beef, cooked pork and beef, sliced cabbage, stale bread and so on. At set intervals I'd pull 'em out and study the extent of digestion."

"It's certainly helping mine. My digestion, that is."

"Don't laugh, dammit! It resulted in the world's first authoritative study of the digestive system. Fact, I've just finished converting my notes for publication. *Experiments and Observations on the Gastric Juice and the Physiology of Digestion.*"

"Sounds trenchant. Is he still alive—St. Martin?"

"Hell, that damned Canuck will live to be a hundred if he doesn't rupture his tender gut jabbing klooches. Reminds me, I examine you for that yet? Rupture, I mean?"

"What else did you forget? Ouch!"

"You're all right there," Dr. Beaumont said imperturbably. "St. Martin went back to Canada in '26. Persuaded him to return in '29 for further study, but he quit me again. Worried about his goddam health. Hell, he'll live a hundred years. So will you. Put on your clothes."

As he dressed, Beaumont rattled off questions. Had his eyes bothered him before? What childhood diseases had he contracted? "Far as I can tell," he said, "there's nothing wrong with you that Old Zeke's prescription of a month's complete rest won't cure. Some of your symptoms sounded like an onset of cholera or even lockjaw, except that they passed quickly. I'd hazard it was a touch of the grippe, no more. Happens when a man's health is undermined."

140

"There's, ah, something else."

"Well, what is it?"

Davis rubbed his jaw, staring at the floor. Beaumont, for all his peculiarities, was brilliant and knowledgeable. And they were friends. Otherwise he wouldn't have considered baring a private matter. But it might mean something, it might contain an answer of sorts.

"It's a dream I had . . ." He described it.

"Hell, nothing startling in that. Everyone mixes past and present in his sleep. You grafted Old Zeke and the fair Sarah K. onto a childhood memory."

"But why?"

"I dunno. You falling in love with the girl?"

"We've been at odds since we met . . ."

"Perversity, m'lad, has been a symptom of that malaise since Adam and Eve cracked the first applejack dram against interdict. If love is budding, you might create a situation with yourself and the girl complete with obstacle, real or improvised. In this case, gruff old papa."

"Could there be another answer?"

"Well, ever hear of Mesmer?"

"Vaguely. Another quack, wasn't he?"

"Very funny. Franz Mesmer, Austrian physician. Postulated a theory he called 'animal magnetism.' Idea that a mysterious fluid which permeates all bodies enables one person to exert influence over another in the form of common vibrations."

"That's the damnedest piece of nonsense I've ever heard!"

"Of course it is," Beaumont beamed. "But a smart boy like you can't be bothered with the ordinary garden-variety explanation . . ."

Davis returned to his quarters. With his luggage stowed on the *Arabella,* there was nothing to do but fret away the four hours before the steamer departed. He told James to occupy himself elsewhere awhile; he wanted a quiet nap. But he wanted to think. Beaumont had bared the issue to the bone.

He peeled off his coatee and lay down, pressing his palms over his eyes. His head ached, he was sweating, he felt altogether miserable. Partly, no doubt, from a flock of evil humors brought on by his illness.

But there was Sarah Knox Taylor too. Undeniably there was Sarah Knox. He seemed to have fallen in love with the girl. *I don't even like her, for God's sake. What kind of a thing is that?*

He slept.

When he pulled himself from the damp gray wool of his nap, he felt no better. Sleep clung like dust to his brain. He filled the washbasin and splashed water in his face.

Someone tapped softly on the door.

He wiped his face and went to open it. Mrs. Taylor stood there, looking pale and worried. "Lieutenant, have you seen my daughter since you and I spoke?"

"No, madam."

"I thought that you might have sought her out . . ." She bit her lip. "I am sorry. I'm distraught. When she hadn't returned to the house after two hours, I became worried . . . I've been all over the village. She is not with Mary Street or any of her friends."

"Your daughter, madam, is accustomed to having her way. She will no doubt come home when it suits her fancy."

"But it's nearly sunset! Lieutenant, I—I wonder if you mightn't . . . if you would help me find her? You have a right to be offended with me. I can only plead the worry my daughter has given me of late. She's not been behaving quite normally. If not for that, I wouldn't be nearly as concerned. But it will be dark soon, and she may have gone off in the woods. The sun is too clouded over now to take one's bearings, and she could well be lost. I thought of asking Lieutenant Gibbs to help, but he is on patrol with Captain McRee, and I can hardly ask the officer

142

in charge to turn out the remaining garrison because my daughter hasn't been seen for a couple of hours. Besides . . . well, I thought that you might have a reason for helping. You did wish to speak with her . . ."

"I still do. Does she have any favorite places? A particular spot she frequents?"

"Oh, several. At least I know the walking trails she likes. The path leading to the French Cemetery, for one. And a portion of the old Sukisep Trail that runs down to the Wisconsin junction. She and the other girls take it for huckleberry parties . . ."

It was agreed that Mrs. Taylor would scour the village again and enlist the help of Knox's girl friends. Davis found Pemberton splitting cedar lengths in the woodyard and told him to scout to the north of town as far as the French Cemetery, then skirt back along the river. Davis would try the huckleberry trail.

He set off south along the trail. The clouds were retreating; a watery maroon glow covered the river. Crickets chirped and sawed in the early twilight; bitterns threw guttural pumpings across the glassy water. Davis halted now and then, cupping his hands to his mouth, bawling: "Hallooo!"

He came to the river junction and swung east, following the Wisconsin upstream. Where its broad outwash poured into the Mississippi, it was immensely wide, pocked with myriad islands, laced with deep sloughs. The trail switchbacked north again, passing some hundred yards from the site of Vitelle Robier's cabin. The forest shadows had a violet depth; he quickened his pace. Daylight was going fast, and he wanted to work back toward the village on the east curve of a broad oval that would cover the ground nearer the bluffs.

His throat was hoarse from yelling; the exertion was tightening a steely constriction around his chest. A paroxysm of coughing grabbed him. When it subsided, his voice was a whisper. His pistol. Why hadn't he thought of it before? He pulled and cocked it, and fired into the air. Reloaded and primed it, walked on another hundred yards, and fired again. He recharged it as he continued on, crossing a humpy belt of prairie and entering another wedge of hardwood forest. The town was just ahead, but cut off by a swell of hills.

He halted and fired off the pistol a third time.

But someone had heard the first shots and was already moving this way. Brush rustled; he heard a weak cry. Sweating and shaking, he sank down on the end of a mossy deadfall and waited.

Knox Taylor came stumbling through a heavy bank of foliage, flailing at it with her hands, head down. She broke into the open and stopped, pushing a straggle of hair out of her face.

"Oh, thank goodness, I . . . *you!*"

"Me."

She moved woodenly to the other end of the deadfall and collapsed on it. She gave him an anguished glare. Her light cashmere dress was bramble-torn, her face red and puffy from crying.

"What are *you* doing here?"

"I dunno. Imagine I merely followed the vibrations."

"The what?"

"Chemistry. Doc Mesmer's vibrations. I was sure you'd felt them too."

She looked at him as though he'd lost his wits, spreading her palms on the deadfall's crumbling bark as if ready to spring to her feet. "Mr. Davis." She swallowed. "Will you tell me what you're doing here, please? What are you after?"

"I? Nothing whatever. Your mother was concerned about you. As your friend Gibbs is on patrol, I was commissioned to look for you."

"Look for me? What on earth for?"

"Well, it's pretty obvious you're not lost."

"Of course not. A little turned around, perhaps." She sniffled. "But I was finding my way out."

"Oh. You didn't hear the shots."

"Of course I heard them. They were *very* superfluous."

"I should have known. May I escort you back to the village?"

"I can find my way, thank you."

She stood up with a hiss of petticoats and began to walk away.

"Oh, Miss Knox."

"What?"

"I suppose you've a reason for heading away from the village, but . . ."

She stopped in her tracks and turned slowly and tautly. "That *is* the sunset in yonder sky, is it not?"

"I believe so."

"Therefore I am walking west toward the river."

"Quite. But you'll come out a considerable ways south of the village. Or"—he shrugged—"a considerable ways north of it."

Tears sparkled in her eyes. "You're trying to confuse me!"

"I shouldn't think that can be done."

She stared at him in a blurry rage, then turned and began to run, holding her skirts high. He got to his feet and started after her. A clot of chokecherry scrub blocked her way. As she tried to scramble around it, he caught her arm.

"Wait. I didn't mean . . ."

"Let go!"

She struck at his face and he caught her hand. She tried to twist away and they were in mid-stride together; her move sent them off-balance. They tumbled to the ground.

She was pressed to him, slim body arched, lips inches from his like small flames. The hollow of her throat pulsed; her eyes darkened. He captured her face between his hands, his mouth on hers. She struggled, not very much. Seconds passed. The struggling ended. Longer seconds. Her body shuddered into surrender.

Her mouth stirred slackly under his and dissolved like a

soft hot ember. The kiss was a universe away from the hard ground beneath; they were lost and drifting in a wild insensible sweetness.

He pulled his mouth off hers and slowly raised himself. She lay unmoving, unspeaking. Her face was very still. All but her eyes; they held a plea and a wonder. He drew her to her feet and held her gently to him. Her eyes closed; he kissed the lids.

"A terribly tough girl," he whispered, "aren't you?"

He kissed her mouth.

A mouth ungiving now, unresisting now. But not lifeless. Trembling. A trembling that ran all through her.

"I need to think," she whispered against his lips.

"How can you think about it?"

"You don't understand. Please."

"I love you. Say that you love me."

"Oh . . ."

"Say it."

"Yes, yes, I love you. I do!"

Her mouth fused with his in a fierce hot clinging. From the river landing, a steamer's bell clanged faintly. Time to embark. And no time at all to say more.

10

Knox sat on the veranda that ran across the front of the fort hospital. More accurately, she was slumped in a way that would have fetched sharp disapproval from her teachers at the Thomas Elliot School, Louisville, and the Pickett School, Cincinnati. By sitting on the top step and bracing her back against a supporting pillar, legs outstretched and heels resting on the ground, she was able to ease her sore knees, tender calf muscles, and aching back all at the same time.

It was good to rest a bit. Away from the sweet-sickish and rancid smells of an overcrowded ward. The groanings and retchings of the sick. All the sights and sounds and smells of a cholera epidemic.

She stared across the river. The bluffs were blue-green in the summer haze; sunlight teased the water with silvery sparks. The prairie grass looked rusty and dry, the scanty late-summer blooming of goldenrod and asters as wilted as the grass. Except for a couple of cold and rainy stretches, it had been one of the hottest and driest summers in Northwest memory. Hot summer, cold winter, she thought. Or was it the other way around?

From an open window back of her came the voices of Dr. Beaumont and the Robier girl. She half-listened to their talk as she inspected her hands, backs and palms. Lordy. Chapped

147

and reddened, knuckles swollen, nails raggedly short and raw at the quick. All from hours of lye-water scrubbing, most of it on her hands and knees.

"*Merci*," Beaumont was saying. "We'll try your suggestions, ma'm'selle. And the herbs you brought. Thanks very much. One day soon, I hope we'll discuss all that secret stuff you're forbidden to blab about."

"You mean the *Medewiwin* cures?" the girl said severely. "Oh . . . you joke."

"On occasion. *Adieu,* my dear."

She came out the door, gave Knox a remote smile, and went down the long slope toward the landing. Just beyond the store-houses, soldiers were laboring blocks of quarried rock into place on a partly constructed building. The entire squad stopped work to watch Ceclie. A sergeant bawled them back to the job.

The little witch, Knox thought. Just look at her, so blatant and shameless. Her piquant golden coloring and brazen thrust of breasts might be nature's doing; the insolent flirt of her hips was not. More renegade behavior from a family of renegades. The father a squaw man. The brother who, it was said, had gone off to join Black Hawk. A good many half-tamed half-bloods had done as much.

"Don't like her, eh? I reckon women wouldn't."

She glanced around. Dr. Beaumont stood in the doorway, resembling a slightly jaded pixie as he curled a Rabelaisian grin around his pipe.

"I imagine," she said evenly, "that you find such a tasteless ooze of sensuality quite appealing."

Beaumont shuttered his tar-spot eyes up and down, grinning. "How did you guess?"

"Fie on you!" Knox laughed in spite of herself. "Distinguished surgeon! Typical male."

"And rip, rake, *roué* to boot," leered the doctor.

"And a surprisingly credulous one. Those ridiculous cures

of hers! Poultice of skunk cabbage leaves. Charred honey-suckle vine in bear oil!"

"Don't forget the plaster of cattail fried in wolf grease."

"Ugh. I wish I could."

"Wraow," Beaumont murmured. "How's your arm these days, Sarah K., I mean the left one?"

"Ha. Next you'll be swinging a calumet or punching a hole in someone's skull to release bad spirits."

"Unh-uh." Beaumont puffed on his briar, the smoke of fragrant burley cutting a generous dead zone out of a cloud of gnats. "Just don't scout all primitive palliatives so handily. Worst of the Indian remedies are no worse than the more palpably inane folk cures of our own race. I could appall you with a recitation of the combined superstition, guesswork, and sheer quackery spouted by respected medical pillars of the civilized branch. In fact I will." He pulled a folded paper from a pocket of his shabby uniform and shook it open. "Letter from Dr. Daniel Drake of Cincinnati, most renowned, mind you, physician in the Northwest. In reply to a query of mine about cholera treatments. 'Would suggest calomel, weak lye, and mustard as purgatives.' Blazes! With the poor victims already throwing up their guts." He grinned at the face she made. "He does subscribe to the animalculae hypothesis, that the disease is borne by tiny invisible bodies; fine—and advises cleanliness, proper diet, drinking in moderation, and wearing of thin flannel. But here: 'In extreme cases I advocate the lancet, not withholding recourse to the jugulars when blood cannot be elicited in quantity from the arms.' *Bleeding!* Shades of Merlin the Medieval."

Knox sighed. "I don't mean to sound contrary, but are there more effective means? Take the sanitary regulations *you've* posted for our garrison. Barracks and mess halls to be scrubbed down, all troops to wear flannel smallclothes, whiskey prohibited. Goodness, I don't see—"

"Neither does your doctor, my dear. No measurable relation

between *any* precautions taken and the way cholera strikes. Nearly half our garrison down sick, hospital wards and village pesthouse overflowing. While only four citizens of the town, whose sanitary habits are *really* deplorable, have taken ill. Animalculae? Perhaps this devilish heat, marshes and lowlands reeking with miasma. I just don't know . . ."

A bitter discouragement tinged Beaumont's words; his face was lined with fatigue. Usually any accessory as meditative as a pipe was foreign to him, his fantastic energy making relaxation impossible. But a day-and-night frenzy of coping with plague had sapped even his vitality.

General Winfield Scott's nine companies, arriving at Detroit on July 4, had apparently carried the Asiatic cholera from the Atlantic seaboard. Within a few days, sixty cases were reported in the ranks . . . then thirty deaths. The sick were housed in the upper story of the territorial capital building while the unstricken troops, proceeding to Fort Dearborn at Chicago, rapidly spread the disease. Twenty Chicagoans dead in twenty-four hours. Green Bay, The Portage, and Prairie du Chien swiftly stricken. The plague had raced across Michigan Territory and into Illinois; death carts rattled through village streets; bells tolled. Till the tolling was ordered stopped because of the effect: hundreds rushing from towns into the countryside were spreading the contagion among their rural brethren . . .

"Thanks for your help today," Beaumont said. "Getting to be a refrain, that. But a deserved one. Wasn't for you and the other ladies helping out where you can, our troubles would be compounded."

Knox gazed ruefully at her ravaged hands and nails. "I'm seeing mops and scrub brushes in my sleep. But it's little enough when there's such a need . . . better than gadding about at quilting bees, carpet tackings, and chicken pluckings."

"All the same you might spare yourself a bit. Look at you. Fine-drawn, hollow-cheeked, circles under your eyes."

"I hope all your lady patients don't find you such an arch flatterer."

"Only the pretty ones. Seriously, you pay more eye to your own health. Around the afflicted, there's always a chance of contracting the affliction; lowered resistance doesn't help."

"How is it that doctors fancy themselves immune to everything?"

"Arrogance helps. Besides, can't shake the laity's faith. Code of hypocrites."

Knox smiled, a bit wanly.

Familiarity with the plague's gruesome realities had numbed her past any fear for self. These two weeks had been a frenetic nightmare. Twice she'd accompanied Beaumont on his rounds of the village and outlying farms, for the frontier's military physician went where he was needed, no stockade around his services. She had seen the sick, the dying, the dead cramped under one roof at one time. Men, women, and children prostrate with vomiting and flux, too weak to rise, bellies hot and distended, arms and legs jerking with spasmodic agony, wailing in fever, begging for water. Skins turning cold and blue while their voices dropped to hoarse whispers and their pulses threaded raggedly out. And sometimes she had seen the swift and awful violence with which death came . . .

"Cometh Ole Persistent and Ever-Hopeful," Beaumont remarked.

She looked up from the frayed stained skirt of her old linen dress. Denny Gibbs was coming up the slope below the fort. Not now, please, she thought. She was worn too fine to cope with Denny. He reached the veranda and greeted them, resting a foot on the step.

"What's new with you?" Beaumont asked. "The usual alarums and excursions? Led any assaults on blueberry patches lately?"

Denny made a wry face. "That's about it. However, I've just come from the adjutant's . . . some dispatches have arrived from Blue Mounds. Appears that Black Hawk is on the run at last. Headed for the Mississippi."

Beaumont took the pipe from his mouth. "Thunderation!"

Little news of the campaign had reached Fort Crawford of late. A wildfire plague had given them more than enough to think, talk and worry about. The war's tight little skirmishes were going on miles to the east; after the early alarms and rumors ebbed, the whole business had seemed rather remote and dissociated.

They knew that weeks ago, General Atkinson, arriving with his army at White Crow's village on Lake Koshkonong and refused help by the Winnebago chief, had built a small fort on the Bark River and set his troops to beating the swampy wilds for Black Hawk's main camp. It did force the Sac leader to break off raiding the border farms. But as the summer wore on and the phantom enemy continued to elude the troops, it had begun to look as if the campaign would stretch into autumn.

"All credit goes to Brigadier James Henry," Gibbs explained. "Atkinson needed provisions; nearest supply point was Fort Winnebago—eighty miles away. He sent Henry's and Colonel Dodge's milish to fetch 'em. They ran into a gang of Winnebagos who offered to lead 'em to Black Hawk's camp. But one of the chiefs, Little Thunder, had misgivings and went ahead to warn Black Hawk. The Sacs slipped away into the Four Lakes region, Henry and Dodge in hot pursuit. Even discarded baggage and provisions so they could hold the trail."

Beaumont puffed zestfully at his briar. "Catch 'em?"

"Finally. After days of foul weather, living on raw meat and raw dough, and nearly all their horses dying under 'em. Black Hawk fled northwest, then cut back due west. He'd apparently decided to abandon hostilities and escape across the Mississippi. A week ago, July 21 it was, the troops finally overtook him on the Heights of the Wisconsin, maybe eighty miles east of here. There was a big fight, I guess a delaying action on Black Hawk's part. He sacrificed some of his men while the rest withdrew with the women and children onto a big hill. At night they built up huge fires to fix the troops' attention. While the milish watched that flank, the Sacs slipped down a saddle on the hill's west side and got to the Wisconsin."

"Ha! Slipped out under their noses, eh? Leave it to that old devil."

"Apparently the Sacs worked all night building rafts. Braves placed the weakest women, children, and old people on the rafts and sent 'em down the Wisconsin. Rest struck west overland toward the Mississippi."

"Sweet Mariah!" Knox exclaimed. "You mean they're headed for Prairie du Chien?"

"Hardly. Black Hawk's had enough; he'll avoid tangling with our garrison. Anyway he appears to be making for a crossing well north of here."

Beaumont bit on his pipestem. "Hope you're right. With half our troops debilitated . . ."

"Black Hawk's worse off than we. Henry's 3rd Brigade numbered six hundred. Dodge's Battalion of Michigan volunteers, about one hundred and twenty men. At least two hundred were too wasted by sickness to join in the Wisconsin Heights action. Yet Henry reckoned they had the Sacs outnumbered nearly five-to-one for fighting men."

"Hope so. What about Atkinson?"

"He's reforming his army at Blue Mounds, pulling in hundreds of regulars and militia troops for the pursuit. To prevent Black Hawk from escaping across the Mississippi."

"He'd better," Beaumont said dryly, "after the unholy botch this campaign's been. Not to single out Atkinson; a lot of career heads will roll when it's over."

"You said some Indians were sent down the Wisconsin," Knox said. "They'll arrive here then."

"Not quite; Captain McRee has dispatched troops upriver to intercept the rafts." Gibbs shifted his weight from one foot to the other. "I wonder, Doc, if I might borrow your scrublady awhile."

"I'm really too busy now," she said evasively. "So much more to do . . ."

"Go along, blast it." Beaumont made a shooing motion with his pipe. "Mrs. Taeger will finish up. Get away from this infernal charnel house for a bit."

Oh thank you, Doctor. What can I say? She took the hand Denny offered and began to stand. The earth and sky spun; both men caught her by the arms as she swayed forward.

"Does it for you, m'girl," Beaumont said. "Get straight home. And tomorrow, blast it, stay there."

"But it's over," she insisted. "It came and went—like that."

"Fatigue and exhaustion. Week's rest is in order. See you get it. Dizzy spells can lead to other complications. Take the case of Jeff Davis."

"Davis?" Gibbs said. "I knew he went on furlough . . ."

"With vast reluctance. And a raw throat, dizziness, headaches." Beaumont crossed to the doorway and turned there, slyly stroking his jaw with his pipestem. "Stomach trouble too. Vibrations, I told him. All in the Mesmeric vibrations."

Knox stared at his back as he disappeared inside. Vibrations? Oh no!

"What the devil does he mean?"

"Who knows? Come on, if you're walking with me."

"But you're to go—"

"For a walk." Beaumont had nettled her to a small rebellion. "Walk along or not, as you please."

They strolled away from the fort buildings, past the brown sugarloaf lodges of the Winnebagos. Naked coppery children were playing around them, their cries splitting the afternoon. Knox's tensions ebbed as they walked by the river. The quiet water flickered with gold-green sunrays; dragonflies burred statically over it. What a relief to get away from the stenches and groanings.

154

Gibbs broke the silence. "Did you happen to see Jeff that day he was here?"

"Saw him, yes."

"Oh."

Was the query casual? It wiped out her moment of serenity. All the drudgery in which she'd submerged herself had failed to touch a deep, nagging restlessness. She wasn't sure of anything. Except that Jeff Davis's kiss as they lay together on the forest mold, mouths sealed, hearts hammering, had sucked up all her emotions in a hot consuming blast.

Thinking of it made her skin gooseflesh.

Did she love him? She wasn't sure of that either. The excited avowal. Or impassioned impulse. Whatever it was. Then he was hurrying her back to the village, kissing her goodbye, running for his boat, leaving her all in a turmoil.

She had thought of him constantly. Wondering whether he was still in Mississippi or whether he'd reported back to his regiment. He needn't have returned to Fort Crawford; he might have journeyed north as far as Fort Armstrong, then gone with a supply boat up the Rock to the Bark River where the 1st was encamped. Or had been; it was Blue Mounds now.

He had aroused her more, and disturbed her more in retrospect, than any man she'd met. But how much did that mean? Denny Gibbs's kisses stirred her too; it was a matter of degree.

All right, admit it. Aren't you afraid of him?

She'd wondered often: Was that all of it? Had it been that from the first, an attraction so violent that it repelled?

Jefferson Davis wouldn't be controlled. He, not she, had seized a role of cool mastery. And she wasn't accustomed to such a reversal. In the folklore of courtship and marriage, the male always took the helm and the initiative. In fact, as Knox knew—she had noted it all her life among her parents' friends, more lately among her own married friends—there were as many kinds of marriages as there were couples. In countless cases, in spirit if not in word, it was the woman who led and the man was secretly glad of it. And didn't it have to be one or the other? If both vacillated, the relation degenerated into a mousy mutual toleration. If both sought to dominate, they were forever at each other's throat. She had seen it again and again. And, on occasion, a superb balance of personalities, a sharing of voices. But rarely.

Knox was her father's daughter. More so than Dick or Betty, certainly more than the gentle Ann. Bob Wood had been strong enough to woo and win Ann away from a strong (and protesting) father. It wouldn't be that way with her, Knox had decided long ago. The man she wed must be—not compliant, but flexible, ready to surrender in a real crisis the lead that she would claim. Otherwise it would never, could never work.

Finding such men had never been a problem. Beaux had been numerous since her fifteenth birthday. Always a few favorites of course: Denny. Charlie Anderson. Sanford Preston.

Jefferson Davis wasn't like the others. He might be reserved, often aloof, but he was never in retreat. He'd bend no more than a ramrod would. A characteristic that must frequently ruffle even those closest to him. Yet his magnetism was a vibrant flood when he chose to let down the gates. Men felt it one way, women another. She had let it overwhelm her, and that was wrong. Her own bedrock nature would reassert itself, and then . . .

"Something amiss?" Gibbs asked. "You're so quiet . . ."

"Just tired. I guess you'd better see me home."

They turned back along the riverbank. Bugle notes spiraled across the cricket-keening afternoon. She halted, touching Denny's arm.

"Listen."

Taps. The silvery loops of sound were coming from the post cemetery; they quivered poignantly and died. A farewell to one or more plague victims. What a melancholy sound taps was these days! For as a salute to death, it could come at any hour, any moment. When you stood in blazing sunlight and listened, the notes were eerie, sad, irreconcilable with the day's bright beauty.

They walked slowly on. Gibbs said frowningly, "Hadn't you better take Doc's advice? You're worn to a shadow, and with plague there's no telling . . ."

A fleeting smile twisted her mouth. Jeff Davis would not have suggested; he would have ordered. And she would have flared up.

"If I were going to contract the cholera, I guess I would have by now. Anyway most all the women are helping where they can. You can't think only of yourself at such a time, Denny."

"What would your father say if he knew you were exposing yourself so?"

"You know as well as I. But he's not here. I have to put up with your helpful offerings instead."

"Knox, I'm . . . I'm nonplused by your behavior of late."

"An unfortunate situation, isn't it?"

"See here!" Gibbs took her by the arm, halting her. "I'm getting a bit tired of being treated in so cavalier a manner. I have a few feelings, and I'm neither an imbecile nor a child."

Knox gave him a surprised smile. This was a step beyond his drollery and diffidence that sometimes pleased, sometimes irritated her. It did not deceive her; Denny was no Jeff Davis. But it was nice to know that she could flay a nerve of temper in him.

"I'm terribly sorry, Denny. You're absolutely right; I apologize."

"I should think so. While we're about it, I asked you some time ago to marry me. You agreed, or have you forgotten?"

"Oh heavens, I didn't say . . . I mean I did say you could consider us engaged. But . . ."

"Well, good Lord, then we'll be married! The question is, when do we announce the engagement? I think, directly your father's returned from the campaign, I'll ask him."

"No!" A bit shrilly; she lowered her voice. "You shan't

do anything of the sort. I told you we must be sure . . . I need more time."

"Time! You've had six weeks. And I've hardly seen you of late. As though you were deliberately avoiding me."

"That's nonsense."

It wasn't, though. She knew it. And felt a needling guilt. She'd gone out of her way to escape his company. Because, she'd told herself, her feelings were in a crucial perspective; she didn't want his presence muddying a doubtful situation more.

A thin excuse. And somewhat less than half the truth. The fact was, she didn't trust herself by a jot these days. Denny had almost swept her away on an emotional tide that night by the river. And she had succumbed totally to Jeff Davis; it was he, not she, who'd pulled them up short.

Just thinking of it made her feel unstrung with shame.

"What is it then?" he persisted. "Why keep me dangling?"

She frowned. "Isn't that a bit crude? I'm doing nothing of the sort."

"Then I think you should prove it. Set a date for our wedding."

"Denny, I . . . I can't. Not yet."

"This is ridiculous!" He threw out his hands. "Either we're engaged or we're not. Which?"

"Ask me another time. When you've remembered your manners."

She turned and walked away, her shoulders taut. She expected him to call after her, to say he was sorry. But he didn't.

She began to run. By the time she reached the house she was crying, great wracking sobs that got all the worse for her fighting them. She reached the veranda, threw open the door, rushed through the parlor and up the stairs. She heard her mother coming from the kitchen.

"Knoxie, wait."

For what, more tart homilies, more domestic repartee that

never reached the root of anything? She ran into her room and slammed the door. In the reflex of habit, for she always changed on returning from the hospital, she tore at the buttons of her dress. Then dropped her hands. Sank onto the edge of her bed and stared desolately at the wall.

Her mother tapped on the door. "Knoxie."

She came in, sat on the bed and looked at her daughter. "If all that business at the hospital depresses you so, you shouldn't go."

"It's not . . . that."

"I didn't think so."

"Oh, Ma! I just don't know how to talk about it."

"Well, you needn't unless you care to. But something's been troubling you most of the summer. We've talked before . . . about womanly matters. Anything of that nature?"

"No. I guess . . . in a way. But it's different. Denny . . ."

"Yes?"

"When I'm with him, I want him to make love to me. *Really* make love."

Margaret smiled. "Perfectly normal. And if you had, you'd hardly be worrying that you might. Is that all?"

"All!" She fidgeted with a pleat in her skirt. "It's bad enough . . . and worse with Jeff Davis."

"Davis—" Margaret paused. "Excuse me; I am trying to adjust . . . when did this begin?"

Knox told her. Not too coherently; she could feel a crying spell coming on. The familiar kind that nobody had seen. Suddenly she broke down and covered her face with her hands.

"Oh, Ma, what's wrong with me!"

"Nothing." Margaret's arm came around her shoulders. "Unless it's growing up."

"But Ann! She's older than me, she always told me everything, she was never like this. Always sweet and obedient, never such a trial as I've been—"

"Until she took us all by surprise and ran off—eloped, if

159

you will—with Bob Wood. Knoxie." She held Knox's face between her hands, raising her head. "It's harder for some than for others . . . that change. For the high-spirited, the ones with intense, deep-running feelings, hardest of all. But that'll pass. All that fine brimming spirit will be tempered to a womanly strength, vivacity and charm. One day soon, I believe, it will happen. And it will be well worth all of this."

Knox sniffled, straightened and wiped her eyes. "What do you think of Denny, Ma? Really?"

"A very good man with several shortcomings. Peccadilloes that, I daresay, may annoy and upset at times. Your father has his share, heaven knows."

"Did it—I mean when you were courting . . ."

"Give me pause? Of course. Even a regret or two since, if you must know." Her lips curled gently up at the corners. "When I was a girl, I met a dashing young officer very like Lieutenant Davis. A golden-haired Adonis in an immaculate uniform. With a dozen sweethearts whom he loved each in her turn. And do you know, each time he believed it himself. The pity was, so did they."

"Did you?"

"For a time, yes."

"What happened?"

"Why, I pined a little while. Then met your father and fell really in love."

With Zachary Taylor. Bluff as a rock hill, not at all handsome, and whose contempt for proper dress was legend. Knox rubbed her hand over the satin coverlet, frowning.

"It might be different. Mightn't it?"

"Dear, I don't know. One thing only. Be sure you don't ask for the moon. Often as not, it's been a woman's lot to marry a man she may never greatly love. The completely right one may never come along. Or may come too late. Even then, quality more than basic attraction should be . . . well, who

160

decides that objectively? I flatter myself as lucky to have both—
to love a fine man."

"Weren't we talking about Lieutenant Davis?"

"And Denny. I don't know Mr. Davis; I *know* Denny's quality. All I'm suggesting is that Mr. Davis is terribly handsome
and terribly dashing. That perhaps—and quite naturally—your
head's merely turned a bit. Is it that, Knoxie? Or is it love?"

She smiled wanly. "If I really knew, we wouldn't be talking."

"Another thing." A taut significance touched Margaret's
words. "Denny has said he'd leave the Army if you and he
should wed."

"Oh, Ma, what difference does that make?"

"A great deal, young lady. As you well know."

Margaret briskly rose, went to the armoire and took out a
clean cotton frock which she laid on the foot of the bed. "Get
out of that awful dress and give yourself a good scrubbing. Then
you can help me prepare dinner. I'll make you some sassafras
tea. That will help cleanse the humors from your system."

Of course, Knox thought. Sassafras tea. Exactly what I
needed . . .

11

The Kickapoo River, snaking south along the western end of Michigan Territory, had sculptured its ancient valley out of the ground floor of time. Its small crooked mud-heavy stream had wound for ages between the same green hills and crumbling bluffs, a tiny patch of country that had remained untouched by the glaciers which had ground across the continent eons ago, crushing and leveling. On the evening of July 30, 1832, thirteen hundred mixed regular and volunteer troops under General Henry Atkinson made camp in the Kickapoo's valley, some thirty miles above its confluence with the Wisconsin River. The camp sprawled for two hundred feet along and back from the streambank.

Men sat in groups around yellow tatters of fire that congealed in oily glitters on the water. Men vitiated by fevers, torpid with exhaustion. Men who had slogged for weeks across bog and prairie, sweating through humid green ovens of wilderness, soaking and shivering through rainy days and nights. Men who had left scores of fever-wasted comrades in unmarked graves—few of them felled by arrow or bullet—while eking out weeks on half rations, quarter rations, and no rations.

Heat and cold. Hunger. Sickness. These were the real enemies. And exhaustion. The leaders quibbled endlessly about the focus of the campaign. Those in the ranks already knew. It was fatigue that etched itself endlessly into every nerve till your whole body screamed for rest.

Lieutenant Jefferson Davis sat on the bank and watched George Wilson splashing in the brown water. The pressures that left everyone else stupefied had only excited Wilson's boundless energy. He was trying to damp it in the Kickapoo.

"How is it, George?"

"No damned good. No good at all. Too damned warm."

Davis rubbed a palm over his beard scrub; he slapped at mosquitoes. Bogs and sloughs bred whining clouds of them; faces of the more allergic had swollen like bladders. Davis's face and hands were covered with bumps and blood flecks. Only a combination of high-ground camp and cool wind kept the pests away. Or the smoky side of a fire whose fumes left flesh and clothes stinking. By now, few gave a damn. They merely consumed tasteless rations, pitched into their blankets, or stared insensibly at the fires. If appetite was gone, it was as well. To negotiate bitter terrain and quicken pace, Atkinson had long ago abandoned all baggage wagons and most of the provisions. What remained was packed on the horses; few were riding any longer.

Wilson came splashing out of the water. He resembled a scrawny and plucked but still highly animate chicken. Robert Anderson, his back against a tree, arms folded and legs outstretched, raised the forage cap tilted over his eyes and studied Wilson.

"Migawd. I've seen more enticing carcasses on hooks in a butcher shop."

Wilson vigorously toweled himself with a rough army blanket. "A Sunday chap, Robert. That's what you are. Want to sit on your bloody tail six days a week. Hullo, Sid."

Albert Sidney Johnston came up, flashing a wry and weary grin at Davis. Two friends who traded confidences as naturally as others traded views on the weather, they'd found little opportunity for solid talk of late.

"Speaking of tails," Johnston said, "you fellows best get yours over to the general's tent."

"Another bloody conference," Wilson sighed.

"But the last, we hope."

The four of them crossed the camp, Wilson struggling with the buttons of his uniform. Men's drool of tired chatter filled the crickety night, the volunteers chewing familiar bones of contention. But the talk had no bite; they were too spent for anything more than the age-old gripes of troops in the field. An army very different, Davis thought, from the one he'd quit a month past . . .

Two weeks of rest at Rosemont, his mother's home near Woodville, another week at his brother Joe's plantation below Vicksburg, had restored him. He had made an early return to the campaign, joining up with a contingent of troops about to embark from Fort Armstrong. At Blue Mounds, Atkinson was regrouping an army gleaned of its dross: large-scale militia desertions had left a hickory-hard core. Morale was high, despite the terrible toll taken by the cholera. Davis had seen it before, but never in plague proportions. No way of isolating troops in field conditions; the Blue Mounds camp was a chimera of moaning stricken men, makeshift hospitals and overworked surgeons. And a pervading stink of disease and death that, in accumulation, was a smell unlike any other.

"Watch out for flying sparks," Johnston commented. "Your beloved leader has been rocking the general's boat again. He and Henry Dodge."

"What's it about?" Davis asked.

"Who knows? Ask your colonel; all on his side."

"Seems to be," Anderson said. "Sometimes Old Zeke is a hard nut to get to the meat of."

"Needn't guess about Dodge's reasons," Wilson observed.

"Politically ambitious, they say. You have to see his bone-picking as nest-feathering."

"Is it true he was once tried for conspiring with Aaron Burr?" Johnston asked.

"Not only that," grinned Anderson. "When a grand jury indicted him for treason, Dodge quashed the indictment by systematically thrashing the nine jurors who stood their ground."

"He's pretty well lived that down," Davis said. "But he raised a little dust with the Army a few years back. Set up an illegal lead-mining operation in the Winnebago country, built a stockade, armed a crew of bullies and held out for a long time in defiance of both the Indians and us."

They approached the headquarters tent. Atkinson, attended by his brigade commanders and most of their officers, was seated at a field table. Zachary Taylor was in the midst of an impolitic tirade: ". . . Sacs should have been stopped flat on the day they crossed into Illinois. They weren't moving so rapidly it couldn't have been done. Not while laden with their families, baggage of various kinds, domestic stock and the like."

A flush stained the general's gaunt cheeks. "Stopped, Colonel, yes. With force and bloodshed while I still had hopes of bringing Black Hawk peaceably to terms. In any case, I hadn't enough troops at Fort Armstrong to either prevent his crossing at the Yellow Banks or to arrest his march up the Rock."

"True," Taylor said curtly. "The garrison was undermanned. Had been all through the fall and winter long after Black Hawk made his threat. The ice was out of the Mississippi by late March. Plenty of time to move three or four companies up from Jefferson Barracks."

Atkinson nodded coldly. "Duly noted. Anything else?"

"At the moment, no, sir."

"We're grateful."

A few more officers joined the group. Atkinson cleared his throat. His face was nerve-drawn in the firelight, etched with the cruel burden of command. He still retained that command only because the cholera outbreak had immobilized Winfield Scott and his nine companies at Fort Dearborn. "We've two goals," he said. "To stop Black Hawk from crossing the Mississippi and to take him alive. To prevent, that is, either his escape or his martyrdom. We're roughly twenty-five miles from the Mississippi. An extremely rugged distance that, with luck, we can cover in two days. The scouts report that Black Hawk isn't over a day ahead. To cross the Big Miss, he'll need rafts and time to build them. Ordinarily I wouldn't count it prudent to overtake and close with an enemy after three days of forced marches and little sleep. But the foe has fared far worse, as we know."

There was a general murmur of assent.

Usually, even under the most trying conditions, the Sacs would carry their sick with them, or if they died, give them ceremonious burial. But the whites had come again and again on shocking evidence of the toll that a four-month campaign had taken of Black Hawk's people. Bodies of the starved and wounded, the dead and dying, marked the line of flight. Men, women, children. Tottering elders and nursing babies. A dying woman had whispered the way of it: when the last cracked corn had been devoured, the last gaunt ponies slaughtered, the hunters unable to find meat enough for so many, the Sacs had resorted to berries, acorns, edible roots. Finally to insects and grass and elm bark.

"As many braves as he's lost to death and desertion," Atkinson said, "we must have ten-to-one odds on him for fighting men."

"How long will it take him to build those rafts, General?" asked Colonel Henry Dodge.

He was a strapping, stocky man of fifty in fringed hunting coat and tall jackboots. Strikingly handsome, with a compressed, tautly full mouth. His eyes, snapping like January ice, were hooded by a busy ridge of brows as thick as his shoulder-length hair. A man of fiery, ruthless drives, he had lived down a bad reputation by helping quell the Winnebago rising of '27 and by

166

leading a battalion of mounted rangers that had protected settlers on the Arkansas border. His inflicting the first defeat on the Sacs at the Pecatonica and routing Black Hawk's band at Wisconsin Heights nine days ago was a double coup that would grease any political path.

Atkinson blinked his cod-lidded eyes wearily. "I might better answer if I knew the present number of his band. Hundreds have died, we know that. I am counting on the raft-building to delay him by at least a day. Meantime, I've sent our best runner, Man-Who-Walks, to Fort Crawford with a message directing Captain McRee to send whatever troops he can spare up the Mississippi to intercept any attempted crossing. He can hardly outfight the Sacs, but he can engage and hold 'em. One good night's sleep for us, then we march day and night to reach the Mississippi."

"And the order of march, sir?" Dodge asked pointedly.

"Why, the one we've followed since leaving Blue Mounds. The regulars under Colonel Taylor at the front. Then Posey's and Alexander's brigades. Brigadier Henry's force bringing up the rear."

"And my Michigan Volunteers?"

"With Brigadier Henry, as before."

"In charge of baggage and supplies." Frost edged Dodge's tone. "Presumably you're aware that since the engagement at Wisconsin Heights, a degree of jealousy has been directed against Brigadier Henry's men and my own. It is, in fact, common talk that we've been deliberately made your army's chore boys."

"I see." Atkinson, always the worried fence-mender, glanced at Brigadier James Henry. "Are you aware of such talk, sir?"

Henry, whose 3rd Illinois Brigade had shared honors with Dodge at Wisconsin Heights, looked quietly distressed. His huge-boned body was wasted by sickness; his hands shook with ague. Steady, modest, resolute, he enjoyed the high regard of all who knew him—and he was a dying man.

"There's always talk, General. I will not shoot taw for a lot of damnfool gossip."

"But your men are disgruntled at being relegated to the rear?"

"Sir, some say you are trying to quiet the jealous ones. Others, that you're rebuking us for letting Black Hawk slip through our hands."

Atkinson nodded unhappily. "Would such talk be squelched if your troops were assigned to a frontal position?"

"It is not necessary, sir."

"That would certainly squelch it." Dodge overrode the aging brigadier's protest with quiet iron.

A resentful stir ran through the regular officers. Taylor's lips tightened to a granitelike seam: from the first, his regulars had occupied the post of honor. Tensions ran deep around the table. The campaign had thrown together men of every stripe. In the ranks, differences were blurred by the common exhaustion that lulled men to an artificial camaraderie. While the leaders, repeatedly humiliated by the stratagems of one old redman, trying to shift blame for command blunders, twanged every latent string of discord.

When the conference broke up an hour later, all plans discussed and a half-dozen more feuds smoldering, Davis, Anderson, and Wilson returned to the tent they shared. Davis's companions said good night and sought their blankets, but he wasn't ready for sleep. He lay on his back on the turf, fingers laced behind his head, staring at the frosty points of starlight.

Restlessness twisted his mind. He thought of the battle soon-to-be. His first. How would he acquit himself? The question weighed on his thoughts with a delicate nerveless pressure, yet was of no real concern. The meaching trickles of doubts that plagued many men, eroding spirit, courage, decision, had never touched him more than superficially.

His big problem . . . what the devil! He loved a girl. Why was that such a problem? He need only proceed with the proper, lengthy, and ceremonious courtship that befitted a young lady of Knox Taylor's station. He was a romantic-conservative in such matters, a stickler for propriety. And was often twitted for it by Joseph, his much older brother whose philosophy embraced a liberal dalliance with Robert Owen's socialist theories and a belief that a woman, provided she paid taxes, should be given the vote. But Joe had been pleased by what Jeff had confided in him. "I'm glad you're finally serious about someone," he'd said.

Taps sounded.

Davis lay with his thoughts as the camp settled down. The fires ebbed to cherry flickers. An owl made a luting, watery call; blossoming locust was sweetly feverish in the night.

He raised his head. A stocky figure of a man was crossing the camp, passing not a hundred feet away. It was Zachary Taylor, heading for his tent.

Davis sat up, firming a decision. Maybe this wasn't the best of times, but it would have to be said sooner or later. Why wait? He was here, so was the colonel.

He walked to Taylor's tent and bent, peering in the open flap. The colonel sat on his blankets, tugging off his boots by the light of a candle stuck upright in its own tallow on a small folding table.

"Sir?"

"Is that you, Mr. Davis?"

"Yes, sir."

Taylor pulled off a boot and dropped it with a weary grunt. "Whatever it is, mightn't it keep till morning?"

"It's rather a personal matter, sir. If you can spare me just a minute . . ."

"All right. Step in. Sit down."

Taylor rummaged in a haversack, found a couple of cigars and tossed one to his aide. Davis thanked him, lighted both their cigars from the candle, stuck it back in the puddle of warm tallow and seated himself cross-legged on the ground, facing the colonel.

Taylor ignored him for the moment, giving the cigar his full attention. The candlelight was cruel to his face, a tired and jowly sag to its craggy beard-stubbled lines: a face like a monument that had weathered and crumbled. A hint of temper there. He was rankled by the new order of march; yet he'd stuck out his jaw and invited Atkinson to swat it. What made him do such things? The determination of a rough-shod and earnest man to see that nothing was swept under the rug? The misguided strategy of an unfathomably sly man trying to advance his career by recklessly and gratuitously humiliating a superior? He had alienated Winfield Scott with such cryptic needlings; he was repeating with Henry Atkinson.

A half-minute with the cigar warmed the edge of his mood. "Pleasant vice, eh? Have to curb it at home. Aggravates hell out of the wife. Now, what's your trouble, mister?"

"Sir." Davis wished he had remained standing; hard saying it properly in the posture of an Indian at a trade parley. "The matter I wish to discuss is of a nature so confidential as to occasion some hesitation, and the time may not be propitious." God, he sounded like a novel of manners. "But you're here, so am I, and I thought . . ."

"Fine, mister, we're both here, what is it?"

"I wish to ask for your daughter's hand in marriage."

The cigar paused short of Taylor's lips. "My daughter."

"Miss Knox—I mean."

Taylor's teeth clicked together. "Now let's just take a sounding here, mister . . . want to make sure I'm hearing right. It has been my notion that you and Sarah Knox were at considerable odds with each other."

"Yes, sir. But when I returned to Prairie du Chien a month ago, well, all that changed. We discovered that we are deeply in love."

"I see. Reciprocal, eh? She confessed to a feeling for you."

"Yes, sir. Several times, clearly."

"Yes. Well, mister, does it occur to you that your way of engaging me on this matter—all out of the blue, before even asking permission to pay her court—is a damned effrontery?"

170

Davis stared at him. Ran his mind frantically back over his own words. Had he said something wrong? All he was sure of was that when the colonel faintly stuttered, as he had now, it was a sharp augur of Taylor temper on the rise.

"Sir, I'm confused. There was no disrespect intended. On the contrary, I'm concerned with your feelings in the matter."

Taylor's teeth tightened on the cigar; his eyes mirrored its coal with red malevolent points. "Very well, I accept your good intentions, you want to hear what I think, eh? My feelings?"

"Yes, sir, I hope—"

"My feeling is that all interests can be best served by your dropping the matter here and now. And not attempting to see my daughter again."

Davis stabbed the cigar into the ground and came to his feet: a blind, stunned, and defensive reflex. He'd been prepared for anything from a growled assent to a cataloguing of obstacles. Not a flat denial.

"I don't understand."

"You're not required to. Good night."

"I'm sorry, sir. I cannot accept that."

"Are you *telling* me, mister?"

"Yes, sir!" He snapped to a heated brace. "I am entitled to an explanation."

Taylor's eyes hooded above his cigar tip. "Suppose I give you one. Will you agree to drop this business and avoid seeing any more of Sarah Knox?"

"No, sir, I will not. I am in love with Miss Knox, and she me. I intend to court and wed her in due and proper course. Nothing will alter my mind. That is my position, sir; I cannot make it clearer."

"Your position, eh? Now you hear mine." Taylor raised the cigar, pointing it like a gun barrel. "The day that you marry my daughter, it will be over my corpse. Furthermore, if you ever raise the subject to me again, I'll break you, mister; I'll break you clear down to your heels. Now get the hell out of here!"

12

For the next two days Atkinson's army struggled west across a rugged confusion of bluffs towering over deep valleys filled with blue haze. Always they penetrated heavy timber. Only twenty-five miles from the Kickapoo to the Mississippi. For an army already debilitated by ague, exhausted to the guts, it might as well have been a hundred. Men dropped out constantly, literally falling in their tracks. The cholera had run its course since the army had departed Blue Mounds, but the usual attacks of summer ague continued to take a devastating toll. Men unable to proceed further were litter-borne to the next camp or rest halt, made as comfortable as possible and left with a few of the less ailing who could minister their needs.

The ones who could still walk and shoulder a gun plodded on. Constantly they came across dying Indians. Of Black Hawk's people, only the young and strong had survived the arduous months of marching and running, moving from one break-up camp to the next, existing on snatches of food. The rest were dropping by the score. Both sexes, all ages. Hollow-eyed, helpless, wasted to skin and bone, covered with sores and lesions. Sitting or lying in the mire of their own filth, indifferent to the columns of whites trooping by, eyes averted, mouths and noses covered against the terrible stench.

The uneven weather that had plagued the erratically hot-cold summer was acting up again. A storm was building. A man could taste it in the thick windless air, wet cottony heat, electric absence of birdsong. Twilight brought relief from the broiling sun, none from the heat. The troops made bivouac on a wooded bluff. They sat in tired groups, muttering and cursing, cuffing mosquitoes, scratching at their louse-infected clothing. They cursed everything from the heat and mosquitoes to their leaders and the Indians and the sullen speckled sky.

General Atkinson called another conference. Man-Who-Walks, the Winnebago runner, had arrived with a dispatch from Fort Crawford. The general read it aloud, a soft exultance rippling his voice.

After receiving word that the Sacs were headed for the Mississippi, Captain McRee had commandeered the services of Joseph Throckmorton, captain of the Army transport steamboat *Warrior*. Daily Throckmorton's boat had cruised up and down the Mississippi to a distance of fifty miles above Prairie du Chien, her only cargo a company of regulars and a six-pounder mounted on the foredeck. Yesterday, after traveling forty miles upriver, Throckmorton had spotted a large party of Indians on the east shore about a mile below the Bad Axe River. They were signaling with a white flag. In the exchange that followed, an Indian claiming to be Black Hawk had requested that the captain send a boat to bring him and others out to the *Warrior*, as he wished to discuss terms of surrender.

Throckmorton, distrusting the savages' intentions, had ordered a load of canister fired into their midst. It had mowed down, as he reckoned, about twenty of their party. Afterward he had steamed back to Prairie du Chien to refuel and report.

McRee suggested that the general bring up his troops in all haste to the mouth of the Bad Axe and take Black Hawk in a squeeze between land and water. Meantime the *Warrior* would continue her daily vigil and give the savages as many more doses of the same as were required to discourage a crossing.

"We'll rest till midnight, then break camp," Atkinson told them. "We'll march all night if necessary to reach the Mississippi before daybreak. *Warrior* or no, Black Hawk might still find a way out, perhaps to north or south. That, gentlemen, we must prevent at all costs."

The last daylight was fading as Davis, Anderson, and Wilson returned to their fire. They sat around it and stared at the flames in a nadir of fatigue, listening to the drone of men's voices, talk washing around them like the lazy currents of a summer river, now hitting an eddy of temper, now sagging in a pool of silence.

"God," Wilson said. "All we've seen . . . those poor dying beggars. Even a truce flag doesn't mean a damn in this bloody damned war. How do we justify it? Any of it?"

Anderson grimaced as he painfully tugged off a boot. "I don't know. Take a page from the redneck gospel, maybe. As far as the milish are concerned, debating the worth of a redskin life is tantamount to arguing which came first, the louse or the nit." He jerked the boot free and stared at it morosely. "Myself, I will merely wait for my dotage. Or till the records start smelling of mildew. Then do all my thinking on it."

Wilson got to his feet and began prowling up and down. "My blasted edge is back again," he muttered. "What I wouldn't give for an icy bath."

He stalked away to walk off his "edge."

Davis lay with his back against a hummock, slapping at mosquitoes. Cries of owls and whippoorwills coasted up from the marshes. He half-listened, his brain again budging tiredly to thoughts of his stormy head-on with Zachary Taylor two nights ago. The colonel believed in keeping his personal and professional lives in clean separation; no further reference was made to the matter, and Davis had carried on his aide duties as if nothing had happened. But it continued to rub him like salt on a raw sore.

Why had Taylor rejected his suit out of hand? He weighed every facet of his behavior since he'd known the colonel. He might be faulted on a few minor scores, nothing that should have earned him such a reaction as he'd gotten. He shifted a thoughtful glance to Anderson.

"Bob, you mentioned that you and your brother grew up with the Taylor girls . . ."

Anderson nodded, massaging his sore foot with both hands. "My pa's home, Soldier's Retreat, is hard by their grandfather Richard Taylor's place at Springfield. Why?"

Davis told him.

"You and Knoxie, eh? Well, the two of you struck sparks off each other from the first. Where there's smoke . . ."

"I know. To continue. Two nights ago, I asked Old Zeke for her hand. I was refused in no uncertain terms."

Scowling, Anderson picked up his boot and gave it a hard shake. "Yeh, he's touchy as hell on that particular subject. I could have told you."

"Hindsight is no doubt a handy virtue. But one I don't happen to possess. Told me what?"

"That Old Zeke swore years ago no daughter of his would ever marry into the Army. Didn't he mention as much?"

"He offered me the largess of his reasons if I'd agree not to see Knox again. Hardly an equal trade."

Anderson reached an arm inside his boot and extracted a small pebble. He eyed it disgustedly. "Imagine the occasion generated more heat than light after you fired your nice double-barreled thunderbolt into Old Zeke's craw. You're not exactly the model of sweet patience yourself . . ."

"At the moment, what little I have waxes exceeding fine. Why would *he,* of all people, object to an Army man?"

"All I know, he's damned if any girl of his will marry one. Unluckily, one of 'em upped and did exactly that. Three years back, Ann, the oldest, eloped with Robert Crooke Wood, an Army surgeon. They're stationed at Fort Snelling now, have a baby, and are, by all reports, deliriously happy. Cuts no ice with

Old Zeke. She might as well be on the moon, for all of him."

"What about Gibbs? He seems to be in solidly."

Anderson smiled. "Sure. But you know Denny. Always open to suggestion."

"You mean he'd resign his commission?"

"Like enough—on request. Would you?"

"Not on condition," Davis said flatly. "In my own time, maybe, for my own reasons. Never because I was dragooned into it."

"Exactly. Colonel's had time to take your measure. I'd guess he sees you for the stiff-neck you are. Takes Gibbs on the same face value."

"I wouldn't be that sure of Denny. I've known him since Academy days. He always struck me more as dedicated than compliant."

"With qualification. A lot of it." Anderson took out his pipe and jammed in a thumb of tobacco. "I knew Denny as a boy. His old man, Judge Whelan Gibbs, would be a martinet if he were Army. Raised Denny 'by hand,' trimmed out all the soft spots, as he put it. All the dedication you see, it's all form, no feeling."

"I don't follow that."

"Denny feels what he feels, thinks what he thinks, because it's how a man is supposed to feel and think. If the esteemed father-in-law-to-be were to suggest he resign from the service, it follows that this were the proper thing. Besides the colonel and Denny's father are old friends; you can lay odds they have an understanding."

"I see," Davis said slowly. "What about Knox? Would she just go along with all this?"

"Against the heart, so to speak? That's a question." Anderson leaned forward and scooped a live coal into his pipebowl. "Ann always seemed the tractable one. Knox, the headstrong, all fire and vivacity. Still—where Knox has bucked her mother, she's always harked to the paternal voice. Understand, we were all children together. I'm talking about then."

"Now, though?"

"Dunno. It was Ann, the meek 'un, who went against the sire's express wish. Knox, who knows? What did she say, she'd marry you?"

"Hadn't time to ask."

"Well, I'd bear in mind that she's had scads of beaux before this, several serious. My brother Charlie for one. Gibbs of course. And Sanford Preston, a cousin on the Smith side, her mother's family. She's like you, a born romantic. And given to flights of fancy."

"Bob, this is no fancy. Not on my part."

"If so—" Anderson shrugged. "Then look out, my boy. A whole lot of sparks are going to fly . . ."

A slow rain began about ten o'clock. The men rested, but got little sleep. They huddled under dripping trees and shivered in wet blankets. Before midnight the rain let up, though a heavy misting continued. At midnight the signal for assembly was given, but what with the problems of loading horses and mules in the dark, confusions of poor liaison, further wrangling over the order of march, it was nearly two o'clock before the trek got under way. Dodge's battalion shared advance column honors with Taylor's regulars, Posey's and Alexander's Brigades filled the middle ranks, Brigadier Henry's troops brought up the rear, still in charge of baggage and supplies.

They were a little over three miles from the Mississippi. But miles fretted by jagged ranges of hills heavily forested from base to crown. As always, it was easiest to move in broad loops around the less overgrown bases of ridges. In spite of the brutal terrain, miserable weather, physical disorders, the general spirit was high.

The powder-gray of false dawn came, the mizzling rain died away. They were close to the Mississippi at last. And heading into a soupy fog. The river bluffs grew out of its grimy curtain like sleeping cougars. The men began to mutter uneasily. How could you fight Indians in a stew like this?

Wary of being ambushed in the fog, Atkinson ordered a halt; Captain Joseph Dickson's company of spies was sent ahead to ferret out the ground. Davis was among the staff officers attending Atkinson and Taylor as they conferred. The conference was breaking up when a leather-garbed scout galloped in with a message from Dickson. The spies had ranged to the rim of the bluffs, but the bottoms were masked by fog. No sign yet of the Sacs.

"Did you see the *Warrior?*" Atkinson asked.

The grizzled campaigner shook his head. "Body couldn't make out a masted sailing ship in that soup. But we hazard we're a mile below the mouth of the Bad Axe. Would put us mebbe a mile above the Ioway on t'other side. Seems dead sure the Sacs is somewhere in them bottoms, but the cap'n ain't taking chances. He is fanning out a search along the bluffs."

Atkinson nodded, gaunt-eyed. "If he abandoned his plan to make a crossing, Black Hawk would try to slip out above or below us. If he didn't, he'll be racing time. Getting his rafts finished and launched before the *Warrior* finds him or we do. Damn the fog! They could still make it across unless it lifts . . ."

A sudden rattle of gunfire tore the mist.

They fell silent, listening tensely. The firing broke off, then picked up again. Shortly afterward, another messenger came racing out of the fog. Dickson's men had encountered a party of braves on the bluffs. After a brief engagement, the Sacs had fallen back.

"Fell back where, man?"

"Toward them near bluffs to the north, Gen'ral. They's heading for the bottoms from there, most like."

"Tell Captain Dickson not to press the enemy closely. They

could be leading him toward an ambush. Tell him we're bringing the army up at once."

The messenger saluted and wheeled his mount away. Atkinson gave orders: Zachary Taylor's regulars would lead the assault; Posey's command would disperse to his right and Alexander's to the right of Posey's. If the river blocked Black Hawk on the west, they must cut off any retreat to north or northeast. Held to a crawl, Brigadier Henry's baggage-laden force had dropped behind. Atkinson sent a runner to tell Henry to proceed with all haste.

"Sir!" said Henry Dodge. "I'd suggest that my battalion be sent to the left—and into the bottoms. There's a possibility Black Hawk may be buying time by leading the army away from his real crosspoint . . ."

Atkinson hesitated only a moment. "Very well, Colonel. We can't cover all points without splitting the army into trickles. But if your gamble sours into a wild goose chase, you could miss all the action."

"I'll take that chance, sir. If you find 'em, send one man to me. I'll do the same."

The metal-hard fire in Dodge's eyes touched Davis with a kindred feeling. Impulsively he turned to Taylor: "Sir! Request permission to accompany Colonel Dodge."

Dodge's heavy brows twitched upward; he smiled. "Honored, Mr. Davis. Colonel . . . ?"

Taylor nodded.

Dodge lost no time. While the main force swung north along the bluffs, he led his company of Michigan Volunteers—by now numbering less than a hundred able-bodied men—down a brush-clogged cleft in the bluffs. They battled through the raking brush, stumbling over rocks and roots. Davis could make out nothing but stony banks on his left and right, nothing ahead but the shuffling file of men quickly lost to sight in the milky haze. The light was growing steadily, but the fog remained almost impenetrable. By the time they reached the slushy footing of the bottoms, the visibility was a little improved. They were in a maze of marsh and sloughs jungled by hummocks covered with dense brush and scrub oak.

These were veteran rangers; many had served in Dodge's Arkansas Mounted Brigade. Without a spoken order, they broke ranks and eased apart, infiltrating the brush as they moved forward. Davis was close to the front. A Sabbath hush clung to the bottoms. Equipment chinked softly; dawnlight shimmered damply on metal. Men's feet made sucking sighs as they tramped through the muck and shallows. Crab-limbed trees loomed all around, looking like ossified trolls in the mist.

Suddenly a crackle of rifle and musketry. The fog came alive with darting forms and cherry blades of gun flame. Buckskin-legginged warriors were spiriting among them like gaunt wraiths, scalping knives and steel-bitted tomahawks made dull flashes, bows twanged. Within a minute, battle was loosely joined over a narrow hundred yards of riverbottom, a turmoil of shots and shouts and shrieks, a swirl of locked, struggling bodies that struck and slashed and rolled back and forth.

Davis fired his musket at a howling brave and missed; he closed with him and wrestled him chest to chest till the tide of battle tore them apart.

Both sides were handicapped by fog and packed brush. But more Indians were pouring into the fray. "Fall back," Dodge yelled. "Fall back!" The rangers formed a ragged line of clubbed rifles and swinging tomahawks and gave ground slowly, moving back toward the bluffs. The Sacs pressed them hard for a short distance, then broke off and withdrew.

Dodge called a halt at the foot of the bluffs. The men sat on hummocks to treat their wounds and recharge their weapons. Dodge asked whether anyone were missing. Only two had been seen to go down; nobody was seriously wounded.

"How do you like that?" Dodge chuckled, wrapping a strip of calico around a nick in his arm. "First I thought we'd hit an ambush. But it was only a rear-guard action, purely defensive. Well, we've found their main body. Major MacConnell!"

A square-faced ranger stood up. "Aye, sir."

"Get to Atkinson. Tell him we've found his enemy for him. Tell the military genius of genii he was following a decoy force. And to move his troops down here on the double."

MacConnell loped away.

Davis sat with his knees pulled up, elbows resting on them. He held a hand in front of his face. It trembled slightly. He looked at it till the tremor ceased. Then he could admit to a cool tingling pleasure: his first action in a real war. He took a paper cartridge from the pouch at his belt, bit off the end, poured the powder down the barrel of his musket, crammed in the bullet and paper wadding, seated it with a thrust of the ramrod, half-cocked the hammer and crimped a percussion cap on the nipple. (The Army still issued flintlock priming; he'd converted to caplock at his own expense.) Finished, he looked at his hands again. Steady as stone.

While his men rested, Dodge stalked back and forth with growing impatience. A dim rattle of noise reached them: men descending the wide ravine leading to the bottom. Ghostly columns of them filed into sight.

Brigadier James Henry plodded up to Dodge at his painful walk. He flickered a ravaged grin. "Well, Dodge. Another feather in your cap, eh?"

"Where's Atkinson?"

"He sent me a message telling me to come up fast, but no battle orders. So when we met MacConnell on the bluffs—he's gone on to Atkinson—I thought we might as well join you straightway."

Dodge smiled. "Well then, James. With your six hundred men, we need hardly wait for Atkinson."

"Attack now, you mean?"

"First—I mean. Man, when you're this close to glory, can't you smell it?"

"Glory!" James Henry's smile held a gray indifference. "Glory and death . . . hand in hand, are they not? Very well; you'd make a handsome governor of Michigan, old friend."

They quickly agreed on deployment of troops: forming a broad crescent whose two horns would stab against the riverbank to either side of the Sacs, catching them in a loose cordon.

Pushing forward, they ran into a stiff resistance from the Sac rear guard. A fusillade of shots hammered the Indians back, but not far. Henry ordered a bayonet charge and fighting was closed at a score of points. It swiftly bogged down in a grinding stalemate, the militia unable to gain ground. The many woody knolls furnished entrenchments for Sac snipers, but most of them were poor shots; heavy moisture in the air caused numerous misfires. Nevertheless, the ferocity of the defenders was incredible. Weak, emaciated, many half-dead of wounds and disease, they repulsed every charge with a desperate vitality. Davis saw a dying warrior throw himself on the bayonet of a charging militiaman. They were buying precious moments of time with the holding effort.

But not time enough. A clamor of charging troops and renewed firing told of Atkinson's arrival. The remaining braves fell back swiftly from tree to tree, giving ground almost to the water's edge. The whites pressed them fiercely, cleaning out stragglers as they went.

A pink wash of true dawn was flooding the bottoms. A golden cloud of fog and powder smoke frayed across the shoreline. The rafts had been launched; now a good half of the defending braves plunged into the breast-deep water and made for several small islands, holding rifles, powder horns, and shot pouches above their heads. The remaining Sacs dug in briefly along the shore, holding the whites in check. When the first wave of warriors had achieved the islands, they began firing in turn, covering the second party's retreat. Davis watched the maneuver in amazement. Executed by a few score of undrilled, undisciplined, half-starved Indians, it was the most flawlessly handled tactic he'd ever witnessed.

The Indians must have worked feverishly through the night to assemble floatable timbers and lash them into large rafts. A dozen or so were well on their way across, poling between and around the islands toward the far shore. Crowding the bank now, the whites opened up at the rafts. But musket fire was ineffective beyond eighty yards, and shredding fog continued to frustrate the deadly accuracy of the Kentucky long rifles.

A steamboat's bell tinkled across the water. A scatter of lusty cheers went up from the troops. The *Warrior*'s low black hulk was gliding into view from behind a long strip of island. The roar of a six-pounder underscored the angry sputter of shots.

The cannon bellowed again and again, pouring lethal showers of grape and canister into the flotilla of crude rafts. Many were wounded or mortally hit. Others sought only to escape the slow-poling concentration of rafts that had turned suddenly to a death trap. One polesman panicked and abandoned his charges, leaping into the water; the rest held their places. A few rafts seemed in a fair way to reach the far bank.

Some braves on the islands seized floats of driftwood and kick-swam themselves out in an effort to aid the women, the children, the decrepit struggling in the water amid the debris and bodies. The rest dug in along the islands' banks, thickly overgrown with willows and osiers. Cover for a last-ditch resistance.

Zachary Taylor shouted and flashed his saber, then plunged into the water, leading some of his battle-blooded regulars in a perilous half-swimming attack on the largest island. Davis followed close behind the colonel, his own saber out. His pistols were empty; he had lost his musket. A ball whistled by his head; another passed through his sleeve.

They struck shallow water and lunged up the bank. Taylor was still in the lead, his stocky form clear to enemy fire; a hurled tomahawk knocked the cap from his head.

His troops splashed pell-mell through the shallows and swarmed up the bank behind him. Bucking through the willow mottes in a solid charge. Cutting down the defenders, trampling thickets underfoot, slashing foliage to emerald confetti, swarming over every yard of the island, shooting to right and left, clubbing empty muskets, stabbing with bayonets, their throats raw with a hoarse and mindless shrilling.

Taylor and those of his officers not caught in the demented fury were tardy in realizing that their men had gone crazy. And getting them under control then was impossible. Davis saw a soldier laughing as he smashed a dead brave's face with the butt of his musket. He swung the flat of his saber against the man's head and watched him reel off, still sobbing with macabre delight.

The bloody pitch of excitement faded.

Davis stared around him. The earth and trampled brush reeked like the floor of an abattoir. Even the raft survivors who had reached the island had not been spared. The bodies of men, women, tiny children, lay twisted and still. Others writhed and bled; screams keened the smoking air. The shooting tapered off to the sporadic popping fire of Army riflemen who were picking off Indians in the water.

The *Warrior* fired a self-congratulatory salute. A salvo of cheers erupted from the men on her deck. The water around her dark squat hull seemed awash with blood. But it was only the crimson dye of sunrise.

The new day had a raw stink. Bodies lay gently in the lapping water and moved on with the current. Soldiers stood about like gaunt Charons inspecting a dawn-red Styx. Or like mere zombies, their faces grimy and streaked and empty. A clear baritone voice said, "Mary, Mother of God," the words dangling with unreasonable clarity above the other sounds. My God, Davis thought, all the women, all the children.

He could not yet believe it. He moved woodenly toward the bank, looking for Taylor. Where was he? Somebody should take charge, someone should salvage a shred of honor from this crowning horror to a four-month fiasco.

Somebody. But not him, Davis thought, not him. A curious numbness had spread through his flesh. Later on, he thought, I will think about these things. Yes, later. Realizing that he still held his saber, he thrust it, clean and water-dewed, into the scabbard and out of sight.

He made his legs carry him down the bank and into the water. Put out a hand to steady himself and closed it over something. Something just beneath the water, cool and pliant flesh over structured bone. A human face.

He snatched his hand back. For a moment he stood as he was, letting his nerves absorb the shock. Then he moved on toward the main shore, not looking at the body. Nothing in the world could have made him look . . .

PART THREE

A Season for Honor

13

Knox Taylor toyed with the food on her plate and ate little. She wasn't hungry, though she should be. She and Margaret had bustled about all day, preparing a soldier's welcome.

Late yesterday a courier had brought word of the Bad Axe victory. The troops were coming home. Colonel Taylor would arrive before nightfall on the *Warrior*. So, with Betty and Dick getting excitedly underfoot, Knox and Margaret set to work. Scrubbing and dusting, cleaning the house top to bottom. They had outdone themselves preparing the dinner: boned grouse baked a golden brown, young potatoes and tender asparagus in melted butter, plumcake, coffee with maple sugar. Candles lighted in tin-backed sconces shed a soft glow across the snowy damask tablecloth, bone china and gleaming silver.

The other Taylors and the sole guest, Denny Gibbs, were enjoying the meal. Zachary Taylor paid grim eulogy to Black Hawk's generalship: "To top it," he was saying, "the old devil slipped out of our hands at the last moment. He wasn't among the living or the dead. What little we've gleaned from prisoners indicates that he and his son Whirling Thunder—along with The Prophet and thirty or so squaws and children—fled east toward the Dells of the Wisconsin. We've dispatched our red allies to every Indian camp between here and there, warning 'em not to harbor the Hawk or his party. Also to assure 'em that should they capture him, they'll be warmed by the Grandfather's favor. And I've sent Wilson to the Dells with a patrol. At least we've got Neapope, the Hawk's good right arm, squarely in hand. A few of the rafts got across, and a party of Sioux attached to our command asked Atkinson for permission to overtake those Sacs. He agreed, with the proviso that they take 'em prisoner. Unfortunately they slaughtered all except a handful. Well, nits and lice as they say. The Sioux did fetch Neapope back sound as a dollar. Had him brought along on the *Warrior,* and he's safe in the guardhouse."

Knox glanced at her mother. Margaret's face showed faint frown lines; she didn't fancy war talk at the table. Knox felt a little ill herself, and had ever since earlier when, tired from the day's work, she had taken a walk by the waterfront. Parties of captured Sacs were arriving hourly, marched down the Sukisep Trail from the north under heavy guard. She had watched them being herded into a hastily erected stockade a little distance from the fort proper. Not in all her life, not even during the worst of the pestilence, had she seen such sights as this. Men, women, children, all of them unbelievably emaciated, skull-gaunt, sunken-bellied. Warriors limping with wounds, trooping single file between squads of musket-ready soldiers. Women and children herded along in huddled bunches. (Where were the babies? Had all the babies died?) Bereaved women. Dozens of them. Wailing with grief, arms and legs gashed and bleeding, bodies and faces and hair smeared with dirt, tokens of bereavement. And that child. The child with a blood-stained rag tied over its eyes being led by a tottering crone . . .

"What's ailing you, miss? No appetite? You look a bit liverish."

"I'm all right, Pa." She forced a smile. "A little tired, I guess."

Nits and lice. As though they were vermin. She had never felt so tempted to challenge that heavy majority opinion. After what she had seen today, she could not even dredge charity from the fact that her father's brother William had died in horrible fashion at Indian hands. Earlier, she had voiced her feelings to her mother—and she felt Margaret's warning glance now. When the colonel was off duty, he expected the pleasures of a cozy household. A hot drink, warm slippers, cheery womenfolk. Margaret always saw to it that these pleasures were undiluted for him.

"I understand that General Scott arrived today while I was on wood detail. I regret having missed him."

Denny spoke with the half-mechanical air of a man making talk. Something else was on his mind, and Knox knew why. He'd been moody and out of sorts since their tiff the other night. She couldn't gracefully put him off much longer; the engagement must soon be either confirmed or broken.

"You didn't miss much," the colonel said dourly. "Old Fuss and Feathers stopped here barely an hour. Long enough to muster out the volunteers, order Atkinson and his regulars back to Jefferson Barracks and leave instructions relative the disposition of prisoners. Then he took the *Warrior* down to Fort Armstrong, I guess to set up negotiations with the different tribes involved. Suppose all treaties with 'em will be reshaped according to their recent conduct."

"Did we suffer many casualties, sir? At the Bad Axe?"

"Thunderation, no. A dozen killed, dozen more wounded. The Sacs fared less well. A hundred and fifty, I should say, died in the battle. At least an equal number drowned when the *Warrior* capsized the rafts. Quite a battle to miss, boy."

"I'm embarrassed, sir."

"Nonsense. You acquitted yourself well, McRee tells me, in a little skirmish last week—"

"Yes, routing a clutch of whiskeyed blanket Injuns who were annoying a picnic party of village belles."

Taylor chuckled and winked. "Well, my boy, the ladies always decide on the garrison hero, so you have no complaint coming. You might have gone through nearly the whole campaign and not seen a mote of action. Mostly we encamped, weighed rumors, kept in touch and generally twiddled our thumbs. Miserable excuse for a war any way you look at it. Only the politicking ones will reap the glory, deservedly or not."

At this point Margaret firmly steered the table talk into other channels. But Knox hardly listened. She continued to worry her food around with her fork and worry her mind with the dilemma that had partly marred her appetite.

Jefferson Davis was back. She had seen him crossing the parade in a hurry, and he hadn't noticed her. But he would have time for her soon enough. And unlike Denny, he would not be put off.

The talk languished for a few moments. And then, abruptly as a thunderclap, Denny laid down his fork and said determinedly: "Sir!"

"Yes?"

"Sarah Knox has done me the honor of consenting to be my wife." Denny's face was pink; his words came in a rush. "I have already decided to resign from the service. I know of your wishes respecting a son-in-law, and I cannot expect to support a family on a lieutenant's pay."

Knox stared at him. He stared back with a kind of nervous defiance. So this was what had been in his mind . . . a brash announcement that he hoped would force her to a decision.

Taylor had stopped eating to hear Denny out. He half-raised his napkin, then wadded it beside his plate.

"Is that the truth, miss? You told Denny you'd marry him?"

"I—well, not exactly. I mean, I said that he could consider us engaged, but I didn't . . ."

Her voice waned under his iron-colored look.

"That's just fine," he said grimly. "Now suppose that you tell us what you told young Jeff Davis."

She stared at him, unable to say a word.

Margaret said sharply, "Zeke, what do you mean?"

"Meant to take this up later. Davis came to me a few nights

ago and asked for Knox's hand. Told me cool as you please that she'd, 'hem, told him of her mighty affection for him. I've no idea what passed between them, but certainly he believed what he said."

Margaret looked straight at Knox. "I will ask you once, and I want a direct answer. Did you tell both Denny and Mr. Davis that you would marry them?"

"Oh, Mother, no! I never said I'd marry either one—"

"Then what did you tell them, pray? It must have been something in each case that led them to . . . Betty and Dick!" The children were open-mouthed. "You're excused from the table."

The two lagged out of the room. Knox gazed slowly around the table. At Denny, his face dismayed, stricken, bewildered. At her father, florid with a thinly contained anger.

"Heavens knows," Margaret said, "that I've tried to be patient. All this flirting from beau to beau . . . I've tried to see it as part of a delicate period. But Knoxie . . . this is too much."

"Ma, it wasn't that way!"

"Then what the devil way was it?" her father snapped. "Just who in blazes are you promised to?"

"Nobody. Nobody at all!" She stood up so quickly that she knocked over her water glass. "Let me alone, can't you?"

She ran up the stairs and into her room, slamming the door behind her. Tears streamed saltily into her mouth as she undressed, throwing her pink cashmere frock, shoes, stockings, petticoats, everything to the floor. Then, still in her chemise, she threw herself across the bed, muffling her sobs in a pillow. Footsteps in the hall. She scrambled under the blankets and pulled the pillow over her head. "Knoxie," Margaret said softly, opening the door. "Oh, Knoxie, for pity's sake!" Small rustlings as she gathered up the scattered clothing. Knox jerked away when she felt a hand touch her shoulder.

"Dear, all this nervous vacillation of late, I've tried to understand, I really have. But honestly, I think you've bred up all manner of unhealthy humors that are . . ."

"Mother, please!"

"Very well." Margaret paused. "But your father is upset as I haven't seen him since . . . well, suffice it to say I shouldn't try his patience too far if I were you."

She went out, quietly closing the door.

Knox rubbed her wet face back and forth on the pillow. They were right, she thought. Wrong in one assumption; for once she hadn't flirted. But here on the border, an indecisive female was as bad as any flirt. Too often men had fought duels over such women; men had died. Suppose she were to cause such a thing . . .

What of Denny then? The oaf, the foolish tactless oaf! But what did she really feel for him? He was man enough to satisfy her, flexible enough to suit her. He was very close to the (for her) ideal choice she had envisioned.

Why couldn't she love him?

Jeff Davis.

The fire and the doubt. The same as before. Strength, forcefulness, self-assurance: he had entirely too much. More than she could live with, more than she could control. Any more than she could control the wild disturbance she felt.

Was that love? Wasn't love more than a mad burning of the senses?

How much more?

Her mind whirled; her head ached. She rose finally, slipped out of the chemise and into an excessively plain flannel nightgown which she buttoned up to her throat. She washed her face with cold water and Boston soap, and returned to bed, burrowing into the blankets. Twilight spread velvet shadow through the room; taps sounded.

An hour later, she still lay awake, her nerves charged and quivering. Her father and mother ascended the stairs and entered their room; she heard faint and fretful discussion. Then there was silence.

Faintly through the window (tightly secured against noc-

turnal miasmas) she heard a tipsy *voyageur* giving rich voice
to a familiar *chanson:*

> *"A la claire fontaine*
> *M'en allant promener*
> *J'ai trouvé l'eau si belle . . ."*

The lonely, hopeful, deep-bass chant was no balm to her
mood. She threw back the hot bedclothes, unbuttoned her damp
flannel gown and opened it. The air felt cool and sudden. She
smoothed her hands along her slim silken thighs and boyish
hips and mild curve of belly; she cupped them beneath her
small pear-shaped breasts.

She felt a self-conscious tingling. How strange, the touching
and the knowledge of herself and her womanhood . . .

A noise.

She yanked the covers up to her chin, heart pounding. Something had clattered against the outside wall by her window.

She heard it again. Realized that someone was pitching
pebbles against the siding, not too gently. Swung out of bed,
hurried to the window and crouched by the sill. A thin sickle
of moon lustered the yard; shadows blotted the scene like pools
of ink. It took several seconds to pick out the erect form of a
man, his face tipped up. She wrestled the sash up a few inches.

"What d'you want!" Hissing the words.

"I want to talk to you." Davis's tone was normal and rather
amused. "Come on down."

"Don't be silly! It's late, everyone's abed. Please go away."

"You won't come out?"

"No!"

"Are you sure?"

"Quite sure. Go away!"

He tossed another pebble.

"Oh don't, you'll wake . . . oh very well! But only for a
moment."

She felt her way through the dark to her closet, then let her nightgown slip to the floor. For a moment in the humid dark, she let her hands sleek over her flesh again: shivered a little. She dressed quickly, threw a shawl over her head and eased open the door, listening. Her parents' room at the end of the corridor was separated from hers by the children's room. She passed silently down the staircase to the parlor, went through the kitchen and out the back door.

She skirted the house hugging the shadow.

She almost ran into Davis's arms. He murmured, "This way," and marched her across the summer-yellowed lawn silvered by moonlight. They were heading toward the oak and beech grove, and she thought, please no, not here, remembering the evening with Denny. But they were moving away from the river, into the moon-fretted motte of trees. It was brush-clean, free of fallen branches, naved by black archings of limbs that whispered in a warm wind. Davis walked her slowly, he kept his arm tight around her waist. She felt a squirm of heat in her veins; she felt moved to protest.

"Please. You're holding me too . . ."

"Sorry."

The arm relaxed, but stayed where it was. They came to the edge of the grove; the white-silver sheen of prairie flowed south to the foot of Sugar Loaf Bluff. Knox jumped at the close belling call of a screech owl. She saw the bird on a low branch, pale as a phantom.

"There's a perfect chaperone." She laughed nervously. "You shouldn't have said . . . what you said to my father."

"So I learned." His voice was wry. "How could I know? Bob Anderson belatedly told me his opinion of service marriages. And about your sister's elopement."

"Yes." She touched her dry tongue to her lips; she felt impelled to talk. "It took us all by surprise . . . Annie was always the quiet, obedient one. It absolutely stunned Pa, but

196

he was a thousand miles away at the time and couldn't do a thing."

"I'm a little puzzled about it all . . ."

"Oh, you'd never imagine the lengths he's gone to in trying to separate his career and home life! And it's just impossible; he's a professional soldier who goes where he's ordered, and practically every assignment has taken him to remote posts. Usually it's been the harshest sort of living—though we occupy very nice quarters here—and Ma's lot is far better than most Army wives know." She was chattering, she realized, but there was a relief in letting her agitation spill out in words. "At home, in Louisville, we've servants and domestic luxuries of every kind. But Pa can't forsake a conviction that he's done badly by us when we've had to share his hardships. Even at Vincennes, you know, where I was born, Pa held Fort Harrison with fifty men, half of them down with ague, against all Tecumseh's Indians and a host of British regulars . . ."

"I think I've heard of that." His tone was amused again.

"I'm chattering," she said honestly. "But it's true; and other times he hasn't seen us for months into years. I guess—while Ann and I were growing up—I heard him vow a hundred times that no daughter of his would ever marry a soldier."

"Your sister did. I should think he'll come to terms with her sooner or later."

"I suppose, yes. But then it will remain the not-quite pardonable act that stays under the face of things. I'd hate that."

They walked slowly along the grove's edge. He hadn't tried to kiss her. He was very serious about this, she thought: she did not know whether to feel disappointed or not. Faintly, from the direction of the stockade, came the low wailing of the Indian women. He broke the silence:

"I imagine, things as they are, he'd be far harder on a second daughter who followed suit."

She glanced at his face under the moon; a shock ran through her. "Oh—"

"What's the matter?"

"You look so . . . fine-drawn."

"You could say that," he said tonelessly. "I suppose you've heard about the Bad Axe."

"I heard how some of our men behaved. It must have been terrible."

"Worse. It was a dastardly business, start to finish."

A warmth stirred her; they felt alike in this. "Whatever some men did can't reflect on you personally. If you acquitted yourself honorably . . ."

"There was no honor at the Bad Axe," he said flatly. "Come, we'll walk back."

His arm turned her firmly; they passed back into the grove. The arm tightened again.

"Please . . . don't."

This time he brought his arm to her shoulder and halted, turning her to face him. "What is it?"

"I—I'm not sure, that's all."

"You said you loved me."

"I've thought before that I was in love. I'm like plum blossoms." She gave another nervous laugh. "I break out every spring, regular as—"

"You're a big girl now, Sarah Knox." He pulled her tightly to him. "And this is a perennial thing between us—"

Her blood drum-rolled hot and cold in her veins. She did not know how long the kiss lasted. When it ended, she still clung wildly to him, her face buried in his throat. Never like this, she thought, never like this . . .

"You know," he murmured.

"Oh, you're so sure of yourself!"

"Yes."

"And of me—"

He kissed her again; his lips nuzzled her ear. "Once and for all, do you love me?"

"Once and for all, yes," she whispered. "Yes!"

198

14

Zachary Taylor mentally phrased a strong lecture to his daughter while he tried to enjoy a good Southern breakfast of waffles with butter and sorghum, ham with red-eye gravy, and fluffy biscuits. He wasn't making much progress at either. His wife and two younger children, always quick to sense when he was out of sorts, knew better than to make conversation between themselves, much less address him directly. Breakfast was eaten in silence, except for Margaret twice warning Dickie not to gulp his food.

Knox leaned her chin on her hand and pushed the food around on her plate, every now and then patting a delicate yawn. She looked tired and downcast and a little sulky.

"Straighten up, miss," Taylor snapped. "Eat your breakfast."

She took a tiny bite of biscuit. He eyed her unsympathetically. She'd always been healthy as a young mare. Now, as if her erratic behavior weren't enough, she was getting as pale and thin as those bleached little ninnies that some of his friends had sired. She'd picked at her food last night too. She looked as if she hadn't gotten an hour's sleep. Margaret poured the coffee, brewed as he liked it, black and strong. He flooded it with thick cream and began to raise the cup to his lips. Then set it down. His mouth pouted grimly.

Margaret knew the signs. "Children, you're excused from the table."

When Betty and Dick had run out the back door, Taylor began dourly, "As you know"—making his point impartially to wife and daughter—"the judge and I have hoped, I won't deny planned, for two years against the day Denny and Knox would make a match of it. We expected, from all signs, that the announcement would come soon. After Missy's display of last night, I'd say the time's come for a reckoning. Just what are your plans for Denny, miss?"

"I'm not going to marry him." She said it sulkily, not raising her eyes.

"I see. Hum." He managed to hold his temper. "Well, I shan't press you, never have where your young men are concerned. Likely been my error. Always felt my daughters should make their own choices."

"With one prohibition," Margaret said quietly.

"Hum." His brows flew together. "Trouble with a woman is, give her the whole hog but for the ears and she'll grab for the ears every time."

"Let's not engage in personalities, Zeke. Or if you must, pray don't put my whole sex under fire."

"Didn't mean to," he growled. "But first it was Ann and now . . ." He stared at his daughter. "You'll tell Denny your decision directly, no damned shilly-shallying. Now. Are you serious about young Davis, or is that another lark?"

Knox raised her eyes sullenly, then lowered them without a word. Another lark, he thought with relief. Blast the girl! Her moods were always clear as spring water, but damned if he'd ever fathomed that cross-grained mind of hers. Of course she'd never been meek. But he'd always been inclined to the opinion that her occasional fiery spates contained more petulance than courage.

"Listen, my girl." He tapped a finger on the table. "Davis is the best aide I've ever had. Even Atkinson's commended him as being as promising a subaltern as you'll find in the Western Army. Worth a score of those fops you've played the courting game with back in Louisville. He deserves better than being another romantic sheep to your infernal Judas goat. You've created friction between that boy and me with your blasted lollygagging, and I want no more of it. Understand me?"

"Yes, Pa."

"While we're on the matter, high time you took steps to purge the gross and impure humors from your system. You should drink more water, pure water. Abstain from meat altogether. Fish, fowl, or cheese will do as well." He sipped his tepid coffee and scowled at it. "Tea will suit you better than coffee. I suggest an ice-cold bath twice a week. Scriptural readings before bedtime and warm weak tea—"

"Oh Zeke, honestly . . ."

"Blast it, madam, those wild humors of hers have drained her nature. She's as pale and peaked as—"

"Of course she is. You'll hear of it in any event, so I'll tell you. After the cholera reached Prairie du Chien, your daughter gave all her days for two weeks, dawn till dark, helping Dr. Beaumont at the hospital."

"Jehoshaphat!" He thumped his cup down. "What in the name of God possessed you to . . . !"

"Please be calm," Margaret said. "You're stuttering."

He pushed away from the table and stamped out through the parlor to the piazza. Reached for his coatee on the hook by the door. What was this? Not the shabbily faded excuse for a uniform coat he'd worn for years. He held it up, staring at the gleaming silver epaulets with gold eagles: the Army's new insignia for a full colonel. He shrugged into it and buttoned the ten close-set buttons to his throat.

Margaret came to the doorway, smiling. "A welcome home gift. And a perfect fit, I see. I made a few adjustments."

He went to her, smiling at her gently flushed face; he kissed her. "Thank you, my dear . . ."

Leaving the house, he crossed to the fort's west gate. Honeysuckle was delicate on the dawn air; sequins of dew reflected the mother-of-pearl sky. The day's beauty should have put an agreeable edge on his mood. It didn't; he brooded furiously all the way to the gate. Two days ago the pleasure he'd shown Margaret would have been unfeigned. Now the new epaulets only served to remind him of another bitter personal problem.

He'd come through the second war of his career and had acquitted himself, within the range of opportunity, as well as he had in 1812. For the Wabash campaign, he'd been honored with the Army first brevet rank; when political enemies had gotten him graded back to captain, he had angrily quit the service. Two years later, friendlier politicians had restored his major's rank. And this spring, after a dozen years as a lieutenant colonel at Forts Howard, Snelling, and Crawford, during which he'd been repeatedly bypassed as higher posts were vacated, he had finally received his brevet colonelcy. At least a brevet brigadier generalcy should await the man who'd spearheaded the field campaign against Black Hawk. During his brief stay yesterday, Winfield Scott had dashed that hope. "Zeke," he'd said bluntly, "you've trod on too many high-placed toes too often; that's your trouble." One intemperate barb directed against the man in the White House had reached Old Hickory's ears, it seemed, and Scott was relishing the situation. Damn. These eagles would wear tarnish before another promotion came . . .

The reveille gun had already boomed. Taylor stood impatiently through assembly, inspection, muster roll, and sick call, spoiling to set the teeth of his anger into the day's work. Post discipline had slackened during the campaign, and Scott had gone out of his way to drop smarting remarks on the helter-skelter state of things. Taylor grimly intended to apprise the garrison that tough campaign or not, nobody had earned a vacation.

While the men were at mess, he summoned all company

commanders and subalterns to his office and issued assignments without the formality of general orders. The companies needed reorganizing. Ranks were gapped by desertion and battle casualties, mostly from post-wound complications. The cholera still raged unabated in the lower river towns where quarantines had been declared against incoming cargo; here the pestilence was on the wane. But the rash of lime-sowed graves in the post cemetery was a stark reminder of the almost hundred lives that the plague had slashed from the ranks of the 1st Infantry, in garrison and in the field. Every man found drunk, Taylor said, would be compelled to dig a grave, since it wouldn't be long wanting a tenant. Thus sparing temperate soldiers the bother of preparing intemperate comrades for burial.

"Zeke," growled Captain Tom Smith, "if intemperance is causing the contagion, I can name you damn strange exceptions."

Everyone smiled, including the colonel.

"It appears to have run its course here at least," Taylor said. "Word's come of a fresh outbreak at Fort Armstrong. Still, Scott left orders I'm to single out the Sac prisoners who are potential troublemakers and have 'em delivered to Armstrong for temporary internment. At least till after the big powwow with the chiefs has adjourned. Forty of 'em will leave tomorrow on the *Winnebago*. Mr. Anderson, you'll be in charge of the guard escort."

"Yes, sir."

"Nothing would please me more than to send along General Black Hawk himself. But he's still at large, and nothing to go on but rumors. Can only hope Wilson turns up something at the Dells."

He gave special orders concerning the care of the prisoners. The rest of the duty roster, already posted by the adjutant, was routine and would be supervised by Captain Smith, as Officer of the Day. He then dismissed everyone except his administrative staff.

They were discussing the procurement of more stone and

timber for the construction work when Lieutenant George Wilson strode in and braced, throwing a salute. He was red-faced and blinking, his jaws furred with stubble.

"At ease, mister. What's the news?"

"Black Hawk has been taken, sir."

A murmur ran around the table.

"That's welcome intelligence, Mr. Wilson. Where is he?"

"On his way here, sir—and no credit of mine. Pair of Winnebago headmen, One-Eyed Decori and Chaetar, captured the old beggar."

"Those two? They're supposed to be friends of his."

Wilson grinned. "I'd guess, sir, that General Street's threat to cut off the Winnebagos' government annuities bears on their sudden cooperation. In any case, they arrived at the Dells ahead of us. You know what a bloody rabbit warren the place is. All sandstone cliffs, ravines, chimney rocks, and the like. Couldn't scare up a bloody elephant if he hid there. As it chanced, the old man spotted 'em coming from the cave where he'd hidden and came out to greet 'em as friends. They seized him and his companions, including the old beggar's son and The Prophet. Were on their way here when we met 'em. They were slowed by the sick ones, so I came ahead to tell you. Their party should arrive in three to four hours."

"Good, all right; go clean up, Mr. Wilson."

Taylor began pacing up and down, hands clasped behind him. Scott's remarks still rasped in his craw; Black Hawk's capture could be the stroke that would recoup his fortunes. The occasion demanded a ceremony, a bit of drama really, that would make it an historic event.

"Mr. Davis, my compliments to General Street and tell him the news; ask that he join me at once for a consultation. Then hunt up that trapper acquaintance of yours, what's his name, Robier, and ask if he'll serve as interpreter at a full-dress council . . ."

The flurry of preparations went on all morning. Taylor

204

personally oversaw as much of it as he could. He was standing on the porch of his office, casting a critical eye over the general fatigue detail as it policed the parade ground, when Lieutenant Gibbs stepped up and saluted smartly.

"May I speak to you, sir—privately?"

Taylor gave him a careful scrutiny. Gibbs's mouth quivered with a pale strain. He wore the staggered, uncomprehending look of a man who had been belly-kicked by a mule.

"Certainly, my boy. Let's step inside."

They entered the stone-walled coolness of the sergeant major's office, went past the busy row of clerks and into the colonel's office, a large room containing a desk, two chairs, a map table and, on staffs in opposite corners, the American flag and the regimental colors. Taylor closed the door, seated himself behind his desk and motioned Gibbs to the other chair.

"Thank you, sir, I prefer to stand. I wish to request a transfer from this post."

"Damn it, boy, don't be proud with a man who jogged you on his knee when you were a tad. Sit down . . . you've spoken to Knoxie, I take it."

"Yes, sir." Gibbs stared blindly at the wall. "Couldn't sleep last night after dinner and . . . what was said. Thought I'd see her first chance I had today. She has rejected my suit. You knew?"

Taylor nodded. He pouted at his steepled thumbs. Damn all females and their everlasting caprice. He and Whelan Gibbs had habitually discussed their children's union as though it were ordained. He knew that Denny had spoken with his father of the possibility of resigning his commission and getting into the cotton export trade. Taylor and the elder Gibbs, mutually pleased by this choice of a lucrative career, had quietly agreed to pool resources and stake the lad to his start. New Orleans, of course; all the activity was there, and the children and grandchildren would be a pleasant river journey away. So much for dreams.

"I'm sorry about this, my boy. As to the transfer." Taylor

paused. He was no coddler of bruised souls, but as a man he could sympathize. "I can put through a request, for reasons of health, let us say, and approve your transfer if it comes through. But that will take months. An earlier departure might be arranged . . ."

"How, sir?"

"General Scott has asked that I review the qualifications of my younger subalterns for a certain job. Seems enlistments have fallen off and the Army wants officers with frontier experience assigned to the posts of itinerant recruiters in the East and South. They'll stump from town to town and sing paeons to the service. Especially the charms, should you chance to think of any, of serving on the border. The recruiter must be young, energetic, personable, persuasive. And prepared to work his tail off."

"Thank you, sir." Gibbs wore the look of a man freed from the rack.

"Thank my abiding faith in the grand Yankee anodyne called work. You'll start for Fort Winnebago directly the adjutant has your papers ready. Thence to Green Bay and Buffalo, and on to Washington City. Suggest you go over to Rolette's post and see if you can engage a *voyageur* to take you up the Wisconsin. If one is obliging, no reason you can't start out this afternoon." He rose and extended his hand. "Good luck, my boy."

"Thank you again, sir."

Gibbs saluted, about-faced and started for the door. Halted and turned hesitatingly. "Sir. Do you think—would you know whether it's serious with Sarah Knox and Mr. Davis?"

"Not as I see it. What did she say?"

"Well, nothing, sir, really. Nothing definite. Naturally I asked . . . thought I might have been turned down for that reason. But she seemed quite vague on the matter and I'm not sure . . ."

Taylor snorted to cover his sudden gust of doubt. "Neither

is Sarah Knox. She has some growing-up to do, that's all . . ."

After Gibbs had gone, he pushed back his chair, stood and circled his desk, hands clasped at his back. Had he too hastily assumed, on the basis of past performance, that the thing with Davis was another fool flirtation? He'd taken Knox's silence for a negative; now he remembered that Ann had never defied him to his face either. She had simply eloped with Bob Wood at the first opportunity.

Damned if he'd let that particular lightning strike twice.

He hadn't liked Davis on first acquaintance; Taylor was Old Army, with a built-in bias against West Pointers. Davis's meticulous habits of dress and grooming had suggested a light-weight popinjay. That he'd turned out the opposite—impetuous yet rock-stubborn, ready to storm hell if you told him not to—had won Taylor over completely. Without liking his aide a jot less, he suddenly saw those same qualities sweeping an indecisive girl off her feet. Good thing if he could get Davis away from Prairie du Chien awhile . . . see how Knoxie responded. Trouble was, all the outside jobs pending had been assigned.

He thumped a fist on the desk. Damn all female children! If God Almighty hadn't put 'em in the world specifically to plague a man, why had he gotten three? Not to mention a bonus of one Army son-in-law and now the rearing threat of another . . .

Toward noon Taylor sent Man-Who-Walks to check on the progress of Black Hawk and his captors. The Winnebago returned shortly, saying that the party would arrive when the sun was highest. Taylor ordered the garrison assembled on the parade. He stood by the flagstaff in the parade's northeast corner and ran a satisfied eye over the companies smartly ranked in muster formation before their quarters. Splendid in full-dress: dark blue coatees and white crossbelts, white drill trousers, bell-crowned shakos bristling with snowy ponpons, red facings, white trimmings. Line officers in white waistbelts, tall jackboots and gleaming spurs flanked their companies. The staff officers, standing to Taylor's left, had exchanged their service sabers for straight dress swords slung from black waistbelts. The color sergeants stood out proudly, the blue silk flag with the U. S. Arms vying with the distinctive colors of the regimental flag.

To Taylor's right was General Joseph Street, U. S. Agent for Indian Affairs, florid and neat in a tall wool hat, plum-colored double-breasted coat and yellow nankeen trousers. Vitelle Robier stood at Street's right. His old-fashioned suit of black broadcloth, wrinkled from long storage, gave his stocky frame a false portliness so that he resembled a stout tradesman. A handful of civilian onlookers, townsmen, *voyageurs,* a few Indians, had gathered in front of the sutler's.

Where the hell were those redskins! The midday heat had made a sweatbox of the colonel's new coatee, the high collar grooving into his underchin; his feet began to hurt. Ah, there they were . . .

Black Hawk was approaching the open west gate, flanked by his captors. Worn and unbent, he was gaunt almost to emaciation, and he walked straight as a war arrow. He and two other prisoners were brought through the gate and across the quadrangle, guarded by musket-armed Winnebagos. At a command from Taylor, two soldiers exited from the guardhouse with a big robust Indian: Black Hawk's sullen fiery lieutenant, Neapope.

Taylor had seen Black Hawk up close before, but the Sac leader's slight stature always surprised him. Meagerly built, he stood six inches above five feet. He wore a suit of white buckskin, a bright blanket flung about his shoulders; the feathered skin of a sparrow hawk dangled at his side. His coppery high-browed dome was plucked except for a coarse plume of scalplock adorned with eagle feathers, each ear rimmed by a row of silver baubles. The skin of his face was taut and unlined with a great beak of a nose, his cheekbones as high and heavy as a Mongol lord's. The deep hollows beneath gave his mouth a pinched, compressed look.

The Prophet was over six feet tall, powerfully built; he wore his long hair in a turban and was conspicuous for the black mustache bisecting his fleshy face. His deep-set eyes suggested at once the Oriental and the savage, the ascetic and the sensualist. The third prisoner was Black Hawk's son, Whirling Thunder, a younger image of his father.

Black Hawk looked at Taylor and spoke.

Robier translated: "Ma-ka-tai-me-she-kia-kiak says, this time it is the eagle chief who has won."

An unsubtle allusion to a rankling incident of another war. "A whole army did the job," Taylor said curtly. "Nobody won."

Robier spoke in Sac; Black Hawk gave a slight, austere nod. Agent Street complimented his Winnebago captors in their own tongue. One-Eyed Decori, who had lost an eye and wore a black silk handkerchief over the socket, said: "My father, you said that if we brought before you these two, Ma-ka-tai-me-she-kia-kiak and Wa-bo-kie-shiek, the dark cloud that hangs over your Winnebagos would lift. Our people are more to us than our friends, but this thing has turned our hearts bad. If they are to be done harm, then first let us go from here." Chaetar, the younger headman, added: "My father, Wa-bo-kie-shiek, The Prophet, is my kinsman. You know, therefore, what a thing we have done. Will the Grandfather's word be kept? Will Black Hawk and The Prophet come to no harm?"

Street replied, then interpreted the exchange for Taylor's benefit: "My children, I am pleased. You have delivered these men to me; I deliver them to this eagle chief who shall direct that they be taken down the Father of Waters to Rock Island, where the chief of all paleface warriors will use them in such fashion as the Grandfather orders. But I have spoken with the tongue of the Grandfather; all that was promised you shall be."

What the Winnebago Judases had been promised was that their own clans would be spared whatever punishment was meted out to Winnebagos at large because some few had aided the Sacs. Black Hawk spoke, his eyes like black holes in a copper mask: "Three times we, the People of the Yellow Earth, sought to give up our weapons and surrender to the Long Knives. First at Old Man's Creek near the Rock River. The Long Knives fired on us and ran away when a few Sacs charged them. Again at the Heights of the Wisconsin, Neapope called out that if the Sacs were permitted to return across the Father of Waters, they would throw down their arms and make peace. The Long Knives did not answer. Finally, at the Father of Waters, when we saw the great war canoe on the water and made the sign of peace, a cannon was fired upon us."

"It was you who broke the treaty," Street countered. "Why did you cross to lands that were no longer yours?"

Black Hawk replied with an old man's crotchety quickness: "I did not put my mark to those pale skins that were signed by old woman like Keokuk, whose bellies were sick with your whiskey. Only one that I was tricked into signing. I gave you Saukenuk, the land of my fathers, for a smile and a trinket and a lie. Gitchee-Manitou made a world for the white man and placed him there; for the red man, he made another world. When is it meet that one should take that which is the other's? The pale skins are of your making; my people do not understand them. Knowing this, you made bargains that took all and gave nothing. But if we had not given you whites the land, you would have taken it with guns. What you do not seize with guns, you sicken with whiskey. You do not scalp the head, you poison the heart."

The conference went on for a couple of hours, along with Black Hawk's recriminations. Taylor found the bitter recital tiresome. He had tried (by his own lights) to be fair with the Indians when he had sat in their councils, he had dispassionately redressed some wrongs done them. All without a jot of sympathy. Maybe they didn't understand the treaties, but they had put their marks to them in knowing ignorance; maybe the snakehead had befuddled them, but nobody forced them to drink it. He himself had cracked down savagely on the whiskey peddlers, but the red man's ways of slaking his thirst at the white man's trough were devious and inexhaustible. There was justice in Black Hawk's tirade, but how to couch a nation's march of empire in any moral terms? He remembered what Senator Thomas Hart Benton had told him: right or wrong, America's sense of her supremacy on this continent was irresistible and irreversible: her manifest destiny. Crushing Black Hawk had closed the last chapter on the red man's power east of the Mississippi. Only the Seminoles of Florida still held forth in their everglades, and it wasn't the same; America's destiny was westward . . .

The caucus ended; Taylor ordered the hot, stiff, tired companies dismissed and the four Sac leaders taken to the guardhouse. The rest of Black Hawk's party joined their fellows in the stockade. As he was issuing the orders, he noticed that Lieutenant Robert Anderson was sweatily pale, gulping wretchedly, and holding his stomach.

"Are you sick, Bob?"

"Not really, sir. Bit under the weather."

"The weather's fine, your color isn't. Get over to the hospital before you collapse. Mr. Davis, go with him."

He was sitting in his office laboring over a report when Davis returned from the hospital. Beaumont had quickly diagnosed the attack as cholera, no way of saying yet how serious. Taylor glumly hoped that this didn't presage another outbreak. He remembered that he'd assigned Anderson to take the Sac prisoners down to Armstrong.

He almost smiled, gazing across his steepled fingers at Davis. "I have a little job for you, mister."

15

Next morning, while an amethyst flare of sunrise still burned away a mist curling off the water, Davis supervised the loading of his human cargo. They filed onto the boat, forty emaciated Sacs limping with illness and half-healed wounds, forty tired, silent men held to be firebrands ready to incite again. Taylor had accompanied the special guards that escorted Black Hawk and his son, The Prophet and Neapope, to the dock. He spoke to both Davis and the *Winnebago*'s captain, warning them not to dally long at any landing.

"No need to put in for supplies," he said. "We've loaded enough pickled beef, salt pork, and corn meal to last you a half-dozen such trips. You'll have to make regular stops for fuel, but most places it's cut and stacked by the banks. Prisoners in this condition should give you no trouble. All the same, Mr. Davis, keep a lookout posted by night and a heavy guard at all times. Always a possibility of a boarding attempt by the Hawk's friends or foes."

Roustabouts wrestled aboard tag ends of cargo; they hauled in the plank. The *Winnebago* paddle-washed into the main channel, its twin stacks belching a murky curtain against the topaz dawn. Davis leaned against the rail of the lower deck, watching Prairie du Chien fall slowly astern.

A white flutter caught his eyes. A girl stood on a knoll well off the bank, a breeze toiling with her light dress; she waved. He'd have waved back, but Taylor was still watching from the landing. He was glad Knox had come to see him off, even if from a knoll where she was cut off from her father's view.

Davis was sure of her feelings now, but her continued vacillation depressed him. Where had all that temperamental spunk gone? She'd objected vehemently when he'd suggested that they make clear to the colonel their intention to wed. Not till time was right, she'd insisted. When would that be? She didn't know. He remembered Taylor's dry relish when he'd ordered him to replace Anderson on this mission. The oblique point: it would separate him from Knox awhile at a time when their relationship was still on shaky ground.

At least the thorn of Denny Gibbs was out of his side; Gibbs had departed yesterday on his recruiting stint. George Wilson, who'd seen Gibbs off, had told him that Denny had volunteered. At their rendezvous last night, Knox had said she'd told Gibbs she wouldn't marry him. Davis was sorry for him. But not that he was gone.

He kept his eyes on Knox as she shrank to a figurine, finally hidden as the *Winnebago* passed behind an island. He sighed and watched white-breasted swallows dart across the sloughs, skimming for water bugs.

He tried to fix on a brighter side. Except for the usual hazards of river travel, breakdown of engines, collision with snags, hangups on shifting sandbars, he should have no trouble delivering his cargo. For the present, the Sacs themselves were no concern; they were interned in a large cabin with guards at the door. The duty was really a prestigious feather in the cap of the officer who drew it. Rightfully, with his seniority, it should have gone to Bob Anderson whose onset of cholera had proved mild after the first rapid symptoms.

For a time he lost himself in the Mississippi's primordial beauty. Between Prairie du Chien and Dubuque, its tan-stained azure was so crammed with side sloughs and wilderness islands that the main channel was almost lost. On the east banks, the hills fell back in easy emerald undulations; forest crowded the shore. On the west side, the bluffs rose vertically from the sloping banks at the edge, towering up to seamed graystone battlements striated by ancient glaciers, crumbled and smoothed by time. He loved the big river; his life had always been tied up with it one way or the other. Here in the North, it was a link to the homeland he loved even more. As a child, he had played along its banks. At the age of nine, returning from St. Thomas Boys School in Kentucky, he had ridden the *Aetna,* one of the three first steam-propelled crafts on the Mississippi. An experience that still ranked as the biggest thrill of his life . . .

With Sergeant Champeau handling such details as feeding the prisoners and seeing to the guard change, Davis found himself with little to do but occasionally look in on his charges, read or nap in the small cabin he shared with Vitelle Robier who had agreed to come as interpreter, chat with him or the captain, or just stand on the hurricane deck and drink in the river. All was pleasant as far as the Fever River; they put into its narrow channel a short distance in order to reach Galena.

Somehow word of the *Winnebago*'s passenger list had come ahead.

Davis worriedly surveyed the mob spilling off the wharf and along the banks. Most seemed merely curious, but here and there clots of well-armed citizens mingled with the general throng. The roustabouts threw out hawsers which were secured by men on the dock; the plank was run into position. Davis assembled his troops on the lower deck and gave Champeau an order. The men covered the rail with a bristling line of muskets and bayonets.

"Be blamed. How-de-do, sojer boy!"

He'd have known that cavernous drawl among a million. And picking out Rafer Beal's flaming hair was easy. Naturally he was at the front of a bellicose group. Davis smiled and raised a hand.

"How 'bout leaving us step aboard for palaver?" Beal called. "Am honing for a friendly word with that bloody ole buzzard."

"I'll bet you are," Davis shouted back. "No visitors this trip." He directed his next words to the hurricane deck overhead. "Captain, tell your men to hurry. Sooner we get out of here, the better."

"Aye, Lieutenant. Shake your skids, you hearties!"

Davis was half-certain of trouble as the roustabouts filed down the plank and pushed a lane through the crowd on the wharf. The general mood, though, seemed tractable, half-bantering, seasoned by an unbearable curiosity. Some restless muttering as the crowd realized it wouldn't be permitted a glimpse of the prisoners. The roustabouts proceeded quickly with the loading.

A bad moment came when someone on shore fired a gun. "Steady," Davis said sharply to his men. The tension dissolved when someone loudly commented that Lando Beauchamp had accidentally shot off his rifle, narrowly missing his big toe. Laughter. The tableau relaxed.

Loading finished, the *Winnebago* cast off and steamed back toward the Mississippi. Davis's innards uncoiled; he gave Champeau a casual nod: "All right, Sergeant. Dismiss the men . . ."

Farther down the Mississippi, the gray limestone bluffs tapered lower to the banks. The forest opened to stretches of prairie splashed with the paisley brilliance of August blossoms. The farther south they went, the less chance of an incident. Davis had the Sacs brought up from the cramped quarters. He gave them the freedom of the deck, posting only a few guards along the rails. The poor, diseased, skeletal creatures were too weak either to overcome their guards or to escape by swimming.

It was easy to pity them. The slaughter of the Bad Axe would brand his dreams all his life, Davis thought. And its aftermath.

Bob Anderson kneeling in the muck of a pothole cradling a tiny Indian girl in his arms, her starved body clinging to a festering life, the red-raw ivory of splintered bone projecting from the ruin of one arm. And the volunteers who carved two long vertical slits in the backs of dead or dying Indians and tore the strips of skin from still-quivering flesh to be cured for razor straps. At the same time, at Barrett's Ferry on the Wisconsin, troops had ambushed the raftloads of sick and weakened Sacs that Black Hawk had sent downriver after the Wisconsin Heights battle. They had killed fifteen, then upset the rafts and drowned the rest. God! Honor at the Bad Axe. The honor of murderers and butchers.

Black Hawk was speaking with Robier; the two approached Davis.

"Ma-ka-tai-me-she-kia-kiak wants to thank the young chief for his kindness."

"Tell him it is my pleasure," Davis said, "and ask him to answer a question, if he will. The Long Knives had him outnumbered many times over. At the end his band was dying on its feet. He must have known from the first that he stood no chance. Ask him . . . why?"

Robier translated to Black Hawk, who replied:

"He asks what the young chief would do if he were head of a nation and a people who were much stronger said, 'Now your land is ours—now you must live our way—now you must do like we say.' Would he tell his people not to fight, not to take up arms for their land, because they would only throw away their lives?"

Davis smiled. "That will never happen, thank God! Tell him I would do as he did. But I cannot say why."

Black Hawk made a brief reply. Robier smiled and turned to Davis. "He says that is because the heart speaks, not the head."

The sun had heeled deeply west as the *Winnebago* ap-

216

proached Rock Island. Banners of magenta and lemon stained the water; the evening cry of a whooping crane dovetailed into the dry chittering of crickets. Black Hawk stood by the rail, his face an austere bronze cameo as his ancestral home grew into view. A home to which he was returning as prisoner. Beyond the parks of slopes and big trees lay his town of Saukenuk whose more than a hundred lodges had been burned, the fields laid waste, by encroaching settlers. He spoke once, as the island wheeled past their bow.

" 'This is sacred ground,' " Robier translated. " 'The bones of our dead lie here.' "

Fort Armstrong crowned a low stony cliff at the south end of Rock Island, its Western blockhouses commanding a miles-long view of the river. Its whitewashed walls were yellow in the glazed light.

"M'sieu," Robier exclaimed softly, "I think we will not stop here. Look."

He pointed at a dead tree projecting from the bluff. On it hung a pennon of bright cloth: an unmistakable cholera flag warning river traffic not to put in. Davis went up to the wheelhouse and told the pilot to hold the *Winnebago* offshore. General Scott should send out an order relative to their next move.

Shortly a skiff put out from shore, two bearded men in buckskin handling the oars. Davis had no trouble identifying the big man in uniform who sat between them. "Old Fuss and Feathers" himself. Black serpents of shadow that coated the river writhed and broke to the skiff's passage. It halted off their bow. Brevet Major General Winfield Scott raised his stern bitter face, scanning the men at the rail. A craggy giant in his mid-forties, he stood six feet four inches; his coatee was bedizened with medals and fancy braid.

"The devil! Isn't that Black Hawk?"

"Yes, sir," Davis said.

"So he's taken. Good! Assume you're in charge of the prisoners . . . er, Taylor's aide, aren't you?"

"Davis, sir."

"Well, Mr. Davis, I'm afraid you'll have to backwater with them. Cholera's raging so virulently here, we've had to suspend all communication with other posts and camps." The wrinkled worry in his face gave Scott the look of a harassed eagle. "Two thirds of the garrison is down . . . men are dying every hour of the day and night."

"I'm sorry to hear that, sir. What of the treaty council?"

"Called off till God knows when. The Indians are dropping like flies wherever a tribe's been touched . . . no time to be treating with the beggars."

"Shall I return Black Hawk and his companions to Fort Crawford, sir?"

"No. I want them taken down to Atkinson at Jefferson Barracks. He'll have the care of them till we decide what to do with them. Which won't be till Governor Reynolds and I get this damned council convened. How are your supplies holding up, mister?"

The *Winnebago* steamed south toward St. Louis. The bluffs dropped away to humpy contours of forest and meadow broken by alluvial marsh flats. Sycamores were pale pen-strokes against hills of gray sedge grass. Crude log cabins and ragged acres grubbed from the dark timber were still common, but painted farmhouses and tidy fields also dotted the east bank.

On the morning of the day they should reach Jefferson Barracks, Davis was congratulating himself that altogether things hadn't gone so badly, when Robier cracked his complacency. The trapper suggested that he look at a couple of the Indians.

A look was enough. The two young Sacs were burning up with fever, their abdomens distended and tender. They admitted to night-long sieges of vomiting; agonizing cramps were creeping through their bellies and legs. Davis isolated both cholera victims toward the stern and did what he could to alleviate their misery. Both were hopeless cases, that was plain; he only prayed that the seizures wouldn't prelude a boat-wide outbreak.

"Vitelle, ask the poor devils if there's anything they wish of us."

One youth was already unconscious. Robier spoke to the other. The boy whispered a dry febrile reply.

"He says that he and his friend must be put ashore. So not to make danger for the rest. I think it is wise; soon they die."

It was the only practical course, but the order was hard to give. The plank was run out to a sandbar protruding from the bank, the two youths and their belongings carried quickly ashore with provisions and water. The steamboat churned back toward the main channel. Sacs crowded the rail, watching in silence. The conscious youth struggled to a sitting position, then half-lifted his friend and cradled his head. He swayed back and forth, chanting in a weak low rhythm. The death song ebbed gradually into the distance.

Davis leaned against the rail, staring at the *Winnebago*'s creaming wake. Robier moved up beside him, produced a stone pipe with a long reed stem and chewed it meditatively.

"Don't think too much about it, m'sieu. That is foolish."

"You're a cynic, Robier."

"Non. A realist. And you are the romantic, eh? Long ago, at the school in Ottawa, I learn' many good English words. You and Black Hawk are alike, my fine young soldier. That is a good one, eh?"

"I admire him for fighting for what he believed. I suppose by your lights, that is foolish too."

Robier shrugged his comma-tufted brows. "A man is as he is. Black Hawk fought a fight he could not win. Because of this, many died. Still, that is nature. Only man makes battles. Man and some ants. But there is war always. The tree takes the sun and its little neighbor dies. *Voilà tout.*"

Would he be so philosophical, Davis wondered, if he knew about his son? Several times he had come close to telling him;

219

he'd told himself he must wait for the right time. Why was it so damned hard?

After the Bad Axe battle, he had found Jean Robier among the dying. What had the young half-breed been looking for when he joined Black Hawk's last fight? Davis did not know. He had spoken to the boy. His only reply had been a look of unquenchable hatred. He lay dying on the wet earth, his white war plumes stained red, proud as an Aztec prince, undefeated even in defeat.

Davis was still tempted to keep silence. Robier need never be sure; for all he might ever know, the son he'd been unable to tame could have escaped into the Trans-Mississippi with other survivors looking for a life far from the white man's rule. But intuition told him that was wrong; the gnawing doubts would never be stilled.

"Vitelle," he said slowly. "There's something . . ."

Twenty-five miles above St. Louis, the fat wild snake of the Missouri River vomited a torrent of yellow-red mud into the Mississippi blue. The Missouri's voracious mouth was eating southward year by year, its racing silt turning the big river ocher-yellow clear down to the gulf. Nine miles below St. Louis lay Jefferson Barracks, training headquarters for the Army's Department of the West. Davis had pleasant memories of his brief stay there before he was transferred to the North. General Atkinson had been an easygoing commander and his Louisville-born wife had made the officers' barracks into a delightful home. Davis usually disliked cities, but St. Louis had been different with its pleasure-loving yet genteel flavor of old France.

Twilight was thickening as the steamer pulled toward the landing. Davis felt the wash of memory, watching the buildings grow to view on gentle rises cloaked by stately groves of oak and hickory. Stationed here four years ago, he had enjoyed letting a good horse out at a gallop through those groves. He glanced toward Black Hawk standing on the lower deck, his slight form muffled in a blanket. He stood alone and watched a golden sky electric with freedom. Wild swans trumpeted; hawks dropped on silent wings and arched upward, their wild whickers ringing across the water.

Freedom, Davis thought. What else is there for a man?

The steamer was made fast at the dock, the plank run out. Davis went ashore to arrange for the disembarking of the prisoners. In twenty minutes, he returned to the boat accompanied by General Atkinson, a party of officers and a company of well-armed troops.

The general said: "You and your men will be quartered and fed, Mr. Davis, till transportation upriver is arranged. Er, aren't you friendly with my aide, Mr. Johnston?"

"Yes, sir, Sid is my closest friend. I was wondering where . . . ?"

"Well, he is down with the cholera."

"Sir—not seriously?"

"Fortunately, no. He's coming along well, the surgeon says. The plague hasn't struck seriously here, but of course the hospital is under quarantine for the present." Atkinson lowered his voice. "However, I might mention that Mr. Johnston's cot is conveniently near the northeast corner window which is open to reduce the forbidding atmosphere."

"Thank you, sir."

The troops marched in two columns onto the dock. At a command, both lines wheeled to face one another and came smartly to attention. The officers strode through the six-foot lane between them and up the boat plank, followed by a sergeant and a half-dozen privates trudging under a weight of balls and chains. "I want these four men shackled, Sergeant." Atkinson pointed in turn at Black Hawk and Whirling Thunder, The Prophet and Neapope.

The four men stood silently as the heavy balls were fettered to their legs. Then Black Hawk spoke. Robier interpreted: "I am an old man. Where does White Beaver fear I will run to, that he chains me like his dog?"

"Sir," Davis said, "is it necessary to—"

"What do you think, mister? This old devil put us to vast trouble and expense fortifying the border and putting thousands of troops under arms. He has destroyed, I should hazard, something over three million dollars in property. He'll have no opportunity to repeat a fling that has cost well over a thousand lives, including eight hundred of his own people."

So he'll be blamed for those too, Davis thought with a bitter weariness. Thank God this job was done; he had hated it.

As soon as he could, he went to the hospital. Albert Sidney Johnston was quarantined at the northeast corner of the hospital ward. They had no trouble carrying on a conversation through the window. Poor Sid was wrapped from neck to foot in heavy wool blankets, his pillow soaked with sweat. He gave Davis a strained grin. "I was drenched with both vinegar and salt before being trussed up to baste. Am also being dosed every hour on the hour with brandy laced by cayenne peppers. In a few days, I am told, I will be allowed a draught of chicken soup. With luck, I may survive both nature and the surgeons."

They talked about the war; Davis mentioned the shacklings.

"Don't be too harsh on the Old Man," Johnston said. "He's in a hell of a stew. The campaign's already been adjudged a mass of blunder and mismanagement. The Old Man's abiding fault is an overcautious streak that makes him an ideal sacrificial ox. A lot of people are to blame, but when the armchair generals in Washington City begin casting about for a scapegoat, the whole ax will drop on his neck . . ."

Davis couldn't really give a damn. He felt disgusted, used up, unutterably tired. All he wanted was to get back to Prairie du Chien. To Knox.

222

16

"Finis . . . Finis. How did you ever come by such a name?"

"It's only a middle name."

"Well, how?"

Knox lay on her stomach in the dry grass, propped up on her elbows and chewing a straw. Davis lay beside her on his back, fingers laced behind his head and eyes closed. The volumes of poetry he had brought along—Shakespeare and Burns and Keats—lay untouched in the grass beside them. Knox took the straw from her mouth and poked at his chin.

"C'mon."

"Oh, Mother was past forty-five when she bore me. They were going to call me Thomas Jefferson Davis, but as it seemed unlikely that she'd bear more children, made it Jefferson Finis Davis instead."

"Oh."

"Expect something dramatic?"

Knox rolled lazily on her back. The sun was warm on her face; a buttery October haze drenched the prairie. Veed in mysterious telepathic grace, a flight of geese honked their way southward. The smell of dry grass and earthrot was like wine. Or aphrodisiac.

"I dunno . . . I was curious. We don't talk very much."

"Well, isn't it all said?"

"I'd think there's more to getting to know one another than hugging and spooning."

She had to smile, thinking back on stolen hours of the past two months. There wasn't much room for talk when the turbulence of young blood almost overpowered you . . . when halting intimacies by lips and hands lent a wonder and quickness to the passing time. A lot of foolish murmured nothings, yes. But nothing serious.

"Anyway I'm curious. I was visiting in the village the other day and one of the ladies showed me a great clumsy cabinet she called a 'Davis'—"

He chuckled. "Carpentry is a pastime of mine. Some wag dubbed the unspectacular fruits of my labor 'Davises.'"

"A man of many parts. See, I've been making queries relative to you, Lieutenant. Bob Anderson told me you 'get off steam' by riding what he calls 'crazy horses.' Claims you've been like to break your neck sometimes—"

"Guilty. What else have you heard?"

"Oh, that you nearly broke records in demerits achieved at West Point."

He cocked one eye open. "Where did you hear that?"

"I just heard."

"Gibbs, I'll bet."

"Never you mind; is it true?"

"I'll have you know I was an honor student at Transylvania University. West Point was different."

She turned toward him on her side, bracing her chin on her fist. "Different how?"

"I wanted to be a lawyer. The idea set poorly with Pa. He used to say that lawyers would circumvent God. Then, he had quite a strong feeling about the country, had fought in the Revolution and helped put legs under us so to speak—"

"Aren't you pretty young to have had a father in the Revolution?"

"He was eighteen in '76. Anyway he used his influence on Congressman Rankin of the lower district of Mississippi to wangle me a commission to the U. S. Military Academy. I was unhappy about it because I was anticipating my senior year at Transylvania, and I wanted to go on to the University of Virginia. My brother Joe stressed the honor of the commission, only one of every thirty applicants accepted, et cetera, and finally prevailed by promising to send me to Virginia if I were still dissatisfied at the end of my plebe year. Then Pa died, and suddenly it was a matter of duty. I accepted the commission three days later. Rather bitterly. I excelled in very little besides French, rhetoric, and carousing."

"I'd have guessed as to the French. Ceclie Robier, h'm?"

"Dead issue."

"I hope so." She stabbed his cheek with the straw. "As to those other two fields, what about all the rest of the girls?"

"What girls? Cadets are forbidden. All our carousing was done at Benny Havens's groggery."

"Aha, which is also forbidden." She tweaked his ear. "Sly dog."

"Stop that. Remember what your father said, you're supposed to let me alone."

"I'll let you alone!"

She seized his hair in both hands and yanked, then scrambled away, laughing. He rolled quickly closing a hand over her loose-coiled mass of hair. Already disarranged, it tumbled like brown silk over his hand. Suddenly all playfulness was wiped from the moment and their bodies were clasped, their lips fused. He pulled his mouth away and looked at her a moment, her head pillowed on her hair, her lips parted. He sat up and locked his arms around his knees.

She lay unmoving, the blood thundering in her veins. The sky swam on a cobbled fleece of clouds; the sun-splashed prairie bristled with goldenrod. Her breasts felt unbearably sensitized, tip-tingling, so that even a slight movement caused

225

the soft material of her chemise to chafe them. It was always the same when they were together: desire gusting through her like raw flame. And she had no idea whether it was the same with the man she loved. They didn't talk about such things. Jeff and his bright, bright honor. What could you say about that?

She sat up and began arranging her hair. The meadow to which they'd come was surrounded by hardwood stands bannering with fall color. Sugar maples cloaked in scarlet deathfire. Quaking aspen and pale birch shrouded in rustling gold discs, the coinage that bought winter sleep. Betty and Dick were playing in the trees; their shouts rang with quick young life. Her pulse slowed; the mundane miracle of fall again fleshed her day with simplicity. She smiled at her man, lying back with his cap tilted over his eyes. She remembered how, at first, she'd clung stubbornly to her theory that they were both too willful to be happy together.

"It just won't work," she'd argued.

And he'd laughed, saying, "Do you think I want a little milk-faced mouse without her proper share of spirit? I've never cared for that kind of woman and I never will."

"But we'll have quarrels. Some terrible ones."

"I'm sure."

She could smile, remembering. You've met your match, Knox Taylor. What's more you like it.

"Speaking of him," Davis said lazily.

"Of who?" Though she knew perfectly well.

"Your beloved sire. When do we tell him?"

"Well, I don't think I'd approach him just now. You know his mood of late. Even Ma has never seen him so irascible. He wanted that brigadiership so much, and . . ."

"I know all about that." He raised the cap off his eyes. "What I really want to know is, why are you afraid of him?"

"Oh rubbish, I'm not!" A smile touched his lips; she fidgeted. "Oh, I suppose I am . . . in a way."

"Why?"

"I . . . I don't know. I hardly even know him. Perhaps that's the reason. I grew up on Grandpa Taylor's estate outside of Louisville. As far back as I can remember, Pa was usually away . . . shuffled from one border post to the next. Except on those rare occasions when we'd pack up the china and the furniture and join him, we'd rarely see him for more than a month at a time. He was ill for two years before this current assignment . . . spent them with us at our First Street home in Louisville. It was like living with a stranger. You know how he is anyway . . . gruff and remote most of the time. When he's around, I still feel as I did when I was a little girl."

"How's that?"

"How do you feel about God? I mean that grim one in the Old Testament?"

"I usually think of Zeus with a fistful of thunderbolts." He sat up frowning, clasping his knees. "I think it's time I talked with him again."

She felt a grain of panic. "I don't think that's wise. After what happened before . . ."

"Now or later, does it matter? From what you've told, his view won't mellow in the next ten years. The sooner he knows, the sooner he'll have to get used to the idea."

"But he doesn't have to, that's the point! He's my father and I'm under twenty-one. Defy him all we like, he can still prevent our marriage. At least, while he thinks it's over between us, we can meet this way . . ."

"Yes, tiptoeing about like a pair of sneaks. It goes against my grain. And how long can you trust children to keep a secret?"

They'd been meeting for some time through a simple contrivance. At garrison social affairs, they had the casual contacts that let them arrange more intimate rendezvous. Knox would take Betty and Dick on long walks across the woods and prairie; Davis would meet them and the children were sent off to amuse themselves.

"Oh, Jeff, you don't know my little brother. 'I won't tell *nobody,* Knoxie.' And he won't."

"What about Betty? Are you still bribing her?"

She flushed. "What else can I do? She'd tell Ma everything. Anyway, how corrupting is the gift of a worn-out shawl or a dab of rice powder?"

"On a seven-year-old's scale of values, who knows? Suppose your mother should find out. Would she tell the colonel?"

"I don't know and I shan't tempt fate, thank you."

He glumly gathered together his cap and books and got up. Knox bit her lip, watching him, then sprang to her feet and pressed herself to him, arms tight around him.

"Jeff, I know we'll have to tell him. But not yet. Please."

"The longer we put it off . . ."

"I know. But please."

"As you say."

She picked up her ribboned bonnet and brushed bits of grass from her green cassimere walking dress. He was disappointed in her. But what else could she do?

"Betts! Dickie! We're going home."

She had to call several times before they came reluctantly out of the grove. Betty had been in a vicious pet most of the day, and it had taken all of Knox's self-control not to shout at her. Betty was inexhaustibly curious and too snippety for her own good. Precocious, with the underdeveloped moral sense of any seven-year-old.

They sauntered across the prairie and down a trail through the woods, the children running ahead, pausing to tussle with each other while Knox and Davis, walking slowly hand in hand, caught up. Hard flat rays of sunset sheeted the birches in pale fire; a litter of acorn shards crunched under their feet.

"Jeff," she murmured, "won't you think some more about prospects outside the service?"

228

"Darling, I've told you, I won't be run out of the Army. That's what it would come to."

"Oh, I know. Your pride. But mightn't you resign for reasons of your own? You told me that you'd really wanted to become a lawyer . . ."

"Once. All that's changed. The service has grown on me, and I can grow with it." After a moment he added moodily: "I might resign all the same, if this South Carolina business comes to a head."

"Oh, is that fat still in the fire?"

"You ought to keep your ears open. There's a big tariff fight shaping up in the South Carolina legislature. If they rule the federal tariff laws void in that state, the President will probably send in federal troops to enforce them. You know what that will mean?"

She sighed. "I can guess."

"There are all sorts of signs these days. Garrison and his Abolitionists spouting like sperm whales, that Nat Turner business in Virginia last year, now this tariff feud. Something's coming to a head in this country, you mark me."

"Oh well, there are always wars and rumors of wars. And the rumors have it by a hundred to one. I could almost hope something does happen, if it makes you quit the Army."

"Thereby knocking your pa's reservations into a cocked hat? I doubt it would; he's a Unionist. I believe in States' rights as set forth in the Constitution. If the government marched troops against South Carolina, I'd have to resign my commission."

"Sweet Mariah!" She came to a stop. "I forgot; I told Mother that the children and I were going nutting."

"Then you'd better gather some. I have to get back for retreat."

He pressed her hand and went on down the trail. She glanced at the children. Betty wore a mulish pout. "Pish posh," she said. "I don't want to pick up nuts."

229

"Betts, please?" Knox forced herself to speak sweetly. "I did give you my figured shawl . . ."

"Can I have some of that cherry paste you put on your mouth?"

"No, you'd have it all over your face. Wouldn't you like a little more rice powder? You're pretty brown, you know."

Betty frowned and ran a finger over her cheek. "I guess so."

The three of them scoured through the groves, gathering the plentiful squirrel cuttings and windfalls of hickory nuts and black walnuts, and the fuzz-husked hazelnuts that could be pulled in sticky handfuls off low-hanging brush. Dick filled his pockets, Betty her apron; Knox added their pickings to her own in a flour sack she'd brought. They left the woods, strolling past garrison fields and orchards that were stripped of their harvest, nothing left but bare leathery cornstalks and withered squash and pumpkin vines.

The sunset gun boomed. They paused to watch the flag descend its pole while the clear notes of retreat were bugled. Knox's glance was pulled to the deserted stockade that had held the Sac prisoners. General Scott and Governor Reynolds, meeting on September 1 with leaders of the Northwest tribes, had stripped the Indians of their remaining lands south and east of the Wisconsin and Fox rivers. Because a few tribesmen had abetted Black Hawk, the Sacs and Foxes were forced to move beyond a line fifty miles west of the Mississippi and cede all their lands except for a tract of four hundred square miles. The survivors of Black Hawk's band were turned free.

The deeds were swelled, the blunders buried. It was finished.

Entering the house, they found their mother in a poor humor as she bustled about the kitchen. "You might be more considerate," she told Knox. "You know how hectic things have been of late. Putting up preserves, winter sewing, entertaining and whatnot. Couldn't you be on time to help with dinner?"

"I'm sorry, Ma. The afternoon just flew."

Knox set the table and lighted the new camphene lamp,

then helped her mother carry in the food. Margaret fretted because the colonel was late and she had roasted a saddle of venison; cold venison was no treat. While her mother's back was turned, Betty edged over to a dish of taffy and filched a piece.

"No you don't, miss," Margaret snapped without looking around. "Put it back and go wash your hands."

"Oh pish." Betty replaced the taffy and licked her thumb and finger, gazing venomously at Knox. "Mother, d'you know what Knoxie did today?"

"Betts," Knox said hastily, "wouldn't you like some cherry paste?"

"No! She's been seeing Lieutenant Davis, that's what, lots of times. She takes Dickie and me—"

"You little carrytale! I'll box your ears."

"Mother!"

"Enough of your shennanigans for one day, miss." Margaret gave Betty a brisk whack across the bottom and pointed her toward the parlor stairs. "Up to your room. Son, go wash your hands."

Betty ran tearfully up the stairs and Dick went out to the washbench. Margaret circled the table, straightening the silver beside the plates. "Cherry paste," she said bitterly. "So you've been bribing the children?"

"Only Betty. Mother—"

"*Only* Betty!"

"Mother, please don't tell Pa."

"If the young man's intentions are honorable," Margaret said crisply, "your father should already know, shouldn't he?"

"It's not Jeff's fault; he wanted to tell Pa. Can't you guess why I asked him not to?"

"He will have to know sooner or later."

"But not yet, please." Knox sank into a chair, kneading her hands together. "You know how he's been lately. Betty won't tell . . . she'll tattle to you, but never to him."

Margaret sighed. "Very well. But when he does find out, I'll be obliged to play a neutral role. You know that."

"Don't I, though. If you think he's right, you argue for him. And if wrong, you say nothing."

"Always." Margaret's voice softened; she came up behind Knox's chair and touched her hair. "Dear, I won't interfere . . . that's all I promise. It is your choice. Mine was made when I vowed to love, honor and obey your father. Once he's made a decision, he's absolutely unshakable. I learned long ago that if you disagree with Zeke, you don't prevail on him to change; you either fight him or keep still. For me, not opposing him is part of wifely duty. You stand up for your man when you can and not balk him when you can't. And lie a little to him now and then, if it saves emotional wear and tear for you both."

"I guess this comes under that category," Knox said in a brittle tone. "If you don't tell him and he finds out, he can't blame you even indirectly."

"You know better than that. I have a duty to my children as well as to my husband. No, Knoxie . . . I shan't tell him because telling him is your duty."

The colonel didn't get home till much later. Margaret had fed the children and sent them to bed. The warmed-over venison was marbled with grease, but Taylor made no complaint. He ate in silence, occupied with his own worries, and didn't even reprimand Knox for her lack of appetite. A dozen times she screwed up her courage to the point of telling him. And each time she retreated. Finally she excused herself, pleading a headache, and went up to bed.

She undressed slowly, stepping out of her garments as they rustled to the floor, dress, petticoats, shift, and pantalettes. She faced her tall mirror and studied the slim white naiad of her reflection. The taper of ankles swelling to dainty calves, the lean yet womanly thighs, the tight waist and flat belly. The dark triangular floss of womanhood and the boyish hips starting to lyre-curve with maturity. The small ivory cones, pointed and rose-spired. She had these things to give her lover. Dear God, how she wanted that. More than anything.

She was his for the asking. But he wouldn't take her outside of marriage. And he was right. It was up to her to force the issue that would defy her father's edict. And she couldn't find the courage.

She blew out the candle, crawled between the sheets and lay shivering until her body built a cocoon of warmth. She thought of Jeff; desire tingled through her veins and climbed to an ecstatic ache in her loins. She pressed her palms over her breasts, massaging the nipples till the nubs were smoothly round and hard. Oh damn your honor, Jeff, she thought suddenly, fiercely. Damn your foolish, stupid honor!

17

Mary Street hugged Davis's arm. "Isn't this fun, Jeff!"

"I suppose so," he said without conviction. "I just wish those four would hurry."

They were standing in a pool of lamplight just inside the wide doorway of Henri Aucoin's barn. The yard was a lake of frozen mud under the frosty moon; Aucoin's house lights checkered the slope beyond. Mary's oval face, framed by corn-yellow curls and a scarlet bonnet, showed plain delight. But Davis felt no happier about the new arrangements.

Since, thanks to the temperamental Betty, he and Knox could no longer meet comfortably on her walks with the children, they'd explored other means. On one evening, their friends Captain and Mrs. McRee might invite them both to dinner at their cabin; on another, Davis might call at General Joseph Street's and find Knox visiting there. At least as often, George Wilson could encounter Miss Street at the Taylor home. Street and the colonel both seemed too preoccupied to notice anything unusual, and their wives kept whatever they thought to themselves. The girls and Wilson enjoyed the clandestine spice of the conspiracy, but Davis hated even an innocent deception.

Sergeant Champeau, wiry body shapelessly muffled by the thick blankets he'd wrapped around him under his greatcoat, spoke from the seat of the big hay wagon that stood ready, the team harnessed and hitched.

"I am getting cold, Lieutenant, and have none of the sovereign remedy in pocket tonight. I hope the others come soon."

"Patience, Sergeant. Lieutenant Anderson is bringing a dram or two."

"Ah, *c'est bien!*"

Champeau, a man of parts, numbered among his soldierly accomplishments a genius for wangling the best of deals for next to nothing. As a favor to the lieutenants and their ladies, and for a modest fee plus cost, he'd managed to commandeer for tonight a wagon and a load of dry fragrant hay. He and Aucoin, whose small farm was on the outskirts of Prairie du Chien, were both of Gascony.

"Here they come," Mary said.

Two men and two girls were coming into sight, their arms linked, their laughter crisply ringing in the November night. Wilson and Knox were accompanied by Bob Anderson and Taisy Watson, the pretty and feather-brained daughter of a grogshop owner.

"Wow!" Wilson said. "I say, it's cold. But not for long, I trust."

"Corn squeezin's." Anderson lifted a double-eared jug on his gloved right thumb; a second jug dangled from his other hand. "Hard cider. Jules?"

Champeau smiled. "How does one choose between vintages so noble?" Anderson passed up the jugs and he laid one gently on the straw, pulled the cork of the other and took a pull. "*Peste!* It is not cognac, but then what is?"

With a good deal of laughter and horseplay, they climbed onto the wagon and burrowed into the straw, three couples in separate nests. Champeau took up the reins and whooped at the team. The wagon clattered across the flinty barnyard toward the beginning of the military road being laid between Forts Crawford and Winnebago. They were quite cozy: the men in greatcoats, jackboots, and fur caps, the girls in wool dresses with thickly lined skirts, warm boots, and wool bonnets. There was hay warmth and body warmth; if the man's hand strayed too far and the lady didn't mind, neither did anyone else.

"Any trouble getting away?" Davis asked.

"No." Knox laughed, nestling into the curve of his body, lips brushing his throat. "Mother was surprised, of course, when George called for me, but she knows what's afoot. Pa offered George a cigar and a drink and didn't think twice about it."

"General Street was away when I came to get Mary. I imagine Mrs. Street had your mother's thought, but nothing said."

Talk ebbed in a flood of kisses and murmurings. A long evening lay ahead, and it was a long drive to Josef Schliemann's farm. Minna, the oldest Schliemann girl, had been married today. Between wedding and bedding, there would be plenty of feasting and dancing, old Schliemann had assured the three lieutenants when he'd encountered them at Jourdonnais's taproom. *Ach,* they all must come, and the girls bring.

The wagon jolted over the stone-hard ruts and crunched through ice-crusted puddles. The night was a panorama of woods and dark earth and moonfrost. Indian summer had ended; trees stood starkly symmetrical against a hard sky. Where the timber gave way to fields, cornstalks were shocked up in spectral wigwams. A fuzz of frost rimed the prairie grass; moonsheen gave it a milky dazzle.

Davis tried to enjoy the night's beauty. But lying warm and close to Knox, his loins ached with wanting her; he couldn't put off the hot knowledge that kissing and fondling no longer sufficed. They were becoming, in fact, shattering catalysts that were spiraling his hunger out of control. He felt Knox's fierce desire like a flame; it had shocked him a little at first. She was as body-ready as he, direct as a young animal in her passion.

He doubted that he could control himself here and now, if it weren't for the others.

Damn! Why couldn't she commit herself for good and all to telling her father? At least, for better or worse, it would start things in motion. He might force her to a decision, but the forcing would come hard; she was willful enough to fight him to a last-ditch stand, and then the bitterness of her agreement would always tinge their whole relation.

Of course the colonel might find out independently: aside from confining their evenings to the activities of the villagers and farmers rather than participate in garrison amenities, they'd taken no particular safeguards. And there was always plenty to do: isolation made the border people a gregarious lot, with their house-raisings, barn dances, and husking bees.

The mood sparkled a little more as the jugs were circulated.

"Squeezin's," Wilson said wistfully. "What I wouldn't give for a jolt of good civilized redeye. Well, for these good things, we thank thee, O Lord."

"I think you're terrible," Mary said.

"So is the chill of November, m'love. Zounds; lively booze, that, Bob. How has your friend managed to shield a backwoods distillery of such potency from the colonel's vigilant eye? Anyway you'll get its warming benefits indirectly, my little mourning dove."

Mary shook her head. "You're really awful."

Taisy Watson took a small nip from a jug; Knox and Mary declined. Davis drank little, since he was to sit on a court-martial in the morning. Wilson said, "I say, either of you fellows hear any more about the South Carolina thing?"

Anderson nodded. "I understand John C. Calhoun's come up with some harebrained nullification scheme. It calls for a state convention to adopt an ordinance of nullification against the tariff. Open treason, if it comes to pass."

"Oh, I'd hardly call it that, old boy," Wilson said, "It's within a state's Constitutional rights to declare a tariff void. But it *is* a radical move."

"As radical as Old Hickory stating he'll meet nullification with force?" Davis demanded. "He's already increased the federal garrison at Fort Moultrie in Charleston."

"True," Wilson said, "but I'd heard he's asked Congress to make further revisions on the tariff. Perhaps a compromise . . ."

"George, you know that tariff law was rammed through to protect New England industry. Federal favoritism to private industry happens to be unconstitutional, besides being ruinous to the South. And Bob, no planter's son should need the principles of Jeffersonian Democracy explained to him. Not on a question of state autonomy. Or maybe we should just scrap the Constitution."

"Look, Jeff, the Constitution was drawn up three generations ago by men who had to allay a mishmash of differences between thirteen colonies. I was taught that the unity should endure, but change too, evolve with time and circumstance . . ."

"Oh, come on, Bob! Who decides what those allegedly desirable changes should be? Andrew Jackson?"

"The President isn't powerful enough to speak only for himself, Jeff; no elected official is."

"Not unless we feed him more power by yielding our own. That's what the doctrine of States' rights is designed to prevent."

"I know," Anderson said. "I just wonder how far the firebrands will carry it. To dissolution of the American Union? Dissension, disunion . . . finally civil war?"

"A state's defense of its sovereign rights," Davis snapped, "is never *civil* war."

"For God's sake, Jeff! Why do you always reduce facts to a prattle of abstractions? Can't you have the foresight to count your costs?"

"Yes—and the cost that concerns me is the loss to personal

liberty. Just how does each state fulfill the individual needs of its people once its privileges are engulfed by the leviathan maw of your infamous union?"

"Need I remind you," Anderson said icily, "that you're wearing the uniform of that infamous union?"

"To me," Davis shot back, "this uniform represents the Constitution of Jefferson and Hamilton. Something I'll not see subverted on the whim of any damned tyrant. If that's treason, make the most of it!"

A frozen silence followed.

"Good Lord," Wilson said in a soft, chagrined voice. "I only raised a topical piece for conversation! Can't you chaps go a bit easy?"

"I declare," murmured Taisy Watson. "You soldier boys do get your risibles up 'bout nothing much at all."

"I agree with Taisy," Knox said. "You two should be ashamed of yourselves."

Davis felt sheepish. "Sorry, Bob . . ."

Anderson grinned. "Me too. Pass that jug, will you?"

The incident was closed. But Davis had the shaken feeling that it wouldn't be forgotten. A few sips of border tonic and the topic itself had bared feelings that shouldn't be voiced between friends. It was like finding a fine webwork of cracks in a prized thing that had seemed shaped for all time.

The wagon swung off the rough road onto a graveled lane winding between the boles of big trees. Saffron squares of lighted windows showed ahead. Josef Schliemann's Teutonic industry and energy had hewn out of this wilderness tract a home that outdid any in the region. His house, built in a grove flanked by fields and pastures, was constructed of massive pine timbers squared and smoothed by ax and drawknife, each course jointed to the next with almost seamless precision. Beyond the house lay a well-ordered maze of barns, stables, and cattle and hog pens. The yard was filled with wagons, the teams tied to the tailgates so the animals could feed on straw in the beds.

Beaming and ruddy, Old Schliemann was at the door to welcome them. "*Ach*, it good is that you came. Schliemann likes soldiers. Welcome, welcome."

Leaving their wraps in the foyer, they entered a big festive parlor, warm and inviting. Big fireplaces of blackened limestone dominated opposite walls; instead of the usual log or puncheon furniture, there were thick, solid, graceless pieces that must have accompanied the Schliemanns from Europe. They found their way through the crowded room to a lavish buffet table; the four Schliemann girls, scrubbed and pretty in snowy puff-sleeved blouses, laced bodices and embroidered full-skirted jumpers, served them from platters of sauerkraut and rich-spiced sausages made as only the Schliemanns made them. A pale and excellent Rhine wine served with the food added a rare glow to the festivity. Soon fiddles were striking up, the bride and groom leading off the polkas and waltzes, jigs and reels.

Davis and Knox danced every set. He admired the rose-warm curve of firelight on her cheek, her hair newly dressed in high-piled curls; she had put on a little healthy flesh too. Her well-cut dress of warm brown merino emphasized her slim waist and saucy bosom. The whole effect limned a blooming poise he'd noticed in her, defining her personality more soberly yet excitingly. The signs of her increasing maturity pleased him, but he wryly wished that more of it showed in her thinking . . .

Her fingers tightened on his arm.

"Sweet Mariah . . . Jeff, look!"

Captain Tom Smith, her father's good friend, was coming their way, threading between the dancers. He was a stocky intense man with a black eyepatch and a crabbed white scar on one cheek, legacy of an arrow wound in the Creek-Seminole War. Usually gruff, he seemed mellow and a little florid from drink tonight; he cut in courteously and danced Knox away. Davis walked to a bench near the foyer and seated himself. When the dance ended, Smith returned Knox to him, bowed his thanks and walked away.

"Oh Jeff! He'll tell Pa that he saw us together."

"I doubt it; the captain's a gentleman. Anyway don't you think it's high time . . ."

At that moment Wilson and Mary danced up close beside them. Wilson murmured, "Clear for action, boy, and brace for a broadside," as he nodded toward the foyer.

Schliemann bustled over to the door. "Herr Colonel," he beamed, "my house honored is. And your good wife too? *Wunderbar.*"

"I must apologize, Mr. Schliemann," Taylor said, sweeping a metallic stare over the room. "We've declined many invitations to your home, and tonight we've come begging your hospitality uninvited."

"*Himmel!* The honor mine is, Herr Colonel. Schliemann likes soldiers."

The rotund host took their wraps; the Taylors came over to Knox and Davis. The colonel was neatly attired in black broadcloth; Mrs. Taylor was slim and handsome in a bouffant gown of pale blue satin. After a grimly polite exchange of greetings, Taylor said, "I trust you can spare a dance for your pa."

"Of course, Pa." Knox was pale, but her voice was steady. "Excuse me, Jeff."

The dancers were squaring off for a quadrille. Taylor swung his daughter into the five-figured dance with a surprising lightfooted ease, never missing a step. Davis glanced at Mrs. Taylor.

"May I get you something to eat, ma'am?"

"We've eaten. A glass of wine will do nicely, thank you."

He brought it and sat down beside her. Margaret sipped the wine and smiled. "You seem thoughtful, Mr. Davis."

"I'm thinking that the colonel is not a man to come uninvited to any social occasion, even if sure of his welcome. Unless he has a strong reason."

"Such as?"

"Such as outflanking an enemy."

"Well, if you're also thinking I told him about you and Knoxie, I didn't. The colonel is merely more aware of most matters than people realize. Then, Knoxie did say where she and Lieutenant Wilson were going tonight." She smiled a little. "Outflanking the enemy indeed!"

Davis glanced toward the floor; Knox and the colonel were trading words. He could guess at Taylor's: Had she come here with Davis? Had she been keeping company with him all this while?

"Ma'am, I'm curious as to *your* thoughts. May I speak frankly?"

"Of course."

"I'd like to know if you have any objections to me as a son-in-law. From what Knox has said, I take it that on the surface at least, you don't disapprove. Yet you won't oppose any stand of the colonel's, however wrong you think he is. How far does your wifely duty extend?"

"Don't be impudent, young man."

"I'm sorry."

"Right or wrong, I *will* stand by my husband. But as you've spoken frankly, so will I. I'm far from sure that Zeke is wrong."

"I think I understand."

"I don't believe you do. If you're thinking of the unpleasantness of last summer, that's forgotten; it was foolish of me. No, it's the matching that concerns me. You and Knoxie are too alike: self-willed, stubborn, bursting with temperament. You may curb those parts of your nature now, during courting, but will it always be so?"

"Ma'am, about myself, I'd plead guilty. But I think you're wrong about Knox. Her high spirits have toned down."

"Yes, I've noticed that. I've hoped she's growing up a little . . . but age doesn't dim a person's real fire. Look at her father!"

242

"I might wish," he said wryly, "that she'd show a bit more fire where he is concerned."

"That, Mr. Davis, is altogether different . . . as Zeke himself is different. I happen to think that he's a great man, or would be if he allowed himself to match his potential. Perhaps that's a wifely puff. But no denying that he's a very strong man. And a distant parent. A twofold fact that's stamped itself on his children's regard. They respect, almost revere him. But only the boy loves him."

"Ma'am, the colonel is a boy's kind of man."

"Yes, but of our children, Knox is the one most like her father. It's so; I know those two better than they know themselves."

Worry shaped her mouth as she gazed at her husband and daughter looping through the caracoles of the quadrille. Tension there. It lay in the colonel's jutting jaw, in Knox's bright angry eyes. Words were passing between them; taut words that locked them in a tense orbit excluding the people around them. And people were taking notice.

Knox broke off the dance and marched back to the bench, her color high. Taylor followed her, his bulldog jaw knotted with strain.

"I think," he said distinctly, "that we'd best have a private talk, all of us. Will you oblige me, Mr. Davis?"

"Gladly, sir."

Taylor beckoned Schliemann over; they spoke briefly. Then Schliemann showed the three Taylors and Davis down a corridor and into the master bedroom. Afterward he bowed himself out and closed the door. The colonel squared around to face his aide, his face mottled with temper.

"I take it that you and my daughter have seen each other regularly?"

"Irregularly is the word, sir. I did ask your permission . . ."

"By God, don't bandy words with me! You asked; do you recall my answer?"

"I do, sir. But I didn't agree not to see her again."

"True; you said nothing. What you did was take to skulking behind my back like a damned dog."

"Sir—" He stopped himself. "I won't dignify that with a reply."

"Then I will!" Knox said angrily. "Jeff wanted to tell you from the first. I insisted on his saying nothing."

"Keep still, miss; I'll have it out with you later."

"No! We'll have it all out here and now. I was afraid of you, Pa. I'm not afraid any more. I intend to marry Jeff. Until then, I'll see him when and where I please."

"Devil you will! You'll stop this damned nonsense and come home with us."

"No, Pa." She moved nearer Davis and slipped her hand into his. The hand was cold; she *was* afraid. "Jeff will take me home, and I'll see him as I choose. You can lock my door, hide my shoes, do your best. Or your worst. I'll still find a way."

"Will you?" Taylor's jaw was set like a sprung trap. "We'll see about that. I suppose you'll also emulate your sister and try to elope first chance you get. We'll see about that too!"

"We have no intention of eloping," Davis said evenly. "We mean to have your consent."

"You'll wait forever then, by God!"

"Why?" Knox said hotly. "I could understand, not forgive but understand, if there were anything objectionable in Jeff's background. But there's not. His family is respected, his brother a self-made millionaire. Is it a fault in his character or conduct? Not by your own stated opinion! Then why?"

"You've heard it a hundred damned times! I'll not see another daughter of mine consigned to a life of scrabbling and minching as an Army wife!"

"Pa, the life under discussion happens to be *mine*. Haven't I the right to decide? I've heard all your objections . . . and all that they sum up is what I've already known and lived—"

"*Nothing* is what you've known and lived!" Taylor strode

244

across the room and back as if four walls couldn't contain his intensity. "You've led an incredibly sheltered life for an 'Army brat.' On one hand, the solid comforts of your grandfather's manor and our Louisville home. On the other, the extras in prestige and comfort that my rank and outside means have assured you during a few sojourns at border posts. The worst you've had to endure—and that bad enough, to my way of thinking—is hardly knowing you have a father. Thunderation, we barely know each other! As to the price a soldier's wife pays . . . ask your mother! She's paid full coin!"

"But you've most always insisted on leaving Ma behind! I'd go where Jeff goes, I'd—"

"Fine! As to *that* course, ask your sister. What has she got besides drudgery, drafty quarters, an overworked underpaid husband, one baby and another on the way, and a miserable make-do existence?"

"She's happy, that's what matters. But she went against your almighty word, affronted your pride—"

"Knox!" her mother said.

"The devil my pride!" Taylor roared. "Ask her again twenty years from now! My God, a redneck lad and his bride starting out with nothing but forty acres, a slab of fatback, and a Dominicker hen have better prospects! Do you know what the odds are against advancement or a decent scale of pay in the abusive, misbegotten mess the Army calls its brevet system? Ever since it began these damned temporary ranks, a service career has been a fool's gamble. As to the rest, being shipped about post to post at the Army's whim, likely to a plains cantonment in the Far West that'd make Crawford a paradise by comparison—who bears all the brunt of hardship? Always the wife. Read glory into his life, never hers! It's she who never knows the meaning, even the memory, of a real home. Who grinds her pride into the dust to make ends meet. Who watches her children grow up playing in hog wallows with Indian brats!"

Davis felt Knox's hand warm and tighten in his: her Taylor

245

fire was up like a red flag. One might as well shout against the wind. Taylor saw or sensed it; he shifted his attack.

"All right, mister. Tell me this. What do you make in a single month?"

"My rank pay is sixty-three dollars and ninety-two cents, my staff pay—"

"Ten dollars. Any private means?"

Like tactics, Davis thought. Strike at the weakest flank. "No, sir."

"What about that rich brother?"

"Sir, I'd never—"

"Of course not. Too damned proud. Fine. In addition, you usually support a body servant—or do you subscribe to the old saw that three can live as cheaply as two."

Davis felt a dull heat crawl up from his collar. "If I found myself unable to support a wife, I'd seek other prospects."

"Oh, would you? What?"

Davis's temper was warming under the sarcasm. But he felt the justice in Taylor's reasoning too; the dilemma had occupied his own thoughts for weeks—a fact that stung him even more.

"That, sir, is my affair."

"Ours," Taylor said with surprising softness: he had hit a nerve and he knew it. "There are other ways of making a livelihood, boy. With your connections—I should say, with your brother's—you could find a good one. Her or the Army . . . there's your choice. But it's one or the other."

"Yes, sir," Davis said just as softly, "if I choose to make one or the other. Or still a different choice. If I choose. And that is the whole point. If *I* choose."

Taylor's eyes narrowed. "And just how do you choose?"

I can't tell you what I haven't decided. The words hung on his lips. It would buy time: time perhaps to come to Taylor's own conclusion. It was a temporary out that was both honorable and reasonable, that he could accept without shame.

What he could not accept was the locked, cold challenge

246

in Taylor's eyes. The bald man-to-man warning flung in his face as plain as a slap.

"I intend to have both," he heard himself say. "I will marry your daughter and I will remain in the Army."

Taylor's weight settled; he rocked back slowly on his heels, watching Davis.

"Let me tell you this," he said. "You are a plain damned fool. And as wrong as a man can be. You're going to find out how wrong."

He strode to the door, flung it open and stalked out.

Davis looked at Mrs. Taylor. "Well, ma'am, you're as good as your word. You didn't say a thing."

Margaret shook her head slightly; she went to the door and stood by it, waiting. Knox brushed a hand across her eyes and walked out quickly. Margaret followed Davis out, firmly latched the door behind them, and without a word went back to the parlor.

"Jeff!" Knox turned blindly into his arms. "It's ridiculous; it's . . . like a bad dream."

"Sarah Knox." He lifted her chin gently. "Do you know what you just did . . . what it means? That you've grown up. You've grown up all the way."

She shivered, pressing her face to his shoulder. "If that's what growing up is, I hate it!"

"I know."

He held her tightly; he felt the sobs break in her throat and wrack her whole body. Sarah Knox, he thought, you don't know it, you won't believe it now, but that was the worst, my darling, that was the acid test. You'll never be hurt again that way, that badly . . .

PART FOUR

A Season for Waiting

18

Leaving the parade ground, Davis angled upslope toward the hospital, hands plunged in his greatcoat pockets, body canted against a cutting north wind. Chickadees and fluffed-up Canada jays huddled in the lee of the building: they stayed close to their pickings these days, and smaller animals moved furtively and by night. Sun pulsed like white flame on a fresh inch of snow that had fallen overnight, preceding today's cold snap. The glare hurt his eyes; the February wind seemed hoarse with death.

He tramped across the long veranda to the wing that housed the surgeon's quarters. When he raised the latch, the wind yanked the door open and swung it inward, hissing a skirl of snow across the floor. Beaumont, sitting at a puncheon workbench, growled without looking around, "Close that goddam thing!"

Davis shut and latched the door, stamping snow from his boots. Walking to the fireplace, he held his hands to the roaring blaze, feeling them tingle and swell; he glanced at the workbench.

"What the devil are you doing?"

Beaumont was whittling at a block of white pine, shavings dribbling in precise corkscrews off his busy knife. His grin was a satiric leer; he nodded at a row of figurines on a shelf above the bench. "How do you like 'em? Fruits of many an idle hour."

Davis inspected the six-inch carved figures. He had no trouble recognizing them: all caricatures of various garrison personnel. Executed with considerable droll skill and lampooning their subjects without mercy. Sergeant Donahue, who'd been broken twice for drinking, his fat body leaning askew, a jug dangling from his fist. Zachary Taylor wielding a schoolmaster's ferrule. Typically, Beaumont had included a figure of himself examining a hole in his own belly.

"Very clever," Davis said. "Where am I?"

"You aren't. You're too sad a case to jest with. The size torch I'd have to carve you holding would bust your arm off."

Davis shook his head with a wry smile and shucked off his greatcoat, dropping it on a stool. "I'd appreciate a quick examination . . ."

"Why quick?" Beaumont scowlingly gouged another curlicue from the soft woodgrain. "What's Old Zeke got you on now?"

"The wood detail again."

"Christ." Beaumont threw down the knife and gazed at him. "You're crazy as a loon or a plain damn fool, I'm not sure which."

"That bad?"

"Must be, or you'd listen for once. To, for example, such trivia as that your health is so undermined as to make you particularly susceptible to wet and cold. But I could shout myself blue in the face warning you not to push your body to stresses it can't withstand. I could howl myself into a goddam paroxysm and foam at the mouth. Wouldn't do a damn bit of good. So why waste valuable time that could be devoted to—"

"Things of real importance." Davis nodded at the littered workbench.

Beaumont gave a barking laugh. "Goddam it, Jeff! That attack you experienced last summer was just a warning sign. Keep driving yourself as you've been and you'll invite worse."

"Look, it's not as though I want—"

"No, you're just plain damned if you'll fold up your pride and pack it away a short season. It's way overworked, boy."

"He's the commander. What do you suggest? That I get myself cashiered for insubordination?"

"Give me the word and I'll put you on the sick list. You'll remain on it at my discretion—and not a damned thing Old Zeke can do."

"Fine," Davis said coldly. "I'll sit in a hospital bed and twiddle my toes. How else does a malingerer occupy himself?"

"Malingerer, hell! You're a sick man. You've developed a persistent cough, have dizzy spells, are nearly dead on your feet. Look. In a matter of days, hours, it could all catch up at once and you'd have a total collapse. One"—he raised a finger—"that could so weaken you that any complication at all, grippe, inflammation of the bowels, anything, could kill you."

Davis began unbuttoning his coatee. "Suppose, Sir Leech, that you stick to your bleeding, blistering, and physicking and let me—"

"All right, all right," Beaumont grumbled. "I'll look you over. But it's like prescribing spectacles for the blind."

From his viewpoint, the doctor's disgust was well-grounded. For weeks, Davis had been incessantly assigned every mean and miserable detail that Taylor could dredge up, some that took him away from Crawford for days at a time. He'd worked and slept out in weather ranging from iron cold to sleety drizzle; he enjoyed no holidays and rarely a free hour. The colonel found fault in all his work, constantly blasting him on one detail or another. He'd taken it in stiff-lipped silence, never uttering a complaint, never betraying a fleck of weakness. He was sure that Taylor's intent was to wear him down to a sodden nub. To a point where, unable to master the fatigue and pain of his flesh and nerves, he'd be forced to one of three alternatives. Resign his commission. Refuse to obey orders and invite court-martial. Or break off with Knox.

The harder he pushed, the harder Davis pushed himself. It

didn't matter what others thought: in his own mind, if he broke, Taylor had whipped him. Beaumont's alternative held no more appeal than the others. It would only afford a temporary reprieve; he couldn't stay on sick call forever. And cut it any way you pleased, it was another way of giving up. Beaten.

Taylor, to do him justice, had at first kept their private quarrel on a strictly private basis. Until a couple of months ago, after an insignificant court-martial. The court had been composed of Taylor, Davis, Captain Tom Smith, and a young lieutenant named Meserve, recently arrived from Jefferson Barracks. Meserve had asked to be excused from wearing his full-dress uniform, which he'd forgotten to pack. Taylor, despite his own penchant for casual dress, was a stickler in matters of military etiquette. He and his old friend Smith had had a bitter quarrel only a few days before, and the captain had taken the opportunity to oppose the colonel's harsh tongue-flaying of the abashed subaltern. Davis had been unable to stay out of the harangue; he'd defended Meserve on principle, but in retrospect he knew that his own simmering feud with the colonel had heated his argument. In fact, he had to admit, he'd been downright rude. Taylor, convinced that Davis had carried their personal difference into a public feud, had tacitly declared all bars dropped: from now on, it was fist and boot. And Zachary Taylor made a bad enemy. Terminating Davis's service as his aide had been only the beginning . . .

Stripped, he seated himself on a stool. Beaumont began thumping his back and shoulders.

"What do you hear from Sarah K.?" the surgeon asked. "Imagine you two are keeping the mail runners overtime on the trail."

"There was a batch of letters a week ago. She's in good health; her aunt still isn't."

Not long after the Schliemann party, Knox had gotten word that her Aunt Elizabeth in Louisville had been taken seriously ill. Knox, as her favorite niece, had been elected to be her nurse and companion through her illness. She had left Prairie du Chien on the last steamer before freeze-up.

Beaumont snorted. "So you won't see her till March at the latest, depending when the ice goes out. And on how long Auntie's vapors last."

"Vapors?"

"Assuming absence makes the heart grow sour, and Old Zeke's assumptions are likely to follow that vein, I see dire hints of a family intrigue, my boy. Auntie Liz *is* the colonel's sister."

Davis smiled. "It crossed my mind. But I don't think so."

"Huh. What Old Zeke hath put asunder, let no man join together."

The heat beating off the firegrate was a soporific; he was yawning when the doctor finished his examination. Beaumont asked him about the dizziness, the constant fatigue, the raw, hacking, persistent cough.

"All right, you bullheaded damn fool, put on your clothes. You know, fighting him on his own terms is sheer lunacy. Worse, suicide. It's no equal contest."

"Are you the referee?"

A wracking cough splintered Davis's speech, bending him almost double. When he straightened, Beaumont was eying him bleakly.

"I've already declared the winner. Old Zeke, by a frostbitten nose. Listen, do me one favor. Take on his damned chores if you have to, but take 'em easy. Avoid physical strain as much as possible. Let your sergeant handle most of the duty."

"He already is."

Beaumont grunted and then, as if embarrassed at betraying any concern, seated himself at his bench, picked up the block and made the shavings fly. As Davis finished dressing, the surgeon muttered, "One day your infernal breastplate of righteousness will crack all to hell."

"That should be an interesting development. Happy carving."

He left the hospital and tramped down the slope. Fatigue made a marrow-deep tug through his whole body. Beaumont was right. It wasn't man versus man; it was a one-sided game of strength with Taylor holding every winning hand. His mouth twisted wryly. *Why?* Not because he needed to show Taylor his mettle. Nor his friends; they knew him already. Himself? But again, why? He couldn't plumb some things in his nature even to his own satisfaction.

Reaching the west gate, he was gratified to find that Sergeant Champeau had the whole detail formed and waiting, the horses harnessed to the sleds. Champeau snapped an order; the men braced to attention. He wheeled and clicked his heels, saluting.

"Ready, Lieutenant!"

"Let's move out, Sergeant."

They headed south toward the abundant mottes of hardwoods above the mouth of the Wisconsin. The sleds ran easily over the thin snow. Last year it had fallen three feet deep by January; this winter there was barely enough to track game by. Another bitter ordeal for the Indians, hundreds of them already subsisting on gruels made of stewed acorns and elmbark. Heavy foraging by troops and war parties last summer had scared off most of the game in the country; the Black Hawk War, six months later, was continuing to inflict a ghastly toll on the tribes. So were the plunging temperatures of this winter of 1832–33; trees creaked with cold and a man's spit crackled on the air.

Davis plodded behind his men, head down, eyes half-shuttered against snow glare. He thought dully of Knox; he thought of her constantly. He wrote her every day, though the few tired minutes he could spare produced a gray uninspired drivel that he was almost ashamed to post. Then he didn't know when his letters might reach her; winter mail was often delayed for months. River traffic ceased; the half-breed dispatch and mail runners, men of incredible stamina who could cover up to forty miles a day in good weather, slogged slowly on snow-shoes, and even in this year of little snow were held to a tardy pace by driving winds and bitter cold. So imagination served in place of news.

Only Army dispatches arrived with reasonable regularity. The garrison, tense with divided opinion over South Carolina's looming break with the Union, had relaxed with the news that Senator Henry Clay's compromise efforts to prevent the tariff issue from coming to a head had been successful. Yet Davis had felt his relief diluted by a nudge of disappointment. Perversely enough, because he might have bowed out of the service as a matter of principle, had South Carolina seceded.

It had been a mere flicker of a feeling, yet it had shocked him a little. Was he having genuine second thoughts about an Army career? Misgivings that he could not—by his own stubborn lights—assay objectively as long as resignation would mean, in a sense, that he had knuckled under to Zachary Taylor?

For whether he liked it or not, Taylor had bared his career prospects in a bitterly realistic light. He'd been accustomed to openhanded living, rarely giving a thought to the future. What he hadn't spent, he'd sent to his mother. He had no other prospects in the wind and no time—now—to think about any. From time to time he'd been caught up in enthusiasms for law or business or farming, but they'd never lasted. The ideal solution was to continue his career and seek such outside investments as Zachary Taylor's tobacco lands in the South. But it took money to make money. Determined to see that Knox didn't suffer the usual privations of a soldier's bride, he'd painfully found that good intentions were hell's paving stones. Marriage demanded all the strategy of a master battle plan. With equal attention to logistics of supply, shelter, morale, and general routine.

He wanted badly to consult with Joseph, twenty-three years his elder, the brother who'd been more like a second father. Joe, having successfully practiced both banking and law in

Natchez and Greenville, was now devoting all his energy to raising cotton and three lovely daughters. His advice and connections would be invaluable. But it wasn't likely, Davis knew, that he could obtain a furlough in the near future; in any case he was stuck fast in Prairie du Chien until the river opened.

They entered the hardwood stands. Blue bars of tree shadow flowed across the tramping detail. They passed the maple grove where Vitelle Robier's cabin was hidden in the trees. At its edge, in plain view, was the log mausoleum that Robier had erected for his son, interring the body above ground in a sitting position after the Sac fashion. He had gone clear to the Bad Axe to find the corpse and bring it home. Since that time, he and his daughter had kept virtually to themselves, never coming to the village except for supplies.

The detail halted in the woods a little above the river junction and set briskly to work. Davis's men were fresh, for Taylor's animosity was scrupulously confined to Davis himself; work details drawn from his troop were rotated regularly. The work went quickly, axmen cutting down and limbing off oaks and maples that were three inches or more in diameter, sawyers bucking them into ten-foot lengths for loading. Uninteresting work to Davis, who had spent his first winter in the Northwest cutting big pines on the Chippewa River, two winters since logging on the Baraboo and the Iowa, rafting the logs down for construction on Forts Crawford and Winnebago.

He tramped up and down, feeling more miserable by the hour. His muscles ached intolerably; the icy wind cut through his clothes. Snow glitter made his eyes sting and water. Rubbing them with his gloved hand increased the irritation. More coughing fits seized him.

He had the thick despairing sense of being close to a cracking point. He fought the feeling with an insensate fevered stubbornness that was no longer aware of itself. He had seen men crack from hidden pressures. In the heat of battle, in icy seasons of the soul. He had never cracked, he wouldn't now.

258

The morning wore on. He no longer paced: he slumped exhaustedly on a stump, head back in a travesty of alertness, avoiding the bitterwhite dazzle of snow. The sun wore a fuzzy halo. His ears hummed with fever and the men's idle talk. Mostly of whiskey and gambling and brothels, the only amenities available to them. Or the endless rehashing of the summer war. The talk drifted in his brain; it seemed faraway and meaningless.

His muscles were strung like cords; tremors began to wrack him. His eyes ached so intolerably, he could hardly bear to open them. The hard shimmer of snowlight filled his vision. He stumbled blindly to his feet. Walk, he thought, walk, damn you.

He took several plunging strides, then half-turned, his eyes wheeling against the sun. What was this?

No. Dear God, no.

He couldn't see. A sludge of spotty darkness had dropped over his eyes. An icy panic congealed in his guts: he stood where he was, paralyzed. He heard the splintering crack of a tree starting its fall.

"Hey, Lieutenant! Watch out . . ."

"Lieutenant, *gare—*"

Champeau must have moved on the heels of his shout. Davis heard his explosive grunt as the sergeant slammed sidelong into him and they went down together. His ears filled with the tree's roaring crash as its impact crushed him flat against the snow and frozen earth. Something struck him across the head, momentarily stunning him.

As awareness flooded back, he knew that his face was buried in snow. A vast weight pinned his shoulders and hips. Men were swearing. The weight stirred on his back. He grunted a little—it did not hurt much.

He turned his face to get it out of the snow. All he could see were watery daubs of black and gray. Enough to tell that, thanks to Champeau, the falling trunk had missed him; only a network of branches held both men helpless as moths. The sergeant's body was cramped across Davis's legs; the limb that had struck his head now prevented Davis from raising it. He tested his extremities; they all moved.

Half the crew labored with cant hooks to partly turn the trunk and give axmen more play to limb off, one by one, the boughs that imprisoned the two men.

Suddenly the pressure was off his back. Hands were turning him over. "Le' me be—" He batted drunkenly at the hands. Shadows of leaning faces spun. *Oh God—my eyes.*

"Champeau," he heard himself say distinctly.

He wanted to tell the sergeant to get him to Robier's cabin, that being the nearest shelter and not far away, but was never sure whether he got the words said.

After a while in the painful rise and ebb of consciousness, he was aware through a nondescript blur of impressions (being carried, jolted as a man stubbed his foot, a sharp curse) that he really was being borne somewhere. They seemed to carry him forever . . .

Then there was easing darkness: the cabin's interior. A limber crackle of straw under his back. Voices conversing in French. Champeau's: "Mademoiselle, it is the second time this has happened to him that I know of . . ."

Ceclie Robier replied. He knew her voice. And that was all he knew, as the fever roared over him like the waves of an endless black ocean.

19

He knew that Beaumont was brought, but had no idea what he did or when he left. And that much later, Robier, who must have been out following his traplines, came home, and that later still, while he thrashed and shouted in delirium, the trapper and his daughter were holding him down. All this in ribbons of faraway awareness that were almost lost in the excruciating tear of contortions seizing his body. It was last summer's attack all over: his muscles seeming to pull against each other, first doubling him up, then arching him backward. As before, the neuralgic anguish centered in his face and fixed its claws in his eyes. Some easing of pain, finally, from laudanum that Beaumont had left. But his fever raged on.

He was wracked by successive chills. Gusts of increasing ague shook him; his hard dry coughing never ceased. Sometime later be began hacking up a reddish-brown phlegm. A spark of sense fraying fast away on the tide of fever told him what that symptom meant: virulent pneumonia. Among his watery crawl of impressions between plunges into the slow ragged drumbeat of delirium was Ceclie always at his side, seeing to his needs, dosing him with innumerable remedies that eventually eased the fever and inflammation.

Often during the hot drift of his sickness, he dreamed a dream.

Always it was the same. He was in a room, a different room than this, moonlight streaming through a window. (He knew the room from somewhere: But where?) And a voice he knew was faintly calling him. He was striving with all his strength to rise (not knowing why, only that he must) and he could not, his muscles were like water, and then he would suddenly succeed, as if a ghostly cord binding his limbs had snapped. And the dream would end . . .

He came slowly back to life. He was awake. But terrifyingly weak, helpless as a baby. He could not even raise his head; his body was one long sore throb. Pain tore at his face and eyes. He forced his crusted eyelids open.

It must be dark. No . . . he could see the windows. Powdery squares of gray among pulsating shadows. Then he remembered. Panic stabbed him to the guts.

"Ceclie . . ." His voice was a hoarse husking whisper. He tried again. "Miss Ceclie!"

Quick steps crossing the dogtrot; the door opened. A flaming white oblong of daylight poured against his eyes. He turned his head quickly, squeezing his lids shut.

"Close the door."

"*Qu'est-ce que c'est?*" she said sharply. "What is it?"

He felt her hands touch him; he caught at them weakly. "Get Beaumont. Bring him here. Tell him my eyes . . . tell him I can't see."

"*Comment?*"

"I'm blind! Don't you understand?"

"Yes . . . yes! I'll get him now . . ."

Her hands pulled away. The door closed again; she was gone. Calm, he thought. Be calm.

"Lord God."

He forced himself to lie quietly. Sun on snow had done the mischief, but how bad was it? His flesh crawled with sweat as he stared at the meaningless swarm of shadows.

262

Blind! He realized that he'd never been really afraid before. Fear, in fact, had always held a quality of subjective curiosity for him. Seeing it at its worst in other men made him feel a puzzled pity. He'd known it as an occasional dryness in the throat, a quickened pulse, never as a blind, unreasoning panic. Now he knew its full meaning. It was an unseen shutter closing in the brain and walling you away from all you knew, all the warm sensate flow of color and outline . . .

It seemed an eternity before he heard steps in the dogtrot. The door creaked open; light penciled through. He pressed a hand over his eyes.

"Doc?"

"Right here, boy. Take it easy . . ."

Beaumont pried open each eye, leaning down so close that Davis felt the warmth of his face.

"Well?" he burst out impatiently.

"Can't be imperative." He felt the face move away. "Miss Robier, do you have a piece of cloth handy? Something soft and thick, preferably cotton or linen."

"Don't be so damned coy!" Davis almost shouted. "Can't you tell me something?"

"Kindly simmer down and let me tell it in my own gruff but kindly way." A chair or bench creaked as Beaumont seated himself. "First, the obvious. Those neuralgic fits, then the attack of pneumonia, weakened a nerve enough to effect your vision. Apparently colds and pneumonia are your bane—the neuralgia recurring when you're constitutionally weakened. Remember last summer? A touch of snow glare now, and the dirty work was done. I'd guess, if we keep your eyes covered awhile, sight will be fully restored . . ."

"You'd guess!"

"Well, I'll be brutally honest. I've heard of permanent damage of a sort in these cases. Those eyes of yours could give you a plague of trouble the rest of your life. Spells of neuralgia, temporarily impaired sight. Anything is possible. And probably avoidable, depending a hell of a lot on you."

"Congratulations," Davis said quietly. "This time you've done it. Put the fear of God squarely in my flesh."

"Where it belongs. Stay afraid. Here . . ." He raised Davis's head. "Got a tasty dose of calomel for you."

Davis took it, shuddering. "You and your damned emetics. Does this stuff really do any good?"

"How in hell should I know? I never take it. By the way, how do you feel otherwise?"

"Weak as a half-drowned cat. Head's spinning. It hurts. Ears ring off and on like plague bells."

"That's the quinine from the Peruvian barks."

"Doc, what about Champeau? Was he hurt?"

"A wrenched shoulder was all. He fared less well than you at that; all the tree fetched you was an abrasion on the head. Could have been worse, could have hit the seat of your brains. That'll do fine, Miss Robier. Raise his head, will you?"

He tied a strip of cloth around Davis's eyes. The relief of thick muffling darkness caused the pain to gradually ebb.

"Leave it on for a week," Beaumont said. "Well, young lady, I'm afraid he'll be all right. Feed him meat or vegetable broths. Skunk stew and turnip soup will do him nicely, anything else that's light and tasty. Also try to keep the debauched fellow from wandering out of bed till he's fully recovered."

Davis grimaced. "Your innate goodness is enough to make a statue weep."

"Merely one of the many qualities that the Almighty and I share in common. Well, boy, you'll have a chance to really get well now. Too weak to move. That'll hold you down, by God. And a lovely young lady in attendance. A typical Davis situation. Must tell you for your post-service memoirs that some of those *Midewiwin* cures of hers are damned efficacious, all the mumbo-jumbo aside. Not supposed to say that. Code of hypocrites. Sign your damned name in blood. Hell!"

Davis heard him walk to the door and pause. "One more thing, Jeff, and that's advice. Get out of the North. Ask to be transferred to your native heath or anywhere that's warm and temperate. But get out of this country or it'll be the death of you. I'll see you tomorrow."

When he had gone, Davis lay for a while thinking about what he'd said. But he was too weak and tired to think long; his throat felt hot, raw, dry as paper.

"Miss Ceclie, would you bring me a drink, please?"

He heard her cross the room. Her hand lifted his head; the rough rim of a clay bowl pressed his lips. He drank deeply.

"Thank you. How long have I . . . ?"

"Eleven days. Sometimes we thought you would die."

"And you wouldn't let me, eh?"

"That was not all my doing, m'sieu. Papa burned gunpowder in a copper dish to keep your throat clear. *Le docteur* gave you the Peruvian barks tea with salts of tartar and red senic. All these things help'."

"I don't remember the other things. You were always here, I remember that."

Her skirt rustled as she straightened up. "*Excusez-moi.* I will make you some broth."

"I'm not hungry. I want to talk. I fear I've put someone out of a bed . . ."

"No, m'sieu. This was my brother's bed."

She returned to whatever it was she'd been doing. He concentrated awhile on trying to ease himself into this new world of darkness and sound and smell. He identified the crackle of burning birch-lengths in the fireplace, a musty odor of drying pelts. But after a minute of trying to assay the small noises Ceclie was making, he gave up.

"What are you doing?"

"I make the moccasins for Papa. First I cure the hide."

"How do you do that?"

She laughed. "I loosen hair and grain with ashes and water. I

265

spend many hours rubbing the hide in brains and fat. So, the hide is slick, I pull it many times across the graining block to make it soft. Then I hang it in the smoke to cure. Now, m'sieu, if you are not well enough to eat broth, you are not well enough to talk. Go back to sleep."

When he woke late in the evening, he felt strong enough to ask for a razor and something to eat. But his trembling hand spilled the broth until Cecile took the spoon and fed him. Afterward Robier shaved him and trimmed his hair. He thanked them, trying to cover his embarrassment at being treated as an infant.

He was weak and shaky for several days. Then he was able to sit up in bed, shave and feed himself. Beaumont kept him dosed with cathartics and purgatives which, if nothing else, kept his plumbing nicely cleared. His recovery was slow; continual stress had undermined his once robust health. Taking seriously Beaumont's warning that another such taxing could prove fatal, he got all the sleep he could. He cautiously exercised his arms and shoulders, but quit at the first hint of a strain.

The days crawled by. He fretted tensely against the time when he could remove the eye bandage. He had frequent visitors. Champeau brought some of his belongings and the best wishes of his troop. George Wilson and Mary Street brought books and garrison gossip. He spent an afternoon with Bob Anderson and goodbyes were said; Bob was departing for Jefferson Barracks to prepare for service with the 3rd Artillery. After Knox, Davis thought often of James Pemberton; he missed the body servant who had been his companion through four years in the Northwest. When he'd been visiting his brother last summer, Joseph's overseer had suddenly died and Davis had left Pemberton to fill his place. He thought of another winter when he'd fallen ill on a logging detail far to the north. How Pemberton had nursed him through, scorning the obvious temptation to take his master's money and weapons and escape across the Canadian border that was so tantalizingly near . . .

He thought the week would never end. When the day came, he waited tensely for Beaumont to arrive. The surgeon was late, probably on some urgent call, and he decided to wait no longer.

Delicately he lifted the thick strip of cotton. Felt a thin panic until he realized that his vision was merely blurry from disuse. Gradually the edges where dark met light stabilized.

He drank in the homely details of the room like a man gazing on virgin territory. Log walls chinked with "clay cats" of mud and straw, hung with hoop stretchers on which fleshed skins were drying. Windows made of hides that had been scraped, rubbed translucent by fat and allowed to dry hard and unworked. His bed built into a corner with posts driven into the ground and rails run against the walls, interlaced with cords of twisted bark for a mattress. The bright trade blanket covering his marsh-hay pallet, the ancient buffalo robe covering his legs, objects he knew so well by touch.

"Ceclie!" he called. "Ceclie!"

She came running in from the room across the dogtrot. *"Qu'est-ce que c'est?"*

"I can see! I can see as . . ."

His words trailed. He gazed at her with a near-shock. Her face was thin almost to gauntness, striped with black paint, her hair hacked off short. Her sacklike calico dress gave no clue to how much weight she'd lost, but her wrists and hands were thin. Suddenly he remembered what Robier had told him, that she was still mourning her brother's death in the Sac fashion, living on water and a little boiled corn.

He recovered, smiling. "I can see as well as ever."

"Tres bien, m'sieu . . ."

An hour later Beaumont bustled in on a flurry of snowflakes. He wore a nondescript fur parka that made him resemble a snow-crusted and slightly baleful cinnamon bear. He set his bag on the table, tossed his coat beside it and came over to the bed at his quick lumpy stride.

"You look like the ghost of Galen, frostbite aside," Davis said.

"By which I take it your eyes are as dewy-fresh as ever and all the girls can offer up thanks. Sorry I'm late. Code of hypocrites. Any pain? Blurring?"

"None."

Beaumont bent, peering at his eyes, holding the lids wide with thumb and forefinger. "Roll 'em around . . . fine. Well, m'lad, you were lucky. That fine, stiff-necked Southern pride nearly tripped you up for fair. But heaven forbid I advise. Never embarrass a man bound to kill himself."

"Not any more, Doc. What's news at Crawford?"

"Not a hell of a lot. Old Zeke's formed the Fort Crawford Temperance Society."

"At Mrs. Taylor's behest, I'd bet."

"You'd win. By the way, you'll be gratified to know your imminence to death's door has had a sobering effect on the old boy."

"I'll bet on that too."

"No, seriously. I told him if he carries this private vendetta with you any further, the outcome will be on his head. I think the warning's found root."

Beaumont prescribed soups and gruels, rest and sleep, dim light, no reading. Davis tried to follow orders, but he'd always been an omnivorous reader; his boredom became so acute that he turned to the books his friends had brought. They knew his tastes: English classics, particularly Shakespeare; Byron, Shelley, Keats, and Scott's Waverley novels. The smoky flickering light of a cowhorn lamp that burned melted fat through a cloth wick invited eyestrain; he rested his eyes a minute between pages. He began trying his legs, hobbling about with the aid of a crotched staff Robier made for him, a little longer each day. First sight of his bony face in a mirror shocked him, though he knew his body had wasted to bone and tendon.

The cabin was a double house, two spacious rooms connected by the dogtrot, a wide roofed gallery; the sleeping and pelt-curing room was purely utilitarian, but the common room that was kitchen, pantry, and parlor was Ceclie's domain, brightened to her taste with whitewash, braided rag rugs, and print curtains. Robier had spent countless hours making the furniture, dressing thin splits of poplar by ax, finishing them with a drawknife, pegging on cross-pieces and legs to make stools, benches, a heavy table for each room. A solid dwelling put together with the loving care of a wanderer who'd finally sunk roots.

Ceclie spent many hours in the sleeping room, working on sets of moccasins for her father. At first he watched her work with interest, the cutting up and sewing of hides with knife and awl and sinew. Then he began to watch her. She'd abandoned the black paint of mourning, was neatly groomed again and putting on weight, filling out her formless calico dresses. She wasn't talkative, but she was good company. Her father, up and out in the murky dawn on the unending rounds of his trap-lines, spent the evenings at the table, skinning his day's catch and stretching the hides on hoop frames, folding and hanging dried hides on pole racks. Most of his cache was prime furs: marten, otter, and muskrat. He showed Davis a darkly beautiful pelt that he called a "sable plus," an exceptionally fine skin. "I hunt always for the best," he said. "Ceclie has come a little way in this white world; she will go farther. When I have the money saved, I will send her to a good school."

Davis's normal energies returned faster than his body strengthened; he had a young man's needs, quick and tearing, and enforced inactivity gave him no outlet. His memory pictures of Knox, once flavored with tenderness, turned hot and sensual. He saw her slim body without trammeling layers of clothing—lovely as roseleaf, sweet-curving, secret-hollowed. It liberated fiercer fancies, bodies annealed in the clasp of love, images that barbed him unbearably . . .

March had brought warming winds, melting snow, patches of bare earth. Honeycombed with warmth, the river ice groaned and cracked, split off in sheets and crawled toward the Mississippi. He extended his short walks outside and around the maple-fringed clearing, feeling spring quicken in his veins. Sometimes Ceclie walked with him, sharing his mood, making him more aware of her. Her ripely vital presence aroused him, stabbing at his loneliness. Sad to think that in a few years that glowing ripeness would thicken to slovenly suet. No *metisse,* no matter how attractive, how schooled by a father's dream, could escape a half-breed woman's lot: wife to *voyageur* or hard-luck farmer, bearing him a dozen children in poverty, some of whom wouldn't survive their first year.

Though far from fully mended, Davis felt he should soon report back to the fort and take on some light duty. He was taking his meals with the Robiers now, and he expressed his feelings at supper one evening.

"What work can you do at the fort?" Robier asked. "Stay awhile longer."

"I think not," Davis smiled. "I've imposed on your hospitality a whole month."

"Pah, that's nothing. You are still too weak even to walk into Prairie du Chien. Wait a few days; I take my furs up to Rolette's post. Then you come with me in the pirogue, eh?"

They were sitting at the table while Ceclie stirred a savory stew in a copper kettle hung from a fireplace lug. She was wearing the scarlet frock in which he'd last seen her at the gumbo ball a year ago. The dress showed no wear; probably she hadn't donned it since. With it, she wore the beadwork belt and mussel-shell necklace he remembered, blending the flavors of her heritage in a way that was primitive and exciting.

She carried the kettle to the table; they filled their copper bowls and dug in with iron spoons. It was good to be on hearty fare again, but Davis tasted the stew rather circumspectly; it was seasoned with herbs unknown to him. He thought the meat was venison, but wasn't sure.

Robier laughed quietly. "It's not dog, m'sieu."

He flushed. "I'm sorry. It's very good."

When they had finished, washing the meal down with strong tea, Robier took out his stone-headed pipe and loaded it with a mixture of tobacco and *kinnikinnick,* the fine-scraped red willow bark preferred by the Indians. "How are your eyes to-night? If they are good, it will not hurt to watch the fire. Have you ever seen the true burning of pine knots?"

"Of course. When I was a boy, we used them to 'shine deer.'"

"We do that too in the hunting. You must watch them burn for themselves, you mix nothing in. I'll show you."

The trapper went out to the dogtrot and returned with a bulky sack. Kneeling by the hearth, he spilled out a heap of pine knots. He'd unearthed them during the thaw, he said, digging in old duff where pines had fallen and rotted, all disintegrated now but the heavy knots preserved by clotted resin where the branches had bent out of the tree. He tucked the knots among the crumbling embers in the fireplace, then extinguished the lamp.

Davis sat on a bench by Ceclie, too aware of how fireglow polished her skin to smoky gold and stressed her breasts with circling shadows. He fastened his attention on the pine knots. Caressed by flame, they began to burn slowly, red, yellow, blue tongues of resin fire washing the gnarled black wood with weird lights. There was something curiously satisfying about the simple ceremony.

"I think about this," Robier murmured. "All that has gone into the pine knots. Sun and water and earth for hundreds of years, eh? Now we watch it turn back to itself."

It was true. And fascinating. A ritual climax to a life cycle, returning the millennium-long distillation to its source. Davis met Ceclie's eyes for a moment. A moment locked in a primal oneness he couldn't define. And on its heels a fierce exploratory sensuality that shook him to the core. But a feeling of guilt undercut the moment. He'd had his casual affairs; what young blood hadn't? But he was under this roof as friend and guest. He looked back at the flames . . .

An hour later he lay in bed watching shadows play on the hewn tamarack joists overhead, restless with his lonely thoughts. Ceclie. Her appeal was old as time, direct as a bullet. And she was close. Too damned conveniently close. All bold ripeness and silky raven beauty. It would be a long night, a hard night to get through. But he'd known other such nights; he would survive this one.

Winter was making a last gusty throb, a shrill yammer of wind tearing at the eaves, snow hissing against the windows. Robier's faint snores drifted from the loft above.

Ceclie pushed open the dogtrot door and entered, carrying an armload of wood. Snowflakes sparkled on the fur-trimmed hood of her parka. He lay quietly, feigning sleep, as she dropped her burden in the woodbox. Afterward she closed the door and "locked" it by pulling in the latchstring that passed from inside through a hole and hung outside. Then went to her bed, built into the corner opposite his and curtained off by a drape of unbleached muslin hung from a joist. He tried not to listen to the small noises she made. But his nerves were prickling and sensitized.

She pushed the drape aside and came out wearing only a faded chemise made of yellow sacking, her shoulders and arms bare. Crossing to the hearth, she knelt and built up the dying fire. When she had a high blaze going, she straightened up and raised the skirt of her chemise. Firelight washed the golden curves of her calves and thighs as she turned slowly, warming her legs; the threadbare chemise clung like a lover's touch. Limning the satiny ripeness of haunch, the full shadow-cleft breasts, the nipples peaking the cloth like hard buttons. She was like a young fertile Astarte, glowing and all-gold. And the pose was for his benefit, he realized, naïvely contrived: she knew he wasn't asleep.

Suddenly she moved; shadows changed. Then she was on her knees beside him, her lips like soft damp moths tracing the lines of his face in little frenzied kisses. He stopped the frantic movements of her mouth by sealing it with his. The kiss was hot and sweet, slashing into the roots of desire like ground fire.

She raised her mouth just a little, whispering against his. "All this time, I want to do that. I am bad."

"No. I wanted it too. But—"

She stopped his mouth; he felt the vibrant lash of her tongue. His hands clasped her shoulders and moved her slightly away.

"Ceclie. There are other people to consider."

He saw her cheeks glimmer and he touched one and found wetness. "Why do you cry?"

"Because soon you go away."

Snow falling in the flue hissed on hot embers. No other sound in the room. Her flesh was warm velvet under his palms. He moved them in a sleeking motion and then her hand was guiding his to her breasts. His fingers cupped one firm globe; the nub-hard tip burned against his palm. Her face came down, her wetly open mouth covered his.

She stood with a lithe swift motion, hands lifting to her shoulders. A whisper of cloth as the chemise slipped down, crumpling around her feet.

"How weak does m'sieu feel?" she whispered.

20

Davis slipped on his greatcoat before stepping out the door into the dogtrot. The late March days were still half as cold as the nights, cold enough to preserve the half a deer carcass hung in the dogtrot shadow out of the reach of wolves. But moving out into the sunlight, he found the morning pleasant enough. Granular mottlings of snow still clung to the ground; chipmunks and chickadees scratched at the bare soil around the clearing. He took pleasure in a fretwork of leafless maple boughs on a scrubbed blue sky, oaks wearing an ocher cling of last year's leaves. He had discarded the staff and in the last couple days had made short excursions into the woods. His eyes seemed as good as ever except for a dry needling ache if he read too much.

Ceclie came out of the common room carrying buckets of maple sap that she'd collected yesterday and strained through flannel to remove bits of dirt and bark. She had half the sugar maples around the clearing plugged with basswood spouts. At one side of the clearing, she'd laid a small fire under a frame of stones supporting a long pan. She emptied the buckets into the pan, then stoked the fire with more sticks, enough to keep the liquid at a slow boil as it browned and thickened.

Kneeling there, she made a pretty picture in her red blouse

and blue skirt with the ornate bead and quill designs. But it made him feel uncomfortable and a little glum. He hadn't known what to say to her since the other night. Maybe there was nothing to say. He did not feel guilty; he had taken a gift freely and pleasurably given. But what did she really think about it? She was a quiet one; even her father admitted he couldn't fathom her thoughts and moods. I should say something, he thought; there has to be a gift for a gift. That thought seemed rather idiotic, but how else could he look at it? He didn't know her at all.

He walked over to her.

"Ceclie."

"Yes, m'sieu?"

He cleared his throat. "Your father has told me that he'll send you to a good school when he has the money. You shouldn't have to wait. I can loan you as much as you'll need."

"You cannot owe me so much, m'sieu."

"Don't be offended, please. It's an offer from a friend."

Her sooty lashes lowered and lifted. A hint of mockery there? "Suppose, m'sieu, that you should need your money? Suppose you should marry? I think you must keep it all."

He felt his face warm. "Nonsense."

"You do not mean to marry?"

"Not at once, no."

"But sometime, eh?"

"Well, yes . . ."

"It will be Miss Taylor?"

How the devil did she know that? "Yes."

"You will need all your money then, eh?"

She gazed at the fire again. He walked away, his face burning. Women! Damn. Why couldn't they stay to the point; why did they personalize every subject that came up? Tomorrow, he thought. Tomorrow Robier would take his furs up to Prairie du Chien, and he would go with him. And of a sudden he was very glad of it.

Robier had pulled in his traplines for the season. This morning, using a scissors-press made of logs and rawhide, he compressed his stores of cured pelts into 100-pound packs of sixty hides each. They were stacked in the sleeping room, ready for tomorrow's trip to Prairie du Chien. He spent the afternoon working in the yard, splitting oak bolts for roof shakes to replace the thick sheets of bark which hadn't proved impervious to rain and melting snow. Davis was helping him, stacking the oak splits into neat piles, when Robier straightened up from his work. He glanced at the straight path he had cut through the trees down to his landing place.

"M'sieu, I think you have visitors."

Davis looked. A canoe was pulling up by the riverbank. A girl sat in the bow. The armful of shakes he was holding clattered to the ground. It was Knox. And the big brown-faced man in the stern was James Pemberton.

Knox had stepped from the bow as Pemberton thrust the craft aground with his paddle. She briefly steadied it as he sprang to the bank, and then she was turning, coming at a run up the path, her face alive with laughter. Davis walked to meet her.

She rushed into his arms and he swung her half-around for balance, or they would have tumbled to the ground. Her kisses were warm and dear on his lips and face. When they stepped apart at last, he still holding her arms, feeling their delightful softness through the sleeves of her gray walking dress, it was all he could do not to sweep her back to him. She was the same, yet not the same. As if their half year apart had shifted a fine balance between the girl and the woman.

She laughed, a little shakily. "Say something, you fool."

"I'm speechless."

Pemberton came up, smiling broadly. They clasped hands.

"Lieutenant Anderson visited your brother, sir, and told him of your illness. Mr. Joseph sent me north on the next steamer."

"How is Joseph?"

"Well, sir, and Miss Eliza too, and the young misses, all well."

"And you were replaced?"

"Yes, sir. There's a new overseer at Hurricane. Will you leave with us? If so, I'll load your belongings."

Davis indicated the sleeping quarters; Pemberton walked on. They stood in the path looking at each other, speaking with their eyes. A mild restraint between them, as if they were learning each other all over.

"How is your aunt?"

"Quite recovered, and sends you her best. Jeff, must you look at me that way?"

"What way?"

"I don't know . . . I feel like blushing all over."

They both laughed; the embarrassment vanished.

"I wasn't sure when I'd see you again. Allowing as how Auntie could very well be trotting out barrel after barrel of vapors . . ."

"Aunt Liz is on our side, my friend. Said Pa's notions are nonsense and if I want to be married, to bring my young man to Louisville. She'll arrange everything and invite a couple score of relatives."

"She must be quite a woman."

"And it's a tempting offer, don't you think?"

"Let's discuss it later. Where did you and James meet?"

"He was on the steamer when I boarded it at Cairo."

Ceclie, who had been drawing water at a spring in the woods, entered the clearing, carrying two buckets from a shoulder yoke. She saw Knox and almost paused, then went on to the cabin.

Knox smiled. "I don't think she fancies me too well. But Mary tells me she took very good care of you. Is that true?"

"Yes. For over a month." He knew his face was coloring and that she noticed it and he wondered, now what?

"Well, I'll thank her another time. Shall we help James collect your things?"

The canoe made slow progress through the maze of sloughs, gliding upriver toward Prairie du Chien. Pemberton dipped the paddle just often enough to lend the craft a faint motion.

Davis was stretched out comfortably with his feet in his gear and his head in Knox's lap, she trailing her hand in the water. They were silent for a time, enjoying the spring air. The banks were greening out here and there, sprayed by a delicate flush of maple flowers; willow-grown hummocks showed yellow budbursts of pollenating catkins. The south wind held a richness of thawed earth.

"Isn't that where we met?" Knox asked.

He turned his head to see where she was pointing. "That's right. The oaks just below that rise. A year ago less three days. Hard to believe, isn't it?"

"Why, that's very good. I hope you remember all our anniversaries that well."

"That's a hard one to forget," he said dryly.

She laughed. "Did I behave very badly?"

"Merely like a brat. Brattishly. How was winter in Louisville?"

She flicked droplets on his face. "I'm glad you asked. Naturally, since no official announcement's been made of our betrothal, I kept the usual string of beaux in attendance."

"Naturally."

"It was wonderful to be back." She untied the satin ribbons of her dove-gray bonnet and took it off, smiling down at him. "So many parties and balls! I even took special lessons from Professor Patrick, dancing master to the *élite*. A black man— and all the rage in Louisville!"

"When did you and James arrive?"

"Only this morning."

"A trifle unexpectedly, I'd imagine."

"Of course. I'm glad you appreciate my cunning ways. If I'd notified Pa in advance, you can be sure I'd have received a military order to remain in Louisville. I really think Pa had high hopes that social distractions would sap my enthusiasms for things hereabouts . . ."

"I suppose he waxed exceeding wroth and minced few words?"

"Does he ever mince them? 'There'll be no more gadding about behind my back with that overdressed popinjay.' I don't think he fancies your tastes in attire, Jeff."

She'd imitated her father's military growl so well that he laughed. "And as an obedient daughter . . ."

"I said absolutely, henceforth I'd meet the popinjay openly. So he forbade me to set foot outside Prairie. At which Ma interposed to tell me of your illness . . . and wonder of wonders, made no bones about being furious with Pa for pushing you as he had. Not half as furious, I assure you, as I was. All I could think was that you might have . . . oh Lord, I was mad!"

He glanced up at her again; a residue of anger flushed her face. So she had found her full courage. Who had been right, he or her mother? Both, in a way. On one hand, her high spirits had gentled; on the other, she could stand up to her father.

"I think the colonel has crossed his own steel," he smiled. "Sorry I caused dissension in the ranks."

"It had to come, didn't it? Not that a vocal tug of war really settles much."

"I think it has."

Pemberton's paddle dipped and stroked; blackbirds rustled in the reeds. A muskrat lazing in plain view as he scrubbed his face and whiskers took to the water in bored precaution, veeing a wake of liquid corrugations. The sun worked into Davis; he began to feel drowsy.

Knox bent and kissed him on the lips. "About Auntie's idea," she murmured.

"When will you be twenty-one?"

"You know very well when. In two years. Less three weeks and, um, five days."

"Meaning he can legally block the marriage or have it annulled after the fact. We can wait. More important, I've given a good deal of thought to what I have to offer a bride. At present, nil—"

"Oh fine, you sound like him."

279

"Well, he's right."

"You're a Southerner and a romantic. You're supposed to think you can live on wasp wings and unicorn milk."

"It can't be did, eh?"

"About as likely as your quitting the service. You're not serious?"

"Not a matter of what I'd like—if Beaumont is right. He says that another siege like the last might put on the finishing touches. That I should get out of the North Countree."

"Oh . . ."

"And that may be impossible unless I get out of the Army first. It's not the only consideration, but taken with the Army scale, the chances for advancement, the prospect of marriage . . . it all tips the scales mightily."

"Why, you're parroting Pa's arguments exactly."

"I had a thought or two of my own before Taylor *père* offered his charming dissertation on the drawbacks. Never said I disagreed with him."

She sighed. "No. You'll just be drawn and quartered before you'll retreat an inch, if it happens to placate him. Very well—leave the Army then! But why should we wait? We can go where he won't find us, we can manage . . ."

"To settle on a turnip patch and live off collards and clabber?" He smothered a yawn. "Trouble with you is, you've never tasted real poverty."

"Have you?"

"Once." He smiled a little. "When I was nine years old, attending the Wilkinson County Academy, I was assigned some memory work I thought was too tough to master. So I walked out. Pa said I had a choice between working with my head or my hands. He offered me a job with his cotton pickers."

"No! Did you take it?"

"For two days. Then went to my father and asked to be sent back to school. Moral: you and I were reared in reasonable comfort. We'll have a hard enough row to hoe whatever we do; I won't compound our troubles by taking a chance on pure misery. I want a certain prospect, any sort of enterprise that will pay and grow . . ."

"Mightn't your brother help?"

"Possibly. I hate to ask, though."

"I can believe it."

"Hope I won't have to borrow." The motion of the craft was making him irresistibly sleepy. "Hopeful he can find me a useful connection or two . . ."

"You're practically napping, sir. Would you like a lullaby?"

"I'm at least as weak as a baby. Why not?"

She began to sing. He'd never heard the melody before—a sweet wild air with a haunting quality. It wasn't exactly sad. Yet he felt vaguely saddened.

"That's a weird whatnot," he murmured. "What do you call it?"

"*Fairy Bells*. Don't you like it?"

"Oh, it's pretty. It's just strange. Go on . . ."

He dropped off to sleep almost before she finished another bar . . .

Apparently Beaumont's warning to Taylor and the colonel's stormy interlude with his womenfolk had had their effect. For two weeks following his return to the fort, Davis was assigned only the lightest of details.

There were no more secret meetings. He and Knox saw each other every evening. He called for her at the Taylor home and she always met him at the door. Several times he quelled the itch to go in and confront the colonel, forcing the welcome that he had a right to expect as Knox's fiancé. But it would be a pointless gesture, and Taylor's temper must be wearing a thin leash as it was. No use provoking an outburst that might invite a reprisal; anything more of that nature would worsen the strain already existing in the Taylor household.

He and Knox visited friends in the garrison and village who

were understanding of the situation; they had few moments alone, which was frustrating but necessary as Davis saw it. He wanted the whole thing kept strictly above board, even public, in the future; the garrison was already buzzing about his feud with the colonel. Any hint of a scandalous aspect would be fuel on the fire.

He wasn't sure what Knox might think or suspect about Ceclie Robier and him. It was hard to hide anything from her. He had been a month under the Robier roof; he and Ceclie had shared the same room. But she avoided speculating aloud, and he decided to be as sensible as she. One emotional incident wasn't worth the harm it would do being dredged up. Just let it be the last. His stiff Southern view of women as two classes had been softened, first by loving Knox, then by Ceclie's dedicated care during his illness. Women had become more to him than mere objects of sentimental veneration or of momentary pleasure.

Meantime he ate well and built up his strength. And continued to wonder what Taylor's next move would be.

His curiosity was relieved by a summons to the colonel's office.

As he entered, Taylor was standing at the window staring out, his hands clasped characteristically aft. Without looking at Davis, he heeled around and walked to his desk, picked up a sheaf of papers and riffled through them. A mere gesture, Davis saw; he wondered what was in the wind.

Finally Taylor shuttled a glance at him. "Your record states that you attended Transylvania University at Lexington before going on to West Point. Familiar with the country thereabouts, are you?"

"Quite well, sir, yes."

"Good. Some time ago, I recommended to the War Department that you be dispatched to Lexington as recruiter for that part of Kentucky. As you likely know, the Army launched a major recruiting campaign last year. It's sending out young officers to every state and territory in the Union. If an officer knows an area and its people intimately—by upbringing or from taking his schooling there—so much the better. Your orders arrived this morning; you'll leave on the steamer *Arabella* tomorrow."

Davis kept his face perfectly composed. If the assignment meant another long separation from Knox, it also meant an opportunity to examine other possibilities for a career. No likelier place to begin than Lexington, a center of culture and business and a city where he knew a score of influential people: specifically fellow alumni of Transylvania, "the Harvard of the South," sons of some of the South's first families. He could also get in touch with Joseph and perhaps arrange a meeting . . .

"How long will the duty last, sir?"

"Until whenever you are assigned another duty." Taylor dropped the batch of papers on his desk, then walked back to the window. "Dismissed."

Davis hesitated a moment. Why not tell Taylor that he intended resigning—for reasons of his own? Before, he had even cautioned Knox to say nothing. Suddenly he felt the foolishness of continuing the posture; he'd proven whatever needed proving.

"Sir. May I discuss a personal matter?"

"You may not. Dismissed."

He gazed at the colonel's back. Taylor's tone rubbed an angry nerve in him. But beyond this, he saw something else: that the spiky antagonism between them had swollen past the colonel's flat bias against service marriages. The matter had split a contented household, even blistered up friction between Taylor and the woman he loved. So far as he was concerned, all that remained between Davis and himself was a bare-boned enmity. Too late to erase all the bitterness said, the bitterness done.

He stiffened in a respectful brace, saluted the colonel's back and walked out.

21

A shitepoke rose out of a reed bed and flapped lazily past the bow of the big *canot du nord*. A *voyageur* grabbed for his musket; the man beside him slammed him in the ribs with his paddle, protesting that *le bon Dieu* protected the shitepoke as he did the albatross, *pas de chance!*

Lieutenant Dennis Gibbs sat in the center of the craft, a hand braced against each gunwale, morosely ignoring the good-natured horseplay of his companions. The order transferring him back to Fort Crawford had come as a bolt from the blue. His eleven-month recruiting stint was up, and appealing the assignment would have been wasted time; a soldier went where he was ordered. He hadn't much taste either for the brawling, noisome company in which he was completing the final leg of his trip. But the soldier assigned to a border post was expected to find his way there by whatever means available: stage, horse-back, boat, or shanks' mare. If he were so fortunate as to draw Northwest duty, he could come most of the way by steamer through the Great Lakes, usually from Buffalo to Detroit, then to Mackinac, Chicago, or Green Bay and points inland.

At Green Bay, a few dollars had bought Gibbs passage with a gang of six merry *hivernants* who were crossing Michigan Territory to explore fur prospects far up the Mississippi. Their thirty-foot craft held the usual traps, gear and provisions—pickled pork, lyed corn, dried peas, tea, and tallow—and still had room for a ton and a half of cargo. The *voyageurs* paddled all day, twelve to fifteen hours in fair water, five miles an hour, forty choppy strokes to the minute, setting the rhythm with songs, ballads, and jingles, usually obscene, all led by the steersman in the stern. They'd made good time coming up the Fox to The Portage, shouldering the big "north canoe" across the neck of land, pausing outside Fort Winnebago for a go at Pierre Pauquette's rum, then slipping swiftly down the Wisconsin. Whenever *la veille,* woman of the wind, was favorable, they'd rigged a light mast and made yet better time.

After an early start this morning, they were nearly to the mouth of the Wisconsin. In a matter of minutes they would reach Prairie du Chien. Cherry blades of sunrise slashed the east; bluffs stood stark against a crisp sky. Birds talked of dawn; water rustled under the paddles.

Gibbs hoped fervently that Knox was no longer at the fort. He'd done his best to forget her with the aid of hard work, hard play, hard drink. Nothing had really helped except time. A little. That and distance. He hoped that chance or whim had taken her back to Louisville and kept her there. He'd had no word of her in nearly a year. In fact had shunned all contacts that might inform him. For he'd built up the painless fantasy of any man disappointed in love. In it, at odd moments, he lived a dream that nothing had gone amiss. At liberty to squander the coin of fancy, he'd shaped her into the most beautiful, the most desirable of women.

False relief. And wrong. Of course. But what the hell?

"Arretez!"

The hoarse whisper came from Lebret, a bowman. His companions sank their paddle blades, halting their momentum.

Lebret pointed. *"Que voyez-vous?"*

They peered downstream. All Gibbs saw was a shallow bank covered with oak and ash, clear unbrushed breaks between. A very ordinary slope. Then he caught a flash of pale gold, a quick dive from the bank, a jeweled spray of water.

"*Mon Dieu!*" murmured a steersman. "*Je l'ai vu de mes propres yeux!*"

"*Si fait, si fait,*" grunted Lebret. He shipped his short cedar paddle and dug in. "*Hatez-vous, mes amis!*"

The *voyageurs* chuckled; six paddles dipped. The craft shot forward through a tangle of lily pads lush with lemon-colored blooms.

Gibbs realized their intent. "Now see here, you fellows—"

"*Arretez!*"

The canoe stopped in a cluster of green-wanded reeds. From here to shore, the water was open. The men sat still, grinning and whispering, watching the sunshot ripples. Suddenly the girl plunged back to the surface. Struck for shore like a tawny eel. She stood up mid-thigh-deep in the slow current. Turning against the pink light, she was like a nubile golden Eve in the dawn of a primeval Eden. She threw back her streaming hair; sunlight silvered her wet body.

Smoothing the hair back from her face, she froze. Stared at the men fifty feet away. She scrambled out of the water; brush slashed their view. From behind it, she shouted furiously, "*Vous etes un pou! Un chou! Cochon!*"

The *voyageurs* howled. They dipped paddles and headed their heavy, high-prowed craft toward the river junction.

"Lice, cabbage, and pigs," Gibbs muttered. "I've spent mornings in more exalted company."

Lebret turned, grinning. "Ah, m'sieu, *enfin la vérité se degage!* You don't find that a tasty piece?"

Gibbs shrugged. "Never could see what some white men find in squaws—or klooch girls—"

Lebret poked him in the ribs, cackling. "You joke, eh? I hear you gentlemen of the South, you have the taste for dark flesh."

"Some so-called gentlemen maybe."

286

The *voyageurs* traded bawdy appreciations.

"It was the daughter of Vitelle Robier," said one. "He lived with Keokuk. He is *un sauvage*."

Robier. He remembered the girl now. Her face anyway. What was her name? Robier . . . Ceclie, that was it. Davis had brought her to the gumbo ball last year.

Shortly the *canot du nord* slipped into the Marais de St. Feriole, the channel separating the island part of Prairie du Chien from the shore area. Fort Crawford's stone buildings stood tan-yellow in the morning sun. They pulled up to the fort landing; Gibbs stepped ashore. He shouldered his gear, trudged up the gravel road to the east gate and crossed the parade to the adjutant's office.

He was told that Colonel Taylor was in Galena on business, that several officers he knew, including Jeff Davis and Bob Anderson, were no longer serving at Crawford. Things were a bit slack in the colonel's absence, and there were no immediate orders for Gibbs. He was assigned his old quarters.

After cleaning up, he made a few purchases at the sutler's and asked a casual question. "Aye," MacDougall said. "The colonel's family is still with him." He winked. "Miss Knox too."

There it was. He couldn't avoid her forever. Might as well have it done with.

He left the parade and walked to the commander's house. Knox was out by the chicken pen, scattering feed. He stopped; sweat broke on his palms. An impulse seized him to walk away. Put it off. Anything. But she saw him. "Denny—" She dropped a handful of corn, then set the feed pan on the ground and came to meet him. She was wearing a crisp calico print; her body filled it with a maturing insistence. She was, he thought, more desirable than any dream.

"Denny!"

Her kiss was pleasant, cool, light as a feather. Disappointment surged through him. What had he been half-expecting? She'd always been a full-blooded girl, her lips warm and eager, no matter how casual the kiss. He stared at her bitterly. Had she changed so much? Yes and no. He no longer had illusions about the adolescent passion she'd felt for him, yet some part of memory had clung to hope.

"Don't look so grouchy."

"I'm sorry."

"Let's walk." She took his arm and started them toward the oak and beech grove, down a path that gave him a gut-stab of memory. "It's been almost a year. Tell me about your adventures in the East."

They walked and talked. He told her about New York and Baltimore, hardly knowing what he said. It was such damned folderol; she knew how he felt. Her light, careful skirting of anything important made him brace for the worst. They stopped under a gnarled oak. She laced her fingers before her and looked at the ground.

"Denny, I'm engaged to Jefferson Davis."

"It was Davis all along, wasn't it?"

"Yes. But I didn't see it for a long time, Denny. I never meant to lead you on."

"That's likely."

"Lord," she said softly. "Men and their burden of pride. You, Pa, Jeff, you're all alike. Men. Can't you be kind and wish me well?"

"I'm sorry. I do wish you well, both of you." Wormwood in his mouth. "The adjutant said that Jeff is in Kentucky on recruiting duty."

"Yes, he was sick this spring. He nearly died. If not for the Robiers—"

"Robiers?"

"The trapper and his daughter." She told him a few details. "I was in Louisville caring for Aunt Liz, you know her, and I'd hardly returned before Jeff was off to Lexington."

He gazed at her miserably. Moisture dewed her skin; shadows

patterned her tipped-up face. Restraint snapped in him. He reached, he caught her by the arms.

"Oh, Knox, I love you so!"

She tried to twist away. Twisted again and broke his hold. She flattened her back against the rough-barked oak, staring at him.

"I didn't mean to," he whispered.

Her hand lifted, her fingertips brushed his cheek. "Oh, Denny . . ." Tears flecked her dark lashes. Pity. God. Compassion. He would rather see fear, anger, hate, anything but that.

"Don't worry," he muttered. "I won't bother you any more. I'll go away. I'll resign my commission, I'll—"

"Denny. Please."

"Sorry for the bitter dramatics. Makes me sound the poor loser, doesn't it? Well, I am."

He turned and walked blindly away.

Back in his barracks room, Gibbs sat at the rough board table, head between his arms, hands rubbing the back of his neck. Reaction blistered him; he despised himself for a weakling. Poets made men die for love. Love. It was a sentimental trap, a bad joke of the gods. Maybe even a disease. But he'd never heard of anyone dying of it.

He rubbed his neck. No good brooding over it. He forced himself to think about composing a letter to his father. A task he always put off. He could never say anything and make his father understand. By letter or otherwise, it never came out right.

He pulled up a sheet of paper and dipped his pen. *Dear Father, I trust you are well and that the business is prospering. I have just ret*— His hand jerked; the paper blotted. He stared at the hand. It was clenched white-knuckled, trembling. He laid the pen down, got up and went to the window. On the parade, a bull-voiced sergeant was drilling recruits. The blacksmith's hammer clanged faintly; a fly bounced and buzzed with vain acrimony against the pane, seeking escape. He noticed these things without being aware of them. The room was a hotbox in the June heat. Christ, he was suffocating. He seized up his shako and strode out of the barracks.

At the stable, he told the sergeant to saddle George Wilson's thoroughbred. Officers had to provide their own mounts, and he had sold his before departing Crawford last year. George, he knew, would not mind.

He put the horse south across the prairie at a brisk canter. Molten-eyed daisies snowed the summer grass; meadow larks and killdeers piped from its deep carpet. A partridge whirred up almost under his mount's feet. Gibbs pulled up at the edge of a plowed field. Green wheat. He was surprised to find anybody farming this particular stretch north of the Wisconsin.

He absently patted the bay's neck. He must be close above the point where the girl had been bathing earlier. He remembered how she had looked, standing in the burnished water. Ripe and golden. Sepia-crested, night-tufted. Hair like shimmering ebony.

He swore quietly. His mood tore at him.

He reined the bay slowly along the field's edge, thinking of the Robier girl. And Davis. How many weeks had he spent in their cabin? She must have been an easy mark for someone like him. No, that wasn't fair. Jeff wasn't a girl-chaser; he'd never had to be. What was it about him? He had sharper passions than any man Gibbs knew, but he held them like trained tigers. Trimmed their claws, minimized each and turned what remained to his use. It was the whole way he could be, had always been. If you saw a shiny-eyed girl at a dance, it was a good bet that Jeff had just left her.

Maybe there'd been nothing between Davis and the Robier girl. It didn't matter, except that plowed ground was always easiest to break. Thinking of that, and how she had looked today, gave a sharp, almost vicious focus to all his swelling frustration. Maybe it had been in the back of his thoughts all the while, maybe that was why he'd ridden this way. Worth looking into. If her old man was about, he'd simply pass the time of day and ride on.

A well-beaten path led off the far end of the field. He followed it into the maple motte till a clearing opened. He saw a large double cabin and, along the clearing's east edge, a truck garden scratched out of the thick humus. Ceclie Robier was moving along the rows with a hoe, loosening the earth, grubbing out weeds.

She saw him and stopped work. Her eyes were a sea-ice green.

"Good afternoon, miss. Could you give me a drink of water?"

"Get it yourself. It's on the bench."

"Merci."

She resumed hoeing. Gibbs dismounted, threw his reins and walked to the puncheon bench by the cabin. He sank the half-gourd dipper into the nearly empty wooden bucket and raised it to his lips, eying her above the rim as he drank. In the past year, trying to drown a memory, he had turned to many outlets. Women no longer abashed and overawed him as they once had. This one was angry with him, she had reason to be, but soft words, the right words, could do wonders with a woman.

"Is Mr. Robier about?"

"He is away with a surveying party. Did you want to see him?"

"Um, no."

Even the drab gray cotton she wore didn't diminish her sleek and burgeoning youth. Its neck scooped to partly reveal, as she bent, two glossy globes of pale bronze. Her feet were bare; she'd tucked the hem of her skirt up in her belt to keep it clean as she trod the soft dirt, her calves flexing with each step.

He filled the dipper again, rinsed his mouth and spat the water out. "'Hem. Miss. Afraid I've drunk all your water. If you'll tell me where to get it, I'll fetch some more."

"That is not necessary."

Her voice had a dark throaty music that hummed a little with irritation. It edged his mood up several notches. He wanted her with a sudden, fierce, loin-stabbing hunger.

"But it is," he smiled. "I insist."

She straightened and dug the hoeblade into the earth, watching him. "Why do you come here, m'sieu?"

Gibbs smiled wryly, slapping the dipper against his palm. "Please don't take me amiss. I felt badly about what those fellows did this morning. I had no part in that; I was only traveling with them. Won't you accept my apologies?"

She stirred her shoulders slightly. "Why should I not?"

"Well, if I'm forgiven, may I fetch the water?"

She eyed him a moment longer. Her eyes had lost the icy lights. "If you must, I'll show you where the spring is."

She untucked her skirt and let the hem fall, then crossed the clearing ahead of him. They went down the path through the maple grove. Her skin, moist from exertion, glistened under an anemic checkering of sunlight. The cling of her frayed skirt to sweat-damp skin hinted at thighs that were ripely round but not heavy. Again he saw her in the water, silver sunstreaks rounding on bold gold curves, swelling hips and saucy buttocks, the jut of high breasts hard-nippled with water chill. His hands began to sweat, his throat felt gummy. God, he thought, take it easy.

They emerged from the maples and crossed a patch of open prairie into a copse of small hemlock that rose like straight ridged pillars. Plumed with lacy foliage, they hooded a central glade in cool green shadow. She pointed to a spring edged by blue sprays of moss-couched violets. Gibbs knelt and dipped the bucket, gazing around him.

"Beautiful, isn't it? Like a cathedral."

She didn't reply. He looked at her over his shoulder. At least she wasn't ignoring him; she watched him steadily, but he couldn't tell if she were still angry or not. He swung up the dripping bucket, his hand aching from the icy water, and set it on the ground. Then got to his feet.

"Could we talk a moment?"

"I don't know what we have to talk of."

"Let me talk then," he smiled. "I did come to see you, I admit it."

"You didn't see enough this morning, eh?"

"That's not fair, Miss Ceclie. I told you how it was."

"Yes, you tell me." She nodded at the bucket. "Now it is full, we go back."

When he did not move, she moved forward to pick up the bucket. As she bent, she wasn't two feet from him. He felt the tight rising surge of desire again. He reached for her arm.

"Please. Listen to me."

She tried to jerk her arm away. Gibbs held it tight. "Listen, can't you?"

She straightened and wheeled, striking at his face with her open hand. He caught her wrist and tried to hold her still. "Listen to me!" She was struggling wildly now and he pulled her against him. He felt the arching heat of her whole body; her face was inches away. He hammered his mouth onto hers.

Her body was tight as a strung bow. Then, almost imperceptibly, her lips loosened. He felt the beginning of response as her body softened into surrender. He cautiously let go of her wrist and felt resistance melt, his other hand freeing her arm now, gentling the kiss a little as he felt her body mold and cling and then her hands moving up his sleeves and locking at his back. Her satiny lips flared open and he tasted the soft wet dart of her tongue. Her response was hot and physical, frank as a child's. Somewhere behind the tide-roar of blood in his ears he felt a flicker of shame, almost of reluctance. It came and went and then his hands were dropping, clasping over her fruitlike buttocks, squeezing and fondling. One hand lifted to the row of wooden buttons down the back of her dress.

She pulled her mouth away, whispering, "Don't." It only

inflamed him; he tore at the dress; buttons popped. She wrestled like a wildcat against his pinning arms, head thrashing from side to side. She was strong, full-muscled with terror; she tumbled them both off balance. They fell to the mossy ground and she tried to scramble away. He caught her and fell on her and held her against the earth.

She was suddenly quiet, staring into his eyes. He felt the heat and tension flood up from her body to his. He dropped his mouth on hers in a grinding kiss. He moved his weight, interposing his hand, bunching a handful of calico, jerking. Cloth ripped; velvet flesh throbbed under his palm.

She said, "Don't, you must not," her lips barely forming sound, writhing and twisting against him as he clawed away the torn calico. Ran his hand over the proud spheres of her breasts, feeling the rubbery brown teats spring erect, the nubs like round hard pebbles. He closed his mouth on one, tugging with lips and teeth. She moaned and arched her body, her hands groping into his clothing. His hand thrust down to the crisp pubic tuft, the swollen lips of her pudenda.

The hard smooth thighs parted for him, he plunged like a young stallion into her silken flowing sheath. Their bodies grappled in the start of a sucking churning rhythm that pumped, that climbed, that soared toward the sweet, aching, unbearable threshold where pain and ecstasy were one: where the wailing cry of a woman impaled at the living core of her being would sear itself for all time into the cells of his memory.

They lay quietly, the loam warm against their backs, bodies not quite touching. Sunlight sprinkled them through the hemlock boughs, a brittle lacework on indigo. A red squirrel ran along a branch, flirting his tail, scolding. She stirred, sighing, under the torn dress thrown over her, and felt for his hand.

He hardly dared look at her. When he did, the dark light in her eyes tunneled back into her thoughts. It had happened so easily for them both, he thought. He could not explain it and knew that she could not. What had begun as near-rape had turned into something often dreamed, often sought, rarely found: the plateau of flesh and mind where passions had met and were fused forever.

My God, he thought.

And murmured: "I'm sorry."

She pressed his hand. "I am not . . ."

Davis leaned against the lower deck rail of the *Arabella,* watching the turquoise water churn by. The steamer was muttering up the Mississippi past the broad island-pocked mouth of the Wisconsin. They were a few minutes from landing; Prairie du Chien lay just ahead. It was now July. Shores and islands wore tumescent cloaks of jade. Flies droned over the black stink of low-water muck; minnows swarmed like brown darts in the shallows. Stiltlike in the water, several great blue herons were feasting. A restful sight.

God knows I need rest, he thought. After the last four months . . .

The recruiting duty had begun pleasantly enough in Lexington. He had renewed a dozen friendships from his Transylvania days. "Athens of the West," the city boasted bookstores, theaters, musical and debating societies. Further duty had transferred him to Louisville, where he'd gone out of his way to meet many of Knox's friends and relatives. He liked her elegant Aunt Elizabeth who'd pronounced herself firmly on his side; he had become friendly with Colonel Taylor's older brother, Hancock. Another ally, he believed. The kaleidoscope of social life had left him pleasantly dizzy. His brother Joseph always brought his frail Eliza to the Northern resorts to escape the torrid Mississippi summers; they'd stopped off in Lexington to discuss Davis's future.

Earlier, Jeff had been approached by a friend, Judson Parker, who was seeking investors in a new enterprise. Some entrepreneurs in South Carolina had been experimenting with a steam-propelled engine that ran on rails of wood and strap iron. Though it seemed of little practical value now, some felt that one day it would revolutionize transportation, industry, society itself, bringing civilization to areas not served by waterways and carrying out produce, ore, and timber. Davis had been fascinated. The Western lands were opening up; a man could grow with such ventures. But Joseph had been cool toward the idea. "This 'rail-road,'" he'd said, "is an interesting toy at best. If you're going to support a wife, you'll have to put aside childish gambles."

Well, Joe should know; he hadn't built a fortune on unsound decisions. What was really dismaying was that there'd been no time to check on other possible lines of endeavor. For widespread cholera had struck for the second summer in a row, hitting a watermark of virulence that made the last one seem a mild romp. It had begun in New Orleans where a vessel from the Orient had brought in a plague that had taken five thousand lives in less than two weeks. From the coast, it had erupted up through the Mississippi Valley, spreading into Natchez, Vicksburg, Memphis, and St. Louis. Towns throughout Ohio and Indiana were ravaged. At Salem, Indiana, one hundred of eight hundred inhabitants had died within a week. Physicians working by day and night were powerless to check it. Fur traders had carried contagion up the Missouri from tribe to tribe; Indians on the plains of the Far West were said to be dying by the thousands . . .

When Lexington and Louisville were hit, Davis had devoted all his energy to helping the stricken. Soon he was supervising burial details. Dozens of them. Helping roll sheets around unwashed corpses (still warm hours after death, temperatures climbing unreasonably, muscles contracting in awful spasms), lifting them into rough slab boxes that were lowered into lime-splashed graves. Elsewhere, he'd heard, bodies were being stacked like cordwood, dumped into trenches and covered; scores were pitched into rivers with rocks tied to their feet. The total number of dead could only be guessed at.

Davis shuddered, trying to block the nightmare pictures from his mind. But it would take a long time. He had more than one reason for being glad of the orders transferring him back to Fort Crawford. Now he had to face telling Knox that all plans of marriage must be postponed; first the railroad idea was scotched, then the plague that had consumed the time he'd have used seeking other prospects . . .

Prairie du Chien was coming into sight. A cannon boomed across the water; fireworks were sputtering and popping all across the incline below the fort. Today, Davis remembered, was the Fourth of July. The whole countryside would turn out to celebrate. A good-sized crowd had already gathered, he saw as the *Arabella* pulled dockside, bell clanging. The bronze cannon on the slope replied, pluming white smoke. Roustabouts ran out the plank; Davis disembarked, sending Pemberton on to their quarters with the portmanteaus.

He plunged into the crowd, looking for Knox, his ears assaulted by the gay holiday atmosphere. Women bonneted against sun and deerflies stood in gossiping bevies; men passed jugs and regaled one another with tall stories. Some were throwing mauls, pitching quoits, playing handspikes; two groups from different "groves" were forming a tug of war. Davis grinned as he passed a circle of grown men on their knees shooting marbles. A medley of high spirits and bumpkin patriotism assailed him from every side—and he enjoyed every bit of it.

He said hello to a number of acquaintances; he asked about Knox, but nobody had seen her. He drifted in the direction of a wooden platform decorated with colored bunting; the regimental band was playing while a group of ladies tried their voices on *Hail Columbia*. He found George Wilson with Mary Street at a table of boards laid across sawhorses. George was bobbing for apples in a tub while Mary shrieked with laughter. He came up with a large apple clamped in his teeth, handed it to Mary, mopped his face with a handkerchief, took his shako from her and chin-looped it on, then shook hands with Davis.

"What a bloody fine surprise! Transferred back, eh? Looking for Knoxie?"

"Have you seen her?"

Mary nodded. "She was with her mother a while ago, over by the barbecue pits."

"Just come off the boat?" Wilson said. "Then you haven't spoken to Dodge yet."

"Dodge?"

"Colonel Henry Dodge, you know, chap who led those Michiganders in the late campaign. He's here; was inquiring after you. Seemed disappointed to learn you weren't here. Any idea why?"

Davis shook his head. "I haven't seen or heard anything of Dodge since last summer."

"Well, he's just come from Washington City following big powwows with Great Father. He and Black Hawk arrived yesterday . . ."

"Black Hawk too?"

"Along with a retinue of his dusky relatives. Officially the old boy is still a prisoner of the government, but he's being treated like visiting royalty. Saw him with Dodge and Street and Old Zeke a bit ago."

"I'll see them later. If you folks will excuse me . . ."

"I believe he finds us superfluous." Mary caught Wilson by the hand. "Come on, the speeches are beginning. I don't want to miss any of those gorgeous liars."

Moving on, Davis paused by the barbecue pits where pairs of beeves and hogs were being roasted. No sign of Knox. He saw Margaret Taylor, but decided against querying her. Idling back toward the platform, he joined Wilson and Mary at the crowd's edge. A blustering ex-militiaman and would-be legislator, Colonel Thaddeus P. Eggers, was speaking. Stout and featureless, bristling with no force, he railed at the blunders and ineptitudes of the Army, proposed reforms, and climbed down to hearty applause from the civilians.

Wilson grinned at Davis. "Ah, democracy."

Black Hawk ascended the platform, accompanied by Agent Joseph Street and a younger man. Street raised a hand for silence. "Today we welcome as friend one from whom, a short year ago, we parted as enemy. Black Hawk will speak for himself; Mr. Antoine LeClaire will render his words."

Black Hawk spoke slowly and deliberately. He wasn't visibly reduced in stature or bearing; yet somehow the blue military greatcoat and plug hat he wore made him seem shrunken and old. His speech was an odd, rambling monologue of his experiences of the past year. From Jefferson Barracks he had been removed to Fortress Monroe, then taken to Baltimore where he'd again met the Grandfather, Andrew Jackson—"a warrior of my own years"—and on to Philadelphia and New York where he had witnessed a balloon ascension, very remarkable; afterward to Albany, Buffalo, Detroit, and Green Bay. Now he was bound for Fort Armstrong where he would be set free; from there to the Iowa River where his people had gone. Keokuk had asked him to live among them and advise them in certain things. Also a white man's book was being made of his life; Antoine LeClaire was setting down his words.

He gazed across the crowd of white faces. His black-pebble eyes shimmered. "A man must go home, my friends. The old days are gone. When I was young, the Sacs were rich and powerful. All the valley of the Father of Rivers was ours, from the Ouisconsin to the Portage des Sioux near the mouth of the Missouri. Today these things are as shadows. I have seen the Eastern places where the Americans are many. Your young men grow as the grass grows. I loved my towns, my cornfields, the home of my people. I fought for them. My fight was a great foolishness. I have lived too long. I want only peace. May Gitchee-Manitou smile on your children and on you."

His voice was reedy and tired; he had made the speech too many times. Street ceremoniously presented him with the sacred medicine bag of his people, which the Americans had confiscated. Cheers. The cannon was fired off.

Davis felt a little sick. He remembered the man Black Hawk had been. Old, tired, battle-broken, but still a man. Defeated yet undestroyed. Now he showed the first fine gray traces of death. A short exposure to the horrors (for an Indian) of the white man's prison. A conducted tour to impress him with the white man's civilization and numbers. Finally the return as a lackey to Keokuk, the Grandfather's obedient grandson.

Davis was turning away when a hand clapped his shoulder. "Lieutenant Davis, by all that's lucky! I was told you were in Lexington."

It was Colonel Dodge; they shook hands.

"True enough, sir. I've been transferred back; only just arrived."

Dodge nodded, his ice-colored eyes snapping. He looked completely at ease in old buckskins and scrubby jackboots, riding crop in hand, gray mane bushing wildly under a slouch hat. "I'd like a talk with you, Mr. Davis, but first you might say hello to Black Hawk. He remembers you most favorably."

"Are you with his party, sir?"

"I've accompanied 'em most of the way, but I'm not his jailer. Major John Garland—that short fellow yonder with Colonel Taylor—is in command of the escort troops. At this point, actually, old Ma-ka-tai-etcetera is more an American idol than a prisoner. Drew a bigger crowd in Baltimore than President Jackson. And a score of New York belles, I swear to God, insisted on *kissing* the old devil."

They joined the group. Zachary Taylor didn't seem too surprised to see Davis; his greeting was courteous enough. Black

Hawk greeted "the young chief who was my friend" with pleasure. Davis shook hands with Major Garland and met Black Hawk's family: his wife Singing Bird, two sons, and a daughter named Namequa, a beauty by any standards. Also Namequa's admirer, a Baltimorean named Gadshaw who'd followed the party from his native city. He was a gentleman, well-dressed and well-favored, probably full of an Easterner's romantic concepts of the noble redman. His ardor, Davis guessed, might chill the first time he saw the lovely Namequa brain a dog for the stewpot.

Taylor gave Dodge a slightly pointed look. "I imagine you'll be wanting to talk with Mr. Davis, Colonel . . . or have you already?"

"Not as yet. A bit noisy out here. I wonder if we might use your office."

"By all means."

Davis felt a rising curiosity as he and Dodge crossed the parade and entered the headquarters building. Dodge must have confided in Taylor, he thought. The offices were deserted for the day; the dense stone walls dimmed the racket outside. In the colonel's sanctum, Dodge walked to the map table.

"What do you know about the West, Mr. Davis, the Far West?"

"Not very much, sir."

"Few Americans do . . . but they'll hear plenty before long. With the Indian menace ended in the Northwest and settlers coming in by droves, we've leisure for turning our attention to this whole area." He swept the tip of his riding crop transversely across the map, from the upper Mississippi to the Southwest plains. "America's western perimeter of defense. Seven forts in a loose line north to south, from Fort Snelling to here, Fort Gibson in Arkansas Territory. A total of three thousand troops, infantry and artillery, to man the entire Western Department of the Army. Some of 'em spread among nine other forts as well as these key seven. Three thousand men to protect thousands of miles of frontier. Not enough by a fraction to handle the job facing us."

"Which is, sir?"

"The same old job, boy. Keeping peace with the tribes and protecting settlers. But a bigger job than ever, and a whole set of new problems posed." The crop raked a jagged circle on the chart. "This whole country between the Missouri and Arkansas frontiers and the Rocky Mountains is the domain of the Comanches and the Pawnee Picts. Tribes that've never recognized U.S. authority. The Osages and Kiowas are constantly warring among themselves in the same region. A highly combustible situation for our people, natives and emigrants." The crop ripped west into Mexican Texas. "And more to come, who'll push even farther—now the Mexican government's thrown open all this empty land and has urged Americans to settle and develop it." Dodge's ice-fire glance swung from the chart. "There's a need here, and President Jackson has filled it. He's given me a special commission to head the first cavalry regiment to be authorized by the U.S. government."

Cavalry! Davis blinked. A Southerner raised to the saddle, he'd always envied European armies for their dashing mounted units. Like many Army men, he deplored the uneasy American conviction that cavalry, the autocratic *élite* of the European military, would menace the heart of American liberty. A fear that, along with the haggling and cost-slashing of a penurious Congress, had long prevented formation of a mounted branch of service.

Dodge grinned. "True, I assure you—by official act of Congress, over and above the bitter protests of our farsighted Secretary of War, Mr. Lewis Cass. I was able to point out that along the Santa Fe Trail in the late '20s, infantry proved so ineffective for escorting and guarding wagon trains that a mounted soldiery became essential. At the time, Congress did establish the Battalion of Mounted Rangers in which, as you're probably aware, I held a major's commission. Brief as its life was, the Rangers demonstrated that even untrained horsemen are more effective on the plains than the best-drilled units of infantry or artillery. Now, thanks to the President's backing, the 1st Regiment of Dragoons is a reality."

"Dragoons, sir? But that's—"

"Mounted infantry. So we'll call it for the nonce—to soften the onerousness. I'm concerned with substance, not titles. I mean to whip out a regiment of such snap and polish as to make those damned Europeans drop their jaws." Dodge leaned his hands on the map table, bending forward with a messianic intensity. "Five hundred years ago, the Great Khan of the Mongols conquered half the known world with three superbly mounted armies. One on black horses, one on white, one on bays. The fierce rivalry thus stimulated between the three generated a matchless prowess in the field. The Khan wanted only to overrun and conquer—his armies, only to outdo one another. The zeal of a divided cavalry brought him closer than any man in history to ruling the civilized world."

Dodge straightened, smiling. "A lesson there, eh? My 1st Dragoons will contain five companies, each mounted differently. Bays, creams, grays, blacks, chestnuts. You know that the Army has been beating the recruiting drums all over the country; I want only the cream of those recruits. Fresh, high-spirited youth, ripe for adventure." His crop tapped Davis's shoulder as if in accolade. "And if you're game, I propose to enlist you in the venture. There'll be a first lieutenancy in it, opportunities for rapid advancement and an excellent scale of pay. You'll also be regimental adjutant."

Davis couldn't believe it. A place in the nation's first regular cavalry unit. Adventure. Citation. Advancement. A half-dozen plums dropped at once into a career he'd believed had reached a dead end.

"I'll be honored to accept, sir."

"Good. Stephen Watts Kearny—he'll be second in command —and I are covering different posts to solicit the officers we want. We're enlisting on a volunteer basis. The Dragoons is a pioneer venture, still on paper, on shaky ground with the Congress too; can't afford to have any deadheads shuffled off on us. I chose you with no hesitation after seeing your mettle in the Black Hawk fracas. Having only a brushing acquaintance with other personnel here, I asked Colonel Taylor whether he might recommend anyone else in your garrison. He suggested Lieutenant Dennis Gibbs."

Knox had written him that Gibbs was back at Fort Crawford; he guessed that Denny was still feeling some heartsoreness, which at least partly accounted for Taylor's recommendation.

"He couldn't have named a better choice, sir."

"Excellent. Gibbs's record is good, but I tend to rely on personal appraisals. I've already spoken to him . . . and the two of you should receive your orders by the end of August. Kearny and I expect to be done recruiting by then, and of course our first base of operations will be Jefferson Barracks. Now then . . . can I interest you in a glass of something better than border squeezin's?"

"Afraid I must decline, sir. I haven't seen my fiancée yet, and . . ."

"Of course. The young lady wouldn't appreciate an indulgence which is bound to show." Dodge chuckled. "So you've found a future helpmeet in Prairie du Chien, eh? May I ask her name?"

"I thought the colonel might have mentioned it," Davis said dryly. "His daughter, Miss Knoxie, has consented to be my wife."

"Wonderful! I met the young lady only today. Lovely girl. No, Taylor didn't tell me. Odd, that. He certainly lauded my selection of you in glowing terms."

"Possibly because there's been no public announcement of the betrothal, sir."

"Ah. Then I take it no immediate wedding plans are in the offing?"

Davis hesitated a moment. "No, sir."

"Good. Settled men are poor bets for bold new ventures. You can well afford to wait until your prospects have stabilized and improved. At least, being Army-bred, Miss Taylor will understand any delay or hardship that's imposed at first. You're a lucky man, my boy . . ."

Outside the building, they shook hands and parted; Davis went looking for Knox again. He passed some boys playing stick-and-hoop. A freckled-faced lad spun a hoop past him; Davis grabbed him, swung him off his feet and set him down.

"Hold on a minute—"

"Lieutenant!"

"Hello, Master Richard. Have you seen Knoxie about?"

"Sure, she's over dancing."

Dick Taylor pointed, then raced off. Davis headed for the scraping jiggle of fiddles. A backwoods quartet was striking up the well-remembered *Weevily Wheat:*

> *"Over the river t' feed them sheep*
> *On buckwheat cakes and barley!*
> *We don't keer what the ole folks say—*
> *Over the river t' Charley!"*

He walked through the onlookers and stopped at the edge of the ring. Wilson and Mary, already whirling in the circle of dancers, made signs to direct his attention. He saw Knox in a dress of fluttering blue bombazet being pirouetted by Lieutenant Mitchell, a good-looking lad about her own age. Davis smiled. This time he had some prerogative for stealing her from a partner. He crossed the ring and twirled her away from Mitchell.

"Jeff . . . oh, Jeff!"

They moved out of the ring and held each other tightly, oblivious to the crowd. For a long moment his whole world was softness and crisp bombazet and a crush of sun-sweet hair against his face.

"Lordy, Lieutenant." She pulled back, laughing. "Isn't this a bit outrageous?"

"Then let's be private. Come on—"

He took her hand and chose a path through the thickest bustle of activity. They came to some tables laden with dishes of beans, boiled potatoes, pones, cakes, pies, and pastries; they took a couple of crullers and munched them as they walked on, heading toward a south meadow which bordered on the woods. The shooting matches were being held there, and the area was a bedlam, men's talk and laughter mingling with a continual roar of gunfire. Most of them were shooting to "drive the nail" —a good score being one out of three hits at forty paces—for prizes of a turkey, a goose, a quarter of beef, and a half-barrel of whiskey.

Knox halted. "Look. There's Pa."

Taylor was standing a few hundred feet away, his back to them, talking with "King Joe" Rolette, the burly Astor agent. They were apparently arguing with the usual bare courtesy, each probably dropping indelicate hints that the other was doing the Indians dirt: Taylor claiming that the American Fur Company wanted to keep the tribes from farms and progress in order to perpetuate the shrinking fur trade; Rolette, that the Army was out to destroy the Indians' freedom and traditions.

"I just realized how God must have relaxed on the seventh day," Davis said. "He spent it arguing with the Devil."

"Jeff!"

"Let's move along while he's diverted."

They passed through a band of birches where some boys were playing shinny with fire-hardened sticks and continued into the whispering, shadowed woods. The festive racket fell behind them. They stopped in a copse of white pine.

"Darling, oh, so long. Now kiss me—"

"My father always told me, albeit in a stern vein, to never disappoint a lady."

He tasted the long hunger of her mouth. The sun had baked a rich resin smell out of the pines; it quivered in the silky air like incense. Suddenly she bit him on the chin and broke away, laughing. She ran, leading him out of the pines onto a prairie slope covered with harlequin spangles of wild roses and ox-eyed daisies. She yanked the scarlet ribbon from her hair; the wind crackled through it. He caught up with her at the meadow's far edge and they tumbled in the grass like children. A flurry of upspilling skirt and petticoats; he saw slim stockinged legs and felt the fierce rise of his blood. Lying together, bowered in the waving grass, they kissed in a soft frenzy. He felt her body slimly uparching, the cool flame of her tongue; his aching need for her scalded his throat. He wanted her here and now, he could have her at a word.

She buried her face against his neck. "Oh, Lordy, Lieutenant, how I love you."

A needle-prick of sanity touched his conscience; he rolled away and sat up. She lay gazing at him, her hair darkly fanned, her lips swollen and poppy-red. He looked away, concentrating on a gray-brown pine siskin which had lit on a small tree to peck at a seed cone.

No sense putting it off, he thought. Tell her now.

"I suppose you've heard why Colonel Dodge is here?"

"Oh, do we talk about that?" She smiled and stretched her arms, plucking a blade of grass. "I understand he's starting a regiment of horse soldiers or somesuch and is looking for officers." She split the blade with her thumb and blew against it. "I could never whistle one of these. Can you?"

"Knoxie, Dodge has asked me to join his new regiment. He wants me as adjutant."

She stared at the grassblade, pulling it apart with her fingers. "You've decided to take his offer. Haven't you?"

"I told him yes, I—"

"Without troubling to consult me. I thought that I had a small interest in your future."

"There was no need to think—or talk. It was one of those things. Directly he'd made the proposition, I knew. This is what I want."

She sat slowly upright, not looking at him. "But your plans. I thought they were all made. You wrote me so less than a month ago."

"The railroad idea, yes, but it was the sort of scheme I couldn't swing without Joe's help and he turned thumbs down. Probably he was right. But before I could juggle any more prospects, the cholera struck. You must have heard."

"I did. I was worried sick."

"I wrote whenever I found time. Didn't you get my notes?"

"Notes, yes. Oh, I know; you were busy day and night. I just wish you'd mentioned . . ."

"I thought rather than disappoint you, I'd wait on another good prospect. But there was no time to even contemplate one, much less go looking. Then I was suddenly ordered back here."

"Very well, I can understand that. I just don't understand how you could throw out all intent and resolution in one moment. You were going to *leave* the service, remember?"

"Yes, but—"

"I heard Dodge tell Pa that his new regiment will probably be assigned to Arkansas . . . perhaps to the line with Mexico. Do you know what that means? We might not see each other for years! Oh, Jeff!"

He knelt beside her and took her hands. "Darling, listen. This has it all over any outside career I might have pursued."

"Does it?"

"Of course. Not only a new branch of service, a whole set of new opportunities. Why, the man who gets in on the bottom today will ride the crest tomorrow . . ."

"I suppose he told you that. Dodge."

"Knoxie, it's not just a glorified version of the old uniform

309

and all the deadwood that went along. It's new, exciting, different—"

"For you, remarkably." She pulled her hands away and clenched them on her knees. "What of me, while you're chasing off on the high road to glory? Waiting, never sure of anything, even where you are or what—"

"But it needn't be that way. There'll be rapid advancement, citation, perhaps a post back East within a year or so."

"Do you know that? Were you promised?"

"Knoxie—"

"Jeff." Her voice was thin and tight. "I have already waited a year. Stealing an hour here, an hour there. Or else not seeing you for months on end. I'm sick of it. Now this. I shan't wait any longer!"

She was close to tears. At least he knew how to deal with that. He drew her into his arms and kissed her. "You have a right to be upset . . . I was wrong not to talk it over with you before I accepted. But it's not vacillation, believe me; it's what I want most. Listen, we'll set a time limit. Two years; give me two years with the Dragoons. If it isn't all I hope—for both of us—I swear I'll resign from the Army for good and all."

"Are you . . . sure?"

"I gave you no promise before. Now I am. Two years. Not a day longer."

She bit her lip and looked at him. "I think I do understand. It's one of those things a man has to do, win or fail. Or it would always gnaw at him." She moved suddenly; she was in his arms, holding him tightly. "Jeff, don't make me wait. Please, let's get married now. Today. I can go with you—"

"No. This horse regiment is being trained for the Far West. Everyone I've heard on the subject agrees that conditions there are next to intolerable—for women . . ."

"Including several hundred Army wives?"

"Knoxie, we've been over a slightly differing version of the same—"

"But you have a fine prospect now. You said so."

"I believe so. I'm not so absolutely certain that I didn't agree to a two-year trial . . . and meantime you'd be chained to a plains cantonment that, in your father's words, would make Fort Crawford seem like paradise."

"Darling, why can't we be wed secretly now? We'll meet like this till it's time for you to depart for Jefferson Barracks. Then I can leave under the pretext of visiting Aunt Liz in Louisville. But I'll get no farther than St. Louis—and the Barracks. And we'll be together openly, all the while you're training for service in the West."

"By which time," he said dryly, "you might have just changed my mind about taking a bride West, eh? Anyway your father could find out by then and start proceedings toward an annulment. Could and very probably would."

"That would take a long time and a great deal of expense. I'd be nearly twenty-one before an annulment was finalized. Hardly worth the effort, even he'd see that . . . and meantime we'd be together."

"I'd hoped," he said glumly, "that the colonel would eventually give his consent. Even his blessing. When he realizes that we've been steadfast, that finally we'll wed with or without blessing, why should he withhold it?"

"Oh Jeff, you know better; you've said it yourself. It's not even the service thing any more—it's you. Nowadays he refuses to even discuss you. It's as though the whole matter had ceased to exist. I say fudge on his blessing!"

"Even so, the idea of eloping sticks in my throat. When we say our vows, I'd hope it wouldn't be after we'd stolen off like a pair of thieves. Then sneaking about afterward to meet one's own wife and husband . . ."

"Darling, please look at my side of it. I'm not a man raging with principles. All I'll have in this life besides the hope of heaven is my husband, my children, my home. If any and if ever. And Jeff, I want them, I want to bear your children, I

311

want to be with you . . . as your wife. Don't make me wait, please."

"Knoxie, be reasonable. Even if we found a clergyman who'd swear to secrecy—"

"We can. You know Father Latour, that Jesuit who lives with a small band of Winnebagos camped a mile or two up the Wisconsin. He's been suspended—I don't know what they call it—from his church for refusing to obey a superior's orders. But he's still a priest and can marry us."

"A pair of Protestants?"

"Yes. In his capacity as a civil magistrate."

"I'd say," he murmured dryly, "that you've examined the matter thoroughly. Only I don't see why he should . . ."

"He will. I know him. Some of we girls have brought food and little gifts to the children in the village. And Father Latour is attending the festivities; I saw him. We can ask him now. Darling . . . ?"

Again her body moved subtly, cuddling into the mold of his, hip and flank a silken warming curve against his arm, lips nibbling moistly over his face. Again he felt the scalding rush of his blood.

"You'd make a formidable Jesuit yourself."

She smiled. Then the smile faded. "You won't do it, will you?"

He shook his head.

She pulled away and got to her feet, brushing wisps of grass from her skirt. "Was the proposal so commandment-shattering to your Baptist soul? I'm sorry."

"It's not that. I told you why."

"It would be improper. Highly improper."

"Yes."

She looked at him. Her face softened and changed. "I don't understand you. You can be so impetuous, and yet . . ."

"Stuffy."

"No, but . . ."

312

"Stealing off to a clandestine rite," he said dryly. "Performed by a priest in bad standing. With, naturally, Winnebago witnesses."

"You needn't elaborate. I have somewhat tawdry instincts, but I understand. Perfectly." Her lips smiled. "Let's return to the celebration. We can celebrate your good fortune."

23

George Wilson got unsteadily to his feet. "Gen'lemen—" he said owlishly, "or in the parlance of good fellowship, all you inebriated sots—may I propose a toast to our friends and comrades-in-arms, Jeff and Denny. May they never lack for those small anemics. Um, emetics. Anemities. Hell. Those li'l things that flag the drooping spirit. On the stark end of whatever nowhere they're next assigned."

"Hear, hear!"

"Also"—Wilson raised a hand for silence—"to that dedicated savant of saw and suture, Dr. William Beaumont. May he never falter in the lists of truth and science, nor lack for new gastric tracts to conquer . . ."

Cups clinked; cheers and laughter briefly drowned the mutter of thunder and drumming of rain. Dr. Beaumont was soon returning to his home in Plattsburgh, New York, to take up private practice, and tomorrow Davis and Gibbs would leave for Jefferson Barracks. They and five fellow officers had gathered on this rainy late-August night at Jourdonnais's, a groggery on the end of a mud lane at the outskirts of Prairie du Chien, for a farewell party. They sat around a table at the back of the taproom, badly lighted by smoky Betty lamps that burned floating rags in pans of oil; cigars and pipes added to the reeking dimness of the low log-raftered room. A fair-sized crowd of *voyageurs* and townsmen occupied the other tables or lined the plank bar, and the din was mildly uproarious.

Davis responded half-absently to the toast. He owed the festivities an appearance, but he was impatient to get away and meet Knox. It would be their last evening together till God knew when. He smothered a yawn; he had spent the day cleaning up the tag ends of a five-year service in the Northwest, fitting in a round of farewells to friends. He and Gibbs would depart in the morning on the *Winnebago*.

The last two months had been the happiest in his memory. He and Knox had whiled away the lazy summer days with idyllic trysts, on outings by themselves or with others, and were regulars at the parties and dances. He was surprised at the light and routine duty he'd pulled and the amount of free time it permitted him. Naturally the colonel wanted to avoid any chance of his taking ill again and his departure being delayed. Reasoning, no doubt, that time and distance, a separation of his daughter and his ex-aide for months and even years, would possibly accomplish what authority had not. They'd amusedly speculated that he might even have persuaded himself that letting them surfeit themselves on each other's company could have a more felicitous effect than prohibition.

In any case, they'd agreed, they would not spend longer than two years apart. By that time Davis could determine whether a future in the U. S. Dragoons was all it seemed to promise; by then too, Knox would pass her twenty-first birthday and be free of any legal opposition her father might pose. He still hoped that Taylor would eventually give his blessing to the match, though Knox pooh-poohed any such prospect. She was still somewhat piqued at Davis's firm refusal to wed now and take their chances on both hardship and her father's temper.

Gibbs was showing little enthusiasm for the libations. He responded indifferently to the toasts and talk, made wet circles on the rough plank table with his cup, and looked preoccupied and a little gloomy. Davis wondered if he were still brooding about Knox. He didn't think so: he and Denny were as friendly as they'd ever been and Gibbs seemed at ease whenever her name came up. But you couldn't be wholly sure. Something had been bothering Gibbs of late . . .

Wilson, sitting beside Beaumont, gave the surgeon a jab in the ribs. "I say, Doc, is it true you're seeking new pastures merely because you've wearied of studying the same old guts?"

"No," Beaumont sniffled morosely. He had a cold; a thick wool muffler was wrapped around his throat and chin. "Of staring at the same silly damned faces."

Wilson hooted. "Stay, Doctor; I shall volunteer my very own viscera to the cause of science. Cleanest guts in the regiment, excoriated by only the bloody meanest of tonsil tonics."

"My boy, may I salute the first truthful thing you've said all evening." Beaumont raised his cup. "Gentlemen—to your collective healths. May you all die in fits of alcoholic megrims complicated by raging satyriasis."

Davis glanced toward the door as someone came in. It was Vitelle Robier, his long rifle balanced on his arm and covered by a sheath of greased buckskin that glistened with raindrops. His gaze swept the smoke-hazed room and stopped on their table. He came across the room, threading between the tables, and halted beside theirs.

"Evening, Vitelle," Davis said. "Won't you join us in a dram?"

Robier's darkly dripping buckskins made puddles around his moccasins; he was hatless, tendrils of wet black hair plastering his brown forehead. And he was staring at Gibbs.

"I want to talk to you, m'sieu. Alone."

Gibbs's lips compressed as he stared back. "I can't think of what we'd have to talk about."

"Can you not, m'sieu? Will you step outside?"

Gibbs hesitated. "No."

"Then I say it here. All will know it soon. My daughter is *enceinte*."

Everyone at the table looked at the trapper. Then at Gibbs. His face was ashy in the bad light.

"Wait a minute, sir," Beaumont growled. "Are you accusing . . ."

"I say what I know. This so-fine officer. This gentleman. He has been by my place different times. If I am there, he passes the time of day, he rides on. Now I know he has come times I am not there."

"The devil!" Beaumont said. "Are you sure she's with child?"

"*Sacré!* I saw my woman twice with child; I know the signs. When they show, I ask my daughter, she admits it. All she does not say is the man's name."

They looked at Gibbs again. He said nothing; the shock in his face said it all.

"I think we'd better discuss this elsewhere," Beaumont said quietly.

Robier made a swift motion that stripped the sheath from his rifle. Oily light stroked the black barrel; he held it unraised, looking at Gibbs. "There is only this to say. I want a husband for my daughter. I will get Father Latour. But it must be now."

Gibbs sat paralyzed, sick-faced. He opened his mouth and closed it.

"You won't say it, eh? I did not think so, but I give a man his chance." The rifle rose and steadied on Gibbs's chest. "Stand up, *cochon*. Walk out the door and give my daughter a husband. Or you die here."

The unheeding talk and laughter went on, its din washing around the still pocket of tension at their table. Robier cocked his rifle; his fist whitened around the barrel. Davis wondered if he could knock it up before the trapper fired. But the piece was probably hair-triggered; the lightest jar might set it off.

Gibbs didn't stir a muscle. His expression went wooden with a squeezed desperate stubbornness. He would not be forced. A savage light quivered in Robier's eyes. For all his volatile French-Canadian nature, he wasn't the kind of man to kill in cold blood. But a wrong word, a wrong move, might tip the scales. They all seemed to sense it. Nobody moved or spoke.

Slowly the tension ran out of the trapper. His face loosened; the rifle sagged downward. He turned and tramped back to the door, threw it open and went out. A wet chill swept the room; someone cursed and kicked the door shut.

Gibbs got slowly to his feet, looking at their faces. "I didn't know," he whispered. "I swear to God I didn't know."

He turned blindly, crossed the room and went out the door.

"I say," Wilson said, "hadn't someone better go after him?"

"Best leave him alone awhile." Beaumont picked up his cup and drained it. "Christ!"

"Did you see his face?" said Lieutenant Belton. "Hell, why all the furor? Everyone dips into a little klooch now and then. Why, I . . ."

"The point needn't be dwelled on," Beaumont snapped. "We all know this room is full of valiant contributors to the half-breed populace of Prairie du Chien. I think, gentlemen, that we should swaddle our errors in the rags of conscience and forget what just passed. Not a word to anyone. Understand?"

There were nods and mutters of agreement. They ordered another round of drinks. The mood was dim and reflective for a few minutes, then picked up again. Davis shared Wilson's concern for Gibbs, and finally the two of them agreed to quit the party and go look for him.

They tramped through the village, fans of rain slashing against their bodies. At the fort's west gate, they queried the guard. Lieutenant Gibbs had come in a while ago and headed for the officers' quarters. They crossed the parade and knocked at Gibbs's door. No answer. They went in; a candle flickered on the table, but the room was deserted.

"He was here," Wilson said worriedly. "But where in the devil . . ."

"We'd better find out," Davis said. "Maybe the sentry at the east gate saw him."

They went down the log veranda that fronted the officers' quarters, left the shelter of the shingled awning and swung across the dark rain-swept parade to the east gate. The guard, shivering and irritable in his damp greatcoat, told them that Gibbs had gone out a short time ago.

"Looked like he had a jug under his coat. I don't argue with no drunk officers; I let him through."

"You'd best curb your tongue, my man," Wilson said. "Did you see where he went?"

"No, sir. I don't collect no drunks."

"Damn your impudence. We're going out to find him and we'll be back shortly. If a word of this leaks into the ranks and I hear of it, I'll have you on report, understand?"

"Yes, sir."

The stables lay fifty yards beyond the stockade; they headed with an unspoken accord toward the line of rain-misted buildings. Increasing rain had turned the compound to a soggy mire that balled their boots. A barn door hung open, and they slogged over to it.

"Goddam mud!" Wilson swore. "Denny, you in there?"

They stepped into the dark aromatic gloom. Straw rustled; a cord of lightning rippled the sky and picked out Gibbs floundering on his hands and knees in some loose hay.

"Wherezat goddam jug," he muttered. "Losta son bitch."

They caught him under the arms and hoisted him upright. He stank of raw whiskey; a worm of spittle inched down his chin.

"Come along, my sweet-smelling friend," said Wilson. "You're luckier than you have a right to be."

"Ole George," said Gibbs. "Ole Jeff. Hey, less finda jug, huh?"

"To hell with your damned jug! If the wrong party had found

you like this, it would cost you those nice shiny epaulets. Come along now, march . . ."

" 'Come, Philander,' " Gibbs sang, " 'let's be a-marching!' "

"Shut up, for Christ's sake! You'll have us all in the bloody guardhouse."

They half-carried, half-dragged him back toward the gate. Before they reached it, Gibbs's sloughing weight threw them off balance and all three went down in the mud. At last they got him across the parade and into his quarters. Davis held him upright while Wilson peeled off his muddy clothes. Gibbs was lax and unresisting, chin lolling on his chest. As they propelled him toward the bed, he lifted his head and said "Goddam!" in a doleful puzzled tone. Then bent over and threw up.

"Christ," Wilson said, eying the mess disgustedly.

"I'll clean it up," Davis said. "You build a fire and boil some coffee. We'd best sober him now or he'll never make the boat tomorrow."

Wilson rummaged on a shelf and found a pot and a sack of coffee. While he laid a fire, Davis wiped up the floor, then covered Gibbs to the chin with blankets to make him sweat. He twitched and groaned as Davis laid a wet cloth on his forehead. There but for the grace of God, Davis thought. The old story. A lonely soldier, a native maiden, a dash of bad luck. And you had any man alive decent enough to feel guilt.

Wilson built up the fire, filled the pot with water, poured in some coffee and set it on to boil. He came over to the bed and gazed down at Gibbs. "What a bloody shame. It will mark him, I suppose; he's the broody kind. Damn that klooch . . ." He met Davis's glance. "Sorry. Forgot she nursed you through a bad time."

Davis nodded dryly. "Better than she should be, George."

"Oh, she's a good enough sort, I suppose. I only hope Denny doesn't get contemplating her old man's notion."

"Marriage?"

"He might, guilt, you know. Can you feature Gibbs as kloochman? Scratching out truck and watching the brats multiply and his lovely half-breed going gradually to suet."

"Gibbs's position and money might make the difference, George. I seem to recall that Pocahontas became the rage of London society."

Wilson snorted. "Miss Robier is not a king's daughter and Denny is no John Rolfe. Granted, she has beauty, charm, and, I should fancy, intelligence. But old Judge Gibbs would disown his son outright, and you know as well as I there's no future in the service for a squawman. Thank God Denny'll be gone from here tomorrow. Leaves him precious little time to think on it . . ."

Davis was late for his rendezvous with Knox. It had taken them nearly an hour to thoroughly revive Gibbs, dosing him with coffee till he threw up again, making him swallow more till he could keep it down, then walking him relentlessly around the room till he could stand shakily by himself, finally allowing him to collapse on his bed and relax into snoring sleep. Afterward Davis hurried to his quarters and changed to dry clothes.

As he approached the hay shed where they were to meet, he saw no sign of Knox.

"Jeff!"

She was standing in the shadow of the hay shed's lee side, muffled in a dark traveling cloak. She came to meet him, throwing back the hood of her cloak. They met and held each other tightly.

"You're late."

"One of the fellows took ill. George and I undertook therapeutic measures."

"A fine excuse. Men!" She shivered. "I'm cold. Let's go inside."

They entered the open-doored shed. It was nearly filled with fragrant new-cut hay. They took off their wraps and lay under them side by side in the odorous crackling dark, arms around each other. The rain had slacked off, but mizzle continued to haze down; glassy puddles reflected dribbles of light and shadow along the log walls. For a while they said nothing, thinking of the months ahead.

He broke the silence. "Imagine you won't find my absence totally insupportable. Not with avid people like Lieutenant Mitchell around to moon, exert charm, and look hopeful."

"Mm-hm. That should give you something to worry about."

"Not really. But it does give you something to worry about."

"Thank you, my pompous love."

She twisted in his arms, moving her body against his so that he was aware through their clothing of the slim parted legs, the tender cones of her bosom. "Darling, darling!" she whispered. They sank deeper into the rustling hay, mouth sealing mouth in a fiery updraft of desire.

He ended it, moving a little back from her.

She lay quite still in the hollow of his arm. And said after a moment: "Do you want anything from your girl on our last night together, Lieutenant? Anything?"

"Knoxie, no. Hush."

"Of course. I can wait as long as you insist. I can also suffer and I will. So will you." Her voice glittered with a dry sudden anger. "I hope you do."

"Do you?"

She buried her face against his shoulder; he stroked her hair in the gloom, new straw heavy-smelling around them, rain whispering on the soaked earth.

"Jeff . . ." Her words came faint and muffled. "You'll be so far away. I'm afraid, don't you see? I can't see ahead, and I'm afraid."

"There's nothing to fear."

"Not for you; you'll be lost in your glorious enterprise—"

"And thinking of you every day."

"Between contemplations of glory, yes. I'll think of you every minute, whatever I'm doing, wherever I am. There'll be no escape for me. Nothing but memories. And I'll need them all to sustain me."

She raised her head. The freckled light played on her tilted face, on her lips and eyes. "Give me a memory, darling. Let me have that much. A real memory . . . a bridal night."

"Not—"

"Here. Now. No matter what happens, whatever is said or done in the future, this will be our night. Our beginning for all time."

He did not move. Not at once. But her fingers were busy on clothing, on buttons, garments sleeking away from pearly flesh. Dusky shadow limned the small and gently pointed breasts. The whipfire in his blood was melting his will and he was seeking and finding her, silken and flowing between his hands, hearing her whispers of love, her murmurs of discovery, her sobs of joy. They moved in a fierce tender grappling and there was now, only now, only here, here and now, now and now and always.

The night cradled them like blue velvet. Thunder growled gently. In all the world, they were entirely alone . . .

PART FIVE

A Season for Doubt

24

Jefferson Barracks, Missouri
September 27, 1833

Dearest Knox,

At last I've found a leisure hour to write you at length, to which task I summon my last energies before Taps. I trust the hasty notes I've found time to post have found you in good health and spirits and that you find in the society of the Prairie enough to amuse if not to please.

It's an exciting time. Day by day one watches the Regiment of 1st Dragoons shape into a reality. This from an unruly broth of boys in the late teens and early twenties—children of the coast slums or itchy-footed farm lads thirsting for adventure— a mixture seasoned heterogeneously with older fellows, some veterans of Dodge's old Ranger Battalion, others at whose antecedents it may not be prudent to guess. They drill on mount and dismount with firearms condemned long ago. The efforts of many at horsemanship are too painful to describe. Their "copious free time" is filled, needless to say, by the meanest of fatigue details. Building barracks and stables (none have been provided) and grooming horses purchased from farms and sales barns all over the country. But the mounts are gorgeous, all thoroughbred, a different color for each of five companies. Each trooper has two horses to groom, his own as well as those of officers and top non-coms and the ambulance animals—an hour above the knees, an hour below. Naturally there's been much grumbling, some malingering, even a rash of desertions. These men enlisted to be cavaliers and adventurers, not carpenters and grooms. Yet they are learning. We are all learning. There is the thrill and pride of belonging to something big and new. In the long pull, I believe, we will make a crack regiment, the Army's finest . . .

I wonder if you have any idea what an indispensable institution is that Mighty Personage, the regimental adjutant. Supposedly one is assigned the post because his most astute commander perceives in him qualities of Leadership, Tact, and Organization. Lamentably, I have learned that this is not the case. The reason that a lowly lieutenant is honored with this position of Immense Power and Influence must be one of pure spite. The adjutant issues (in his commander's name) all orders, conducts all official correspondence, assigns quarters, keeps guard and fatigue rosters, makes recommendations for all leaves and furloughs. It is his duty (privilege? let me disabuse you of that idea!) to demand (in his commander's name) written explanations of any officers (including superiors) derelict in their duty. In spite of this, the adjutant is expected above all to preserve harmony! He must see that all and sundry abide in love even if he becomes the target (as he does) for everyone's vituperation. Still, he's the Army tribe's Man of Big Medicine. He sees that all complaints brought to him (and all complaints are) find solution through Official Channels, be it the sutler's small dog seizing on the fat nether limb of Sergeant O'Hooligan's wife or Major Martinet's gaunt spouse raging against a badly drawing chimney. Through channels! Can you conceive of such errant nonsense?

Fortunately one finds moments, though few, to enjoy Society. Sidney Johnston and Bob Anderson are here, and as I mentioned before, so is the Great Love of your girlhood, Bob's brother Charlie. A lively lad, fresh out of West Point and full of fun. He seemed delighted as well as surprised to learn that I'm engaged to his "dearest friend." Our convivial meetings have led to my inviting him (since he lacks decent lodging) to share my quarters temporarily to the end that I may pump him dry of childhood memories. Stout lad, Charlie!

Taps has sounded and I must close. Why do the things I want to say most bog down in a welter of trivia—all of which is extraneous to you and me? I will say them all in another letter. Meantime, I trust that your mother's cold has improved and that Dick's pet raccoon has survived captivity, civilized provender, and the colonel's temper. C. Anderson and D. Gibbs send their affectionate regard. I begin to feel like a middle man for S. K. Taylor's thwarted lovers.

The heartsease remains as bright as ever.

> Adieu, ma chère,
> très chèr amie.
> *Jeff*

Jefferson Barracks
November 10, 1833

Dearest Knox,

Today General Winfield Scott arrived for a surprise inspection of troops. Fortunately, our new uniforms have arrived, and Colonels Dodge and Kearny used the occasion for a proud review of Dragoon dash and discipline. Despite the cold and blustery weather, we spent hours riding up and down in columns of fours, performing maneuvers. We cut a brave spectacle, I should say, in our full-dress outfits. Our double-breasted coats are dark blue, our trousers gray-blue with yellow stripes down the outseams. Our caps are ornamented with gold cords, silver eagles and stars, and bright orange pompons. We belt our sabers over braided sashes of yellow silk. Our white gloves were spotless, our spurred ankle boots rubbed to gleaming.

329

The general, with his well-known love of pomp and show, was quite impressed.

Speculation has been running high as to whether orders will come soon and what our first duty will be. The general has satisfied our curiosity. We're to proceed to Fort Gibson in Arkansas Territory and strengthen its garrison. Ours will be the task of patroling a thousand square miles of wilderness on the rim of the Western border . . .

Fort Smith, Arkansas Territory
December 15, 1833

. . . After all those days on the Arkansas River, our steamer has docked at Fort Smith on Belle Point, halfway across the territory. Twenty years ago, as Milady may be aware, the government forced the Five Civilized Tribes to give up their homes in the Carolina and Tennessee mountains and move beyond the Mississippi. The fifty per cent who survived the "Trail of Tears" and made new homes in Arkansas found themselves beset by the resentful Osages. Fort Smith was built on the old Osage line to protect them. Ten years ago the line was redrawn forty miles farther west, so Smith has served its time. We found the old billet in ruins from last spring's flood, the worst in Arkansas Valley history. Nearly everything was washed away, torn loose or buried in silt. A single company of the 7th Infantry is quartered here to inspect boats coming past Belle Pointe for spiritous cargo. The prohibited traffic with the Indians is unfailingly brisk.

We encountered an interesting character in a local grogshop. Ben Poore, a fifty-year-old mountain man who used to scout for Dodge's rangers. He's a colorful eccentric who's been everywhere from England to the Orient, everything from buccaneer to wagon guide. He married into the Creek tribe and wears the regalia of a Creek chief: a beaded white doeskin shirt, gaudily decorated yellow leather leggings and a silk turban of brilliant hues. He was quite agreeable to Dodge's offer of the job of chief scout for our regiment. As he puts it, "This child got an itchy foot that only ridge-topping ever scratched."

The steamer captains have refused to proceed above Fort Smith. Seems the Arkansas is at low water and forms a submerged sand bar across the mouth of the Neosho which must be bypassed to reach Fort Gibson. It is over sixty miles to Gibson by the military road which is still snow-free, but Poore advises us that a "hell-dimmer" of a storm is brewing and we'd do well to lay over a few days. Yet Dodge insists on starting out tomorrow. It's bitter cold and the wind off the plains is terrible . . .

The road was slick and ice-rutted, the Dragoons' mounts weaving side to side in broken straggles as the icy shifting wind buffeted them. The sky boiled in gray turmoil; needles of sleety snow slashed like birdshot at troopers' faces. Following them were a few baggage wagons and a slender entourage of officers' body servants, among them James Pemberton.

Davis hunched his back against the near-gale, his gold-corded cap askew. God, what a country. Even five years of soldiering in the bleak Northwest did not prepare a man for the raw wind-torn immensity of these plains. They made him feel depressed and minuscule. Only a short-topped scatter of crabbed and twisted blackjack oaks broke the smooth snow-blown reaches. He wondered what drove men with wives and children to leave soft and pretty regions for such a land. Thank God he hadn't yielded to Knox's arguments . . .

The land grew more hilly and forested; post oaks and other hard scrubs mingled with the blackjack. Dusk had grayed the white scape when Dodge called a halt at a well-timbered site.

Davis sat by his wind-tattered fire, reading over a letter from Knox. It was creased and smudged from much handling. *. . . Ma taught me everything she knows except how to worry, but I learned that from her too. I feel a fear I can't put a* *name to. It must be that I'm already falling into the condition of a soldier's wife. Her whole life a series of long separations and short reunions . . .*

A sprig of yellow heartsease, a wild pansy, lay in a fold of the letter. He fingered it, smiling a little as he remembered her giving it to him before he'd boarded the boat.

"Heartsease," she'd said, "to ease the heart."

And he'd laughed. "What a pretty posey for a soldier to carry . . ."

He carefully folded the letter and tucked it away, then glanced at Denny Gibbs squatting on the other side of the fire, warming his hands to the blaze. His stubbled face was gaunt and faintly lined. Guilt was a hell of a thing, Davis thought. Gibbs was a man torn two ways. By pride of blood, the sense of family duty, the conviction that he must live up to a demanding father's expectations. On the other hand, by a tormented feeling that he'd deserted the girl who carried his child. The knowledge of Ceclie Robier's pregnancy coming on the eve of his departure, being suddenly removed from the scene that would have forced the decision he'd had no time to make, had dug his shame deeper. He hadn't stopped brooding on it all these months. Could he be in love with the girl? If so, there was nothing a man might tell him that would help . . .

Pemberton lifted a bubbling pot from the fire. "Coffee now, sir?"

"Yes. Thank you, James . . . Denny?"

Gibbs nodded and held out his cup as Pemberton poured. Colonel Dodge and Ben Poore were sauntering this way, talking. Davis caught some of their conversation.

" . . . Colonel, you serious about the gov'ment sending you hoss soldiers to treat with the plains Injuns?"

"It's true, Ben. General Scott told me we'll be sent at least as far as the Wichita Mountains."

Poore whistled. "Smack in the Comanch' and Pawnee Pict country."

332

They came up to the fire.

"Good evening, gentlemen," Dodge smiled. "Mr. Davis, we smelled your man's fragrant brew and, as you can see, have brought our cups to beg hospitality."

"By all means, sir."

The two squatted by the fire; Pemberton filled their cups. Ben Poore drank off the scalding coffee like water and smacked his lips. "'Y God, that's prime enough to trade for a plus o' plews." Spare, tall, oak-hewn, Poore had the worn yet preserved look that made years insignificant. He was deeply grizzled, weathered dark as old leather; even muffled in his vast buffalo coat, he moved with a panther's grace.

Davis said: "Sir, did I hear you mention an expedition?"

Dodge sipped his coffee and nodded. "The first of its kind. A mounted force of U.S. soldiery meeting the nomadic horsemen of the plains on their own ground. It's not a punitive expedition, however. The Comanches have been ranging far and fiercely of late. One band attacked several settlements to the south. We merely want to demonstrate to them and to the other plains tribes that the arm of the Grandfather reaches far."

Ben Poore dug out his pipe and scowled into its sooty bowl. "Looka-here, old hoss. Your five hundred Dragoons won't stand no show out there. That's their country—the Comanch'. They rule ever'thing south of the Arkansas and east of the Pecos. They taken a stick one time or t'other to the Utes, Pawnee, Osage, Tonks, 'Pache, and Navajo, all of 'em. *Komantcia* means enemy. Making a Comanch' a show of force on his own ground is a goddam foolishment."

Dodge smiled. "Wait till you've heard it all, Ben. We'll show peaceful intent by taking along two Indian girls to trade for young Matthew Martin."

"You mean Jedge Martin's boy? Pappy had his hair lifted by Pawnee last summer?"

"The one. Andy Jackson has promised his relatives that the Army'll try to recover him."

"Wagh. Think I know two gals you mean. Live down on the Lovely Purchase. Kiowa, fifteen grasses. Pawnee, eighteen. Got lost to their bands some way when they was babies."

"So I was told. Anyhow they'll accompany us. Ben, all we have in mind is to invite the chiefs of the Comanche, Kiowa, and Pawnee to a big council and to dicker for the boy. Can you see any harm coming of that?"

"Well, any trade is good sign. Injun savvies trade talk best." Poore poked his horny fingers into the fire and dropped a live coal in his pipebowl. "When's this she-bang set for?"

"Oh, we won't set out before the coming June . . . or July. The Department will send definite orders."

Poore stabbed his pipestem at the colonel. "You hark to some medicine word, old hoss. Let that tree-tall brass back in St. Looey know you ain't gadding across no high plains in the dead o' summer."

Dodge looked a trifle annoyed. "I'm hardly a stranger to the territory, Ben . . ."

"You ain't see that country beyond the Washita and past the Cross Timbers, come dry-up. She ain't a spit'n'swaller this side of hell. No timber. Damn little grass or game, and 'most none in the hot spells. Waterholes few and far between, all small streams gone bone-dry. Even without a man mentions these Dragoons of yourn are greener'n spring grass."

"Their officers aren't. The troops have been drilled and disciplined to a fare-thee-well. Morale couldn't be higher, all considered. That's what holds an army together, not whether the going is rough or soft."

"Long throw between parade dress and seasoning. Take my word, time to start out is early spring or early fall."

"The Indians make out all seasons. So can we." Dodge finished his coffee and stood up. "Thank you, gentlemen . . ."

For two more days they followed the military road northwest through the Cherokee Nation. Close to Fort Gibson, the hilly oak scrub mingled with cedar brakes; lone holly trees and big cypresses dotted the bottoms. The wind howled eternally, sinking through men's clothing; their faces reddened and chapped. By midafternoon of the third day, most of them were in bad shape from the battering by icy wind. Some, like Private Haver of Davis's company, were suffering acutely from frostbite.

Reining back beside the column to see how Haver was doing, Davis saw that the boy's skin was bluish white. He was beating his hands together trying to restore feeling. In sudden panic, he began to bang his half-frozen feet against his bay's flanks.

"Hold up, Haver," Davis said sharply. "I'll ask the colonel . . ."

But the bay, made skittish by the drumming, shied out of the column, caracoling in short jolting circles, jouncing Haver up and down like a sack of meal. Some of the men laughed, Captain Raoul Masson came trotting up the line, swinging his shot-tipped quirt.

"Dammit, soldier, your antics are disgracing the company! Get that nag under control!"

"I'm, I'm trying, sir—"

"Trying, hell! Give him the bit!"

But Haver could hardly hold his reins. Boneless with cold and fatigue, he began to slip from his saddle.

"Plague take it! You're drunk."

"No, sir, no, I'm not. I can't hold on . . ."

"Devil you can't! Straighten up!"

Masson quartered his horse up by Haver's and flicked his quirt across the boy's shoulders. Haver gave a choked squeal, tipped sideways and rolled out of his saddle. Dodge came down the column at a gallop. He shouldered his mount into Masson's and thrust his riding crop swordlike against the captain's chest. His stare was like frozen flame.

"Damn your gall, sir! How dare you take a whip to any man in my regiment?"

Masson glared. He was a slight man of forty, narrow as a lath; a black patch covered his right eye. His coal-black hair and side whiskers bristled like the hackles of a feist.

"The fellow is malingering, Colonel. Surely you can see—"

"I see what I've seen since we departed Jefferson Barracks. That you have the soul of a churl and a bully. If you ever strike one of my men again, I'll have you spread-eagled and bull-whipped. Is that clear?"

"Yes, sir!"

Masson threw a salute and wheeled away. Haver climbed to his feet and staggered to his horse. With a painful fumbling effort he got his foot in stirrup and heaved himself astride.

"Can you hold on, lad?" Dodge asked. "Less than four miles to Gibson."

Haver shuddered himself spine-straight. "Yes, sir. I can make it."

The column moved on. Dodge, Davis thought, could lead men into hell if it suited his purpose. And they would follow him to a man. Ben Poore came cantering up from the column's rear on a rawboned speckled roan that was the most unsightly piece of horseflesh Davis had ever seen. He jogged alongside Davis for a minute, then said: "That Masson got one mean burr under his tail."

Davis nodded wryly. "I had one fall-out with him at the Barracks. He kept an exhausted and half-frozen man on punishment all day, carrying a fifty-pound log back and forth across the parade. Kept him at it past retreat, when all punishment details cease. Took it on myself to send the poor fellow to his barracks. Masson was furious. More so after we took the matter to Dodge and he upheld me . . ."

"Hunh." Poore sucked at his cold pipe. "Ever hear his story?"

"A word here, a word there. Something about his showing the white feather in the field."

"Kind o' thing folks out here don't forget about a man. Masson was a desk soldier 'fore he got sent West. Five-six years ago some Osages rampaged and burned out a slew of settlers 'fore troops cornered 'em on a hill. Masson got ordered to lead a charge. Shot hisself in the foot with a pistol. Accident, he claimed. Nobody believed it. Turned him salty as brine."

The column moved along briskly, its pace quickened by thoughts of a cozy barracks, a hot fire, a slug of rum for chilblains. The hills were dropping away to canebrake-choked bottomlands, and they could see the Arkansas again. The unending winds kept the river open all winter, thrashing its surface to a mud-colored lather. Poore pointed out the mouth of the Neosho, a crystal stream that rushed into the sluggish chocolate of the Arkansas. "Fort Gibson is a soft whoop and gentle holler above them swamps and brakes yonder; road swings way around 'em."

"How old is the fort, Mr. Poore?"

"Must be ten year ago they moved the garrison up from Fort Smith. Winfield Scott sent Colonel Matt Arbuckle up the Arkansas to locate a new stockade. Old Matt spent two year building Gibson."

"I understand they call it 'the graveyard of the Army.' Someone said several hundred men have died there."

"Mite exaggeration, hoss. But a lot of sojer boys won't never leave Gibson."

"Indians?"

Poore snorted. "Mostly croup and grippe this time year. But that ain't what takes 'em like flies. It's the goddam 'intermittent' in summer. Comes and goes. One day a man is full of sap and bark, next he's took with ague and fever. I warned old Matt agin building here. Fine landing, but these damn bogs and brakes don't never dry up. Full o' mosquitoes and miasma. Ain't nothing old Matt can do but post them blamefool sanitary regulations and advise temperance."

Davis smiled. "I thought the prohibition was strictly enforced in this territory."

"Hell, man as lief try to fly as dry up Arkansas." Poore dug a flask from a deep pocket of his buffalo coat. "Snort, hoss? Cert'-fied to make your whiskers smoke."

"No, thanks."

They had come nearly three miles from the river junction when Dodge halted the column. He ordered muster formation by companies. When the mounted troops were assembled, blinking against the windy flurries of snow, Dodge wheeled his horse out in front of them, whipping the cold, slack, tired men with words. Gradually they straightened up, their faces stiffening, pride masking misery. "In a few minutes," he concluded, "you will ride into the billet that will be your first duty and your home for perhaps years. You will not ride in looking like a gang of ragpickers mounted muleback. You are the 1st Regiment of United States Dragoons. *Act it.* Bugler . . . sound advance!"

They clattered up the road in string-straight columns, pennons snapping. The crystal cut of the Neosho, hidden by the swamps, came back into view, running wide and deep as it crooked around the inclined elbow of land where Fort Gibson sprawled. A broad ledge of rock formed a natural landing. The fort proper was a big palisaded square, each corner fortified by a squat blockhouse. Between the log stockade and the low riverbank were forage barns, stables, storehouses, carpenters' and farriers' shops, the sutler's store and warehouse. Around the fort's other sides, winter-bare rows of elms, oaks, and pecans failed to relieve the barren cheerlessness of the site. Here were officers' quarters, homes of married soldiers, mess halls, a hospital, and the regimental headquarters. Some buildings were protected by indifferent coats of whitewash, others crumbling into decay. They should have named it Fort Desolate, Davis thought.

They rode into the parade with a numb flourish. General Matthew Arbuckle, commander of the 7th Infantry, came out with his staff to greet them. He was a rheumy-eyed old man with a mild, absent, rather prideless air. After introducing his staff officers, he said: "Well, heh, it's a day for white owls, Colonel; I'd as lief carry on by a warm hearth with a warming glass. Will you and Colonel Kearny join us in my quarters? Captain Lawton here is quartermaster; he'll show your troops their barracks."

"Beg pardon, sir; would like to see those myself. We'll join you afterward."

"Ah, yes. Your pleasure, Colonel . . ."

Captain Lawton led the column through the north gate to a row of tumbledown barracks at the far end of the post. The roofs gaped with holes; wind whistled between unchinked logs that had been attacked by damp rot.

"Captain," Dodge said icily, "these buildings are not fit to house swine. I demand that my men be given decent quarters."

Lawton gave him a jaundiced stare. "There are no other accommodations, sir. We aren't set up for visiting royalty."

Dodge assured him that he'd damned well attend personally to securing adequate shelter for his troops. After directing company commanders to pitch tents on the hummocky plain south of the fort grounds, he rapped off names of several officers, including Davis, to accompany Kearny and him: enough to match Arbuckle's staff contingent. Lawton led the way to the general's large and comfortable quarters back of the regimental offices. They sat or stood about the blazing fireplace; Arbuckle's orderly distributed cigars and whiskey. Dodge stated his complaint with a flinty arrogance.

"Well, Colonel," Arbuckle said affably, "I shan't object if you care to salvage materials from the old buildings and throw up your own barracks. Gibson was originally a five company post, much too small for the present garrison. Some of our own troops are already scattered in the hills above the fort, others are at Bayou Menard some seven miles east. Now, on the matter of the Rangers . . ."

"What Rangers?"

"Why, bless me, I thought you'd been told. The Arkansas Mounted Rangers, six companies of them. They were recruited for the Black Hawk War, heh, but somehow ended up here at

Gibson. They're to be merged with your Dragoons. Rag, tag 'n' bobtail gang, but they'll bring you up to full regimental strength. They can ride and shoot, have good horses, but you'll have to drill the devil out of them."

"Sir!" Dodge's eyes glinted like ice chips in his wind-chapped face. "Months of painstaking work have gone into honing this regiment to an *élite* outfit. Assimilating a pack of unruly frontier scum will . . ."

"Oh, you'll whip them into shape." Arbuckle spat across his pendulous underlip into a battered spittoon. "As to your duties. You're aware that the flow of settlers into Texas has increased the likelihood of trouble with the Comanches, Pawnees, and Kiowas. It's been my practice to send an escort of Rangers with each wagon train that takes the Texas Road. That task now falls to you."

"Nursemaiding gangs of pilgrims?"

Arbuckle smiled. "I think you'll find it beats cleaning stables or digging latrines. However, you could see more sinewy action before long. It's fallen to my lot to attempt persuading the Osages to move into territories north, where lands have been set aside for them. Otherwise, the government fears, there'll be full-scale risings against the Cherokees, Creeks, and other newcomers. As the Osages are loathe to obey, we're proceeding delicately; but the situation could deteriorate overnight. Oh, and I should warn you about the 'blind tigers.' Nearest settlement, Three Forks, is five miles up the Verdigris, but a man need hardly venture so far for a turn with vice. Bless me, no. The half-breeds operate a variety of gaming and drinking places back in the hills. Gibson remains unserviced by the sweet ladies of the world's oldest, but the Cherokee maidens down on the Lovely Purchase are not of stubborn virtue."

"Surely, General, these places are off-limits . . ."

"Um, yes. And the edict sternly backed by threat of stocks and wooden horse. Heh. Though I imagine some of the tender but late-realized presents our lads bear home from their dusky conquests quite outdo these punishments." The general's eyelid drooped. "I fear there's no damping man's ardor for that most cherished of prizes, even with beasties and unmentionables."

Dodge did not join in the laughter. "With your permission, sir, I'd like to see to the bivouacking of my men."

"Certainly. I've given orders that the commissary is to supply your immediate needs . . ."

The troops were having the devil's own time setting up tents on the wind-savaged prairie. Driving stakes into frozen earth was impossible; they anchored the guy ropes with stray rocks. Canvas whipped and popped furiously; frozen sleet blew like splintery hail against their faces and hands. Davis went from group to group, lending a hand where he could. Damn Dodge and his fanatical pride; even those gutted barracks would be preferable in such weather.

He swung toward three men who were having trouble shaking out their canvas. Davis seized a loose snapping corner; Captain Masson also hurried up to lend a hand. The blast of wind bellied the heavy fabric like a swollen cushion, almost yanking the five men off-balance. A trooper lost his grip and stumbled into Masson, causing him to slip and fall on one knee.

"You clumsy cabbagehead!" he snarled. "Lay hold and keep hold!"

The soldier, a raw German recruit named Diedrich, had poor comprehension; the gale roar of wind further dimmed his comprehension. Unsure of the command, he stood with a worried little grin on his face and didn't move. Which increased Masson's ire. He seized Diedrich by the ears for a "wooling"—a favored punishment among officers of little patience. Shaking a man by the ears did not smack of excessive brutality, though in fact it was painful as hell.

Diedrich yelled. In the pure reflex of pain he gave Masson a shove that sent him sprawling. Scrambling to his knees, the captain jerked a pistol from his belt and leveled it on the German.

341

Davis, seeing his thumb whiten to the cocking pressure, didn't hesitate. A sweep of his boot knocked the pistol from Masson's hand.

Masson stood up, swaying against the wind, cuddling his skinned hand. "You'll get broken for that, Davis. By Christ, I'll see to it!"

"If Dodge hears about this, Captain, he'll likely 'wool' you himself . . . in front of the whole regiment."

Masson's face was pinched and white. He picked up the pistol and returned it to his belt. He stared at Davis. "You will regret this," he said distinctly.

He turned and stumbled away. Davis looked about to make sure that no others had seen the altercation. Then glanced at the three troopers. "Keep your mouths shut about this," he told them. "Or it will mean trouble for all concerned. Understand?"

They nodded.

Seated in his tent that night, he tried to compose a letter to Knox. Staring at the shadows flung on the dirty canvas by a guttering candle, he thought back on the long day and wondered tiredly and dismally what he could tell her.

> *Fort Gibson*
> *December 17, 1833*

Dearest Knox,

Today we arrived at our new billet. It is no more paradisiacal than one might expect, but I think that our main concern will be how to avoid dying of boredom . . .

25

"What does he say, Knoxie?"

Knox was curled up on the parlor settee, a faint smile on her lips as she read Jeff's latest letter. She glanced at Betty who was sitting on the floor, legs tucked under her, a pile of crochet work in her lap.

"It doesn't concern you, snip."

"I don't care. I want to hear it."

"Well, I'll read you parts of it. But you'd better get to that crocheting. He writes, 'Be assured your letters are read and reread, carried through a soldier's day to grace his few restful minutes. It seems that *my* lines, like the beggar's day, are dwindling to the shortest span!'"

"Mm, that's beautiful," Betty said. "Like something you read in school."

"Do you want to hear this or not?"

"Oh yes!"

"'I observe your concern for my health, but there's no cause for worry. We're well-supplied with physicians. There is a post surgeon at Gibson, but the Dragoons have their own surgeon and each company has an auxiliary sawbones or an individual possessing some medical skill.

"'Since I last wrote, I have been appointed morale officer,

343

meaning that I'm expected to bolster the troops' spirits. I've taken over the Cherokee agent's great council house two or three times a week to put on skits. They not only entertain the garrison, but keep some of the boys occupied at writing and learning parts. Our playlets, I'm afraid, are a shade too coarse to bear description, but some of our satire is worthy of Pope.' "

"Pish!" Betty broke in. "That's nothing. Read the good parts."

"Would you like to leave the room, miss?"

Betty's underlip, a cherry-red replica of her mother's, pouted exactly like her father's. At nine, she was a lovely hoyden with a hint of expectancy if not pubescence to her gangling body. She would be the genuine beauty of the family, Knox thought, and she acted like it already.

"Oh, all right. Go on."

" 'Even in the dead of winter, curious souls seem drawn to this dreary country. In recent weeks we've played host to the redoubtable Sam Houston and some of his Cherokee friends, the crown prince of a watch-pocket European monarchy, and Mr. Washington Irving, author of that delightful *Sketch Book*. He seems so effete a person that I wondered he put himself to the rigors of such a journey. I believe that Mr. Irving would agree.

" 'Otherwise there's little of interest to relate. There is talk that the eastern part of the Territory will soon break away and enter the Union as the state of Arkansas, whereupon the western half will be designated as Indian Territory. Also, General Arbuckle's health has deteriorated to where he has submitted his resignation. His replacement, we understand, will be General Henry Leavenworth who built Fort Leavenworth up in the Indian lands and has a reputation for spit'n'polish. Meantime we continue the routine patrols in the Creek, Cherokee, and Choctaw Nations. The Osages seem less restless. Outside of a surfeit of buffalo meat and what passes for a broth made from it, we cannot complain. The occasional steam packet up from Fort Smith supplies us with provisions, equipment, mail,

344

and a dash of amenities. But being inundated in buffalo is small anguish next to the delays in the letters from loved ones that are a soldier's chief solace . . .' "

She read on in silence, smiling a little.

"That's a good part, isn't it? Read it, Knoxie, please!"

"I am. But not to you."

"C'mon, please!"

"No. I'll read you the closing. 'Finally, my every good wish to your mother and the siblings and yes, to the colonel too. Yours ever, Jeff.' "

Betty edged over to the settee, an avid curiosity in her face. "What's 'siblings,' Knoxie?"

"You and Dick."

"Oh."

Betty sprang up, snatched the letter from her and ran. Knox overtook her at the door and unpried her fingers from the crumpled sheets, then slapped her on the rear. "Get back to your crocheting, miss."

"You'll be sorry," Betty wailed.

Knox went up to her room and knelt by her armoire. She slid open a panel at its base that hid a small compartment where she kept her personal letters and other items she didn't want Betty rifling through. She placed the letter inside, closed the panel, stood up and went to the window, gazing out. Pale sunlight filtered warmly through the glass. The March chinooks had blown and the snow was nearly gone; the Mississippi ice sheet was cracking, splitting away in jagged floes. These days she felt spring in her blood like a voiceless cry. In other springs, it had made her want to shout and run. Now it brought only the sad, tearing stab of loneliness. *Jeff* . . .

She ought to get away from the house awhile. A ride would be pleasant. Provided it weren't spent in the impossible company of Sanford Preston, her courting cousin. Sanford had come up from New Orleans last fall; a winter-long guest, he had occupied his time loafing in taprooms, ogling village belles, entertaining the burghers with the lives of a Southern squire and, as far as she was concerned, making a trying nuisance of himself. Sanford was in love with her, so he said. She did not sympathize. He hadn't been around all afternoon; if she were lucky, she could slip out of the village without encountering him.

She changed to a blue cashmere riding habit, put on her fur toque and then, carrying her gloves and crop, went down to the kitchen. Margaret was on her knees by the hearth, raking a thick crusty pone of cornbread out of the ashes.

"Do you mind if I go for a ride, Ma?"

Margaret, her face heat-flushed, glanced up with a smile. "Of course not. I've told you to get out more often. You've been working much too hard . . ." She paused. "I hope you're not thinking of calling on those Robiers again."

"I might. Would that be so terrible?"

"I've never chosen your friends, Knoxie. I just feel . . . you've called rather too often on those people."

"Ma, I've visited them exactly four times in six months."

"Well, but considering . . ."

"That Ceclie Robier is about to bear an illegitimate child. We needn't sugar our words, Ma. Everyone knows it."

Margaret's mouth tightened. "Delicacy is not sugaring. And I'm not a sheltered violet in these matters, Knox. I joined your father at Green Bay in 1816, when he was on assignment at Fort Howard. You wouldn't remember. You were two then, Ann only six. There were virtually no white women in the border garrisons in those days . . . and it was common practice for officers to share their quarters with squaws and *metisses*."

Knox sighed. "I can't see that anything's changed. It merely goes on less blatantly."

"Blatantly or secretly, right is right and wrong is wrong. That girl did wrong. I can remember when you didn't even like her and made no bones about saying so. Now that she's disgraced herself, you befriend her. Why?"

"I don't know . . . I suppose because she needs a friend so badly. Are you forbidding me to go there, Ma?"

"Of course not. I merely think it's a bit improper . . ."

"Is it proper or improper to befriend someone in need? Or to put it another way, is it more Christian or un-Christian—"

"You needn't recite Scripture to me, young lady. I taught you that particular bit of gospel, remember? And of course you're right."

Smiling, Knox went to her, bent and kissed her. "Thank you, Ma. Now if I can just elude Cousin Sanford . . ."

"I wish you'd be a little kinder to Sanford," Margaret said. "After all . . ."

"After all Sanny is nothing but a pompous turnip. He's gotten on your nerves as much as mine, and don't deny it."

"I know," Margaret said resignedly. "You'd think your father would learn. Instead he's encouraged Sanford exactly as he did Denny Gibbs—"

"Suggesting to him that I'm merely being coy or that a little more persuasion will turn the trick."

"Yes, and I'm tired of it. Tired of living in a household that feels like a state of armed truce."

"Well, I shan't accept the blame for that."

"But you are partly to blame, Knoxie. You're quite as stiff-necked as your father . . . and your whole attitude toward him has been anything but ingratiating."

"I don't care. He has no right . . ."

"On the contrary. He's your father and he has certain well-defined rights." Margaret sighed. "And you're his daughter, with all his honesty, fire, and stubbornness. I suppose it was bound to be like this, once you found yourself and something happened to put the two of you at odds. I just wish you'd try to unbend a little."

Knox looked at her. "I will, Mother. I promise. I didn't realize how upsetting it must be for you."

"Thank you, Knoxie. That's all I ask." Margaret kissed her.

"Now go along with you. And give my regards to the Robiers."

Knox went to the stables and had her chestnut saddled. She rode around the fort quadrangle which echoed, as it did all day, every day but Sunday, with the racket of saw and hammer. The colonel was pressing for completion of the construction that had gone on for four years. George Wilson was supervising a gang of soldiers as they labored a block of quarried stone into place. He idly saluted her and Knox reined over by him.

"Hello, George. Think you'll ever finish it?"

"The purpose of this fort," Wilson said wryly, "is to serve notice on the reddies that a Christian nation is here to stay. So we quarry stone from the Mississippi bluffs. We cut pine logs on the Iowa and the Chippewa, we saw lumber at our mill on the Yellow, and we burn lime at that coulee across the river. And do you know why, m'lass? So we can take another five to ten years getting it finished, by which time the country'll be thoroughly settled and we'll be ordered to abandon the works. Then we can back-slap ourselves numb, having once more vindicated the forces of Liberty and Civilization, and roll on westward over a million or so more redskin corpses."

"Lordy, you're in a cheerful way today. Are all grooms soon-to-be this rapturous?"

Wilson grinned. "Why, I'm ecstatic. Why not? In two weeks I'll be out of the bloody Army and Mary and I will be wedded and on our way to St. Louis."

"Without Papa Street's blessing?"

"With his grudging consent, at least. Plus my unexpected pleasure at shedding the blasted service after seven years. I've discovered I haven't the strength of character or hardness of head to endure a lifelong pyrrhic dance of the soul. Anyway with Jeff and Bob and Denny and lovable Doc Beaumont all gone, the place isn't the same. Any news from Jefferson?"

They chatted for a few more minutes, then Knox said goodbye and rode down the river slope. The landing was crowded with the usual motley spring array of rivermen, *voyageurs,* and Indians. She rode past the last houses and tapped the chestnut with her crop, lifting him into a trot. Snow patches still clung to the buff-colored hills; blue windflowers poked from the dry grass. The sun had unlocked a brew of wine-quick smells. Her mood was improving when a voice hailed her. It was Sanford Preston, coming across the long rise at her back, spurring his copper-bottom bay up beside her.

He tapped his tall wool hat with his crop. "Ah, Cousin Knox! Fancy running into you on the prairie."

"Yes, fancy it," she snapped.

At thirty, Sanford's boyish chubbiness had recently turned distressingly portly. His yellow side whiskers and Vandyke failed to lend an intended air of rakishness. A few years ago he had seemed funny and dashing and not unattractive. But since his father had died last year, leaving him heir to the Preston estate, considerable cash and a fortune in Louisiana cotton lands, he had turned bullish and officious in a cheerful, maddening way. As she tried not to encounter him unless in company with others, he'd become intolerably sly in his attempts to waylay her when she was alone.

He beamed undauntedly, reined a little nearer and seized her hand. "Knox—dear!"

She snatched her hand away. "Sanny, you're the worst—oaf! Haven't you any pride at all?"

"Not where you're concerned, my dear. I humble myself at your feet, I—"

"Oh, stop it. You're as arch as a turtle."

"I apologize." He caught hold of her bridle, forcing her to draw rein. "But do think about it again, won't you? About marrying me?"

"Sanny, I've told you before . . ."

"I know, but think about it, at least. Promise me you will."

"Very well, I promise. Now will you kindly—"

"Of course." Sanford released her bridle. "May I ride with you?"

349

"You may not. I want to ride alone."

"Milady!"

Grinning, he tapped his hat again and swung back toward the village, pushing his spur-galled mount at a reckless run, crop rising and falling. I hope to gracious he falls off and breaks a leg, she thought. And riding on, was sorry for thinking it. Sanford wasn't wholly to blame. She'd been glad to see him when he'd arrived last fall. Sanny had always been an amusing fellow; his presence had promised to enliven the tedious winter months. She'd flirted with him tongue-in-cheek as she always had, never dreaming he would take it seriously. Now she could hardly wait for him to leave . . .

She was riding into the familiar arm of oak woods where she and Jeff had met two years ago. The chestnut high-pranced a little as though he remembered pitching her off at this spot. They passed through the woods, crossed another prairie rise and dipped into the valley where Vitelle Robier's bare stubbled wheatfields lay. She was surprised to see the trapper out with his oxen and bull-tongue plow, breaking the half-thawed soil. As she rode up, he halted his team and sleeved sweat off his face.

"*B'jour,* m'a'mselle."

"Good afternoon. Isn't it much too early to be putting in a crop?"

"I only break up the ground. It is something to do."

"How is Ceclie?"

"The same." He stared across the hills. "Her time is close." Knox hesitated. "Sir, it's none of my affair, but . . ."

"Say it."

"Perhaps I shouldn't. I think of you and Ceclie as friends, yet I've come to visit such a few times . . ."

"This I understand." Robier's tone was sharply bitter. Then he looked at her. "That was wrong. I am sorry. You have been a friend. It's good that a girl like you, her own age, has been sometimes to see her. She does not say so, yet I know it has meant much."

"Well then, I'll speak frankly. Are you going to blame her forever?"

"*Sacré,* I don't blame her. I blame the *cochon* who did it to her."

"Do you know his name?"

"I know it." He stared at her steadily. "He is far away now."

"There's no chance he might . . . make amends?"

"Marry her, this means? No. No, m'a'mselle. Not that high-born pig." He looked away. "I say too much. He does not matter, he is nothing. You are right. Once we were close, Ceclie and me. Now it is hard to say what I feel. I wish to see her save' from the fate of all the half-breed girls. It could have been. The good schooling, then the good marriage. Now she's only another klooch left *enceinte* by a white man who was no good." He gave a jerky nod. "Go down to the cabin. I will be along when I have put up the oxen . . ."

Knox rode through the maple motte and into the clearing. Ceclie was in the yard scattering feed for the chickens. Knox descended from her saddle with a pleasant greeting. As usual, Ceclie had little to say. Her sacklike dress rounded over the heavy bulge of her pregnancy and she moved at a slow graceless waddle. Her hair hung forward over one shoulder, an inky tangled rope that she hadn't bothered to brush or braid.

Robier came from tending the oxen and invited Knox inside. While they sat at the table and made small talk, Ceclie prepared coffee, going about the task with a slow, heavy-bodied indifference. It was not just the pregnancy, Knox thought; she acted as though she no longer cared.

As she was carrying the coffee to the table, she halted midway across the room. Caught at her stomach and grimaced. Then she proceeded to the table and set the pot down carefully.

"Are you all right, *petite chou?*"

"I think it is time, Papa . . ."

Robier got up and helped her through the dogtrot into the sleeping room. He eased her down on her bed, then glanced at Knox standing in the doorway. "M'a'mselle, you know Madam Gignoux, the *sage femme*? If you would be so good, ride quick to Prairie du Chien and fetch her . . ."

Knox stepped into the room, taking off her toque. "Do you know anything of delivering babies, sir?"

"*Sacré,* would I ask for a midwife then?"

"I'll need hot water." Knox began rolling up her sleeves. "Plenty of soap, a piece of string, all the clean cloth you have about . . ."

"*Sacré mil de tonerre!* What do you know, a soft little high-bred thing like you?"

"Enough. I helped a black granny woman on my grandfather's farm deliver many a baby. Even if there's time to fetch Gignoux, she's like as not busy elsewhere. *Pressez-vous,* Mr. Robier—"

Knox washed her hands with soap and hot water. She undressed the laboring girl and washed her all over with warm water. She replaced the blankets on the bed with clean ones and covered Ceclie, then combed out her snarled hair. She was thinner than she should be, but her youth and sturdy build should carry her through easily, barring complications.

"What will you call the baby? Have you thought of a name?"

She moved her head on the pillow, her face glistening. "I don't care . . ."

Knox bent over her, holding both her hands tightly. "You must care. You must think strong and beautiful thoughts to make a strong beautiful baby. That is true whether it's a boy or a girl."

"Oh, he is a boy. He kicks so hard."

The pains began coming harder. Knox's hands ached from Ceclie's grip. Now and then she relaxed, sighing, and Knox wiped the sweat from her face. She could feel her own skin dampening with tension. She had never managed a birthing on her own. Suppose it's a breech birth, she thought. You've seen it done, but even so.

Ceclie thrashed in a sudden painful spasm. "Denny!" she cried. "Denny—"

Dear God, Knox thought. She looked quickly at Robier and met his hard intense stare. He said nothing . . .

An hour later, it was over.

Knox tied the umbilical cord in two places, cut between and spanked the baby into squalling life. She sponged him, wrapped a bellyband around him to protect his navel, swaddled him in clean sacking and laid him in his mother's arms. He squirmed, red and fretful. His scalp was already covered by fine black hair, but he was white, white enough to escape a quarter-blood heritage. But enough to escape the stigma of bastardy?

Knox went to the door and opened it. Hot and sweaty, she stood a moment letting the air cool her. A rose-lemon sunset stained the sky, edging the clouds with topaz fire. Old world, she thought, old world, you're good to be alive in.

Poor Denny. She knew him well enough to know that he would live with his guilt. She hadn't been able to quell a faint needling suspicion, remembering that Jeff had spent a whole month under this roof. But that was a year ago. And shortly after Denny Gibbs had returned, she had seen a change in him, Denny had been pleasant and easy to talk to, his thoughts no longer on her. Gradually, though, he had changed again, turning worried and morose. Had he known—then—about the baby? Or had he really loved Ceclie, had he brooded on whatever future they might have?

She turned back into the room. Robier was bending over the baby, nudging his pink palm with a calloused thumb. He looked suddenly at Knox and grinned. "*Sacré*, a husky one, is he not?"

She smiled. "He's beautiful." You ought to see him, Denny. Your son is beautiful.

26

The creek had dried down to a sallow trickle in the August heat. The men squatted in the streambed and dug holes and watched them slowly fill with water that muddied at a touch. But travel between watering places had stretched into days, and they were not finicky. While some of the troops were digging, the rest held the thirst-crazed horses to prevent their drinking at the slime-covered hollows where buffalo had wallowed. The animals began voiding their bladders and bowels with juicy splattings that filled the air with a ripe green stink. It had been that way every rest halt, and the men ignored it.

Sitting on his heels by the hole he and Gibbs had scooped out, Davis rolled his shoulders against the itching torment of a woolen blouse that was stiff with dirt and sweat, staring across the hot shimmering plains at the jagged blue sweep of the Wichitas. His ears hummed with a slight fever. He soaked a handkerchief, ran it over his sun-boiled face and scrubbed at the dusty beard caking his jaws. Then he dried his hands, took an oilcloth packet from his pocket, opened it and removed one of the letters it held. He unfolded and reread the three frayed sheets, though he knew them by heart. It was the usual sort of letter Knox sent, chatty with the small doings of home and garrison. It was dated nearly five months ago and he'd received it a month after that.

He had not heard a word from her since.

Carefully refolding the letter, he tucked it away in the oilcloth and returned it to his pocket. Gibbs, squatting a couple of yards away, cleared his throat. "Look, boy, you got to quit worrying on it. There's an explanation. Has to be. Any number of things . . ."

"That's the hell of it."

"You know damn well if something had happened, someone would write you. Mary Street would, or George."

"We've been over that. I told you I wrote them . . . sent letters to both months ago. No answer. If all the mail to or from Prairie du Chien has been stalled somewhere, why was Colonel Dodge still getting letters posted there a week before we left Gibson?"

Until late March, the irregular mails had always brought a fat batch of Knox's letters. If she'd suffered an accident or illness of some sort, any number of their friends would have sent him word. Common sense ruled out any clumsy mischance of all their letters going astray. He'd unwillingly considered the possibility that Knox was holding deliberate silence and had told their friends to do the same.

But why would she? Another man? Impossible. And if it were true, she simply wasn't the kind to keep him in ignorance. If he'd unwittingly let drop some remark or other that had hurt or angered her, she wasn't the thin-skinned sort who'd brood in hateful silence. Imagination, though, was an unsparing goad. No matter how many times he told himself that his swarming doubts were beneath contempt, they'd merely cropped up again in a hundred miserable guises. He'd continued to write her, urging her to tell him what was wrong. But no answer had yet come by mid-June, when the Dragoons had started out on their expedition to the Wichitas.

Gibbs cupped his hands, scooped up some muddy water, drank and made a face. "Jesus. Is that what these Western people mean by sand in your craw?" He splashed more water on his face, then stood up, swaying a little. Davis eyed him with concern. His face had a blotched and puffy look; his eyes were glazed and thick-lidded.

"You ought to rest awhile. You look like hell."

"Nothing. The damned heat."

"Probably the 'intermittent.' You'd better see Surgeon Haile."

"Hell, I'm all right. Got to walk the kinks out. Too long on a damn horse."

Gibbs walked away, a little unsteadily.

Davis glanced around him. At the scrubby rib-gaunt horses. At the groups of silent, sun-blackened men whose uniforms hung like bleached rags on their scarecrow frames. They had accomplished their mission. Established a historic milestone. Unquestionably. But what a price they had paid . . .

It had started well enough. The 1st Dragoons had spent this spring of 1834 grading and corduroying a road from Fort Gibson to Fort Towson, a new cantonment being erected to the south. Afterward they'd freighted tons of stone to the Towson site. Their *esprit de corps* had worn thin, but returned in a burst of exuberance once the expedition was under way. On June 15 they had ridden southwest from Fort Gibson belly-in and chin-high, glorying in their restored identity, a mile-long procession of mounted troops, ambulances, and baggage wagons. But the pomp and strut of parade had faded as the mission had bogged down in one misery after another.

They'd been three days out from Fort Gibson when troopers had begun complaining of sore bellies and headaches. By nightfall, many had been too sick to hold saddles. They lay in their blankets burning up with the "intermittent," fever and unquenchable thirst turning to teeth-chattering chills, then fever again. So it had gone through the early days, men dropping out in daily batches, the sicker ones loaded into ambulances, and when these became overcrowded, onto baggage wagons. The mildly ill had been isolated by being ordered to ride at the rear of the column, behind the wagons.

They had reached the Canadian River on June 25. General Henry Leavenworth, the new commander at Gibson, was already encamped there, having departed Gibson on the twelfth with a reconnaissance unit. He'd decided to accompany the Dragoons part of the way. The force had pushed on, leaving twenty-seven sick troopers in bivouac at the Canadian crossing. Buffalo had been sighted almost daily; Leavenworth had become increasingly excited at each appearance of a herd and had finally set out to dust off a bull bison. His horse had thrown and injured him; an Indian-style travois was rigged and the general lashed onto it. Two days later the column had limped into Captain Dean's camp on the Washita River where, nearly two hundred miles from Fort Gibson, two companies of infantry garrisoned in tents formed the last American post on the edge of the Great Plains.

By far the roughest part of the journey had lain ahead; with Leavenworth out of his head in fever, all decision had rested with Colonel Henry Dodge. Half a hundred men had been too sick to go on; nearly as many had been on the verge of collapse. At least eighty horses and mules had been too disabled to take up the march. General conditions and the brutal distance remaining to be covered plus the return journey meant that nobody would blame Dodge for turning back. He'd decided to go on, weeding out those unfit to continue and leaving them in Dean's camp with a pair of company surgeons . . .

Ben Poore cantered up to the cutbank on his ugly raw-boned horse. He was in charge of the regiment's four picked bands of scouts and hunters drawn from the Seneca, Delaware, Cherokee, and Osage tribes. Lather and dust crusted his mustang's rippling coat, but the animal was in far better shape than the high-strung thoroughbreds who had begun to drop soon after the mission was under way. They'd had no bottom for the poor forage, bad water and killing heat to which the scouts' plains-bred ponies had stood up easily.

Poore swung his leg forward over his pommel, dropped in a

lithe motion to the ground and light-footed down the cutbank. He gave Davis a laconic hello and settled on his haunches beside him. He took a mouthful of gritty water, rolled it on his tongue and spat it out, then dug out his pipe, his Mexican tinder cord and flint and steel *eslabón*. He struck a spark into the tinder cord and puffed his pipe alight, nodding toward Gibbs who was pacing heavily up and down.

"Best watch your friend close. He run out of pee and vinegar kind o' sudden."

"We're all pretty depleted, Ben. Except you and the scouts, of course."

"Wagh!" Poore's face puckered up like seamed leather. "Dodge should of got this fandango on the trail two month earlier, like I said. High summer with green troops. Jesus. And them dress-parade thoroughbreds of yourn." He jerked a nod at his own mount. "This child's hoss may be shy on looks, but I caught him on these same high plains. Goes for days on naught but spit 'n' buffler grass. Less he gets, tougher he gets. Could of seated your whole command on mustangs. Should of."

"I know. I've heard you and the colonel pass enough warm words on the matter."

"Wagh. Old hoss, he got too big for his buckskins. Throwed 'em away for braid 'n' fancy cloth. Throwed away his good sense too."

It was hard to argue the judgment.

Sixty miles beyond the Washita River, the Dragoons had struck into the Cross Timbers, a thick sunless belt of blackjack timber where whole acres of trees had blown down in jackstraw tangles. Impenetrable underbrush had sprung up, much of it thorns and brambles that had shredded clothing and flesh at a touch. For three days, the Dragoons had hacked their way through the cross-fallen trees with firewood axes, through the dense thickets with their sabers, opening up by slow yards a road for the wagons. Beyond the Cross Timbers finally, they'd had their first view of the true Great Plains. A billowing sea of tawny grass, muddy rivers, glaring skies, and hot eternal winds, it shrank all of a man's pretensions and crushed him mentally to his knees. While Dodge was insisting the troops would become acclimated, the health of the whole command had continued to deteriorate under the blasting advance of the plains summer. Men's bowels were on fire; fits of flux and vomiting attacked nearly everyone. Countermeasures had proven useless; dread became tinged by panic.

Dodge and Kearny had maintained discipline by adherence to a strict and unvarying routine. Four o'clock brought the night halt. Grass and bushes were systematically beat for snakes, an average of four or five being turned up and killed at each camp. A man bivouacked in one of four uniform lines that formed a square, picketed his horse and scoured up a supply of buffalo chips. At the first rosy smudge of dawn, company buglers blasted away the shreds of sleep; the troops unlimbered a legion of sore muscles, breakfasted and were on the march by eight. The butt sores and chapped thighs of the early journey began to harden, a mild solace.

The weirdly hovering rim of the distant Wichitas had grown slowly nearer. On July 14, smoke of Indian signals had appeared above the near foothills. The scouts had agreed that a Comanche village lay just ahead, but whether the smoke talk was peace or hostile, nobody could guess, though Dodge had sent messengers ahead to apprise the tribes of their coming and their purpose. A party of fiercely painted warriors had met them in full battle array. After some tense minutes, the Dragoons had been escorted to the village, where Dodge and his staff had held council with the chief and his headmen.

With Poore translating, the colonel had explained their mission. The Grandfather desired that the roving bands of his plains children be called to a great council whereat delegates should be chosen and sent to Fort Gibson to meet with emissaries from Washington. Useful gifts of cloth and tools would be exchanged for the tribes' agreement to let American wagon trains pass unmolested through their lands. Would the Comanche sit in council with the Kiowa and the Pawnee? The Kiowa were their brothers, the chief had replied, and he did not object to sitting with Pawnee.

Thus the first ticklish ground had been broken in a historic treaty: the first between the United States and the tribes of the Far Western plains. The War Department had instructed Dodge to make direct overtures to all the Comanche and Pawnee leaders; unless these powerful bands were won over, negotiations with other plains tribes would be futile. The main town of the Pawnee Picts lay one hundred miles east of the Comanche village. If he could deliver the two Pawnee and Kiowa girls to their families, success would be assured, Dodge had felt. And the political relatives of the Martin boy, nine-year-old Matthew, had rallied enough voices in Washington to make his recovery a must.

Dodge's command had been broken and wasted by rampant fever; thirty-nine men were too sick to go on. The spent and feverish columns had little force or glitter left with which to impress Indians. But Dodge never hesitated. Leaving twenty-seven volunteers to care for the stricken, he'd gathered up his remaining hundred and eighty-three Dragoons and pushed out across the late July furnace of the Great Plains. The foothill terrain had grown steeper and more irregular, slashed by deep gullies that forced sweeping detours. Horses had gone lame on sharp rocks; summer drought had caused an exodus of game; no way to supplement dwindling rations. At last, high in the Wichitas, they had found the plateau where the main band of the Pawnee Picts had their village. The Comanche had sent runners ahead to apprise them of the whites' intentions.

After a fierce display by half a hundred Pawnee braves who had come streaming up at a gallop, whooping, brandishing bows and muskets, they had been made welcome by the aged chief, We-ter-ra-shah-ro. Corn, beans, and buffalo meat were traded for tobacco, trinkets and such extra clothes as the whites could spare. Young Matthew Martin had been brought forth—dirty, deeply browned, and reluctant to go home—and handed over to the Dragoons. Only then had Dodge broached the subject of a council whereat the Americans and plains people might speak together. We-ter-ra-shah-ro had proved agreeable to such a council and to the prestigious idea of its being held in his town. Runners had been sent to all the Comanche, Kiowa, and Pawnee bands. The Dragoons had recuperated somewhat in the relative cool of the plateau, established facilities for care of their sick and carried on a friendly concourse with their dusky hosts.

The Indian delegates had begun arriving within a week. As the council had opened, they had voiced a common concern as to the white man's territorial ambitions, but the prevailing wish was to avoid trouble. Dodge had told them that the United States was at peace with all white nations; these would never dare molest tribes who had treaty with the United States. More, if Americans were permitted to set up trading posts in their midst, they need no longer be dependent on the Spanish in Santa Fe for such civilized goods as they coveted. Finally, if the bands represented here would choose delegates from among those present to return with the Dragoons, treaties could be drawn up. After a week of debate, fifteen Kiowa, three Pawnee, and one Comanche chief had agreed to return with the soldiers; others had promised to send emissaries . . .

"Anyway, Ben," Davis said, "we did accomplish something."

Poore snorted quietly. "Wait and see, boy. You don't know Injuns."

"I flatter myself that I do, Ben."

"Hunh-uh. You don't think Injun. They want to keep things like they are, but they don't want no ruckus with the Americans. White man fights for glory and land, Injun for glory and the pure fun. What they want is to keep raiding and making war agin each other the old way and keep outen trouble with whites."

"Well, that's all we'd hoped for, isn't it?"

"Hoss, it'll work that way awhile, but not long. Some of them butt-sprung wise men in Washington'll knuckle under to a pack of stinking investors who want for one reason or t'other to grab off some treaty lands. Then the gov'ment'll sic you bluecoats on these people and tell 'em to move where they say or fight. I seen it before." Poore snapped his teeth on his pipestem, shaking his head. "All this fooferaw for nothing. Jesus, boy, look around you. How many men we lost so far? And we ain't home yet. Christ. All for nothing."

Davis shook his head. "I don't know . . ."

Maybe Poore was right. Follow through on the pattern that history had made east of the Mississippi and you'd have another Black Hawk War. A score of them. One thing was sure. This expedition would be remembered as one of the grimmest and costliest in peacetime military history.

Captain Raoul Masson tramped past them, limping slightly. The wound of his old disgrace always showed when he was tired. He flicked a short stare at Davis and walked on, swiping at his dusty trousers.

"Mean-eyed bastard, ain't he?" said Poore. "Always eyeballs you like he's waiting for your foot to slip once. Man's like a damn cat."

"I won't play his mouse," Davis said.

Poore knocked his pipe clean on his horny palm and stood up. "Well, I best report to Dodge. There's a lot worse ahead. Take care, boy."

He tramped away. Davis listened awhile to the vacant underpitched talk of the men, the blubbery voidings of the horses; flies sang in the stench. Gibbs had joined a group of officers and Davis got up and walked over to them.

"So you served under Old Zeke Taylor at Fort Crawford, eh?" one of them was saying to Denny. "Interesting. Just before I left Louisville, all society was a-twitter about the forthcoming marriage of his daughter. Quite the social highlight of the year."

Gibbs said: "His daughter . . . Sarah Knox?"

"Yes. Do you know her?"

Gibbs turned his head. "Jeff—oh here you are."

"I heard," Davis said. He stared at the officer, a green lieutenant named Brixton who'd been assigned to the Dragoons less than a week before their departure from Gibson. "I know Miss Taylor. You wouldn't happen to know who the man is?"

Brixton gave him a pleasant, quizzical glance. "A cousin on her mother's side, I believe. Talk was that she *was* engaged to some Army chap, just before, but Old Zeke didn't take kindly to the match. So it was broken off."

The humming in Davis's ears climbed to a whining pulse. "You're a damned liar."

A startled flush rose from Brixton's collar. "What do you mean?"

"I'll tell you over pistols or sabers. Take your choice."

"Jeff, easy!" Gibbs said.

"You're crazy!" Brixton burst out. "I have no quarrel with you."

Davis's hand lashed across his face. "Now you have."

Brixton took two steps back, holding his jaw. "I say—are you sick or what?"

Talk had broken off around them. Men were staring. Captain Masson came up the streambed at a trot, alert as a cat. "What's going on here?" His single eye made a glittering appraisal. "Mr. Brixton! Did Lieutenant Davis strike you?"

"No, sir. Had the misfortune to stumble and fall."

"Your mouth is bleeding, mister!"

"Quite so, sir. Cut my lip."

Masson's face darkened. "You're lying, mister! I intend to put both you men on report."

"Sir!" Brixton said. "Should the captain report this as other than an accident, I shall be obliged to deny it."

Masson stared at him. "You'd call me a liar?"

"No, sir. I would regrettably feel compelled to state that the captain was in error."

Masson's gaze slashed across the men around them. Their

faces were stony. Davis and Brixton were well-liked; he was not. They had shut ranks against him and he knew it. Stiff-backed, he wheeled and strode away.

Davis walked off from the others and sat down heavily against the bank. God, God, he thought, it can't be. A pair of muddy boots stepped into the lowered angle of his vision. He looked up at Brixton.

"See here," the subaltern said. "I didn't know that *you* were . . . listen, I'm damned sorry."

"Yes," Davis said.

"Gibbs just told me. Damn! I really am sorry."

"I ought to thank you. It was white of you to take my part after . . ."

"Forget it. Nothing at all. That Masson is a devil. Everyone knows he has it in for you. Anyhow I thought you were in fever . . . out of your head, you know. No holding that against a fellow."

"I wonder . . ." Davis paused, rubbing his eyelids. "Is there any possibility you're mistaken about . . . ?"

"Afraid not. The talk was that Miss Taylor yielded to Old Zeke's importunities and agreed to the engagement. Anyhow news of the betrothal was in all the Kentucky papers—Louisville, Lexington, Springfield, all the rest. Social event of the season and all that."

"It would be. A cousin, you said?"

"Yes. I heard or read his name somewhere. Let's see . . . Preston, I think. That's it. Sanford Preston . . ."

The return journey to Fort Gibson made the first part of the trip seem a picnic by comparison. Having somewhat recuperated during two weeks' rest on the Pawnee plateau, they'd made brisk time the first week. Achieving their sick camp at the Comanche village, they'd found that most of the stricken had succumbed and been buried in shallow rock-filled graves by those who could manage it. Dodge had ordered the survivors loaded onto wagons, they would pick up the others left in fever camps along the way. But the sick list continued to swell daily. Again the wagons creaked to overloads of moaning, stricken men. Again sick camps had to be set up at each waterhole, provisions and a few well men left with the ailing till they died or recovered enough to take up the journey.

The plains heat of June had been sweltering and sticky. The heat of July and August was dry and baking. By nine o'clock in the morning, a man was roasting in his own airtight corner of hell: the Army blouse of heavy wool. By afternoon, sweated almost dry, his flesh prickled and ached with heat rash. The sun poured like blistering fluid over the trudging column. Brittle grass powdered under the wheels and shuffling hoofs; the tawny-tufted undulations of scorched prairie swelled and shimmered to the horizon where, from time to time, mirages quivered.

Sweated and punished by implacable heat, more men fell ill; the sick list doubled. Erratic start-ups of hot, dry, hard-blowing wind increased their misery. Dust billowed in tan choking clouds that hung for hours over the column. Covering fifteen stubborn miles a day, every man became bred to the bone with exhaustion. The pace of the column began to limp. More and more of the emaciated thoroughbreds were dying on their feet. A stench of sickness simmered like a palpable miasma along the plodding line of men and animals . . .

Food became as big a problem as water. Rations were halved, then quartered. The Indians reconnoitered daily for game, but the results of their foraging never sufficed to fill so many bellies. At last, close to the Cross Timbers, a large herd of buffalo was sighted. That night they ate well—those who could still take food. Much of the flesh was jerked and stored against the days ahead. Spirits somewhat renewed, the Dragoons again bucked the jackstraw wilderness. The trail slashed out on first crossing cut their time in half, but it was still rugged going. Here, as throughout the whole trip, the man who shamed all complainers into silence was George Catlin, the artist who had accompanied the mission by special permission of the Secretary of War. Though burning with fever, Catlin continued to toil with sketchbook and paints, capturing all his subjects with a vivid power.

Finally they reached Dean's camp on the Washita. Here they learned of General Leavenworth's death. When he'd failed to show improvement, the ailing officer had been placed in an ambulance and started for Fort Gibson, only to succumb within a few miles. After resting three days by the Washita, the Dragoons resumed their trek. Their hope of easier travel east of the Washita was dashed. Ovenlike temperatures had clamped fists of drought on the plains; waterholes were reduced to stagnant puddles. The men dug holes in streambeds where dampness survived. Horses mad with thirst had to be fought on an iron rein. The parched and impatient troopers had to be watched too . . .

Denny Gibbs had fought off the early qualms of his fever. But he'd refused to be left in a sick camp, and day by day he'd grown weaker. The night after they crossed the Washita, he was burning up again, tossing restlessly in his blankets, his eyes bright and hot, all his faculties sensitized. He was barely able to sit his horse next morning. He rode all that day slumped almost insensibly across its withers, and Davis stayed close to his stirrup.

With only a hundred miles to go, the column was on its last legs. Good water, fresh meat, a few days of rest, were essential before the men and remaining animals fell in their tracks. Dodge ordered a slight detour to the northeast and a crosspoint on the Canadian where, Ben Poore said, were meadows and wooded ridges.

Long before they reached it, Gibbs had joined the other sick on a jouncing wagon, rolling and tossing in delirium. The fever seemed to have run its course; no more troopers fell ill. But those already afflicted continued to slip into coma and death. The trail became dotted with fresh graves.

The Canadian was a lively river that ran clear as glass till it found a muddy terminus in the Arkansas. They made camp in the shade of lush old cedars and staked their animals out on the lush grass. Davis took over the care of Denny Gibbs and did what he could to make him comfortable. He cut cedar boughs, built a half-shelter, floored it with springy cuttings and spread blankets over them. Gibbs fell into a hot twitching sleep.

Davis sat beside him, hugging his drawn-up knees. His thoughts were like a slushy stew. Fat flies droned in the heat. Whistle-songs of parakeets mingled with the throaty somnolent clucking of pigeons in the bottoms. Men sat about, stunned by days of shattering sun, their faces blackened dusty masks, voices muted and sullen. They ignored the flamelike sunset; they'd seen a hundred pretty spasms like it between the blistering days and desolate nights. Dodge came through the camp at his stocky driving stride, inspecting the situation, listening to medical reports, his face grim and haggard.

Gradually the men roused a little. Splashes of fire began to blossom in the plum-colored twilight. Gibbs tossed in the deepening throes of fever. Will he live? Davis wondered dully. And then: Does he care? He wondered about that. For a year Gibbs had dug himself a rut of guilt. Now he had pushed himself unreasonably hard, past all endurance.

Davis stared at the fire. It mirrored the fires, false rippling beacons that swam together and died. How many men had merged their lives for this mission and how many had died or would die? Close to a fifth of the regiment would never see home again. And if Ben Poore were right, as no doubt he was, it had all gone for nothing. Nothing. It made you wonder if life had any value at all beyond its apprehension of itself . . .

Oh, they'd learn. The plains cavalry of the future would benefit from the ignorance, the bad preparations, the blunders of the 1st Regiment of Dragoons—of whom half or more might have to be mustered out as unfit for further service. The glory, if any, would belong to those who followed. And they would. The years ahead would be exciting ones. The fervent expansionists would see to that, even if they destroyed a whole race of red-men in the process.

That's the price, he thought. You are a patriotic American, you believe in your nation, its ideals and its goals, and you like the Indians too and admire many of their qualities and much that's inherent in their way of life. But you can't have it both ways, my boy, and you are starting to see that. You can love your country, but you can't go on helping it rob and exter-minate a people who are only defending what's theirs. You owe the Army a good deal, no doubt of it. It's tempered your body and your mind and it has put some hard gray steel in that too-romantic nature of yours. But I think the time is almost ripe for the Army and you to part company.

That was what Knox had wanted. But his decision had noth-ing to do with her. If she had tired of waiting, if she had decided the man he was and would always be was not for her, that was her right. He had misjudged the woman she was, that was all, and hurt as it might, it was better this way.

Sanford Preston. What kind of a man was he? Quit thinking about it. It explains everything, doesn't it? The letters that never came. The bitter truth your friends couldn't bring themselves to tell you. What does any of it matter now?

"Jeff . . ."

Gibbs was awake. His eyes seemed sunken, the skin taut and shiny across the bones of his face.

"How are you, old fellow?"

"Pretty bad, boy. Water . . . ?"

Davis tilted a cup to his cracked lips. He drank less than half the water and lay back. "Many thanks. Afraid I've made an ass of myself again. A big bloody ass, as George would say."

"Easy, Denny. Try to sleep, will you?"

"Always had a knack for doing the wrong thing. My father tried to break me of it. Break me by hand. I loved him, Jeff. I wanted him to be proud of me. I tried to live up to all he expected of me. God, how I tried. But we could never talk . . . I could never talk to him. I don't know why." His eyes glittered wetly in his chalk-hued face. "Then I failed with Knox and it all pulled loose in me and I had to prove my manhood. I proved it, all right. With Ceclie. I loved her, Jeff, did you know that? So I failed her too. Right in character."

He fumbled a hand inside the breast of his coatee, pulling out a sealed envelope that was stained and creased and dog-eared. "I'm sorry. Sorry for what I did to her. Sorry for being such a damned coward. I wish I could tell her . . . but this will have to do. I hadn't the courage to help her outright, but I wanted it found on my body if anything happened to me. It's a simple bequest . . . wills what little I can claim for my own to her and the child. See that she gets it, Jeff."

Davis put the envelope in his pocket.

"Lord God, boy. I can't see so well. Getting cold too . . ."

"The sun's gone down, Denny."

He didn't add that a stifling quilt of heat still clung to the plains. He pulled Gibbs's blankets up to his chin and fetched his own and spread those over him too. Gibbs slipped back into fevered sleep.

Later he woke and babbled of cold, terrible cold, though his skin was dry and hot. Surgeon Haile came and looked and shook his head. All that Davis could do was stay by Gibbs and moisten his lips with a wet rag. Some of his disjointed mumblings were coherent, others weren't. Twice he said Ceclie's name. A little after midnight, he lapsed into unconsciousness.

Davis fought off sleep as long as he could. At last, face bent against his knees, he slept soundly.

He woke slowly, coming stiff-jointedly back to life as a pink pulse of dawn sculptured the land in gentle relief. Then he jerked fully awake.

"Denny . . ."

Gibbs was cold and stiffening in his blankets. He had been dead for hours.

They spent five days by the Canadian and then pressed across the last brutal stretch to Fort Gibson. The aftermath of fever continued to wither their ranks. Men died daily. Wagons creaked with their burdens of groaning sufferers. Within a couple days, few of the remaining horses were capable of bearing riders. Men still able to walk plodded on foot, leading the gaunted animals.

On August 24, the squat and blocky buildings of Fort Gibson emerged into sight. As they came across the flats, the garrison marched out to meet them, the band blaring, the men cheering. But the music and the cheers dimmed and slowly died off altogether. The 1st Regiment of United States Dragoons had returned. But there was nothing to serenade in its return. Nothing to cheer. Unless it was the fact that some of the troopers could still walk at all . . .

27

"A year or two at Mr. Cadle's school will do wonders for you, Ceclie," said Margaret Taylor.

"If you think so, ma'am."

"Indeed I do. The Cadles are friends of ours and will take you in without question if we recommend you." Margaret smiled, glancing up from the Afghan squares on which she was sewing. "You're Catholic, I suppose."

"No, ma'am. Papa did not like the black-robe teachings. Or any others. He said I must decide for myself one day."

"Well, we shan't try to influence you, though we're all Episcopalians—except for the colonel, who's of your papa's opinion—and as it happens, Mr. Cadle's is an Episcopal school. He and his sister will probably try to convert you, so be warned. The important thing is that you and little Jean-Pierre will be well-treated. You'll have good schooling and the best instruction in speech, manners, and deportment that one might wish."

Knox, seated beside Ceclie in the porch swing, almost smiled. The girl's thoughts were less than wholeheartedly on the Reverend Richard Fish Cadle's fine school at Green Bay. These days her attentions centered around the cooing, kicking baby she held firmly in one arm while she patiently spooned into his mouth a concoction of cooked berries and wild honey on which she was weaning him.

"Of course," Margaret added, "you'll have to guard yourself around the young soldiers at Fort Howard."

"Yes, ma'am."

"I don't mean to imply you wouldn't; it's only that young ladies are still a scarce commodity around border garrisons. And with that figure, my dear, you can depend on being stormed off your feet."

Which was no exaggeration, Knox thought. The baby hadn't pulled Ceclie down one bit; his coming had put meaning back in her life and she was as healthy as ever, lovely in her maturity. Margaret and Knox had tried most of their dresses and some old ones of Ann's on her in the hope that one or two might be sewed over for her, but the Taylor women tended to willowy slimness; Ceclie curved like a milkmaid, with a generous breadth to her shoulders and hips. So they'd cut and sewed to prepare a small wardrobe that would serve for her introduction into civilized society, simple calicoes that decorously brought out her natural charms. Her inky hair shimmered in a fashionable chignon. But with all her dresses, she retained her beaded Indian belt and mussel-shell necklace as if to say that everyone could accept her by these tokens or not at all.

Margaret, rather reluctantly surrendering to Knox's contention that Ceclie's beauty and natural intelligence should not go to waste in consequence of one mistake, had consented to her spending a good deal of time under the Taylor roof for instruction in dress and deportment. Quickly impressed by the girl's potential, Margaret had decided that her education should be furthered at the Cadle school. Though her mother insisted that her sole interest lay in the concern of any Christian woman for a pair of wilderness waifs, Knox knew that she'd grown genuinely fond of Ceclie and the baby.

Knox drummed her fingers on the swing-arm, gazing restlessly across the river. Early October had turned the forested areas of bluffs and islands to vistas of molten color. Sadness twisted in her: the shape of autumn, she thought. The chromatic hues of shut-off life, the pulsing odors of dry fallen leaves and decay. The bone-reaching chill of fall nights: warranties of some hybrid mood of death and heart-soreness. But she'd never felt it so poignantly.

The shrill clang of a steamer's bell drifted from downriver.

Knox almost sprang to her feet, but caught herself. She rose casually, saying, "That would be the *Arabella*. Guess I'll walk down and see if there's any mail."

Margaret gave her an understanding half-smile. "Why don't you?"

Knox sauntered down to the landing, kicking her feet through a crackling windstrew of leaves. The afternoon was mild and smoky-blue, sweetened by the fragrance of huckleberry and wild grape and pawpaw. Please let there be some word, she thought. Anything, even one note. But something, please . . .

Jeff's last letter had come a full seven months ago. It had held no hint of a suggestion that he might not write again. But he had written; of that she was positive. As she was positive that his letters hadn't vanished into thin air. If something had happened to him, Denny Gibbs or Colonel Dodge would have surely let her know.

At first she'd felt only a heart-sore bitterness. Coupled with suspicions that did her no credit. Gradually, as she'd thought it through, suspicion had found a fresh focus. All letters and dispatches brought by runner came through the sergeant major's office. Since it was her father's wont to personally sort out any mail addressed to himself or members of his family, he'd had ample opportunity to confiscate the ones from Jeff. Would he do such a thing? He might; he'd reason as a soldier: severing the enemy's line of communication was a fair tactic. She had queried the sergeant major: Did he remember any letters? His negative hadn't satisfied her. If the colonel *had* intercepted the letters, he'd have dropped a cautioning word to the SM, a man fanatically loyal to his commander. But some mail came by steamboat; since Prairie du Chien had the only post office north of Galena, such mail was turned directly over to the postmaster here. For months Knox had kept a painstaking check on both postmaster and steamer captains, and this too had yielded nothing.

The *Arabella*'s white-painted hulk passed majestically into view and chugged up to the landing. Captain Terence, blue-coated and white-haired, saluted Knox from his hurricane deck. When the roustabouts had made the craft fast, she went up the plank as the captain descended to the lower deck. At her request, he went through the mailbag in his cabin, but there was nothing for her except a letter from Mary Wilson.

"Is this all?"

"Faith, girl, I thought the young lady was your best friend."

"You know well enough what I mean, Captain Terry."

"Your young man, eh?" Captain Terence pulled meditatively on his briar. "Have you any idea, my fine miss, how many ways a letter might go astray between here and the far end of Arkansas?"

"I think so; you've told me often enough. You and others. But we're not discussing one little old letter, Captain. What I'd like explained is how all the letters I've sent my young man since March, and the ones he's sent me, could have been taken by the same misfortune."

"Aye, a caution, ain't it? Unless the answer's so plain you can't see it, or won't."

"We've been over that too, haven't we?" Knox smiled. "Really, Captain, isn't it more likely that some of the mail you've carried has fallen into the wrong hands?"

A frown touched Captain Terence's kindly face. "You'd not be hinting any shoddy behavior of myself and my fellow captains?"

"Not really. But I do have some justification for wondering into whose hands my mail has passed."

"Not into the care of any dockhand, I'll take vow. It's myself, no other, that delivers all posted material entrusted me into the hands of the head postmaster at St. Looey." He sighed, tipping back his head as a wedge of geese veed over, gabbling like old women, following the Mississippi flyway south. "Eh, it'll be chilblains and sore bones before long."

"Will you be returning downriver soon?"

"Aye, soon. But it's on to Fort Snelling tomorrow, and I'm due to pick up a party of gov'ment surveyors at the Falls of St. Anthony's. Afterward it's back to St. Looey for the old tub, and N'Awleans and winter quarters for this tired salt."

"Will you stop at Prairie on your way back? I'll have a letter or two . . ."

"Aye, we'll be picking up a bit of cargo here."

Knox returned to the house and sought the privacy of her room. Remembering that she'd queried Mary as to any word the Wilsons might have received from Jeff, she quickly opened the letter.

> *St. Louis, Missouri*
> *October 1, 1834*

Dear Knoxie,

You ask if we have heard anything from Jeff. Indeed we have. But his letters, though dated this spring, have only now caught up with us. A good deal of our mail has suffered delay in consequence of our moving so far from Prairie du Chien and having no permanent residence until recently. As you can see, Jeff sent a letter to me and one to George—and the subject of both is you and little else. I enclose both . . .

Heart pounding, Knox leafed through the pages of Mary's thick letter. She extracted the two single-page letters by Jeff and read through his familiar script with hungry haste.

So it was true. He had run the same bitter gamut of doubt and fear and anger. She wanted to laugh. Or cry. With trembling hands she picked up Mary's letter again.

I cannot understand why both you and Jeff should fail to receive one another's letters unless someone is intercepting them

*from both ways. As to that, I can draw no conclusions that you
cannot draw equally well. I've sent your letter on to Jeff with an
explanatory note. However your mail to him has been tampered
with, the solution is simple. Henceforth, send letters destined
for Jeff to our address; we'll be your go-betweens. I have given
Jeff similar advice . . .*

The rest of the letter was devoted to describing the Wilsons'
new house, George's growing law practice, Mary's flower garden, and the baby that was due in six months.

Knox seated herself at her tiny writing desk; she dipped her
pen, but did not touch it to paper. She leaned her chin on her
hand and stared out her second-story window at the blazing
band of sumac that hooded a near hill. What do you do now, she
wondered, just let it go by? A breeze arched the India chintz
curtains. Gazing past them, she had a fair view of the town and
waterfront. She saw Captain Terence's stocky form coming up
the road from the landing at his slightly rolling gait that was
the legacy of a lifetime spent at sea. At the fort gate, he spoke
to the sentry and was passed in.

Knox got up and stood on tiptoe by the window; her angle of
view cleared a barracks roof. She saw Terence cross the parade
and enter the headquarters building. She sat back in her chair and
tapped the pen against her teeth, frowning. She hadn't seriously
entertained the possibility of a collusion between the steamer
captains and her father. But why not?

Why not indeed?

All her life, wherever he'd been stationed, it had been Zachary Taylor's unfailing custom (if weather allowed and the waterfront were no great distance) to stroll down at crack of dawn
to the docks, amble about, examine boats and cargoes, watch
the bustle of activity and, above all, chat with the captains. For
these men of many ports were mines of information on the
subjects that most interested him—the state of crops, political
currents, and so on. Over the years he'd struck up fabulous

friendships with riverboat masters up and down the Mississippi Valley.

Now that she thought of it, the three captains who handled Prairie du Chien's incoming and outgoing mail—Terence of the *Arabella,* Moline of the *Winnebago* and Ahearn of the *Galley West*—were all close friends of her father. A thin smile touched her lips. It was easy to construct the hypothetical conversation; she could almost hear him: "You know my daughter, Captain . . . headstrong girl. Got herself engaged to a young rapscallion of an officer. Overdressed, pompous, dandified fellow, always playing around. I want to save her from herself and this blackguard. I wonder if, as a personal favor to me . . ."

The more she considered the possibility, the more convinced she was that none of her letters had left Prairie du Chien. That all of Jeff's had arrived and been delivered into the colonel's hands. If she confronted her father without proof, of course, he'd simply roar her down. She could circumvent him in the future by following Mary's suggestion. But he had a large trove of letters that were rightfully hers.

Unless he'd destroyed them.

The longer she thought about it, the angrier she became.

The feeling stayed with her through the day as she went about her tasks. At dinner, she was too upset to more than toy with her food, and she couldn't bear to look at her father. She retired to her room early and sat down to compose a letter to Jeff. But her thoughts wouldn't jell. Neither would an attempted letter to Mary. She tried to lose herself in Irving's *The Alhambra,* but reading was impossible too.

From the next room, she heard her mother's low musical voice reading the children a bedtime story. In a few minutes the prayers were said, then sleepy good nights; Margaret went to her own room. Knox lay face down on her bed awhile longer, hugging her pillow. Finally she came to a decision. Her father, as was his habit, would remain in the parlor at least another hour, reading.

She left her room, went down the hall to her parents' room and tapped on the door. "It's me . . . may I come in?"

"Of course, dear."

Margaret was in her dressing gown by the mirror, brushing out her hair. Knox seated herself on the bed, watching her mother's reflection in the glass.

"I want to talk with you, Ma. It's . . . a terribly personal matter."

Margaret turned on the stool, still brushing her hair. "Yes, Knoxie?"

"Exactly how far do you think Pa would go in his efforts to spare me the lot of a soldier's wife?"

Margaret lowered her silver-chased brush; her brows sickled quizzically upward. "That's quite a question. May I ask what brought it on?"

"You know that I've written dozens of letters to Jeff this last year and that he sent me fully as many . . . until seven months ago. Since then, not a word."

Margaret sighed. "Dear, we've been over it all before. I know how terribly you've been hurt, but you can't go on brooding forever. I've told you before and I'll tell you again . . ."

"I know. Young men—certain young men—fall out of love as easily as they fall into it."

"Yes. What else can I say?"

"You needn't say anything. Just listen to me, please. The letter I received today was from Mary. Jeff has written to both George and her, as I have. The letters were delayed reaching them . . . and now Mary tells me that Jeff hasn't received my letters either."

"Oh? That's very odd."

"I thought so. You were on the veranda this afternoon. Did you see Captain Terence stroll up to the fort?"

"Of course. He always drops in on your father."

"Even before he's attended to his cargo and other duties that you'd think would come before pleasure calls."

"Why not? They're very old friends. What are you trying to say?"

"Only that I'd barely spoken to old Terence before he'd hied up to the fort and into Pa's office."

"With dispatches from St. Louis, no doubt."

"And perhaps a letter or two—or a dozen—from Jeff."

Margaret stared at her. "Do you realize what you're inferring? That your father is no better than . . . than a sneak thief?"

"Very well then! Give me another explanation. What happened to our letters?"

"I'm sure I don't know, but . . ."

"There is no other explanation, Mother. None that makes a rag of sense."

"Fiddlesticks! So far as sense goes, how much is there to what you've inferred? Assuming Zeke were capable of what you suggest, he's certainly no fool. Of all the clumsy and foolish devices he might employ, purloining your mail would be the—"

"Oh, Ma! As a parent, he is clumsy! And blind and bullheaded too. I believe he'd do it and never think his way to the end till it was too late."

"That will do, my girl."

"No," Knox said hotly, "not by half! If he has the letters, you can find out. Can't you?"

"Oh, I daresay. But you needn't think that I'll even consider such a thing. The very idea!"

Knox rose and walked to the door, her back taut.

"Knoxie . . . what do you want? What do you expect of me?"

Knox turned and looked at her. "Nothing. No matter what happens, the peace must be kept, mustn't it? The colonel's happy home must be maintained according to his taste. I am merely his daughter, you're merely his wife. Good night, Mother."

She marched back to her room, shut the door behind her and pressed her cheek against the smooth wood, trembling. I shouldn't have done that, she thought. What good will it do? But I had to say it. I had to.

She began to undress, thinking that all comfort had gone out of the world she knew. She slipped into her nightgown and into a cold bed. She lay restless, sleepless; loneliness bit at her.

Jeff . . . oh Jeff. I need you so . . .

Four days later, the *Arabella* put in again at Prairie du Chien. Knox accosted Captain Terence at the landing and gave him two letters. The envelope addressed to Jeff contained blank paper; the one for Mary Wilson held Jeff's letter. At least he would get this one, she thought. But her mind held bitterly on the letters he had never seen, his letters that she hadn't seen.

She walked back to the house. Ceclie had come to the village today, Jean-Pierre slung in a cradleboard on her back. Margaret had set up a quilting frame in the yard and was showing Ceclie how to sew a flower-garden design. Knox seated herself on the stoop and gazed across the river, avoiding her mother's eyes. They'd had little to say to each other since the other night. A vast thrashing of wings grew overhead; the women looked up. A southward stream of passenger pigeons darkened the sky, blotting out the sunlight, throwing a kind of twilight gloom over the land. Jean-Pierre, secure in the cradleboard leaning against the stoop, gurgled with delight and stretched his small arms upward.

The flight of pigeons passed; Knox lowered her eyes. And saw Captain Terence coming up the road from the landing. The old hypocrite is wasting no time, she thought. Margaret was watching him too, keeping her eyes on him till he passed through the fort gate. Then she turned back to the quilting frame.

"Take care you sew along the lines of the design, my dear, thus . . ." Margaret paused, biting her lip. Suddenly she stood up, untied her apron and dropped it in the chair. "Well, Knoxie, shall we see your father? Go on with the quiltwork, Ceclie; you're doing fine."

For a moment Knox couldn't believe it. Then she hurried after her mother. They crossed the parade to the headquarters building and entered the sergeant major's office. The SM looked up in surprise, then came quickly to his feet.

"I'm sorry, ma'am, the colonel is occupied at the moment—"

"You needn't trouble to announce us, Sergeant."

Margaret swept past his desk without pausing, opened the door to the commander's office and walked in, Knox behind her. The colonel was standing behind his desk, grimly smiling at Captain Terence who sat in a chair, legs crossed and fingers steepled, smiling too. Both men started in surprise. A drawer was open by the colonel's left hand; he slammed it shut in a kind of unthinking reflex.

Without a word, Margaret walked straight to the desk and around it.

"What the devil, madam!"

The colonel perceived her intent, but moved too late to prevent her yanking open the drawer; he seized at it, knocking it from her hand. It clattered to the floor, upended, and flooded papers over the planks. Knox stared at them, seeing the scatter of unopened letters among them. She came quickly around the desk, dropped to her knees and fumbled through them. They were all here. All the letters she had sent to Jeff. As many from him that she'd never seen, addressed in his sharp nervous hand. She hardly heard Captain Terence's soft and unobtrusive, "Well, folks, I best be going," as he slid out the door and gently closed it behind him.

"Well, Knox?"

"They're . . . they're all here, Ma."

Margaret wheeled on her husband. "How small of you, sir! How small and foolish. And how very petty."

"Damn and blast, madam!" The colonel's face was turgid. "It was for her own damned good!"

"How easily you must have persuaded yourself of that! All that I fail to understand is how a conscience which permitted a man to steal his own daughter's love letters prevented him from destroying them."

"I didn't even open the damned things! I ask you to view the matter reasonably—"

"Reasonably! Such a request from you, sir!" Margaret's tone had a chipped-glass quality; spots of color burned in her cheeks. "Knox. Leave us, please. Take the letters."

She gathered them up with trembling hands and left the room, closing the door before she hurried out past the sergeant major and the line of awed clerks.

Up in her room, she tore open and devoured the letters one by one, scanning them quickly. She felt a bitter shock on learning that Jeff had heard of her falsely announced engagement to Sanford Preston . . .

Sanford himself, being the oaf and blockhead that he was, had been directly responsible for the item. He'd construed one thing or another that she'd said as an oblique confession of love. Returning south this spring, he'd stopped off in Kentucky to spend some time with kinfolk and to spread with a swollen ebullience the fiction that he and Knox would wed shortly. Chance had favored the story being picked up by the newspapers and widely circulated before Knox's Aunt Elizabeth, dismissing it as utter rubbish, had sent her niece copies of the item. As quickly as packet mail could bring word and take back Knox's reply, Elizabeth had begun a militant one-woman crusade to see that every newspaper which had carried the story printed a retraction. It hadn't occurred to Knox that the story might have somehow reached Jeff.

She felt sick at the bitter, distracted, overwrought tone of the letters, but forced herself to read them all. She came to his taut description of the 1st Dragoons' disastrous summer trek. And then to a passage that stunned her. She ran it over twice, numbly: *Hard as it is to relate, I must tell you of the death of Denny Gibbs. He came down with fever during the journey and died on August 18th, at our camp on the Canadian. I did what I could, but to no avail . . .*

"Oh, Lord, no."

Tears blinded her; the pages slipped from her fingers to the floor. She sat on the bed a long while, sobs of grief tearing at her. Finally she made herself pick up the pages and read on: *Since in your next to last letter, you indicated that you believed Denny to be the father of Ceclie Robier's baby and that you felt he owed her a responsibility, I can tell you that before his passing, he gave me a paper which is a bequest to Ceclie and the child. However, because of the misfortunes that plague my letters, I shan't risk its loss by enclosing it here, but shall hold it until I hear from you.*

I will have to tell Ceclie, Knox thought. She loved him. And he must have . . .

A soft knock at the door.

She wiped her eyes. "Come in."

Margaret entered and stopped. "Knoxie . . . why, what's the matter?"

Knox handed her the letter. Margaret sat on the bed, an arm round her daughter, and read it through. "Oh, Knoxie." She was crying too and they held each other for a minute.

"I understand a good deal that I didn't before," Margaret said, drying her eyes. "I think, Knoxie, in consideration of all that's happened . . . you and Mr. Davis should wed as soon as possible."

"No, Ma. I want Jeff to be sure of himself. And he isn't . . . not as yet. I think he's disillusioned with the Army. Even with his precious Dragoons. But we agreed to wait for two years and I won't urge him to break that agreement. He must decide for himself what's best for him."

Margaret nodded. She gazed at the letter, shaking her head gently. "Poor Denny. Poor Ceclie. Were they in love, Knoxie?"

"Yes, Ma."

"Dear God. The things we do to ourselves in the name of . . . duty. Honor. Is that it, or am I wrong again?"

Knox smiled a little. "Right . . . and wrong. Don't we live by duty, one way or the other? All of us?"

"Of course. We have to. But it's a terrible taskmaster. It has driven your father all his life . . . so fiercely that at times it's blinded him to other values."

Knox's lips compressed. "I'll never forgive him for this. Never."

"Never is a long time. Oh, what he did was exactly as churlish and insensitive as you said. But his feeling on the thing runs so deeply, so painfully, that next to it, any other course would be—to him—the lesser evil."

"I don't understand . . ."

"You've heard his reasons for being so set against service marriages a hundred times, haven't you? The reasons he'll offer in explanation, that is. The real reason is one of which he won't even speak. Do you have any memory at all of Bayou Sara?"

"I think . . . yes. But I was terribly young then."

"It was the summer of 1820, and you were six. You and your three sisters and I spent that summer with friends at Bayou Sara in the Louisiana Delta, while your father was on duty in the North. And all five of us came down with the bilious fever. You and Ann were lightly stricken. I nearly succumbed—"

"Yes," Knox said softly, "and little Maggie and Baby Octavia died. I remember being terribly sick . . . but that's all."

"Zeke blamed himself, but I didn't know till we were together again. I think there can be nothing worse than seeing a strong man break down before your eyes. He blamed himself for leaving us in 'that foul miasmic hole.' For being so wrapped up in a thousand details of his career. For not being there to see after us."

"But what could he have done?"

"Nothing, of course. But that blind iron sense of duty wouldn't let him accept the fact. I believe now that he wanted me to say something, anything that would absolve him in my eyes and his own. But I—God forgive me—my babies were dead, and the words wouldn't come then. Later, when I tried to say them, he silenced me. 'The matter is closed, madam.' Just that flatly. And of course it wasn't closed; it will never be."

"Ma," Knox whispered, "why didn't you ever tell me this?"

"I suppose because your father and I could never speak of it even to each other. All grief heals with time, the scar remains. But people live with their scars, live and love in spite of them. I only regret the hardship that ours has worked on you and Ann. You asked how far he'd go to see you spared the lot of a soldier's wife. The answer is, to almost any length. Knowing that, Knoxie . . . can you forgive him?"

"I think so." She forced a smile. "I'll try, Ma."

28

Davis sat at the battered desk beside his bed, writing rapidly, covering sheet after sheet of paper with sharp close-written script. Lieutenant Mulady, acting company commander, stood by the fireplace warming his hands to the blaze. He gave Davis a surly glance and said: "Look, I have to tell Masson something. What will it be?"

Davis laid his pen down and shifted around on the stool, flexing the fingers of his writing hand. "You might tell him to go to the devil. Ever consider it?"

"Please don't be funny. You weren't present this morning for roll call and weren't listed on sick call. When Masson saw the reports, he blistered my ass and demanded an explanation. I'm here to get one."

Davis smiled faintly. Mulady was plump, officious, and middle aged; he had the round boiled-looking face of a peevish infant. A desk soldier by nature, he harbored a festering hatred for the bureaucratic indifference that had transferred him from a comfortable clerk's job in the departmental headquarters at Jefferson Barracks to the cruel privations of a border post.

"Read your regulations, Whit. During inclement weather, rolls are to be called in quarters by heads of squads."

"I'm more familiar than most with the book, Jeff. Will you

kindly not play the latrine lawyer with me? The rest of the company went out in that bastardly drizzle to stand roll. If sickness was your excuse, why didn't you report to the hospital?"

Davis got up, went to a window and opened a shutter, gazing out at the misty buildings and steel-colored sky. For two days a late October rain had wrapped the plains in a smoky blur. And tomorrow might bring rolling fog or icy northers, hail or sleet or even mild and sunny breezes. That was Arkansas. He shivered and closed the shutter.

"Nice day, isn't it?" He turned. "I don't feel particularly febrile, Whit. As it happens, though, I'm highly susceptible to cold and wet. I nearly died of pneumonia two winters ago and I'm prone to neuralgic attacks that, aside from being damned painful, have a nasty tendency to rob me of my vision for indefinite periods. I didn't think it worthwhile tempting fate by an unnecessary soaking in cold weather. Now, think you can explain all this so that even Masson can grasp it? Assuming that regulations give me a little leeway . . ."

Mulady barked a laugh. "You could be coughing up blood and bile, my boy, and our dear captain wouldn't give a solitary damn in hell if you could stand on your feet. Niceties of regulations or not." He buttoned his damp greatcoat up to his neck and jerked his cap down almost eye-level. "I'll convey your message."

"And general sentiments?"

"I'll leave that to you. I'm sure our acting son of a bitch commander will give you the opportunity very shortly."

Mulady smiled dourly and tramped to the door. A cold wet gust swept the room as he went out.

Davis went back to his writing. He wasn't feeling half as chipper as he'd inferred. His head ached, his eyes moved grittily in their sockets, fever simmered in the back of his brain. Two days ago Masson had sent him with a patrol to clean out a "blind tiger" ten miles away and he'd returned wet and chilled. Perhaps he should have gone on sick call, but hospitalization would merely mean endless dosings of Surgeon Porter's doubtful emetics.

He had a resignation to write out and this was as good a time as any.

He'd done a good deal more thinking about his decision to leave the service. Denny Gibbs's death, the tragic fiasco of the summer expedition, his state of mind over losing Knox, had wrought on him to such an extent that he'd put off his resignation, feeling these things might distort his perspective. He'd needed time to think and weigh. Had he wanted to quit for reasons of genuine principle or merely out of private disillusionment? He'd discussed his feelings with Colonel Dodge, who had suggested he postpone his decision at least a year, broadly hinting that a regimental adjutant who gave a good accounting of himself might expect another hitch in rank and a transfer back to St. Louis or even to Washington City.

He smiled thinly. There was a subtle corruption in that dangling of promotional plums; it no longer moved him. He'd continued to perform his duties with impersonal efficiency, waiting for his emotional state to stabilize. When he was sure it had, he'd found his feelings unchanged. His ardor for the military life had faded; valor and glory without principle meant nothing. Different if the nation were at war or involved in international disputes that threatened war. But there was only the Indian problem; his repugnance on that score held firm.

Many had already resigned from the Dragoons on more practical grounds: broken health, a disgusted conviction that they'd been misled about their own ambitious prospects, or simply because they couldn't take the gaff. Kearny and a hundred troopers had been dispatched northeast to the Des Moines River to build Fort Des Moines; meantime Dodge, concerned for the future of the Dragoons, had departed for Jefferson Barracks and consultation with Winfield Scott. Captain Raoul Masson, next in seniority, had been left in temporary command of the regiment.

Davis's statement of resignation flowed out swiftly under his scratching pen; his command of logical language made the task easy. But the nail-driving pulse in his temples continued; the writing began to blur. He laid down his pen and focused his gaze on the far end wall of the deserted officers' barracks. The timbers, salvaged by Dragoon carpenters from the tumbledown buildings, groaned in the wind. Rain hitting the roof began to crackle and thud, freezing to sleet. Betokening another winter of howling cold, brutal rigors, privations and boredom of winter garrison that would suck the weaker dry of soul and sanity, swell the desertion rate and add to the roster of regimental swillheads. Six winters of it, he thought, was enough for any man; it would be good to return to the slow-summering deep South. But the mills of government ground slowly, and his resignation would not be finalized for months. Winterlocked again . . .

He picked up a letter on his desk and reread the first part of it: *My dear brother Jefferson: Cherish ambition, cherish pride, and run from excitement to excitement. It will prevent your ever-preying melancholy, it will blunt your sensibilities and armor you against all afflictions . . .* He smiled. Advice from Florida Davis McCaleb, a seventeen-year-old girl. Not his sister, but his brother Joe's oldest daughter and only nine years Jeff's junior. She understood him only too well.

The smile faded. Easy to fatalistically philosophize about one's loss. He'd done so at first, trying to minimize the pain. But all the memories stayed sharp as knives, hot colors on a blurred summer canvas of sun and warm earth and laughter: no furious dissipation of surface energy could blunt the memories. His few letters written and sent had been taut, impersonal ramblings. The many he'd written and torn up had been labored, much-blotted scrawls whose tone hovered between formality and heartsickness and made no sense at all.

And never a reply. Why couldn't she at least reply?

As a last resort, he'd sent James Pemberton to Kentucky to

inquire among her relatives. Always a chance that her engagement had been reported erroneously. Or was a blatant rumor blown up by some news-hungry tabloid. But these were thin possibilities. Hadn't Robert Anderson once mentioned a Sanford Preston as a suitor of hers? James's return, he thought bleakly, would merely confirm the truth.

He took out the fragile bloom of heartsease she had given him, the petals dry and splintered now, crumbling to the touch. *To ease the heart. Knox, Knox, Knox, why did you do it?*

The door opened; young Barstow, Masson's striker, poked his wet face in.

"Beg pardon, sir. Captain says you're to report to him on the double."

"Very well, Trooper. I'll be along directly."

Barstow pulled his head out and shut the door. Davis stared moodily at the wall. He was getting damned tired of tiptoeing around Masson's acid proddings of him. The acting commander had used his new authority to exact petty vengeance on everyone against whom he held one grudge or another. Officers assigned long brutal patrols in bitter weather, men who drew harsh punishment for a faulty detail of dress or equipment—you could be sure they'd all touched Masson's wrath one way or the other. The man was unstable and a fool, and God knew what he had in mind now.

Davis got up and pulled on his greatcoat and cap. He felt a wave of nausea and swallowed against it, then opened the door and stepped out on the veranda. Gusty brooms of rain and sleet veiled the buildings and campus. The barracks lay a hundred yards from the headquarters building whose south end housed the offices of the 7th Infantry and General Arbuckle, who'd returned from his Arkansas Valley plantation to resume command following General Leavenworth's death. The Dragoon offices occupied the north wing. Maybe he could escape a soaking by hugging the lee side of buildings between here and the headquarters. He dashed across the soggy ground to the hospital, seventy feet away, eased along under its eaves to the corner, then ran for a long low building that housed the families of married officers. He paused on its veranda and knocked the water from his dripping cap. A short run across a boot-chopped mire seamed with rust-colored puddles would bring him to the Dragoon offices. He stepped off the veranda and plunged his foot into a deep pool of muck. Trying to pull free, he lost his balance and fell full-length in an icy puddle. He floundered to his feet, covered with mud, soaked to the skin. He started back toward the barracks, then changed his mind and slogged on to the headquarters building.

He entered the commander's office, a large neatly ordered room with a big fireplace. Masson was seated behind his desk, one booted foot propped on a chair as Barstow, on his knees, polished it. Ignored by Masson, Davis stood chilled to the bone, teeth chattering. He looked at his hands and saw they were bluish-white with cold. He walked to the fire and held his hands to the warmth.

"Mr. Davis!"

Davis did not even glance at him.

"Look at me! What the hell do you mean by reporting to me in such a condition? And come to attention!"

Davis turned and snapped a muddy arm in salute. "I'm sorry, sir. God damn your eyes, sir."

Masson looked at his striker. "Did you hear him, Trooper?"

"Yes, sir," Barstow said uneasily.

Masson drummed his fingers on the desk; his one eye shone like a cat's. "That bit of insolence, plus your failure to report for roll, should be good for a court-martial."

"Yes, sir. And would you oblige me, sir, by going to hell?"

A furious buzzing filled his ears; the objects in the room seemed to tilt and swim. He had the feeling that in another minute he'd pass out on his feet. Masson said something he didn't catch. He stared at the captain's mottled face.

"I beg your pardon?"

"I said, goddammit, you're confined to your quarters!"

Davis smiled. Fine. He heeled stiffly around and started for the door. A clinging mist seeped into his brain. He was aware that he was on the porch, holding to a roof column for support. He tried to step off the porch. And a lake of mud was rushing up to smash him in the face: he knew that much. Then he knew nothing.

In the weeks that followed, he was rarely out of the post hospital. He was felled by one round after another of colds and grippe, with various complications. Fever consumed him; the old optic neuralgia struck again; spurting pains tore at his face and eyes. But this time he had the sense to take to his bed at once. He recovered quickly, but his general health remained low, his spirits lower. Nothing, not even the list of charges and specifications that Masson had drawn up nor the fact that he was to be arraigned before a general court, touched his interest.

When he wasn't in the hospital, he was kept confined to his quarters. Which eminently suited him, for deep winter had gripped the plains and his neuralgia continued to act up, though not intolerably. He filled the hours with plenty of sleep, a little reading, chitchat with fellow officers. His feud with Masson had won him a good deal of sympathy, but he found little solace in company. He thought a lot about Knox: no solace there either. He'd never felt so bitterly depressed in his life.

On a raw, blowing day in late November, he lay abed in the deserted officers' barracks and thumbed through a slim volume which Captain Lawton had handed him that morning, saying simply, "You're in a book." Its title was *The Life of Black Hawk, with an Account of the Cause and General History of the Late War, His Surrender and Confinement at Jefferson Barracks, and Travels through the United States, Dictated by Himself*. Of his journey to prison, Black Hawk had said: "We started down to Jefferson Barracks in a steamboat under the charge of a young war chief who treated us all with much kindness. He is a good and brave young chief, with whose conduct I was much pleased. On our way down we called at Galena, and remained a short time. The people crowded to the boat to see us; but the war chief would not permit them to enter the apartment where we were—knowing, from what his own feelings would have been if he had been placed in a similar situation, that we did not wish to have a gaping crowd around us."

The old man had mated tact and irony in the book's dedication: *To Brigadier General H. Atkinson.* Atkinson, who had commanded the Bad Axe massacre, who had chained and humiliated him! It was the last paragraph of the long dedication that really caught Davis's attention: "I am now an obscure member of a nation that formerly honored and respected my opinions. The path to glory is rough, and many gloomy hours obscure it. May the Great Spirit shed light on yours—and that you may never experience the humility that the power of the American government has reduced me to, is the wish of him who, in his native forests, was once as proud and bold as yourself. Black Hawk. 10th Moon, 1833."

Davis laid the book aside. "God," he murmured. "The poor old devil . . ."

His eyes were starting to ache; he covered them with a strip of dark flannel. The building shuddered as the everlasting prairie wind started up again, drilling in trickles between the logs where chinking had cracked, howling dismally down the chimney, whipping the fire, clawing loose a roof shake and skittering it away. The noises frictioned his sensitized nerves. That wind . . . it was enough by itself to swamp anyone in despondency.

He thought some more about the court-martial he must face sometime this spring, accused by a superior of "conduct subversive of good order and military discipline." He ought to rouse himself to mustering some sort of defense. Many had witnessed Masson's repeated goadings of him. Insubordinate or not, his refusal to report for roll call that rainy morning had been technically correct. If that base to Masson's charges were undermined, what had happened afterward would be thrown into a different light. To be found guilty would mean dismissal and disgrace . . . unless his resignation happened to come through first.

He thought about it without much interest, his thoughts slipping into a gray drift of sleep. He dreamed. The old dream again. He was in that dark room he knew and yet could not place. A voice was calling him and he almost knew whose it was. Almost. He fought to rise and could not . . .

He jerked awake as an icy draft flurried through the room. Someone had pushed open the slab door. He raised the cloth from his eyes as Ben Poore jammed the door shut and came across the room, shedding his heavy buffalo coat. He shook it free of snow, tossed it over the foot of the bed and squatted down on the packdirt floor.

"Wagh. This child's half-froze. That old north wind is on a blue tear. Lights still troubling you, hoss? Know an old Ree remedy mought help."

"No thanks. Been out?"

"Just come from taking a party after buffler. Old Matt Arbuckle, George Catlin, a Russky archduke, and some muckymuck senator. Catlin painted His Dukeship on the spot today. Duke got him a fine bull."

"That we'll be gnawing on for a month. A wonder we don't all grow humps and briskets."

"Wagh. You got to eat buffler like the Injuns and us *hivernants* used to. 'Member one winter, '23 it was, up the Missouri with General Ashley's brigade. Tom Fitzpatrick, me, young Jim Bridger, and some other he-cats lived out the season on naught but choice tongue, liver, and smoked backfat. Man ain't lived without he has sampled gall on raw liver and sweetbreads."

Davis grimaced. Poore dug out his pipe and ruminatively chewed the stem. "When's this court fandango of yourn being flung?"

"Anyone's guess. Not for months."

"You ought to get up more sap 'n' bark about it. Ain't nothing to whup but a sorefoot yaller pup name of Masson." Poore shifted on his heels; something crackled in his pocket. " 'Most forgot, old Matt give me this to give you."

He handed Davis a letter. It was addressed in a delicate backhand slant that he knew. He sat bolt upright and opened the envelope. Carefully, for his hands were trembling. The letter was dated over a month ago. Knox had written it, he discovered, on the day she'd confirmed that her father had been intercepting their mail.

He read the last paragraph twice: *As things stand, I feel that to remain under this roof even one more week would be unbearable. Sooner or later I must forgive Pa what he's done, and I think it will be a long time before the words do not stick in my throat. I am taking passage for St. Louis, where I will remain with the Wilsons awhile. Mary has invited me many times and I can help her with the household until their new addition arrives. Then I'll go on to Louisville and stay with Aunt Liz, I think until you and I can make definite plans . . .*

"Not bad news, hoss?"

"No. I wonder, Ben, if you'd bring me a book or two from the post library."

He gave the titles of several law texts. Poore got up and shrugged on his coat. "Sounds like you plan on boning up for Masson. Aim to argufy your own case?"

"Exactly that."

"Must o' been a heart-tickler, that letter," Poore said dryly . . .

PART SIX

A Season for Love

29

Knox came to the open door of the summer kitchen and looked in. Fragrant steam filled the small building; her Aunt Elizabeth and Sally, the black cook, were bustling about preparing dinner.

"Aunt Liz, may I—"

Knox broke off as a steamer clanged its bell in the distance, putting in at the Louisville landing. She tilted her head, listening, then smiled at Elizabeth. "May I help?"

Her aunt, a tall strong-boned woman with spectacles, peered at her sharply. "Nonsense. Stay out where it's cool. You look crisp as sugar. If that packet's bearing your young man, you can't greet him looking like greens wilted in vinegar. Besides, way you're mooning about, you'd burn yourself sure . . ."

Knox walked on along the pink-scarlet rows of Prairie Queen roses, shears in hand. The rose bushes were trimmed to low groomed hedges that squared off the rioting beds of camellias, daffodils, and violets. Bees burred in the sweet sun-blaze. The big white two-story house with its many dormers and green shutters was the headquarters of Beechland, Aunt Elizabeth's prosperous farm. Elizabeth had married a cousin, John Gibson Taylor, and borne him a large family. Now widowed, she'd carried on her husband's enterprises so vigorously that she comfortably supported a flood of "occasional" guests as well as her children.

Knox walked slowly, snipping off cuttings and laying them in the basket on her arm. Often her gaze would stray down the Louisville road. It wound like a dusty snake through checkered fields that were green-tasseled with corn, wheat, and timothy, past Beechland's barns, carriage sheds, slave quarters, and orchards. Leading up to the house was a broad lane lined with sycamores, beeches, and hickories that drooped in the splintery heat of June. But it was cool under the silver aspens that dotted the three-acre lawn, their leaves making a rainy whisper in the mild wind. She hummed as she walked—her favorite tune *Fairy Bells* which Jeff had never been sure whether he liked or not.

A year and ten months. It seemed like an age. She had filled the time with work and the usual distractions: teas and soirees and balls. But the social kaleidoscope had lost its glitter long before she'd received the letter from Jeff telling her that in March he'd defended himself at his court-martial and won. That he could bow out of the service with honor, directly his papers arrived. For several weeks she'd been giving a start every time she'd heard a steamer belling its way up the Ohio. Any boat, any day now, might be the one. She smiled at her impatience. Even if Jeff were on today's boat, he'd have to disembark, arrange for his luggage, hire an equipage and journey the three miles to Beechland.

He'd told her to go ahead with whatever wedding preparations suited her; she and Elizabeth had already made practically all arrangements. She wanted nothing pretentious; she liked the idea of being married at Beechland, a place that held treasured memories of her girlhood. She had sent out hand-written invitations to their closest relatives and friends, but she guessed that few, if any, of Jeff's family would find it convenient to attend. Many of her own relatives lived in easy traveling distance. The wedding date had been set for June 17 to allow Jeff ample time to conclude his business and arrive at Beechland. He'd been vague as to whatever plans he had under way—she guessed to spare her disappointment should they fail to materialize. All he had told her was that as soon as he was free of the Army, he was journeying to Vicksburg and a conference with his brother Joe.

There was a mar on her happiness. A letter she'd received last week from her mother. Heartfelt in its loving best wishes. Yet disappointing. Her parents would not attend the wedding. She knew why. And harbored no resentment toward her father; she'd forgiven him long ago.

She'd really expected his refusal to come. Yet it stung, it hurt. Deeply and bitterly.

Musing for many minutes, she forgot to anticipate. She gave a quick start as she heard a gig roll briskly up the road. She was bent over a bush, shears in hand, facing away. She straightened and turned, heart pounding. The gig swung into the house lane where a gateway pierced a rambling picket fence. The trees hid her view as it rolled up the lane, but she had glimpsed its occupant and dropping the shears, catching up her skirts, she ran toward the front of the house.

"Jeff! Jeff—"

They had no chance to talk then, or for hours afterward. Elizabeth and her children monopolized Jeff. They remembered him as a welcome and witty guest from his visits to Beechland during his Kentucky recruiting stint two summers ago. As always, Aunt Liz laid a generous Southern table, and Knox was pleased to see Jeff do justice to the dinner of molasses-cured ham, sweet potatoes, spoon bread, and peach puffs. He should, she thought critically; he was quite thin. Striking, to be sure, his cheek hollows ascetically deepened. Older and self-assured. It seemed strange to see him in civilian clothing, but he cut an undeniably handsome figure in his brocaded waistcoat and long-tailed blue coat with brass buttons; he turned a fine leg in tight-fitting trousers of pale nankeen held by straps beneath his insteps. She was glad when Elizabeth ushered the children off to bed, freeing them to stroll in the garden.

The twilight was dry and cool; Knox hugged a light Spanish shawl about her shoulders. She was finely conscious (because she knew he was) that her plain dress of plaid linen, snug at the sleeves and bodice, affirmed the subtle fullness of her arms and shoulders, the breasts that were deeper and rounder than he'd remember, the waist that his hands could span as easily as ever.

She broke the silence as they strolled. "Guess who I heard from last week. Ceclie Robier. She's at school in Green Bay . . ."

"So you wrote me. Is her baby well?"

"Very well, and she's met a trader named Gaston Malotte . . . they're to be married. Apparently he's prosperous, kind and not too old. She took Denny's death quite hard, and I had to be the one to tell her. But now she seems content, at least. I'm glad things turned out well for her."

He halted her by a rose-twined arbor. For a moment they looked at each other. A cloying musk of flowers filled the air; her throat thickened. "Darling—darling—" The ripe fire of the kiss drove everything from her mind but the moment. The long months, the loneliness, the doubts, melted away. Gone in a meteoric instant. Gone wherever night dreams went.

They walked slowly on. After a while he talked at length about the feelings that had prompted his decision to leave the service. "And there was no lack of practical considerations, if I'd taken them into account. The Army has become a poor prospect. Most Point graduates of the last two years have been unable to get assignments anywhere. Promotions are harder to come by than hen's teeth. Half the junior officers at Fort Gibson resigned last year. I've just turned twenty-seven, and what have I to show for seven years of service at border posts? I've served more than the term requisite to pay the government for my Point education. Then there was the court-martial. Acquitted or not, the shadow of it would remain on my career."

"Yes, I'd like to hear about that court-martial. Your letter merely mentioned—in a monument to brevity—that you'd defended and won your case."

He smiled. "It was pretty dry doings. Technically, all I did was vindicate myself by showing that Captain Masson's original complaint was invalid. Paragraph 11, Article 2, General Army Regulations states that roll must be called in quarters in bad weather. I called Surgeon Porter to testify that my health was poor, and a Lieutenant Northrop as witness that the weather had been bad that morning. I brought out that I'd nearly died in the Northwest under conditions of cold and wet, and I submitted a letter from old Doc Beaumont testifying as much. I also called Captain Perkins and Lieutenants Mulady and Bowman to testify on Masson's treatment of subordinates. Mulady then testified that Masson had never given an order specifying that all officers should attend reveille—Masson claimed he had—and that I'd never been absent from a company roll before. In short, I did a pretty thorough job of showing Masson up for a brute and bully and discrediting his word. The Judge Advocate returned my sword and told me to resume my service . . . and he subjected Masson to as harsh a verbal lashing as I've ever heard."

He paused, shaking his head. "I hated doing it . . . but the man was sick. He had no business being in command of troops . . ."

"Don't think about it any more." She hugged his arm, rubbing her cheek against his shoulder. "Let's talk about your new career. I'm so excited! Did you have any trouble persuading your brother? You once told me that he, as much as your father, wanted you to make the Army your career . . ."

"Well, he's changed his mind thereunto. Joe's an isolationist now—feels America ought to steer wide of military ventures, particularly European entanglements. No future, he agreed, in the Army."

"But what did he think of your plan to go into cotton?"

"He wasn't overjoyed. He marshaled a host of hazards. Boll

worms, army worms, Mississippi floods, skittery markets, the perils of inexperience. He tried to argue me into studying for the law. And, quoth I, spend ten years building a practice that he hadn't hesitated to abandon once he became aware that cotton-planting was far more lucrative? I pointed out that he owns sixty-eight hundred acres of peninsula and has only five thousand under cultivation, leaving the south end of Davis Bend wholly untilled. I further pointed out that Pa had willed me a part interest in his slaves, all of which Joe had taken over. I offered to sign over my interest in those slaves in exchange for eighteen hundred acres of the south peninsula. Finally, I pointed out that I'd have the best mentor in the world—him—and the best of overseers in James Pemberton."

She laughed. "He's a Davis; he must have offered an argument."

"Certainly. The gist of which was that I'd be strapped for equipment, animals, workers, a hundred things I'd need. I observed that his use of my slaves for eleven years ought to be worth something. Maybe I *should* have gone into law. With formidable eloquence, I persuaded him to give me a long-term loan and throw in a gang of workers. 'It stands to reason,' I told him, 'that you can't afford to spare any effort in protecting such an investment. You can't ask for better collateral than that.'"

"Why Jeff Davis! I vow, I'd pitch you out on your ear if I were he . . ."

"I'm sure the impulse occurred. But blood was thicker than choler. He even offered us the use of his plantation for our honeymoon. His 'Liza is a New York girl . . . takes poorly to our Mississippi summers. Joe always takes her to the Northern resorts for the hot months. He said it might amuse us to play master and chatelaine during their absence. And suggested that we stay on as guests at Hurricane till I've cleared my land, gotten in my first crop, and have a house standing that's fit to bring a bride to."

"Oh Jeff! That's wonderful . . . but really, we can't—"

"Why not? Do you want to offend Joe by rejecting his wedding gift?"

She shook her head, smiling. "You imposed on him shamelessly, didn't you?"

He laughed and pulled her close. "I'm afraid so. But Joe was pleased, though he wouldn't quite say so. They've plenty of room, servants to handle the imposition . . . and you'll be company for 'Liza while Joe is showing me how to be a planter."

"Jeff, I'm glad you asked him for help. I'd never have believed you would."

"Foolish pride runs a pretty poor second to you. I've seen what loneliness can do to men. They drink themselves into stupors. Break down and cry like babies. Even run amuck. I saw, but never felt—until those two years away from you—what loneliness really is."

"Oh Jeff . . ."

They stood quietly, arms tight around each other, as the twilight sobered toward a beige dusk. "It all seems too wonderful to be true," she whispered. "If only Pa . . ."

"Did you tell him I was leaving the service?"

"I wrote Ma. He knows. He has no reason at all for not relenting. None except that mountain of crusty pride."

"Time wears down any mountain."

"Not his. I did want his blessing, Jeff."

"So did I."

"Well-brought-up children do not contract marriage without parental consent." She tried to say it with light irony. "And we're proper children."

He felt the hurt in her; he held her tightly. "Knox . . . Knoxie."

"I won't cry. I've done my crying. Just hold me, Jeff."

In spite of that disappointment, the days that followed were happy ones. The guests began to arrive and Knox prepared her wedding gown. She and Jeff spent hours riding over the summer-lush Kentucky countryside, on horseback or in Elizabeth's carriage with its team of matched iron-grays. Often they drove into Louisville, down the old streets of crushed limestone lined by handsome brick houses and rows of cool locusts, and she delighted in pointing out her childhood haunts, her family's former home on First Street. They both enjoyed idling along the bank of the glass-clear Ohio or loitering in the dock area, watching the steamboats load and unload. Jeff confessed that he'd never gotten over a childhood fascination for the big steamers. He'd boarded the *Aetna,* one of the first Mississippi steamers, at this same dock in 1817 when he'd left St. Thomas School at Springfield. "It sounds like ancient history," she teased him. "And that's a Catholic school, Baptist. You're not fibbing me, are you?"

On court day, when the justice of the peace arrived for his monthly docket, they went to town to acquire a wedding license and to enjoy the carnival atmosphere on Jefferson Street: gigs, coaches, and barouches jamming the avenue curb to curb; vendors of glass, tinware, and secondhand furniture shouting their wares from improvised stalls; medicine men in frock coats and beaver hats hawking their patent panaceas.

At the courthouse, they found the county clerk, Mr. Pendleton Pope, reluctant to issue a license without written proof that Knox, who had turned twenty-one on March 6, was of legal age. He told them he'd been threatened recently with a lawsuit by an incensed father for issuing a license to his daughter who'd falsely sworn herself of age in order to elope with a scoundrel. Might there be mention of Knox's birth in the county records? No, she'd been born in Vincennes; her birth was noted in the family Bible which her Uncle Hancock was bringing from Springfield for the wedding, but he hadn't yet arrived. However, her family was well known in Louisville and her aunt, Mrs. Gibson Taylor, was highly respected in this city. Somewhat reluctant still, Mr. Pope made out the license.

Elizabeth Gibson Taylor liked entertaining in the grand manner; her large house was soon overflowing. Hancock Taylor and another uncle, Joseph Taylor of Woodford, arrived with their families. So did Knox's sister Ann with her husband Dr. Wood and their two little boys. The older, Johnny, four-going-on-five, took an instant fancy to Jeff and followed him everywhere. Jeff was accepted easily and completely into the clan by everyone.

Almost everyone, Knox thought. Oh Pa, why?

On a Tuesday afternoon a week before the wedding, Knox sat on the veranda with Ann and Sally Strother Taylor, the cousin who would be her bridesmaid. While they were chatting, Jeff and "Doc" Wood and Nicholas Taylor—another cousin whom Jeff had asked to be his best man—came out wearing hunting togs and carrying fowling pieces.

"I believe we're being deserted," Knox said.

Jeff smiled and kissed her. "We'll be back for dinner. With any luck, we'll bring back dinner."

"Hail the mighty Nimrods," Sally said mockingly. "Hying forth to kill some helpless little bob whites. For shame!"

They watched the three men tramp away across the fields. "I *do* feel deserted," Knox laughed.

Ann smiled. Slender and dark-haired, quiet-natured, she had her father's quick gray-blue eyes. "You'll soon be used to it, Knoxie. You have to remember one thing about men: they enter into marriage with misgivings they never quite lose. The whole institution runs counter to their essential natures. With us it's all home and family; with them, a form of comfortably furnished cage. A rather frequent requirement of which is the illusion of escape."

"A safety valve?"

"That and a reassurance of their manhood. It's necessary, believe me."

The girls chatted and sipped glasses of chilled strawberry negus. Knox's gaze wandered to the Louisville road where a

407

plume of dust marked the wake of a gig coming from the direction of town.

"Is that another guest?" Sally wondered.

"I hope not," Knox said. "To think I wanted a small quiet wedding . . ."

The equipage turned in and rolled up the tree-bordered drive. Knox came to her feet, a strange tightness in her throat. "Pa," she whispered. "Ann, it's Pa."

Zachary Taylor stepped from the gig, told the driver to wait for him, and came up the brick walk. He halted at the foot of the steps and removed his tall hat. He looked stocky and indomitable, a little grayer than Knox remembered, and somehow, in his neat suit of dark broadcloth, almost like a stranger.

"Howdye, Miss Sally," he said with a dry smile. "I trust you're well."

"Very well, thank you, Uncle Zeke." Sally dropped a pert curtsey. "You're looking exceptionally fine."

"Thank you." He cleared his throat. "And you, Ann?"

"Quite well, Father. As are my husband and children." Her coolness melted; she descended the steps and hugged him. "I'm glad you came. But you'll want to talk to Knox . . . Sally, shall we go inside?"

They entered the house. Taylor climbed the steps and seated himself at the table, setting his hat on it. After a moment Knox sat down opposite him. Her gaze moved to the gig. "You're not staying?"

He shook his head. "My steamer leaves within the hour. Army business took me to Jefferson Barracks and I had some private business to transact in Louisville. I . . ." He cleared his throat again. ". . . decided I would see you."

"That was thoughtful of you, Pa. But I fear you'll find it a wasted visit."

His face compressed into the familiar bulldog lines. "Lord God, girl. You seriously think that at this stage I'd come hoping to sway your mind?"

"I can't really say. I'm sure you haven't changed yours."

"Not by a jot. He's left the service, hasn't he?"

It took her a moment to grasp his meaning. Hesitatingly, not quite daring to believe, she touched his hand. "Pa . . . do we have your blessing then?"

"You can have it in writing if you like," he said gruffly. "Here . . . you're not going to be the eternal female and start weeping, are you?"

She shook her head, too overcome to speak. Finally she wiped her eyes and groped for words. "I just thought . . . I thought you hated Jeff . . . now."

"The devil! I never hated him. Worst I ever thought of him was that he was a damned bullheaded pup who wanted a sound thrashing. My pa thought as much of me at times. Ah, I was hard on Davis, I admit; it was one of those things that starts up between men, it gets growing, it grows out of hand. Then things happen you never looked to happen . . ."

"Oh, Pa! Couldn't you have said this before?"

"It was all pride, Sarah Knox." His broad mouth twisted. "Your mother said it. 'You know you're wrong,' she told me. 'Why, for once in your life, can't you admit it?' Well, it took time and reflection; I shan't grind the details fine. Suffice it to say I'm here. I'm sorry, Sarah Knox. I regret what I did to you both. What more can I say?"

"Nothing, Pa," she said gently. "I only wish you could stay and say it to Jeff. He's gone hunting with Doc and Cousin Nick . . ."

"I'll say it another time. Meanwhile you'll give him my congratulations and best wishes."

"Of course . . . but can't you stay for the wedding?"

"Sorry, no. I'm on special leave and must get back to Prairie du Chien directly. Been a little trouble between the settlers and the Sioux north of the Falls of St. Anthony's and we'll be moving part of the garrison up there to calm things down." His jaws clamped, bulging against his side whiskers. "Understand, I feel no differently about service marriages. If my original objection still stood . . ."

"I know. You wouldn't be here."

"And you set out to wed without my permission. Don't think I sanction that, by thunder! Though it's not sufficient reason to withhold my blessing now." He shook his head, gazing at her. "Ann defied me in order to marry Wood, but behind my back as it were. You stood up to me as a man might—wouldn't budge an inch. I fear I've never understood you."

Smiling, she closed her hand tight over his. "You should, Pa. You of all people. Whose daughter am I?"

"You look ravishing, Knoxie," Mary Wilson said. "I vow, every woman present will be absolutely green."

Knox laughed. "Every woman appears ravishing on her great day, or so I'm told."

"Just look at yourself," Mary insisted, drawing her over to the tall Adamesque mirror.

She studied herself. Her wedding dress was a pale full-skirted taffeta, accented at the waist by a ribbon of red velvet; the net-covered throat of her puckered bodice veed into the cleft of her bosom. The skirt just exposed the tips of her dainty kid slippers; her hair was arranged in a shining chignon. "I shouldn't like that hair if I saw it on a dog," she murmured.

"Oh Knoxie! We've spent hours—"

"I'm joking, dear." Knox turned and gave her a quick hug. "You and all the girls have been a marvelous help preparing me for the day . . . and with preparations in general. I'm grateful, believe me. And terribly happy that you and George could come after all."

The Wilsons had arrived only two days ago. Earlier Mary had written that George had an important case pending and they'd probably be unable to attend the wedding. Their arrival made the occasion as complete as she might have wished, except for her parents' absence. She smiled at her best friend. Mary was actually a shade buxom, and her crackling blue frock of Afrique silk testified that George wasn't doing half badly at law.

"Shall we go downstairs?" Knox said. "The guests will be getting restless . . ."

"I'll go," Mary said firmly. "Your aunt and the rest of us can handle any last-minute details. Jeff will return any moment and you mustn't see each other before the ceremony."

"Don't be silly," Knox smiled. "When have I had bad luck? Only three years of waiting and now . . ."

"You shan't wither on the vine for waiting another hour. I'll be back here in less time than that."

"Please. I'll need all the moral support you can muster."

Mary left the room. Knox walked to the window and gazed down at the flowered lawn. The morning was bright and clear; mockingbirds chattered from the aspens. Guests were standing about in groups on the dewy grass; some of the children were frolicking with a spotted dog. What a beautiful day for your wedding, Sarah Knox Taylor. Sarah Knox Davis. Mrs. Jefferson Davis. Yes, I like that best; I shall keep it for my own.

She walked to her dressing table and sat down, drew up a sheet of stationery and began to write.

> *Beechland*
> *June 17, 1835*

My dear Mother,

It is a lovely day in more ways than I can well express. As I write this, we are awaiting the arrival of the minister, Reverend Christopher Ashe of Christ's Episcopal Church. Jeff and George Wilson have gone to Louisville to fetch him. We shall be wed in the east parlor where I spent so many happy hours as a child. I am very happy that Ann is here as thus I feel less destitute for the absence of yourself, Pa, and the children.

I can hardly describe my happiness at Pa's visit to Beechland and his freely given blessing if not his express approval. The fact remains that I formed the connection without his consent.

I cannot but feel that despite his professed admiration for Mr. Davis, Pa wrestled so deeply and insistently with himself to break down that immutable wall of Taylor pride, that he retains a degree of bitter reserve toward the match. Though the old wound be mended, a scar remains that I pray time may soften. As you once told me, we live and love in spite of all scars. My deepest regret is that the circumstances leading to this day have been so lengthy and trying as to work a hardship on you, my dearest Ma.

Do tell Pa again how grateful I am for his generous gift. Did he tell you that he left with me a sack of gold double eagles in the amount of five hundred dollars with the explanation that he is no shakes at selecting presents? This after he had already given me a gift finer by far—the very best I could have received.

He expressed some misgivings at learning that Jeff and I will make our home in the Delta country. I know that he was thinking of that tragic summer fifteen years ago at Bayou Sara. Please assure him once more that the peninsula owned by Jeff's brother is, by all reports, in a most healthful region and that there is no cause for concern.

We will depart Louisville on the New Orleans packet Gayla Marie *at four o'clock this afternoon. I shall write again directly we arrive at Davis Bend. I am sending you a gift by Ann, a new bonnet which is the very best I could find. Give my deepest love to Pa and the children. Believe me always your affectionate daughter,*

Knox

As she finished writing, an equipage came clattering up the graveled drive. Stepping to the window, she saw the carriage careen to a stop by the brick walk. Jeff was at the reins, Wilson and Reverend Ashe beside him. Jeff leaped down from the seat and ran up the walk. Oh Lordy, she thought, something's gone amiss. She caught up her skirts and hurried from the room. As she descended the staircase, Jeff was standing in the hall by the foyer, talking to Elizabeth and Hancock Taylor. She ran to them.

"What is it? What's wrong?"

"I don't know." Jeff's voice was brittle. "We'd picked up Mr. Ashe and were coming back on Jefferson Street when Pendleton Pope hailed us. He wanted to see the license he'd issued us. I handed it to him and without looking at it he told me it was invalid. That he'd been informed you're not of age and that your father is intensely opposed to the marriage. Then he tore the paper to bits and walked away."

"But that's nonsense! Who could have told him such a thing?"

"That's hardly important now," said Hancock, a portly man in his mid-fifties with great muttonchop whiskers. "We must get this matter straightened out at once."

George and Reverend Ashe entered. The minister was tall, pale, silver-haired; he looked faintly worried. "Good morning. An unfortunate incident . . . I hope there's no basis to Mr. Pope's charge."

"None at all," said Hancock. "Merely a wedding joke that went too far. My niece, sir, is definitely of age and I can tell you that my brother gave his personal blessing to the match."

"Ah." Mr. Ashe looked relieved. "So Mr. Davis assured me. Wilson suggested taking, um, heroic measures to persuade Mr. Pope of his error. I felt it best that we proceed quietly, to avoid any hint of public scandal."

Elizabeth's eyes flashed behind her spectacles. "That clerk should be horsewhipped for his impudence," she snapped. "Hank, we must get these children married today."

"Of course." Hancock surrounded them with his mellow smile. "We'll simply oblige the dutiful county clerk to make out another license. We have the family Bible with its record of Knoxie's birth and I'll give oath that the record is valid."

The Bible was brought; Jeff and Hancock climbed into the gig. Jeff gave the team a smart touch of the whip that sent them rattling away down the drive. Knox watched from the veranda as they swung onto the Louisville road. Something had to go wrong, she thought. Didn't it just have to.

"Don't be distressed, Knoxie," George said cheerfully. "They'll straighten matters out. Or Jeff will bloody well straighten out Mr. Pope."

Knox smiled wanly. George was no longer such a tense and wiry bantam; he had added a few pounds and filled his double-breasted pearl-gray suit with an easy elegance. "I'm glad you're here, George. You do exude sunshine."

Mary frowned at her husband, then put an arm around Knox. "Such a petty, clumsy trick for someone to play. Who'd do such a thing?"

Knox shook her head. "I can't imagine any guest being responsible."

"I believe," Elizabeth said grimly, "that I'd nominate Mr. Sanford Preston. After I squelched that betrothal rumor he started, I sought the fellow out and gave him a dressing-down he'll not soon forget. This, I'd hazard, was a little revenge for his pique. That fool Pope has been a-twitter ever since he was almost sued by an angry parent; he'd swallow even so nonsensical a charge without thinking."

Knox went up to her room to wait. Ann, Mary, and Sally accompanied her, telling her not to worry; it was such a little thing and should be easily set aright. She smilingly assured them she didn't doubt it, yet knew that she was visibly upset. She'd wanted this to be the one perfect day of her life.

An hour later Jeff and Hancock returned with a new license. Pope had argued bitterly but had finally agreed to issue it provided Hancock swear under oath that his niece was of lawful age and that he go Jeff's bond for the sum of $166.67. The bond had been posted, the oath duly recorded in the county records; the wedding could proceed.

The guests filed into the big east parlor. Jeff and Nick took their places; Elizabeth struck up a chord on her pianoforte.

The shadowy mar on Knox's day vanished as she entered on the arm of her Uncle Hancock. Jeff was the handsomest man in the room, she thought: his wedding suit of black broadcloth fit him like a glove, the long-tailed cutaway open to a white cravat and flowered-silk waistcoat. And he had eyes for her alone. She took her place beside him. There were snifflings and muffled sobs, even from the men: sentiment was the order of the day, as much on solemn occasions as in letters and poetry.

"Mama, everyone's crying but them," whispered Mary Louise Taylor, Hancock's eleven-year-old daughter.

Her mother shushed her; another woman tittered nervously. Knox hardly heard them. She was aware only of the soft voice of Mr. Ashe intoning the Episcopal service. Then it was done and her lips sealed to Jeff's.

The newlyweds and the guests moved across the hall to the west parlor where a fine table of red walnut had been extended full length and laid with white damask, china, and family silver. Iced melon was served, trays of sliced turkey and hickory-smoked ham, meringues and macaroons frosted with pink sugar webbing. Wine was brought in chilled glasses, a light burgundy that was Hancock's gift, and from Elizabeth's cellar the last bottle of a fine old Madeira that had been a present from her brother Zachary at her own wedding many years ago. Toasts were drunk to the long lives and happiness of bride and groom.

Knox's eyes met Jeff's above their slim-stemmed glasses. The toast they made was unspoken. I'll never again be as happy as I am this moment, she thought. And the thought frightened her a little.

30

Knox woke languidly. Stretching an arm, she found herself alone in bed. It didn't disturb her. Jeff was always up before she, but he was still in the house or close by; he never left for the day's work until they'd breakfasted together. She yawned, swung her legs out of bed and pulled the bell-rope. Dawn filled the room with a shell-pink glow and made a pearly sheen on the big Sheraton fourposter bed and the marble-topped pier table and mirror.

She slipped a swiss muslin robe over her nightgown, went to the window and threw open the curtains. Sunbeams slashed the gloom. She opened the tightly secured windows and stepped out on the balcony, savoring the dawn-cool fragrance of honeysuckle and yellow jasmine. Cardinals and sparrows twittered from the lawn. Hurricane. The great three-storied house surrounded by its broad galleries seemed bulky and graceless next to the lavish mansions in Natchez with their clean classic lines. But it made up in solid roominess what it lacked in grandeur; a big two-story annex connected by a pergola contained facilities for dining, amusements and concerts. It's a monster really, she thought, but I like it. Joe Davis had named it after a disastrous storm that had struck the peninsula in 1827, but the name seemed inappropriate to the quiet beauty of the setting. The house was built on a rounded rise of ground facing the Mississippi; a grove of stately oak that mantled the rise had been thinned to let better specimens flourish and to give a panoramic view of the river. Creamy spangles of magnolia and red bursts of camellia mingled with imported tropic shrubs that blazed with soft brilliance in the morning shadows.

When Joseph Davis had first come to this peninsula thirty miles below Vicksburg, he'd found eleven thousand acres of cane-and-brier wilderness with a few stumped-off and plowed patches of farmland. But he'd seen its potential. Shaped like a giant fist, the peninsula clenched belligerently into the Mississippi, causing it to loop off course by a good twenty miles. Whenever the great river belched a yellow fury of floods across the jut of land, another layer of rich gluey soil was added to the black and odorous soil. Aided by a younger brother, Isaac, Joseph had bought out the handful of settlers, consolidated their holdings, cleared more land and brought five thousand acres under cultivation.

Knox could see only part of the eight acres of peach, fig and apple orchards that bordered the fens to the east. The retreating miasmic fog that had crept up from the night swamps still blanketed the rest, hanging like a saffron shroud in the flat sunrays. She shivered involuntarily. The mist was beautiful. But there was death in it. Enough to kill armies. You kept your windows secured until the sun had burned it off.

The door opened and Zerline entered. A lovely toast-colored quadroon, she had been born in Haiti and trained in New Orleans. "Good morning, *maîtresse*." Her precise English was French-flavored.

"Good morning, Zerline. Will you lay out my riding costume, please? The red corduroy one."

"Yes, *maîtresse*."

Knox seated herself at the pier table and picked up her silver-backed brush. She'd hardly begun her hundred strokes before Zerline firmly took the brush from her and continued the count.

She smiled ruefully. After a life spent on Army posts or in the homes of modestly well-to-do family and relatives, she felt shamefully pampered by life at Hurricane plantation.

Like an English squire, the wealthy Southern planter was lord of his manor and acres. He and his lady were served hand and foot, every wish and whim catered to. They entertained, hunted, traveled, and indulged every taste to the full. An affluent unhurried existence attuned to play rather than work, it was designed to be savored, not bolted. Her husband, Knox knew, found the leisure and refined amusements of plantation living less gratifying than she. She was learning that Jefferson Davis was a divided man; half of his nature welcomed the contemplative life, books, quiet thoughts. The other half of him seethed with restless energy. A good thing, since lovemaking had been his sole outlet during their two honeymoon weeks, that her quick young ardor was a full match for his . . .

It had been an ideal honeymoon. First the journey from Louisville to Vicksburg on the *Gayla Marie,* a floating palace of luxury. The Wilsons had accompanied them part way. Knox and Mary had found a hundred things to engage their fancies, from exclaiming over the fourteen-mile view of the crystal Ohio at Fort Massacre to learning all they could about the passengers up in the ladies' cabin. Davis and George had whiled away hours over chess and whist in the men's cabin while sipping whiskey toddies served by white-jacketed stewards. There had been delightful hours of exploring the river towns where the packet laid over for a day or so to unload cargo and take on fuel and fresh cargo. At Cairo, where the translucent Ohio ran into the mud-heavy lower Mississippi, the Wilsons had arranged for passage north to St. Louis, promising future visits. A hiatus of sightseeing at Memphis where the *Gayla Marie* stopped to refuel and down the Mississippi past the vast Arkansas cypress swamps. Hours of standing at the rail watching the riotous half-tropic growth crowding the banks grow more lush as the packet foamed southward. Knob-kneed cypresses and moss-

418

dripping oaks mingling with a rank profusion of cane thickets and green briers. Herons and pelicans fishing the shallows, tanagers and cardinals making flicker-flames in the dark undergrowth. Explosive sunsets of crimson and indigo. Most of all there had been the long nights when, the fusion and fury of their young love exhausted, they lay in each other's arms, listening to the mutter of engines and churning of paddle wheels, watching the speckled dance of river light on their cabin's walls and ceiling, talking of the future that would be . . .

"*Maîtresse* has beautiful hair." Zerline gathered Knox's glossy chestnut hair atop her head and studied the effect in the mirror. "I should like to put it up in the Creole style."

"Like yours, Zerline?"

"Yes, *maîtresse*."

"Very well."

A dash of difference wouldn't be amiss. Especially today. Jeff had promised her a tour of their half-cleared homesite and she was looking forward to the adventure as eagerly as a child. "We'll saddle two horses, pack a picnic and make a day of it," he'd said. "Not a lot to see, I'm afraid, but we've cleared enough to give you an idea of how the grounds will look. We'll give the boys a day off and have the place to ourselves." Which was the real excitement: an opportunity to spend a day alone with her husband.

Not that she felt neglected, really. It was only that since the day over two months ago when they'd docked at Davis Bend, their lives had ceased to be private. The rest of their honeymoon days had been spent hosting a constant flood of in- and outgoing guests, mostly old friends of Joseph's. They hadn't really minded; their love had waited so long on fulfillment that all selfishness and exclusiveness had been winnowed out. They could entertain one and all, the witty and the dull, with gracious warmth. Knox had looked forward to the return of Hurricane's rightful master and chatelaine from the Northern resorts. She and Jeff would have their time together. But directly

Joe and Eliza Davis had returned last week, Jeff had turned with pleased zest to the business of clearing his eighteen hundred acres at the south end of the peninsula. Up at every sunrise, he'd restlessly prowl the house and grounds until, breakfast concluded, he could get to the daily round of touring fields and barns and gin with Joseph, who liked to keep a personal eye on everything. Jeff would ask hundreds of questions and mentally file thousands of details. At one o'clock he and Joseph would return to Hurricane for dinner with their wives and guests, then relax on the veranda with tall mint juleps. Afterward Jeff would hurry off with James Pemberton and a gang of workers to the south peninsula and spend the afternoon clearing trees, burning brush, and dredging ditches. Totally exhausted, he usually retired soon after supper. When Knox left the Joe Davises and their guests to come to bed, he would be sleeping like a log.

Face it, she thought. You do feel neglected. Lately she could have almost envied the wife of slave or sharecropper. She'd had to remind herself that Jeff was putting footing under their future. Meantime he wasn't insensible to her feelings; he'd suggested this outing.

The quick-fingered Zerline finished her task and stood back with a pleased smile. "There! *Maîtresse* is beautiful, so . . ."

The result was becoming, Knox thought; the high Creole style suited her full oval face. "It's very nice, Zerline. Thank you."

She dressed and left her room. The wide hallway was quiet and morning-shadowed as she crossed it to the staircase. In the style of the affluent planter, Joseph had set aside the entire third floor of the house for guests; a full dozen and their body servants could be accommodated. None were up as yet, but Joseph and Eliza, always early risers, would join Jeff and her for breakfast.

Knox descended to the first floor and went to the doorway of Joseph's office to glance in. Jeff sometimes spent the pre-breakfast hour reading, but he wasn't here. She ran a glance over the crammed bookshelves that lined every wall. Books! She had never seen so many. Joe had the walls of his office, annex sitting room, and garden cottage packed with shelved books, many of them expensive first editions, gilt-edged and leather-bound. She loitered through the deep-carpeted parlor with its French wallpaper, cut-glass chandelier, red-satin portieres, and rosewood and mahogany furniture upholstered in flowered Belfast damask. Through the oak-paneled dining room with its long cherrywood table and gilt-backed chairs, silver candelabra, glass-fronted cabinets filled with silver and crystalware and bone china. Finally into the kitchen with its gleaming gamespits and pothooks and rows of iron and copper pots. James Pemberton's mother already had the fires built and the pots boiling. A grizzled hawk-faced woman and a whirlwind of energy, she had presided over the household for many years.

"Good morning, Mammy Pem."

The old woman barely muttered a reply as she bustled back and forth. "Lazy good-for-nothing Nigra wenches," she grumbled, referring to the two girls who helped her. "Both of 'em got with child and not worth a lick when they ain't, got to do ever' blessed thing myself . . ."

"May I help you?" Knox spoke without thinking and immediately regretted it.

The tall Creek woman turned a fierce, shocked glance on her. "This here is my kitchen, Miss Sarah. You can't do one lick in here. Best you go sit yourself and wait breakfast."

Smarting with the rebuff, Knox retreated to the dining room and took her place at the table, leaning her chin on her fists. It wasn't just the kitchen, she thought. It was everything. Had been from the first. She had looked forward to assuming the chatelaine duties at Hurricane until Eliza Davis returned. Duties far different from the wifely tasks for which a conscientious mother had trained her: cooking, sewing, smoking meat, making butter, cheese, preserves, soap, and candles. But she'd been sure that she could take hold, given a chance. However, the grimly industrious Mammy Pem had decided that the responsibilities with which Miss 'Liza had temporarily entrusted her would not be surrendered to an upstart stranger. She'd refused to give up the storeroom keys, had continued to manage gardens and servants, supply medicines, nurse ailing slaves, and train the black children. Knox had refrained from forcing the issue; so much of Hurricane's smooth routine hinged on Mammy Pem that the old woman could easily sabotage it out of pique. Knox had tried to fill her days with seeing to visitors' comfort and pleasure, improvising games, acting charades, giving mock concerts in the annex music room under the stern eyes of Davis family portraits. With Eliza's return, even that diversion was erased. By now, ashamed of her own uselessness, bored to distraction, practically husbandless for weeks, she could regard today's outing as a godsend.

"What! Brooding on such a beautiful day?"

Knox fashioned a quick smile as Joseph entered. "Good morning, Joe. Does it show?"

Joseph laughed as he took his place at the head of the table. At fifty, he cut a figure of trim elegance that matched Jeff's. His wide forehead, generous nose and sensitive mouth gave him a striking resemblance to pictures she'd seen of Shelley. But Joe, however some of his liberal notions might raise eyebrows among his fellow planters, was no poetic radical. It was hard to reconcile his reputation as an astute financier and lawyer with the retiring scholar and thinker he always seemed and was.

"Of course it shows. No blame to you for that. Between Pem and 'Liza—"

"I'm hopelessly outclassed," Knox smiled.

"Nonsense. Disadvantaged at Hurricane, to be sure." Joseph shook out his napkin, giving her a keen glance. "Well, you're a fetching sight this morning. Jeff mentioned a holiday; it'll do him good. And you too."

"I have fond hopes."

Joseph grinned. "You'll hold your own in any arena—never doubt it! I've seen the difference in Jeff. That old carefree hang-tomorrow attitude of his has been replaced by a drive and purpose I've never known in him. It's all for you and because of you. Never doubt that either."

Eliza came in and gave Knox a pleasant good morning. The former Elizabeth van Bentheysen of New York's old Dutch stock, she was frail, gentle, unattractive, half her husband's age and completely devoted to him, as she was to Joe's three daughters by his first marriage. She went to the kitchen to order breakfast brought in. While Mammy Pem was serving toast, boiled eggs and Havana coffee in thin china cups, Jeff joined them, looking lithe and jaunty in black broadcloth and riding boots, carrying a white planter's hat. Knox felt her mood lift; she ate a good breakfast and enjoyed the lighthearted talk.

It would be a wonderful holiday, she thought as she and Jeff left the house and walked toward the springhouse between the bright beds of daffodils, white lilacs, and purple heliotropes that checkered the great lawn. They packed a hamper with a cold boiled ham, half-loaf of good bread, butter and cheese, and a bottle of white wine, then continued on to the sprawl of white-painted barns and stables east of the house. The stables contained thirty stalls of blooded horses, some of them brood mares, the rest reserved for use by family and guests: fast rackers, carefully broken, gentled for riding. A young Negro saddled their mounts, Knox insisting on a burnished blue-gray with dark markings and a more spirited gait than Jeff approved. They stopped by the slave quarters, a neat hamlet of white-washed cabins, chicken runs, and vegetable gardens. Men and women came out to shake their hands; they held their horses tight-reined to avoid injuring a dozen or so toddlers who streamed out of the plantation nursery and stretched up tiny hands, crying, "Howdye, massa." Afterward they rode on past forge, smokehouse, buttery, corncribs, and storehouses, down an oak-shaded bridle path past orchards and truck gardens of pumpkins, squashes, beans, turnips, corn, and potatoes. Except for such amenities as ice, mail, books, and so on that were brought by river steamer, the plantation was self-supporting.

Beyond the gin and the broad cotton acres lay rank tropic growth through which Jeff and his crew had slashed a road. It was wagon-broad, boggy in places, uneven with stumps and potholes. "One day," he told her, "we'll grade and gravel. Ditch along the sides and trim out the brush. Make it pretty as a drive through an English park." She thought it was a lovely ride already, winding through an amber gloom of giant old trees bearded with Spanish moss, oak and ash and hickory mixed with hackberry, mulberry, walnut, sweet gum, flowering redbud, and dogwood. Ferns and mosses and magnolia tulips cushioned the forest floor. They rode by dark pooling sloughs where hundreds of brilliant waterfowl flapped among the reeds and yellow lilies. Blue and white cranes stood in grave stiltlike dignity, darting the water with quick inquisitive bills.

"Is it much farther, Jeff?"

"Just ahead."

"Good!" She tapped the blue-gray into a run.

"Have a care of the stumps!"

She emerged suddenly into the bright blaze of a vast clearing that bristled with stubs and stumps. As yet it was hard to see a homesite in this ugly crazy quilt of lopped-off groves and thickets. Trees and brush had been felled in what seemed aimless tangles; elsewhere slashings had been stacked in piles for burning. The torch had been put to some, crumbled heaps of smoldering, smoking char.

Hearing Jeff rein up beside her, she turned in her saddle. "I didn't realize you'd done so much . . ."

He was bowed forward across his pommel, his face waxen. "Darling, what is it?"

"It's nothing. I feel a little warm . . . a bit queasy. Let's get down and walk. I'll be all right."

They left the horses at the clearing's edge. She kept a worried eye on Jeff as they walked slowly across the raw acreage. Still pale, he was cheerful and animated as he discussed the progress made. The work, he admitted, had proved far more costly, tedious, and time-consuming than he'd dreamed. Hundreds of acres of bottomland remained to be cleared. Scores of giant trees must be marked for landscaping, for lumber, for fuel. Impenetrable jungles of cane and brier must be burned. Ditches must be dredged, the wet heavy soil broken to plow. He showed her a small area that had already been cutover, burned, cleaned and grubbed out. He picked up a handful of the soil and crumbled it to show her its black richness.

"To think," she murmured, "that I'll be chatelaine of these acres."

"No yearning at all for town life?"

"Never. Not for a minute. Why?"

"You've been accustomed to it for much of your life." He gave a wry nod around them. "Not a very encouraging prospect as yet."

"Close your eyes, darling. See it all as it will be."

"How do *you* see it? Our home will be yours to plan."

"Oh, I haven't really thought on it."

"What comes to mind? Anything?"

"Roses. I want roses everywhere."

"Let's lay out a flower garden then. Where?"

"By the house, of course. But we need a house first."

"That oak rise yonder would be a choice site. Well above the bogs, last place a flood will reach. Good view of the river and plenty of room behind to set out gardens, orchards and outbuildings."

They climbed up the flat-topped ridge. It was crowned by a grove of oak as splendid as that which surrounded Hurricane. The long rise ran down almost to the riverbank and the breeze that swept up it was cooling; dappled shadows quivered. Knox looked around her. How peaceful it is, she thought. Watching the small-boy intentness of Jeff's face as he talked, she felt the rush of her love like a sweet choking. What was hell, she wondered, if it weren't simply the loss of heaven? Nothing could be worse, once you'd felt such transports of love, than losing it forever.

" . . . a one-story building that'll blend with the rise and the trees. We can cut most of the timber we'll need within a few hundred yards, next the river—I'll want to clear for a landing. As an old sawmill operator, I'll supervise personally."

"I'd like a large hall," she said, "with plastered walls. And the other rooms paneled in cypress."

"Good. Double doors six feet wide to open on that hall—facing the river to make the most of good breezes."

"A gallery of paved bricks with latticework. And roses."

"We'll build our own kiln and fire bricks as we need 'em. What about a veranda that opens off both parlor and master bedroom?"

"Wonderful. And a gilt mahogany bed, a big one. All mantelpieces of black Italian marble—"

"What'll we call this wonder abode? You decide."

"Kublai Khan's pleasure palace?"

He chuckled. "Afraid that smacks a bit of Natchez-under-the-hill. Why don't you think about it? Meantime we'll lay out your rose garden, a whole field of roses if it suits—"

"That's it! A field of roses, briers, we'll call our home Brierfield. Isn't that fine? Handsome but prickly, like J. F. Davis, Esquire, himself."

"I'll ignore that and merely suggest that we toast the name on this spot. I'll fetch the wine—"

"Let me. I'm too excited to stand still."

"All right," he laughed, "run all the way. Meantime I'll walk off some of the lines and dimensions of this proposed manor."

She hurried across the cutover, her voluminous skirt picking up black streaks from charred slashings it brushed. She didn't care; she'd never felt such happy excitement. They'd left the hamper in the shade near the horses. She might as well bring the sandwiches too; she felt hungry already.

Her arm was aching from the hamper's weight as she trudged back up the rise. She found Jeff sitting on a moss-crumbled deadfall. He was bent over, his face in his hands. She ran to him, dropping on her knees beside him. He lowered his hands. His face, shining with sweat, looked as if the blood had been squeezed from it.

"I exaggerated before. Don't feel so warm and queasy as I do hot and sick."

"You've felt so all this while? Oh Jeff!"

"I thought it was something I ate . . . that it might pass directly. Seems to be worsening. Didn't want to spoil your outing."

"You should have said something. Is it that neuralgia again?"

"No, nothing like that. More like the grippe." His face muscles twitched; his eyes were varnished with fever. "Funny . . . feel cold now. Stomach is boiling like one of Mammy Pem's kettles. We'd best get home while I can still hold a saddle . . ."

By the time they reached Hurricane, he was slumped almost insensibly over his pommel. As they rode up to the house, Joseph hurried out. He and Knox helped Jeff off his horse and into the house. Joseph called Mammy Pem; she came from the kitchen.

"Pem, find James. Tell him Mister Jeff is sick. He's to ride posthaste to Vicksburg and fetch Dr. Fabares. And have one of the boys bring some ice from the sawdust pile by the landing."

"Yessir." Pem stared at Jeff's pale face. "If that's grippe that's got the young mister, bes' thing for it is herb and marshmallow root tea."

"Whatever you think best. Now hurry!"

They got Jeff upstairs and into bed. Knox drew the heavy window drapes against the light and came to stand by the bed with Joseph. By now, Jeff was only half-conscious, mumbling quietly. Sweat was already darkening the pillowslip around his head. Knox stared at his gleaming face, biting her lip.

"Joe . . . do you think it's grippe?"

"Let's assume so for now."

"Pray God it isn't the bilious! It's so much like the grippe in the early stages . . ."

Joseph squeezed her arm gently. "Try not to worry. Louis Fabares is the best physician in Vicksburg."

"How long will it take James to fetch him?"

"It's thirty miles, you know, to Vicksburg. He can't possibly arrive before tomorrow. Meantime we'll do what we can. Ice crushed for packs will reduce the fever . . . and Pem has an endless store of remedies that I've seen accomplish wonders."

By nightfall, Jeff was seized in the first violent surge of ague. And they knew it wasn't grippe. Mammy Pem brewed up another strong tea of sage mixed with whiskey and forced small doses down Jeff's throat while Knox held his head. Through the hours that followed, he tossed in intermittent seizures of fevers and sweats, then shuddering chills. Knox never left his side.

Dr. Fabares arrived at noon the next day. He seemed unfazed by a long hard ride; he was a short dark Creole, full of pugnacious energy, who reminded Knox of Dr. Beaumont. He confirmed the attack as malarial.

"It will run its course," he told them. "The usual fever and chills, periods of consciousness, great weakness."

"I know," Knox said. "I had some form of the bilious when I was six. It was a light attack . . . but two of my sisters died of it."

"Ah. And your husband . . . has he been stricken before?"

"I don't know. Do you, Joe?"

Joseph shook his head. "He never mentioned as much, but it would be like Jeff not to. My brother served in the Army for nearly seven years, Louis. All border service, in Michigan and Arkansas."

Fabares grimaced. *"Peste!* I know of the wilderness places. Most soldiers who go there sooner or later contract the bilious. And a host of civilians besides. Whole families bilious, sallow, sapped of energy, from grandmothers to tots."

"I've seen it, Doctor," Knox said quietly.

"I am sorry, madam. You know the standard treatments as well as I. Calomel and Peruvian barks which I shall leave in quantity. Plenty of chicken soup, of course, when he can take it. All that you can get him to eat."

"And feed what's left to a black cat, I suppose?"

Fabares bristled slightly. "Please, madam! Yes, if you hate waste and own a chicken soup-eating black cat. Do me the justice of assuming that I try to winnow the dross from folk myth. It sickens me how little we are able to do. How little we know. Miasma, animalculae, humbug! Even quinine can only palliate *febris acuta,* not check it. But how to find a cure without isolating cause?"

"I don't know," Knox whispered.

All she did know was that she wanted her man on his feet again, well and whole.

31

He was dangerously sick. That much he knew. Sometimes in warm valleys between hot peaks of delirium he was aware of Knox close by. Always there, hazel-eyed tender, always near. But her voice seemed to come from a distance and her face to draw always away from him.

At such times he backfloated on a delirious sea that rolled veil-like above his face: he knew a reality that was shimmered and distorted. The trees and shrubbery banked beyond his window were masses of dazzling green. The baking tropic air quivered with heat and hallucination. Now and again Dr. Beaumont's words *get out of the North or it will be the death of you* trailed like a dwindling thread through his brain and he laughed in his delirium.

Again he would drop into a red-hot vortex of fever that whirled him along tracks of memory where past and present twisted and crossed. The walls turned to rough logs hung with pelts that were alive and snarling, wolves wailed beyond the walls, Ceclie Robier ministered to him like a tender-eyed ghost.

He was awake. Reality abrased him. The sickish-sour smell of the room. Sweaty sheets cooling against his body. His hands feeling unbearably harsh and dry resting on the satin coverlet.

A candelabra on the commode flickered weak spears of flame.

Far off, thunder rumbled.

A finger of rainy air poked under the window sash and blew like cool silk across his face. The candles guttered sallowly; shadows swam. A slow rain rattled like falling pods on roof and galleries. He smiled dimly. As a boy he'd liked lying awake and counting the first fat raindrops as they hit . . .

Knox.

His lips tried the name, but no sound came out.

Knox . . .

The name whispering out rasped his throat. He tried again and made sound.

A latch tripped softly. The door connecting the bedroom to an adjoining one opened. Zerline entered, holding a finger to her lips. "Sh, *maître*. You must not call her. She sleeps now. And you are better?"

"Where is she?" he said hoarsely.

The girl tilted her head toward the chamber she had left, then lightly shut the door and crossed the room to him. Her face was pallid and strained.

"How long . . . ?"

"A week, *maître*. She was never out of this room until . . . until two days ago—" Zerline's voice broke. "Oh—oh, *maître!* She is so very sick!"

"Sick," he said stupidly. "Couldn't be . . . saw her not an hour ago . . ."

"No—no! The *maîtresse* is with the ague too!"

A chill bit into the hot humming of his brain.

I must go to her. He didn't know whether he said the words or not. He tried to raise himself on one elbow. Mustered only a twitch of response. Sank back with a groan . . .

Day followed day. The two young Davises continued together in their illness. Joseph Davis wore himself fine between the glum freight of plantation routine and gnawing worry for the brother who was like a son to him. Dr. Fabares paid several more calls, but his palliatives had no effect. Neither did Pem's various remedies. Davis and Knox didn't worsen; neither did they improve. They oscillated between high delirium and periods of weak consciousness. Such lucid moments as they had rarely coincided. Then they were so drained by fever that talk was meaningless.

Joseph consulted with Dr. Fabares.

The two couldn't continue much longer in their present condition, the doctor ruled. Both were growing weaker from repeated sieges of fever and their inability to take much nourishment. A trip on the river, he suggested, the motion of water and change of scene, might help cleanse them of debilitating humors.

Steamers docked at Davis Bend on the average of twice a week. Joseph collared the captain of the next boat and put the proposal to him. Would he be agreeable to taking on the sick couple and their body servants for an indefinite period? The captain gave reluctant assent, with the provision that the Davises remain isolated from other passengers and their needs be attended to solely by James Pemberton and Zerline.

Knox was conveyed to the boat on a litter. Weak as he was, Davis refused to be carried. He walked beside the litter, leaning on Pemberton's arm. They went aboard and were installed in a cabin. The captain gave a bull-voiced order; the *Delta Queen* cast off.

Her destination was New Orleans. As she paddled southward, the September days were hot, the September nights warm. The Davises hardly knew the difference. They remained in their cabin day after day, too weak to move, tended in every way by the two servants. The quarters were cramped and muggy; no physician was available. It was soon apparent to Pemberton and Zerline that not only were their master and mistress failing to improve, they were sinking perceptibly . . .

Davis's impressions flickered like splinters of colored glass. He knew of paddle-washed waves chunking against the boat's hull. Of nights like warm sable. Of tropic birds screeching and the feral bellowing of bull 'gators. Mostly he knew of a red sea of fever where silver sunbursts collided . . .

There was a time when he knew violet twilight and a weak lucidity. Pemberton was beside his bed, talking quietly.

"We are approaching Bayou Sara on the Louisiana bank, sir . . ."

Bayou Sara. The name had a familiar ring.

He gave his thoughts a sluggish fillip. Yes. His widowed sister Anna lived in Feliciana Parish, and he'd always disembarked at Bayou Sara when visiting Locust Grove, the plantation willed to Anna by Luther Smith, her late husband.

"Are you thinking," he whispered, "of taking us to my sister's place, James?"

"Yes, sir. Directly we dock, I'll rent a wagon and move you and Miss Sarah to Locust Grove."

"Very well, James. We're in your hands."

Pemberton left the cabin.

Knox stirred, murmuring, "Jeff . . ."

Their bunks were set against opposite walls of the cabin. He lay quietly a moment, gathering his strength. Slowly he sat up, swung his legs to the floor and stood, palms braced flat against the wall. Holding his legs stiff and leaning on the wall, he made his way to her bunk. He knelt on the floor and took her hand between his.

Her skin, the skin that had been fine velvet to the touch, was hot and parched. Her forehead was dewed with sweat, the structure of her facial bones limned painfully taut and shiny. Her hair, thanks to Zerline's tireless care, shimmered with a healthy luster.

"How do you feel, dearest?"

"So . . . terribly weak."

"Listen. Soon we'll be off this boat, you'll be in a house

again, a quiet place with a soft bed. We'll lay in directly at Bayou Sara and go straight to my sister's . . ."

"Where? Where did you say?"

"Bayou Sara. Why . . . is something wrong?"

"No, nothing." She smiled. "It's nothing."

He gathered her into his arms, rocking her back and forth gently. The wasted frailty of her body sent a shock of fear through him.

"It's nothing, Jeff. Really."

"I know."

"But you're crying. I never saw . . ."

"Knox. Oh Knoxie!"

Her thin arms circled his shoulders. "Don't be afraid, dearest. Nothing can hurt me while you're with me. Nothing . . ."

On their arrival at Locust Grove, Anna Davis Smith took brisk charge of everything. Sixteen years older than Jefferson, she'd surrounded him with a tenderly fierce care through his babyhood when their mother had been invalided. Now she brought the same untiring devotion to caring for him and Knox. Two spare beds in adjoining rooms were cleaned, aired out and made up with fresh linen. The widow of Dr. Ben Davis, a deceased brother, lived nearby; she came to assist with the nursing. They tried to administer stews and soporifics, but all the patients could keep down was small doses of medicinal teas. Anna and her sister-in-law tried teas of bloodroot and wild ginger, molasses and sulphur powder, chinaberries and whiskey. At first husband and wife seemed to sharply rally. But it proved only an "up" phase in the erratic fluctuations that had so far attended their illness. As suddenly as it had dropped, the fever rose.

Ragged flakes of sensibility told Davis of the fight being waged for his life. He tried to fight too. But the raging waves of ague sucked the will out of him. The time came when he gave up, gave himself to the singing flow of death and let it drift him down dark rivers toward a calm sea.

But he did not die. His fever broke. And he slept for a long time . . .

When he woke at last, he was so saturated with opiates and sleep that he had to fight for a dim patchwork of impressions. Colors shifted and ran together; he was dizzy, his ears ringing, from overlong doses of quinine.

He heard Anna's voice. And a strange masculine one. It seemed to be a doctor's. But he couldn't be sure. Both voices seemed unreal, disembodied echoes.

"Frankly, I'd despaired of them both," the doctor said. "But at least he . . ."

Anna made a shushing noise.

He tried to hold on. To cry a question. But the irresistible tide of darkness rose again. Blotting out sight and sound and thought . . .

He woke in the pause between sunset and twilight. The clock in the hall had struck the hour. Golden light rimmed the window sill with warm amber. Nobody in the room. That was unusual. Even the tireless Anna must have finally given in to her exhaustion.

Thirst. His tongue was sour and crusted. He swallowed; his throat rasped like a file. The stuff of sleep was still packed thickly around his brain.

The words he'd heard before dropping off came back. *What did they mean?*

Knox?

He raised on his elbows, only to fall back. Twice more he tried to raise himself. The strain shot prickles of energy through his flaccid muscles. He dragged himself to a sitting position. Set one foot on the floor, then the other. And stood.

Holding his legs stiff, he edged toward the doorway between

his and Knox's room. Nausea erupted in his throat, sweat crawled on his face. Reaching the doorway, he leaned his shoulder against the jamb and rested. Then felt blindly along the door and opened it. He entered the next room, holding onto furniture to keep himself upright. Zerline was curled up in an armchair in the corner, asleep, a worn quilt thrown over her legs.

He made his way painfully to the bedside, dropped on his knees and clasped Knox's wasted hand to his cheek.

"Knox. Oh, my darling."

He was aware of Zerline's hand. It was tugging gently at his arm. "*Maître*. You must not wake her . . ."

"Leave us. Please."

The hand went away.

Knox's lashes stirred. "Jeff."

She was awake, yet not awake. Her eyes were open with a kind of gentle, questioning awareness that frightened him. It was a peacefulness that erased the ravages of fever. As if she clung to her diminished body with a half-will.

"Jeff."

"Oh, Knox." He dropped his face against the quilt. "Knox, dear God!"

"Don't be afraid, darling." Her hands touched his hair. "I'm not afraid. Not any more. I knew . . . could tell almost from the beginning."

"Knox. Oh, God. No."

"I didn't want you to know. You might have stopped caring to live. You must care. And darling, please try not to grieve for me too long. I know you so well. I'm afraid . . . afraid of what your life will be if you do. Don't try to face the future alone. At times you pull away from people so. And you mustn't."

He could no longer hold back a storm of weeping.

"My poor darling." Her voice began to drift. "We had such a little time, didn't we? And we were so happy . . ."

Sometime later, he wasn't sure when, his sister and sister-in-law came. He struggled weakly as they took him back to his room. His system was sodden with drugs; he'd fallen into a crumpled sleep by Knox's bed. Now, fight it as he might, the resistless urge to sleep dragged him back and down. Into a dreamless oblivion.

When he woke again, the room was dark. Something had wakened him. He didn't know what.

He heard it again. A woman's voice, soft, soft, yet rising in a high sweet treble. *"Fairy Bells, Fairy Bells . . ."*

Knox's song from their courting days. Knox's voice, wild and unearthly. Singing.

He stumbled from his bed and staggered toward the straw of light at the bottom of the connecting door. He threw the door open. Zerline was bending over her mistress. She stood aside as he came across the room.

He knelt by the bed.

Her eyes were wide open, her soft-wild song went on. She did not know him. He took her in his arms and held her close.

Her voice ebbed. Flickered away like tailings of dusklight on an outrunning tide. Ended. She was quiet in his arms.

The hall clock tolled the hour. Long gonging strokes. A knell for midnight.

EPILOGUE

The loss of his bride of three months almost unhinged Davis. Adding to the shock of his grief was a conviction that he was to blame for her death. For marrying her against her father's wish, for bringing her to the Delta country. Still dangerously ill, he insisted that the funeral service be held in his sickroom. The family feared for his life. Then he began to slowly recover. He returned to Hurricane, only to be violently depressed by surroundings that reminded him of Knox. Physically too weak to continue the land-clearing that would have diverted him, he heeded the urgings of his brother Joseph and "got away from it all."

In the year that followed, accompanied by James Pemberton, he journeyed to Havana, Cuba, then to New York and Washington City, where he was introduced to the workings of a role in which he would never feel comfortable: politics. Returning to Davis Bend, he resumed the work of wresting a plantation out of wilderness. He built Brierfield as he and Knox had planned it. He became a recluse. His sole companion was James Pemberton. He studied, he worked, he prospered.

He rarely left the peninsula and then only when necessary. That was his life for seven years.

In the fall of 1843, disturbed by his brother's prolonged withdrawal from society, Joseph Davis urged Jefferson to enter state politics. In December of the same year, while visiting his niece Florida McCaleb, Davis met Varina Anne Howell. Varina was beautiful and intelligent; she had fantastic energy, persistent hypochondria and a temper. She was then seventeen; Davis was thirty-five. They were engaged a month later and were married on February 26, 1845, at her parents' home in Natchez, Mississippi.

Afterward they journeyed by riverboat to Anna Smith's home at Locust Grove on Bayou Sara. They honeymooned in the very house where Sarah Knox had died. In a visit to the Smith family cemetery where she was buried, the newlyweds laid flowers on the grave and stood for a time meditating over the brick and marble tomb with its simple inscription:

Sarah Knox Davis

Wife of Jefferson Davis

Died Sept. 15, 1835

age 21

It is not difficult to guess at Varina's meditations. Little wonder that she was upset by her husband's deep attachment to his first love. Or that through the forty-four years of their marriage she would never cease to feel a tinge of jealous resentment toward a girl long dead. Considering her possessive and volatile nature, Varina lived with the fact quite creditably. In 1890, a year after her husband's death, she published her biography of his life, two large, highly detailed volumes in which she restricted mention of Sarah Knox to a charitable but very brief passage.

In February 1845, while journeying downriver to Natchez to his second wedding, Davis experienced the shock of an unexpected meeting. On the same boat was General Zachary Taylor, on his way to the duty of guarding the disputed border between Texas and Mexico. It was the strangest of times and places to encounter the father-in-law who had bitterly opposed his first marriage, for there'd been no communication between them since Knox's death. But ten years had passed; time had softened the edges of a grief which now forged a common bond. And the beginning of a deep friendship that both men cherished until Taylor's death.

When war with Mexico broke out in 1846, Davis marched to Texas at the head of nine hundred Mississippi volunteers and was welcomed into Taylor's army. At the Battle of Buena Vista, Davis saved the day for Taylor with an inspired V-formation. Both returned home as heroes, Taylor to ride a wave of popular adulation into the presidency of the United States, Davis to receive an appointment as U. S. Senator from Mississippi. On July 9, 1850, when Zachary Taylor lay dying in the White House, surrounded by his wife, two daughters, and three sons-in-law, his last distinct words were spoken to Davis: "Apply the Consitution to the measure, sir, regardless of consequences."*

Davis's close relations with the Taylor family continued through his life. Zachary Taylor's son Dick became a prominent general in the Confederacy and wrote a highly regarded history of the Civil War. Dr. Robert Crooke Wood, husband of Ann Taylor, became Surgeon General of the Union Army; his sons, John and Robert, went over to the Confederacy, and John became Davis's aide. Another lifelong friend was Betty, Knox's younger sister, who grew up to be an "unspeakably agreeable and lovely" young woman. Betty waited until she was twenty-four to meet "the perfect man"; she found him in Major William Bliss, who had been her father's aide in Mexico. "Old Rough and Ready" did not oppose this match. It was one of the final ironies of Zachary Taylor's life that he, who'd sworn an oath that no daughter of his would marry a soldier, had lived to see all three of his daughters take soldier husbands.

If there is a single pivotal event on which a man's early life

* According to Varina Davis in a letter to her mother dated July 10, 1850

turns, for Jefferson Davis that event was the death of his young bride. It changed his whole character and in a sense his whole life. For seven years afterward he was a recluse who bore his grief by developing a stoical and austere front that was later interpreted by many as coldness or disdain. Even sympathetic observers failed to guess the truth.

One such was Robert Anderson's young brother Charles, who had roomed with Davis at Jefferson Barracks in the fall of 1833 when the 1st Regiment of U. S. Dragoons was being trained for the West. Years later Charles Anderson wrote that one day as he was sitting in the headquarters parlor with General Henry Atkinson, Lieutenant Colonel Stephen Kearny of the Dragoons entered to discuss "a delicate business" with the general. That business was to enlist the support of Atkinson, who enjoyed good personal relations with Zachary Taylor despite their professional differences, in urging Colonel Taylor to assent to the marriage of Lieutenant Davis and his daughter Knox. Young Anderson was astonished to learn of the romance between his roommate and "my early playmate and best friend." What came of Kearny's request he did not record, but his amazement was doubled by Kearny's and Atkinson's agreement that Davis was "one of the brightest and most promising officers in the whole Army."

For, in Anderson's words, "whilst I did think him one of the most humorous, witty, and captivating gentlemen whom I had ever met, I did not think he showed to me any signs of such sober abilities . . . One reflection still often presses itself on me: what change of manners must have occurred in him from that joyous and sportful humorist of *my* impressions into the sober, grave philosopher-thinker and statesman of his after developed character?"

It never occurred to Charles Anderson that the first and perhaps primary reason for the change in Davis was the death of his bride, Anderson's own "best friend" and childhood sweetheart, Sarah Knox Taylor.